Case Studies in Contemporary Criticism

MARY SHELLEY

Frankenstein

Case Studies in Contemporary Criticism
SERIES EDITOR: Ross C Murfin

Emily Brontë, *Wuthering Heights*
EDITED BY Linda H. Peterson, Yale University

Kate Chopin, *The Awakening*
EDITED BY Nancy A. Walker, Vanderbilt University

Joseph Conrad, *Heart of Darkness*
EDITED BY Ross C Murfin, University of Miami

Nathaniel Hawthorne, *The Scarlet Letter*
EDITED BY Ross C Murfin, University of Miami

James Joyce, *The Dead*
EDITED BY Daniel R. Schwarz, Cornell University

James Joyce, *A Portrait of the Artist as a Young Man*
EDITED BY R. B. Kershner, University of Florida

William Shakespeare, *Hamlet*
EDITED BY Susanne L. Wofford, University of Wisconsin–Madison

Mary Shelley, *Frankenstein*
EDITED BY Johanna M. Smith, University of Texas at Arlington

Edith Wharton, *The House of Mirth*
EDITED BY Shari Benstock, University of Miami

Case Studies in Contemporary Criticism

SERIES EDITOR: Ross C Murfin, *University of Miami*

MARY SHELLEY
Frankenstein

Complete, Authoritative Text with
Biographical and Historical Contexts,
Critical History, and Essays from
Five Contemporary Critical Perspectives

EDITED BY

Johanna M. Smith
University of Texas at Arlington

Bedford Books *of* St. Martin's Press
BOSTON • NEW YORK

For Bedford Books

Publisher: Charles H. Christensen
Associate Publisher: Joan E. Feinberg
Managing Editor: Elizabeth M. Schaaf
Developmental Editor: Stephen A. Scipione
Production Editor: Tara L. Masih
Copyeditor: Cynthia Insolio Benn
Text Design: Sandra Rigney, The Book Department
Cover Design: Richard Emery Design, Inc.

Library of Congress Catalog Card Number: 90–63557

Copyright © 1992 by Bedford Books *of* St. Martin's Press

Manufactured in the United States of America.

0 9 8 7 6 5
l k j i h g

For information, write: St. Martin's Press, Inc.
175 Fifth Avenue, New York, NY 10010

Editorial Offices: Bedford Books *of* St. Martin's Press
29 Winchester Street, Boston, MA 02116

ISBN: 0–312–04469–0 (paperback)
ISBN: 0–312–06525–6 (hardcover)

Published and distributed outside North America by:

MACMILLAN PRESS LTD.
Houndmills, Basingstoke, Hampshire RG21 2XS and London
Companies and representatives throughout the world.

ISBN: 0–333–57557–1

About the Series

Case Studies in Contemporary Criticism provide college students with an entrée into the current critical and theoretical ferment in literary studies. Each volume reprints the complete text of a classic literary work and presents critical essays that approach the work from different theoretical perspectives, together with the editors' introductions to both the literary work and the critics' theoretical perspectives.

The volume editor of each *Case Study* has selected and prepared an authoritative text of the classic work, written an introduction to the work's biographical and historical contexts, and surveyed the critical responses to the work since its initial publication. Thus situated biographically, historically, and critically, the work is examined in five critical essays, each representing a theoretical perspective of importance to contemporary literary studies. These essays, prepared especially for undergraduates by exemplary critics, show theory in praxis; whether written by established scholars or exceptional young critics, they demonstrate how current theoretical approaches can generate compelling readings of great literature.

As series editor, I have prepared introductions, with bibliographies, to the theoretical perspectives represented in the five critical essays. Each introduction presents the principal concepts of a particular theory in their historical context, and discusses the major figures and key works that have influenced their formulation. It is my hope that these introductions will reveal to students that good criticism is informed by a set of coherent assumptions, and will encourage them to recognize and examine their own assumptions about literature. Finally, I have compiled a glossary of key terms that recur in these volumes and in the discourse of contemporary theory and criticism. We hope that the *Case Studies in Contemporary Criticism* series will reaffirm the richness of its literary works, even as it introduces invigorating new ways to mine their apparently inexhaustible wealth.

Ross C Murfin
Series Editor
University of Miami

About This Volume

The text of *Frankenstein* reprinted in Part One is based on the third edition of 1831, the last version overseen and approved by Mary Shelley. I have retained this edition's spelling and punctuation, correcting only glaring errors and misprints; where appropriate, I have made these corrections in accordance with the 1818 text as edited by James Rieger. Although there was some sentiment for reprinting the 1818 version in this volume, thus making it more readily available to those interested in comparing the two versions, it was decided to use the text most familiar to readers and critics. At one time I had hoped to produce an edition including the earliest drafts of the novel and Percy Shelley's emendations; time and other considerations forbade, but perhaps another Shelley scholar will be inspired to pursue this worthwhile project.

Part Two consists of five essays, specially commissioned for this volume, that apply to *Frankenstein* the methodologies of reader response, psychoanalytic, feminist, cultural, and Marxist criticism. Although each piece is intended to be exemplary of one critical method, there is some overlap among the essays; this eclecticism seems to me not only characteristic of much contemporary criticism but one of its strengths. In choosing the theoretical modes to be represented, I was sometimes guided by already existing work. *Frankenstein* has received so much psychoanalytic criticism, for instance, that a Lacanian reading seemed the next logical step. Similarly, in my feminist essay I attempted to build on previous feminist readings. In my other choices I was guided either by the dearth of previous readings—Mary Lowe-Evans's reader-response essay is, I believe, unique in *Frankenstein* criticism—or by the opportunity to add to the small but intriguing bodies of work in cultural and Marxist criticism of the novel.

Acknowledgments

My first debt of gratitude is to the four colleagues who contributed essays to this volume. Under difficult circumstances they responded promptly and with alacrity to editorial suggestions; what might otherwise have been an onerous task for me was much lightened by their patience and good humor. I am also grateful for the abundance of these qualities in the editors at Bedford Books; in particular, Steve Scipione and Tara Masih cheerfully put up with the delays caused by my transatlantic sojourns. In addition, Steve, Tara, and copyeditor Cynthia Benn gave the manuscript extremely thorough and useful readings, and the efficiency of Kimberly Chabot in development and Laura McCready in production was much appreciated. I would also like to thank Ailsa Brookes at the London office of the American Institute for Foreign Study; by giving me access to fax and computer facilities, she eased my burdens considerably. Dr. B. C. Barker-Benfield, Assistant Librarian at the Bodleian, and the staff at the British Library were unfailingly courteous and helpful. I thank Lord Abinger for permission to cite from the Abinger manuscripts at the Bodleian. I benefited from early conversations with Phil Cohen and Dabney Townsend about possible directions for this volume, and from later ones with Eva Cherniavsky and Andrew Miller about my difficulties with it. Finally but first in time, I want to thank Ross Murfin, model colleague and editor, for involving me in this project, for insightful criticism of all the volume's essays, and for his encouragement and friendship.

Johanna M. Smith
University of Texas
at Arlington

Contents

PART ONE

Frankenstein:
The Complete Text

Introduction:
Biographical and
Historical Contexts

"July 24: Write my story." This laconic entry in Mary Shelley's 1816 journal is her first reference to the fifteen-year process of writing and rewriting *Frankenstein*. She began it in mid-June of 1816 as a short ghost story and gradually expanded it over the next year; in January 1818 *Frankenstein; or, The Modern Prometheus* was published anonymously in a three-volume edition. In 1823, to capitalize on the success of Richard Brinsley Peake's stage adaptation, *Presumption; or, The Fate of Frankenstein*, Mary Shelley's father arranged for a reprint two-volume edition. A copy of this edition contains her notes for possible revision, but no changes were made in the novel until 1831, when Bentley and Coburn published the revised *Frankenstein* in their Standard Novels series. In her introduction to the new edition, Mary looked back on her own history as well as the novel's to answer a "very frequently asked" question: "how I, then a young girl, came to think of, and to dilate upon, so very hideous an idea" (Introduction 19).

Looking again at this dual history will enable us to place author and novel in their context: both Mary Shelley's conflicted revolutionary heritage and the period from 1789 to 1832 during which England oscillated uneasily between revolution and reform. In many ways both Mary Shelley and *Frankenstein* figure a revolutionary age. Mary agreed with the radical ideas of her parents Mary Wollstonecraft and William Godwin, and by eloping with a married man she further defied social convention. The sections of *Frankenstein* attacking injustices in Britain's political and social order are additional testimony to her radicalism. Yet other elements of Mary Shelley's life and work are quite orthodox. She not only became a wife but accepted many of her culture's constraining views of women's nature, and *Frankenstein* suggests that society produces monsters not so much by systematic oppression as by inept parenting. These latter, more conventional elements indicate the reformist rather than revolutionary impulse in Mary's thought, the desire to change certain *aspects* of her culture's systems rather than do away with those systems entirely. The difficulties in choosing between these alternatives are also apparent both in the lives of her parents — radicals though they were, both experienced problems in living out their revolutionary principles — and in Mary's culture during the years between 1789 (the beginning of the French Revolution) and 1832 (the passage of the Reform Bill, which enfranchised sections of the English middle classes for the first time). *Frankenstein*'s chronology — the first version published in 1818, when violent revolution was still a possibility in England, and the revised version published in 1831, when revolution seemed imminent if Parliament failed to pass the Reform Bill — places it firmly in this context of balancing between revolution and reform. Beginning with the divided and often contradictory relation between theory and practice in her parents' lives and work, we can move through Mary's equally conflicted sense of this heritage to an understanding of *Frankenstein* as revolutionary yet reformist text.

Mary Shelley was born on August 30, 1797, the daughter of radical feminist Mary Wollstonecraft and radical philosopher William Godwin. Both her parents were prominent in revolutionary movements that peaked in the late eighteenth century. Although Wollstonecraft died in childbirth and so did not personally supervise her daughter's early education, by her teens Mary Shelley was supplementing that education by reading her mother's works. Now best known for *A Vindication of the Rights of Woman* (1792), Wollstonecraft had previously impressed her contemporaries with *A Vindication of the Rights of Men* (1790), the first full-length response to Edmund Burke's conservative *Reflections on the Revolution in France* (1790). In this work and in her 1795 *An Historical and Moral View of the Origin and Progress of the French Revolution*, Wollstonecraft countered Burkean attacks on the Revolution and its English sympathizers (known as Jacobins), in part by enumerating the "continual miseries" that impelled the poor toward revolution (*Rights of Men* 151).

Wollstonecraft's feeling for the working poor came from personal experience. Although her father rose from master-weaver to gentleman farmer, his drunkenness and general fecklessness impoverished his family, and before she turned to writing Wollstonecraft worked variously as lady's companion, seamstress, director of a girls' school, and governess. This hand-to-mouth existence doubtless influenced her view that more professions should be open to "honest, industrious women" (*Rights of Woman* 148); moreover, as a working woman she recognized that women and workers were equally oppressed by the current political order. At this time voting eligibility was restricted to men and depended on property ownership; out of a population of 8.5 million, then, only 11,000 — men of the propertied class — elected representatives to the House of Commons. Wollstonecraft called this system "only a convenient handle for despotism" (147); under it, she said ironically, women are "as well represented as a numerous class of hard-working mechanics, who pay for the support of royalty when they can scarcely stop their children's mouths with bread."

Rights of Woman consistently linked an argument for women's rights with attacks on political oppression. Here Wollstonecraft joined a long tradition of feminism that not only demanded education and other rights for women but did so in political terms. In *Some Reflections on Marriage* (1700), for instance, Mary Astell had demanded women's equality in marriage by arguing against political absolutism: "if absolute Sovereignty be not necessary in a State, how comes it to be so in a Family?" (qtd. in Ferguson 192). At a time when royal and paternal authority were still for the most part considered equivalent, such demands for women's equality were potentially revolutionary. Indeed, in her poem "The Woman's Labour" (1739), the working-class Mary Collier not only argued that women domestic servants and field laborers worked at least as hard as men of their class (since they did the domestic work of wives and mothers too) but also complained that all workers were robbed of the fruits of their industry. By the 1770s and 1780s such feminists as Catherine Macaulay Graham were making women's claims more vociferously, in part because challenges to political tyranny—the American Revolution of 1775 and the French Revolution—seemed to promise new liberty for women.

Wollstonecraft took this view in *Rights of Woman*. Women must be treated as "human creatures, who, in common with men, are placed on this earth to unfold their faculties" (8); hence, instead of being taught to obey and please men with "gentleness, docility, and a spaniel-like affection" (34) commonly "supposed to be the sexual characteristics of the weaker vessel" (9), women must be educated to foster the "strength, both of mind and body" that will make them "respectable members of society" (10).

But Wollstonecraft supported this position with contradictory arguments that suggest the difficulties of conceiving a revolutionary feminism. On the one hand, she attacked "tyrants" who "*force* all women, by denying them civil and political rights, to remain immured in their families" (5), and she argued that a woman should be "prepared by education to become the companion of man" (4). On the other hand, she concluded that such an education would make women "more observant daughters, more affectionate sisters, more faithful wives, more reasonable mothers — in a word, better citizens" (150). This is a complicated argument: while Wollstonecraft was clearly concerned to improve women's position as "members of society" and "citizens," she also saw that position as rooted in their traditional domestic roles. It is true that in 1792 educating a woman to be her husband's companion and friend rather than "play-thing" (24), "humble dependent" (29), or "upper servant" (40) was still a fairly revolutionary aim, but nonetheless Wollstonecraft's argument tended to define women not as "human creatures" but by their domestic relations to men.

Similar contradictions appear in Wollstonecraft's life as a feminist. Although she warned her readers that "love, from its very nature, must be transitory" (30), she clung to her affair with the American adventurer Gilbert Imlay; the relationship was stormy, to say the least, and Wollstonecraft twice attempted suicide over Imlay's affairs with other women. The paradox of this passion is well stated by Muriel Spark: "The distracted exponent of the rights of women was driven to attempted suicide for the sake of her lover" (6). Wollstonecraft experienced other problems as she tried to work out how to live in the new world that revolution and feminism promised. For instance, while her marriage to Godwin left her independent (they maintained separate households), there were hitches. In a note asking him to settle a business matter, she said, "I am perhaps as unfit as yourself to do it, and my time appears to me as valuable as that of other persons accustomed to employ themselves" (qtd. in Grylls 4); the sharp tone hints the difficulties of living out the principle of equality and shared responsibility in marriage. While Mary Shelley might not have known of these day-to-day difficulties, she would certainly have known of her mother's troubled relations with Imlay from reading Godwin's 1798 *Memoirs of the Author of A Vindication of the Rights of Woman*. She also would have known the penalties a feminist suffered for an unconventional sexual life: Godwin's revelations about Wollstonecraft so shocked many contemporaries that one critic feels the book "made it impossible for a respectable English woman openly to associate herself with Mary Wollstonecraft's feminist views" (Mellor 3). Like Mary Shelley, however, many less "respectable" women carried on those views: in 1834 Frances Morrison, coeditor with her husband of the radical union journal *The Pioneer*, "beautif[ied]" its Woman's Page with an extract from *Rights of Woman*.

I have discussed the contradictions in Wollstonecraft's thought and life at length because they profoundly affected her daughter. Mary Shelley knew her mother's history, if not from Godwin directly then from his *Memoirs*, which she and Percy Shelley often read. Her journal shows that they also read her mother's works over and over, and Mary was in fact rereading *Progress of the French Revolution* and *Rights of Woman* while writing *Frankenstein*. We will see how the mixed signals of Wollstonecraft's life and books appear in Mary Shelley's novel and her own history.

The legacy from her father's works was perhaps less problematic, but it too suggested for Mary Shelley the dangers and contradictions in living out a political ideal that she would both encounter in her life and explore in *Frankenstein*. The son of a Sandemanian minister, Godwin was also a preacher in this dissenting sect, but he later became an atheist and turned his attention to ethics and politics. With his *Enquiry concerning Political Justice* (1793) and his novel *Caleb Williams; or, Things as They Are* (1794), he surpassed even Tom Paine as a spokesperson for radical ideals; "wherever liberty, truth, justice was the theme," William Hazlitt later recalled, "his name was not far off" (qtd. in Spark 8). Godwin was one of many in England who initially welcomed the French Revolution of 1789 uncritically. Wordsworth's *Prelude* records the euphoria of this time when "Reason seemed the most to assert her rights" against moribund institutions, and Wollstonecraft's was only one of some thirty enthusiastic defenses of the Revolution. Radicals formed "corresponding societies" to discuss how best to extend the French example into England, and the phenomenal sale of Paine's *Rights of Man Part Two* (1792) — 200,000 copies by 1793, or approximately one for every fifty Britons (Thompson 117) — further testifies to the revolutionary fervor of those days.

But the year of *Rights of Man* also began a period of repression that made it more dangerous for Godwin and other Jacobins to publicly support the French Republic. In December Paine was outlawed from England and his book banned as seditious libel; in February 1793 England declared war on France and moved no less harshly against the Republic's English adherents. Booksellers were prosecuted for selling *Rights of Man*; leaders of corresponding societies were arrested; habeas corpus was suspended in 1794, large public meetings without permits were banned in 1795, secret organizations were outlawed in 1797, and Combination Laws against workers' associations were passed in 1799. It is not surprising that in May 1793 the government considered prosecuting Godwin for *Political Justice* — a prosecution that, if successful, could have resulted in his being drawn and quartered. Eventually the government decided not to proceed, but clearly it had not agreed with the *Critical Review* that a book "which of its very nature and bulk can never circulate among the inferior classes of society" could do little damage (qtd. in Locke 60). While by no means as successful as *Rights of Man*, Godwin's book went into three licit and two pirated editions; the "inferior classes" often pooled their money to buy one copy, which was then read aloud, so Godwin's revolutionary ideas "circulated" farther than the sales figure of 4,000 might suggest.

But in some ways *Political Justice* is antirevolutionary, and a brief consideration of its contradictory political philosophy will prepare for the contradictions of Mary Shelley's and *Frankenstein*'s politics. In 1800 Godwin recollected: "My heart beat high with sentiments of liberty [in 1789]," but, he added, "I never for a moment ceased to disapprove of mob government and violence" (qtd. in Locke 40). *Political Justice* displays this same ambivalence toward the process of political change. As a radical, Godwin insisted that all government is pernicious. Not only is it "indebted for its existence to the errors and perverseness of a few," but it is perpetuated "by the infantine and uninstructed confidence of the many" (125), for the lower orders confuse the reverence *due* a superior in wisdom with the obedience *enforced* by a superior in rank. The upper ranks have "usurped certain advantages over us to which they can show no equitable claim" (123), and Godwin stated that revolutionaries "angry with corruption, and impatient at injustice" are motivated by "the excess of a virtuous feeling" (139). The key word here, however, is "excess," for it signals how the radical Godwin can also be conservative: revolutionary disruption suspends the "patient speculations" that will gradually produce "salutary and uninterrupted progress" toward "political truth and social improvement" (137–38). Yet revolution and violence are not simply destructive, he concluded, for often they have led to "important changes of the social system" (139). In one sense, then, Godwin *was* a revolutionary: his view that the gradual decay of government is a "euthanasia" devoutly to be wished (125),

like his statement that revolutionary violence may be useful, was unlikely to cheer proponents of the status quo. Yet he was also antirevolutionary: what he desired was *gradual* progress toward a state in which
government is unnecessary because, "the plain dictates of justice" having become evident to all, "the whole species [has] become reasonable
and virtuous" (221).

Unavoidably, such a summary oversimplifies Godwin's position,
and he underestimated neither the length of time required for progress
toward political justice nor the difficulties in educating humans toward
this goal. Yet he had moments of sunny optimism that his daughter,
despite her agreement with some of his ideas, could not share; she was
rereading *Political Justice* as she wrote *Frankenstein*, and her politics are
in part an answer to her father's. If we now turn to Mary Shelley's life
and her conflicted view of her dual heritage, we can move toward an
understanding of her and *Frankenstein*'s revolutionary yet reformist impulses.

Wollstonecraft died of a puerperal infection ten days after Mary's
birth in 1797, so Godwin raised her and her half-sister Fanny (Wollstonecraft's daughter by Imlay) alone until 1801, when he married
Mary Jane Clairmont. Up to this point he appears to have been an
attentive father, but he often said that he felt "totally unfitted" to educate his daughters without Wollstonecraft (qtd. in Grylls 11), and he
gave this sense of "incompetence" as "one among the motives" for his
remarriage (qtd. in Mellor 8). Yet Godwin's second wife was not fully
committed to Wollstonecraft's educational aims, and she seems to have
taken more interest in educating her own daughter, Jane (later Claire)
Clairmont, than Wollstonecraft's. At this remove it is hard to know
whether she was in fact a Wicked Stepmother, but certainly Mary felt
that the new Mrs. Godwin was jealous of her predecessor's daughter
(Mellor 13) and resented Mary's "excessive & romantic attachment"
to her father (*Letters* 2.215). In addition, this attachment to her father
did not console Mary for the loss of her mother. Godwin himself admitted that as a busy father he was apt to command his children "in a way
somewhat sententious and authoritative" (qtd. in Spark 16), and Mary
gradually began to spend more and more time with Wollstonecraft's
books at her grave. In the summer of 1814, when she was seventeen,
this favorite spot also became the site of her meetings with Percy
Shelley.

Long an admirer of Godwin's principles, Percy Shelley had introduced himself to Mary's father in 1812 and was soon dining regularly

at the Godwins' with his wife Harriet. In his usual quixotic manner, in 1811 nineteen-year-old Percy had married sixteen-year-old Harriet to rescue her from a tyrannical father and also, in his own words, to "cultivat[e]" her (qtd. in Sparks 20). Later, he told a friend, he decided that this "rash & heartless union" had become "loathsome and horrible" and he "speedily conceived an ardent passion" for the "genuine elevation and magnificence of [Mary's] moral nature" (qtd. in Sparks 20–21). He and Mary declared their love to each other but at first agreed to part; after Percy threatened before the entire Godwin family to commit suicide, however, an alternative plan was adopted: on July 18, 1814, they eloped to France, taking Mary's half-sister Jane/Claire with them.

Mary Shelley later recalled the next eight years as "happy, though chequered" (*Journal* 430), and checkered seems a mild description. As Percy Shelley's mistress she suffered the same kind of social condemnation visited on her mother's affair with Imlay: even though she married Percy in December 1816 (after Harriet Shelley's suicide), she never entirely escaped the effects of her early indiscretion. Furthermore, although their financial position later improved, Percy was always strapped for cash: over the years Godwin wheedled £4700 from him, and Percy was also generous to the unemployed lace-makers near their home at Marlow. In addition to money troubles, Mary's years with Percy were marked by intermittent domestic disturbances. Claire's continued presence in the household was often an irritant and sometimes worse. Claire had an illegitimate daughter by the poet Byron, and she entangled both Mary and Percy in her schemes to get custody of the child from him; furthermore, Mary was deeply distressed by recurring rumors that Percy and Claire had had an illegitimate child whom Percy bundled off to a foundling hospital. And finally there were the deaths of Mary and Percy's children: two daughters died in infancy, the death of their 3-½-year-old son William led to a depression so deep that Mary felt she "ought to have died" too (*Letters* 1.108), and a mid-1822 miscarriage caused another depression and also an estrangement from Percy. His infatuations with Emilia Viviana and Jane Williams cannot have been easy to take either, so that when he drowned on July 8, 1822, Mary's grief seems to have been heightened by guilt over their recent differences.

But more enduring was her sense that Percy Shelley had helped her to fulfill the promise of her heritage. Wollstonecraft's "greatness of soul" and Godwin's "high talents," she wrote a friend, "have perpetually reminded me that I ought to degenerate as little as I could" from them; Percy not only "fostered this ambition" (*Letters* 2.4) but "supported & brought me forward" (*Journal* 555). This was especially true of her writing: although she felt it natural that "as the daughter of two persons of distinguished literary celebrity, I should very early in life have thought of writing." Percy too was "very anxious that I should prove myself worthy of my parentage and enrol myself on the page of fame" (Introduction 19–20).

Yet one suspects that Percy Shelley's encouragement could be something of a burden. He appears not to have noticed that the time he urged his wife to spend writing would have interfered with "the cares of a family" (Introduction 20) — which of course fell on her and not him. Nor can it have been entirely bracing for her to have her husband "for ever inciting me to obtain literary reputation . . . not so much with the idea that I could produce any thing worthy of notice, but that he might himself judge how far I possessed the promise of better things." To be encouraged only to be judged, in other words, may have reduced rather than heightened Mary Shelley's confidence. The same result is suggested by her recollections of the evenings she spent listening to Byron's talks with her husband: although *Frankenstein* later developed the ideas the men discussed, at the time Mary's "incapacity & timidity" prevented her from joining their conversations (*Journal* 439). Even after fulfilling "the promise of better things" with *Frankenstein*, the author seemed unable fully to escape a sense of incapacity: in her 1831 introduction the sentence that begins with a snappish assertion — "I certainly did not owe the suggestion of one incident, nor scarcely of one train of feeling, to my husband" — concludes meekly and perhaps generously that she would not have developed her tale "but for his incitement" (23).

This lack of confidence, as Mary Shelley herself felt, stems from being a woman (writer) who requires masculine approval. Understandably, it emerges with particular force in her journal entries after her husband's death. Although at one point she vows to pursue self-improvement and "literary labors" (*Journal* 431), more characteristic are the entries where she desires only to be "a faint continuation of *his* being, & as far as possible the revelation to the earth of what he was" (*Journal* 436). Of course such statements display the excess of first grief, and in fact Mary Shelley produced an impressive body of work after her husband's death: five novels, nineteen short stories, a travel book, several biographies of scientific and literary figures, and critical editions of Percy Shelley's poetry and prose. Indeed, Percy's early encouragement may have helped her continue writing after his death. As a widow trying to support herself by writing, Mary had to contend with her father-in-law's rigid ideas of feminine propriety: Sir Timothy Shelley consistently forbade her planned biography of his son and after she published her novel *The Last Man* he suspended the income he had allowed her, because he objected to his son's widow bringing herself before the public (*Letters* 1.521n). Yet she continued to write, and this productivity suggests that Percy's encouragement may not have been wholly deleterious.

But Mary Shelley's journal nonetheless testifies to the dependence on Percy Shelley that appeared in her 1831 introduction to *Frankenstein*, and even later. In a low-spirited letter of 1835, for example, she laments, "I was always a dependant thing — wanting fosterage and support — I am left to myself instead by fortune — and I am nothing" (*Letters* 2.246). These desolate musings reflect not just her personal grief but also a conservative ideology of femininity. The letter includes her general reflections on women as "weaker" than men and lacking in their "higher grades of intellect"; later she records that she has been "unable to put myself forward unless led, cherished & supported" because she has "the woman's love of looking up & being guided" (*Journal* 555).

Such conservative statements suggest that Mary Shelley failed to live up to her parents' political radicalism. Katherine Powers believes that she was "in no sense a feminist like her mother" (34), while Lee Sterrenburg sees a "gravitation toward conservatism" and away from her "utopian and radical heritage" as early as *Frankenstein* (143). And there is some truth to these claims. Unlike such feminist contemporaries as her friends Caroline Norton and Fanny Wright or the French socialist Flora Tristan, Mary Shelley was never a public campaigner for women's rights. Nor was she long a Jacobin: the young girl who in 1814 enjoyed "frighten[ing]" away a bore by "talking of cutting off Kings heads" (*Journal* 23) is by 1817 decrying "the worst possible human passion *revolution*" (*Letters* 1.49). In 1830 she rejoices that "the stains" of the French Revolution (*Letters* 2.118) had been "wash[ed] off" by France's July Revolution (a bloodless coup dethroning the Bourbon Charles X and instituting a bourgeois republic under Louis-Philippe). By 1838 Mary is recording her "revulsion" from the English Radicals, whom she had once supported but whom she now stigmatizes as "violent without any sense of Justice" (*Journal* 555). In 1848 she shares a prevalent fear of the Chartists, the sometimes revolutionary political movement that planned a massive demonstration on April 10: "the Chartists are full of menace," she writes, for they presage "tyranny & lawless-ness" (*Letters* 3.336). And it is unpleasant to read the classist remarks of the letters written after her son had inherited his grandfather's title and estate. One hears neither Wollstonecraft nor Godwin in Mary Shelley's plaint about "the number of Maids one must keep in the country," or in her self-satisfied conclusion that employing these maids is "giving work to the industrious" and thus "one of the best ways in the world of doing good" (*Letters* 3.347).

Against all this evidence for Mary Shelley's betrayal of her parents' and her own early principles, however, we should remember that neither Wollstonecraft nor Godwin was uncompromisingly revolutionary. And Mary's late assumption of the role of Lady Bountiful should not obscure her early radicalism or her lifelong sympathy for the poor. Her shifting views are better approached as symptomatic of England's troubled industrial development.

Early in the 1700s England had begun to move jerkily from a predominantly small-scale agricultural economy to large-scale and mechanized agriculture and thence to an increasingly industrial economy. By the mid-eighteenth century, hitherto "common land," which had been cultivated collectively by small farmers, was being bought up by great landowners. This process of enclosure enlarged an underclass of the landless poor. As enclosure accelerated during the early nineteenth century (from 1809 on there were over 100 Acts of Enclosure annually [Halevy 192–93]), many small landowners, tenant farmers, and laborers were slowly squeezed out of agriculture and began to migrate to the new industrial centers. Joined to 300,000 soldiers discharged when the Napoleonic Wars ended in 1815, this influx of displaced workers doubled and sometimes trebled the potential local work force and so kept wages down. In addition, the boom–slump cycle of early capitalism caused intermittent but chronic unemployment, further exacerbated in such industries as cotton by competition from the more efficient mechanized Continental producers (Foster 18–20). This growing class of unemployed was considered unfit for Parliamentary representation by virtue of its lack of property, education, and couth; as one commentator put it in 1797, "in times of warm political debate, the Right of Suffrage communicated to an ignorant and ferocious Populace would lead to tumult and confusion" (qtd. in Thompson 26). Not surprisingly, this "Populace" sought redress for its economic grievances through extra-Parliamentary agitation. Between 1790 and 1810 there were 500 riots protesting the price of bread in districts like Nottinghamshire, which was also the center of the 1811–1813 Luddite risings when unemployed workers smashed knitting frames.

Percy Shelley was familiar with this district, and the desperate conditions he saw there in 1811 in part inspired his 1812 poem *Queen Mab*. This is the book he gave Mary in 1814 as a sign of their love, and for a time at least she shared its political vision. In her early letters she speaks of her "radicalism" (*Letters* 1.131) and condemns England's "enslaved state" (*Letters* 1.136) under its rulers' "despotism" (1.124). Although the already cited letter of 1817 shows her fear of "the worst possible human passion *revolution*," another letter of the same year expresses her compassion for an unemployed seaman who had starved to death (*Letters* 1.54). Decades later her letters record similar concerns: an 1845 letter states her disgust with Lord Norfolk's suggestion that starving Irish laborers drink hot water and curry ("very warm and comfortable to the stomachs of the people," he explained, "if it could be got cheap" [*Letters* 3.268]), and in 1847 she notes the large sums she and her son are spending to relieve the "bitter want" of the poor (*Letters* 3.305).

It is possible to fault Mary Shelley's sympathy for the poor as the sort of Dickensian sentimentality that gives liberals a bad name, but the example of Lord Norfolk is a salutary reminder that there are worse attitudes than compassion. And it is her *oscillation* — between fear of the revolutionary working class and sympathy for the laboring poor — that is of interest, for it illuminates not only her own politics but those of *Frankenstein*, especially its (and our) shifting judgments of the monster.

It is significant that the novel was reissued in 1831, at a time when "[t]he burnings, the alarms, the absorbing politics of the day render book-sellers almost averse to publishing at all" (*Letters* 2.120). The "politics of the day" to which the author refers are the increasing, and increasingly violent, public debates over a Reform Bill whose early version would have enfranchised a portion of the working as well as the middle classes. As I have said, the former's fitness for the vote was already in question when *Frankenstein* was first published in 1818. By 1831 the issue was bitterly disputed; the propertied class feared to lose its exclusive legislative power to the propertyless rabble, a fear exacerbated when the working-class supporters of the Reform Bill rioted each time the House of Commons voted it down. We can locate Mary Shelley's novel in the historical context of this debate by looking at the characteristically double view of the Reform Bill presented in her letters. To one correspondent she says, "it looks as if the autocrats would have

the good sense to make the necessary sacrifices to a starving people"
(2.120). To another she writes,

> *Progressiveness* is certainly finely developed just now in Europe —
> together with a degree of *tyrant quellingtiveness* which is highly
> laudable — it is a pity that in our country this should be mingled
> with a *sick destructiveness;* yet the last gives action to the former —
> and without [it], would our Landholders be brought to reason?
> Yet it is very sad — the punishment of the poor men being not
> the least disaster attendant on it. (*Letters* 2.122)

Clearly Mary Shelley favors "progress" and "tyrant quelling," but
equally clearly she fears the "sick destructiveness" that propels these
potentially revolutionary movements; yet this destruction seems a cor-
ollary to progress, and perhaps the only way to force landowners into
giving up their exclusive right to the vote; "yet it is very sad." One
could see this passage as waffling, but it would more usefully be considered as an effort, like Godwin's in *Political Justice,* to come to terms with
England's impulse to revolution.

If we see *Frankenstein*'s monster as a figure for this impulse, we can
locate the novel in the context of its conflicted times.[1] In Victor Frankenstein's view, the monster is like the "ignorant and ferocious Populace": he has no rights and no claim to the recognition he demands
from his superior. Yet when the monster asks nicely — for sympathy, for
understanding, for a mate — Victor can recognize the justice of his
claims, just as the more benevolent middle- and upper-class liberals
would consider requests for the vote from the respectable working
classes. But when Victor imagines the consequences of ceding control,
of passing his power to create life to the monster and monsterette, he
fears the "sick destructiveness" that they, and especially she, might en-
gender. Here the danger of a woman uncontrollably "putting herself
forward" — as Mary Shelley did as a woman writer — heightens the danger of a working class that might be equally uncontrollable if ceded the
vote. Victor then withdraws his concession and justifies himself by arguing the monster's unworthiness (Chapter XXIV), just as opponents of
enfranchising the working classes justified themselves by arguing that
the lower orders were "helots" quite capable of "set[ting] fire to London without anxiety for helpless beings at home" (qtd. in Thompson
894–95). In Victor Frankenstein's self-justification, as in Mary Shelley's
delight in "the boldness of [the] measures" that finally excluded the

---

[1]For another such reading, see Williams xiii–xv.

working class from the 1832 Reform Bill (*Letters* 2.133), is relief that revolutionary monsters are disempowered.

But Mary Shelley's representation of the monster can also be read as a radical's support for rebellion against class oppression. The monster's analysis of the origins of poverty draws on Volney's *Ruins of Empire,* an extremely influential book in radical circles (Thompson 107–08). Volney's picture of a privileged class parasitic on the laboring class finds an echo in the Mary Shelley who excoriated "this wretched system of things" (*Letters* 1.173), and the fact that she revised only a few words of the monster's narrative for the 1831 edition indicates that this view at least had not changed. Against Frankenstein's belief that his creature is inherently monstrous, she places the monster's argument that his culture has made him monstrous, an argument in line with both elements of her radical heritage: Wollstonecraft's view that women's capacities have been stunted by men who treat them as "alluring objects for a moment" (*Rights of Woman* 8), and Godwin's view that human character and behavior are the product not of "innate principles" but of "circumstances and events" (*Political Justice* 28).

If this is so, if Frankenstein and his culture have created the monster, then there are clear grounds for two claims: that a society and not its outcasts creates revolutionary violence, and that the monster's rage is, as Godwin put it, the revolutionary's "excess of a virtuous feeling." This tension between fear of revolution and sympathy with the revolutionary reveals Mary's personal ambivalence, but it does more than that: by making both the conservative and the revolutionary arguments, *Frankenstein* dramatizes the tension between the two that characterized England in the years between 1789 and 1832.

I have been discussing *Frankenstein*'s biographical and historical contexts by focusing on Mary Shelley's doubled view of her parents' radicalism and by locating these contradictions in nineteenth-century politics. In so doing I have been making a case for reading the novel in a certain way, one of the many ways possible. Reader-response critics might object that my case leaves out of account *Frankenstein*'s intended and actual effects on real readers, while psychoanalytic critics might say that I have paid too much attention to Mary Shelley's politics and not enough to her less conscious motives. A feminist critic could plausibly fault me for sliding over the author's difficulties in developing the public voice and persona more easily acquired by men. Cultural critics might point out that I have discussed only the political element in her culture, and a Marxist critic could argue that I have ignored class structures and economic issues in the novel. Part Two of this book adds to Mary Shelley's *Frankenstein* and that of this introduction five more versions, all of which are open to modification or displacement not only by the others but also by each new reader. It is to be hoped that these essays, like the endlessly proliferating movie and television adaptations of the novel, will move their readers to produce more *Frankensteins*.

WORKS CITED

Ferguson, Moira, ed. *First Feminists: British Women Writers 1578–1799.* Bloomington: Indiana UP, 1985.

Foster, John. *Class Struggle and the Industrial Revolution: Early Industrial Capitalism in Three English Towns.* London: Methuen, 1974.

Godwin, William. *Enquiry concerning Political Justice.* 1793. Ed. K. Codell Carter. Oxford: Clarendon, 1971.

Grylls, R. Glynn. *Mary Shelley: A Biography.* London: Oxford UP, 1938.

Halevy, Elie. *A History of the English People in 1815.* 1924. London: Ark-Routledge, 1987.

Locke, Don. *A Fantasy of Reason: The Life and Thought of William Godwin.* London: Routledge, 1980.

Mellor, Anne K. *Mary Shelley: Her Life, Her Fiction, Her Monsters.* New York: Routledge, 1988.

Powers, Katherine Richardson. *The Influence of William Godwin on the Novels of Mary Shelley.* New York: Arno, 1980.

Shelley, Mary. *The Journals of Mary Wollstonecraft Shelley.* Ed. Paula R. Feldman and Diana Kilvert-Scott. Oxford: Clarendon, 1987.

———. *The Letters of Mary Wollstonecraft Shelley.* Ed. Betty T. Bennett. 3 vols. Baltimore: Johns Hopkins UP, 1980–1988.

Spark, Muriel. *Mary Shelley.* Rev. ed. London: Sphere-Penguin, 1987.

Sterrenburg, Lee. "Mary Shelley's Monster: Politics and Psyche in *Frankenstein.*" In *The Endurance of "Frankenstein."* Ed. George Levine and U. C. Knoepflmacher. Berkeley: U of California P, 1979. 143–71.

Thompson, E. P. *The Making of the English Working Class.* 1963. London: Penguin, 1988.

Williams, Gwyn A. *Artisans and Sans-culottes: Popular Movements in France and Britain during the French Revolution.* 1968. London: Libris, 1989.

Wollstonecraft, Mary. *A Vindication of the Rights of Men.* 1790. Gainesville: Scholars' Facsimiles & Reprints, 1960.

———. *A Vindication of the Rights of Woman.* 1792. Ed. Carol H. Poston. New York: Norton, 1975.

Frankenstein

or

The Modern Prometheus

Did I request thee, Maker, from my clay
To mould Me man? Did I solicit thee
From darkness to promote me? —

Paradise Lost [X. 743–5]

TO
WILLIAM GODWIN
Author of Political Justice, Caleb Williams, & c.
THESE VOLUMES
Are respectfully inscribed
BY
THE AUTHOR

INTRODUCTION

The Publishers of the Standard Novels, in selecting "Frankenstein" for one of their series, expressed a wish that I should furnish them with some account of the origin of the story. I am the more willing to comply, because I shall thus give a general answer to the question, so very frequently asked me — "How I, then a young girl, came to think of, and to dilate upon, so very hideous an idea?" It is true that I am very averse to bringing myself forward in print; but as my account will only appear as an appendage to a former production, and as it will be confined to such topics as have connection with my authorship alone, I can scarcely accuse myself of a personal intrusion.

It is not singular that, as the daughter of two persons of distinguished literary celebrity, I should very early in life have thought of writing. As a child I scribbled; and my favourite pastime, during the hours given me for recreation, was to "write stories." Still I had a dearer pleasure than this, which was the formation of castles in the air — the indulging in waking dreams — the following up trains of thought, which had for their subject the formation of a succession of imaginary incidents. My dreams were at once more fantastic and agreeable than my writings. In the latter I was a close imitator — rather doing as others had done, than putting down the suggestions of my own mind. What I wrote was intended at least for one other eye — my childhood's companion and friend; but my dreams were all my own; I accounted for them to nobody; they were my refuge when annoyed — my dearest pleasure when free.

I lived principally in the country as a girl, and passed a considerable time in Scotland. I made occasional visits to the more picturesque parts; but my habitual residence was on the blank and dreary northern shores of the Tay, near Dundee. Blank and dreary on retrospection I call them; they were not so to me then. They were the eyry of freedom, and the pleasant region where unheeded I could commune with the creatures of my fancy. I wrote then — but in a most common-place style. It was beneath the trees of the grounds belonging to our house, or on the bleak sides of the woodless mountains near, that my true compositions, the airy flights of my imagination, were born and fostered. I did not make myself the heroine of my tales. Life appeared to me too common-place an affair as regarded myself. I could not figure to myself that romantic woes or wonderful events would ever be my lot; but I was not confined to my own identity, and I could people the hours with creations far more interesting to me at that age, than my own sensations.

After this my life became busier, and reality stood in place of fiction. My husband, however, was, from the first, very anxious that I should prove myself worthy of my parentage, and enrol myself on the page of fame. He was for ever inciting me to obtain literary reputation, which even on my own part I cared for then, though since I have become infinitely indifferent to it. At this time he desired that I should write, not so much with the idea that I could produce any thing worthy of notice, but that he might himself judge how far I possessed the promise of better things hereafter. Still I did nothing. Travelling, and the cares of a family, occupied my time; and study, in the way of reading, or improving my ideas in communication with his far more cultivated mind, was all of literary employment that engaged my attention.

In the summer of 1816, we visited Switzerland, and became the neighbours of Lord Byron. At first we spent our pleasant hours on the lake, or wandering on its shores; and Lord Byron, who was writing the third canto of Childe Harold, was the only one among us who put his thoughts upon paper. These, as he brought them successively to us, clothed in all the light and harmony of poetry, seemed to stamp as divine the glories of heaven and earth, whose influences we partook with him.

But it proved a wet, ungenial summer, and incessant rain often confined us for days to the house. Some volumes of ghost stories, translated from the German into French, fell into our hands. There was the History of the Inconstant Lover, who, when he thought to clasp the bride to whom he had pledged his vows, found himself in the arms of the pale ghost of her whom he had deserted. There was the tale of the sinful founder of his race, whose miserable doom it was to bestow the kiss of death on all the younger sons of his fated house, just when they reached the age of promise. His gigantic, shadowy form, clothed like the ghost in Hamlet, in complete armour, but with the beaver up, was seen at midnight, by the moon's fitful beams, to advance slowly along the gloomy avenue. The shape was lost beneath the shadow of the castle walls; but soon a gate swung back, a step was heard, the door of the chamber opened, and he advanced to the couch of the blooming youths, cradled in healthy sleep. Eternal sorrow sat upon his face as he bent down and kissed the forehead of the boys, who from that hour withered like flowers snapt upon the stalk. I have not seen these stories since then; but their incidents are as fresh in my mind as if I had read them yesterday.

"We will each write a ghost story," said Lord Byron; and his proposition was acceded to. There were four of us. The noble author began a tale, a fragment of which he printed at the end of his poem of Mazeppa. Shelley, more apt to embody ideas and sentiments in the radiance of brilliant imagery, and in the music of the most melodious verse that adorns our language, than to invent the machinery of a story, commenced one founded on the experiences of his early life. Poor Polidori had some terrible idea about a skull-headed lady, who was so punished for peeping through a key-hole — what to see I forget — something very shocking and wrong of course; but when she was reduced to a worse condition than the renowned Tom of Coventry, he did not know what to do with her, and was obliged to despatch her to the tomb of the Capulets, the only place for which she was fitted. The illustrious poets also, annoyed by the platitude of prose, speedily relinquished their uncongenial task.

I busied myself *to think of a story,* — a story to rival those which had excited us to this task. One which would speak to the mysterious fears of our nature, and awaken thrilling horror — one to make the reader dread to look round, to curdle the blood, and quicken the beatings of the heart. If I did not accomplish these things, my ghost story would be unworthy of its name. I thought and pondered — vainly. I felt that blank incapability of invention which is the greatest misery of authorship, when dull Nothing replies to our anxious invocations. *Have you thought of a story?* I was asked each morning, and each morning I was forced to reply with a mortifying negative.

Every thing must have a beginning, to speak in Sanchean phrase, and that beginning must be linked to something that went before. The Hindoos give the world an elephant to support it, but they make the elephant stand upon a tortoise. Invention, it must be humbly admitted, does not consist in creating out of void, but out of chaos; the materials must, in the first place, be afforded: it can give form to dark, shapeless substances, but cannot bring into being the substance itself. In all matters of discovery and invention, even of those that appertain to the imagination, we are continually reminded of the story of Columbus and his egg. Invention consists in the capacity of seizing on the capabilities of a subject, and in the power of moulding and fashioning ideas suggested to it.

Many and long were the conversations between Lord Byron and Shelley, to which I was a devout but nearly silent listener. During one of these, various philosophical doctrines were discussed, and among others the nature of the principle of life, and whether there was any probability of its ever being discovered and communicated. They talked of the experiments of Dr. Darwin, (I speak not of what the Doctor really did, or said that he did, but, as more to my purpose, of what was then spoken of as having been done by him,) who preserved a piece of vermicelli in a glass case, till by some extraordinary means it began to move with voluntary motion. Not thus, after all, would life be given. Perhaps a corpse would be re-animated; galvanism had given token of such things: perhaps the component parts of a creature might be manufactured, brought together, and endued with vital warmth.

Night waned upon this talk, and even the witching hour had gone by, before we retired to rest. When I placed my head on my pillow, I did not sleep, nor could I be said to think. My imagination, unbidden, possessed and guided me, gifting the successive images that arose in my mind with a vividness far beyond the usual bounds of reverie. I saw — with shut eyes, but acute mental vision, — I saw the pale student of unhallowed arts kneeling beside the thing he had put together. I saw the hideous phantasm of a man stretched out, and then, on the working of some powerful engine, show signs of life, and stir with an uneasy, half vital motion. Frightful must it be; for supremely frightful would be the effect of any human endeavour to mock the stupendous mechanism of the Creator of the world. His success would terrify the artist; he would rush away from his odious handywork, horror-stricken. He would hope that, left to itself, the slight spark of life which he had communicated would fade; that this thing, which had received such imperfect animation, would subside into dead matter; and he might sleep in the belief that the silence of the grave would quench for ever the transient existence of the hideous corpse which he had looked upon as the cradle of life. He sleeps; but he is awakened; he opens his eyes; behold the horrid thing stands at his bedside, opening his curtains, and looking on him with yellow, watery, but speculative eyes.

I opened mine in terror. The idea so possessed my mind, that a thrill of fear ran through me, and I wished to exchange the ghastly image of my fancy for the realities around. I see them still; the very room, the dark *parquet*, the closed shutters, with the moonlight struggling through, and the sense I had that the glassy lake and white high Alps were beyond. I could not so easily get rid of my hideous phantom; still it haunted me. I must try to think of something else. I recurred to my ghost story, — my tiresome unlucky ghost story! O! if I could only contrive one which would frighten my reader as I myself had been frightened that night!

Swift as light and as cheering was the idea that broke in upon me. "I have found it! What terrified me will terrify others; and I need only describe the spectre which had haunted my midnight pillow." On the morrow I announced that I had *thought of a story*. I began that day with the words, *It was on a dreary night of November*, making only a transcript of the grim terrors of my waking dream.

At first I thought but of a few pages — of a short tale; but Shelley urged me to develope the idea at greater length. I certainly did not owe the suggestion of one incident, nor scarcely of one train of feeling, to my husband, and yet but for his incitement, it would never have taken the form in which it was presented to the world. From this declaration I must except the preface. As far as I can recollect, it was entirely written by him.

And now, once again, I bid my hideous progeny go forth and prosper. I have an affection for it, for it was the offspring of happy days, when death and grief were but words, which found no true echo in my heart. Its several pages speak of many a walk, many a drive, and many a conversation, when I was not alone; and my companion was one who, in this world, I shall never see more. But this is for myself; my readers have nothing to do with these associations.

I will add but one word as to the alterations I have made. They are principally those of style. I have changed no portion of the story, nor introduced any new ideas or circumstances. I have mended the language where it was so bald as to interfere with the interest of the narrative; and these changes occur almost exclusively in the beginning of the first volume. Throughout they are entirely confined to such parts as are mere adjuncts to the story, leaving the core and substance of it untouched.

M. W. S.

London, October 15, 1831.

PREFACE

The event on which this fiction is founded, has been supposed, by Dr. Darwin, and some of the physiological writers of Germany, as not of impossible occurrence. I shall not be supposed as according the remotest degree of serious faith to such an imagination; yet, in assuming it as the basis of a work of fancy, I have not considered myself as merely weaving a series of supernatural terrors. The event on which the interest of the story depends is exempt from the disadvantages of a mere tale of spectres or enchantment. It was recommended by the novelty of the situations which it developes; and, however impossible as a physical fact, affords a point of view to the imagination for the delineating of human passions more comprehensive and commanding than any which the ordinary relations of existing events can yield.

I have thus endeavoured to preserve the truth of the elementary principles of human nature, while I have not scrupled to innovate upon their combinations. The Iliad, the tragic poetry of Greece — Shakespeare, in the Tempest and Midsummer Night's Dream, — and most especially Milton, in Paradise Lost, conform to this rule; and the most humble novelist, who seeks to confer or receive amusement from his labours, may, without presumption, apply to prose fiction a licence, or rather a rule, from the adoption of which so many exquisite combinations of human feeling have resulted in the highest specimens of poetry.

The circumstance on which my story rests was suggested in casual conversation. It was commenced partly as a source of amusement, and partly as an expedient for exercising any untried resources of mind. Other motives were mingled with these, as the work proceeded. I am

by no means indifferent to the manner in which whatever moral tendencies exist in the sentiments or characters it contains shall affect the
reader; yet my chief concern in this respect has been limited to the
avoiding the enervating effects of the novels of the present day, and to
the exhibition of the amiableness of domestic affection, and the excellence of universal virtue. The opinions which naturally spring from the
character and situation of the hero are by no means to be conceived as
existing always in my own conviction; nor is any inference justly to be
drawn from the following pages as prejudicing any philosophical doctrine of whatever kind.

It is a subject also of additional interest to the author, that this story
was begun in the majestic region where the scene is principally laid, and
in society which cannot cease to be regretted. I passed the summer of
1816 in the environs of Geneva. The season was cold and rainy, and in
the evenings we crowded around a blazing wood fire, and occasionally
amused ourselves with some German stories of ghosts, which happened
to fall into our hands. These tales excited in us a playful desire of imitation. Two other friends (a tale from the pen of one of whom would be
far more acceptable to the public than any thing I can ever hope to
produce) and myself agreed to write each a story, founded on some
supernatural occurrence.

The weather, however, suddenly became serene; and my two friends
left me on a journey among the Alps, and lost, in the magnificent scenes
which they present, all memory of their ghostly visions. The following
tale is the only one which has been completed.

Marlow, September, 1817.

Frankenstein
or
The Modern Prometheus

LETTER I

To Mrs. Saville, England

St. Petersburgh, Dec. 11th, 17—.

You will rejoice to hear that no disaster has accompanied the commencement of an enterprise which you have regarded with such evil

forebodings. I arrived here yesterday; and my first task is to assure my dear sister of my welfare, and increasing confidence in the success of my undertaking.

I am already far north of London; and as I walk in the streets of Petersburgh, I feel a cold northern breeze play upon my cheeks, which braces my nerves, and fills me with delight. Do you understand this feeling? This breeze, which has travelled from the regions towards which I am advancing, gives me a foretaste of those icy climes. Inspirited by this wind of promise, my day dreams become more fervent and vivid. I try in vain to be persuaded that the pole is the seat of frost and desolation; it ever presents itself to my imagination as the region of beauty and delight. There, Margaret, the sun is for ever visible; its broad disk just skirting the horizon, and diffusing a perpetual splendour. There — for with your leave, my sister, I will put some trust in preceding navigators — there snow and frost are banished; and, sailing over a calm sea, we may be wafted to a land surpassing in wonders and in beauty every region hitherto discovered on the habitable globe. Its productions and features may be without example, as the phenomena of the heavenly bodies undoubtedly are in those undiscovered solitudes. What may not be expected in a country of eternal light? I may there discover the wondrous power which attracts the needle; and may regulate a thousand celestial observations, that require only this voyage to render their seeming eccentricities consistent for ever. I shall satiate my ardent curiosity with the sight of a part of the world never before visited, and may tread a land never before imprinted by the foot of man. These are my enticements, and they are sufficient to conquer all fear of danger or death, and to induce me to commence this laborious voyage with the joy a child feels when he embarks in a little boat, with his holiday mates, on an expedition of discovery up his native river. But, supposing all these conjectures to be false, you cannot contest the inestimable benefit which I shall confer on all mankind to the last generation, by discovering a passage near the pole to those countries, to reach which at present so many months are requisite; or by ascertaining the secret of the magnet, which, if at all possible, can only be effected by an undertaking such as mine.

These reflections have dispelled the agitation with which I began my letter, and I feel my heart glow with an enthusiasm which elevates me to heaven; for nothing contributes so much to tranquillise the mind as a steady purpose, — a point on which the soul may fix its intellectual eye. This expedition has been the favourite dream of my early years. I have read with ardour the accounts of the various voyages which have been made in the prospect of arriving at the North Pacific Ocean through the seas which surround the pole. You may remember, that a history of all the voyages made for purposes of discovery composed the whole of our good uncle Thomas's library. My education was neglected, yet I was passionately fond of reading. These volumes were my study day and night, and my familiarity with them increased that regret which I had felt, as a child, on learning that my father's dying injunction had forbidden my uncle to allow me to embark in a seafaring life.

These visions faded when I perused, for the first time, those poets whose effusions entranced my soul, and lifted it to heaven. I also became a poet, and for one year lived in a Paradise of my own creation; I imagined that I also might obtain a niche in the temple where the names of Homer and Shakespeare are consecrated. You are well acquainted with my failure, and how heavily I bore the disappointment. But just at that time I inherited the fortune of my cousin, and my thoughts were turned into the channel of their earlier bent.

Six years have passed since I resolved on my present undertaking. I can, even now, remember the hour from which I dedicated myself to this great enterprise. I commenced by inuring my body to hardship. I accompanied the whale-fishers on several expeditions to the North Sea; I voluntarily endured cold, famine, thirst, and want of sleep; I often worked harder than the common sailors during the day, and devoted my nights to the study of mathematics, the theory of medicine, and those branches of physical science from which a naval adventurer might derive the greatest practical advantage. Twice I actually hired myself as an under-mate in a Greenland whaler, and acquitted myself to admiration. I must own I felt a little proud, when my captain offered me the second dignity in the vessel, and entreated me to remain with the greatest earnestness; so valuable did he consider my services.

And now, dear Margaret, do I not deserve to accomplish some great purpose? My life might have been passed in ease and luxury; but I preferred glory to every enticement that wealth placed in my path. Oh, that some encouraging voice would answer in the affirmative! My courage and my resolution is firm; but my hopes fluctuate, and my spirits are often depressed. I am about to proceed on a long and difficult voyage, the emergencies of which will demand all my fortitude: I am required not only to raise the spirits of others, but sometimes to sustain my own, when theirs are failing.

This is the most favourable period for travelling in Russia. They fly quickly over the snow in their sledges; the motion is pleasant, and, in my opinion, far more agreeable than that of an English stage-coach. The cold is not excessive, if you are wrapped in furs, — a dress which I have already adopted; for there is a great difference between walking the deck and remaining seated motionless for hours, when no exercise prevents the blood from actually freezing in your veins. I have no ambition to lose my life on the post-road between St. Petersburgh and Archangel.

I shall depart for the latter town in a fortnight or three weeks; and my intention is to hire a ship there, which can easily be done by paying the insurance for the owner, and to engage as many sailors as I think necessary among those who are accustomed to the whale-fishing. I do not intend to sail until the month of June; and when shall I return? Ah, dear sister, how can I answer this question? If I succeed, many, many months, perhaps years, will pass before you and I may meet. If I fail, you will see me again soon, or never.

Farewell, my dear, excellent Margaret. Heaven shower down blessings on you, and save me, that I may again and again testify my gratitude for all your love and kindness.

Your affectionate brother,
R. Walton.

LETTER II

To Mrs. Saville, England

Archangel, 28th March, 17—.

How slowly the time passes here, encompassed as I am by frost and snow! yet a second step is taken towards my enterprise. I have hired a vessel, and am occupied in collecting my sailors; those whom I have already engaged appear to be men on whom I can depend, and are certainly possessed of dauntless courage.

But I have one want which I have never yet been able to satisfy; and the absence of the object of which I now feel as a most severe evil. I have no friend, Margaret: when I am glowing with the enthusiasm of success, there will be none to participate my joy; if I am assailed by disappointment, no one will endeavour to sustain me in dejection. I shall commit my thoughts to paper, it is true; but that is a poor medium for the communication of feeling. I desire the company of a man who could sympathise with me; whose eyes would reply to mine. You may deem me romantic, my dear sister, but I bitterly feel the want of a friend. I have no one near me, gentle yet courageous, possessed of a cultivated as well as of a capacious mind, whose tastes are like my own, to approve or amend my plans. How would such a friend repair the faults of your poor brother! I am too ardent in execution, and too impatient of difficulties. But it is a still greater evil to me that I am self-educated: for the first fourteen years of my life I ran wild on a common, and read nothing but our uncle Thomas's books of voyages. At that age I became acquainted with the celebrated poets of our own country; but it was only when it had ceased to be in my power to derive its most important benefits from such a conviction, that I perceived the necessity of becoming acquainted with more languages than that of my native country. Now I am twenty-eight, and am in reality more illiterate than many schoolboys of fifteen. It is true that I have thought more, and that my day dreams are more extended and magnificent; but they want (as the painters call it) *keeping;* and I greatly need a friend who would have sense enough not to despise me as romantic, and affection enough for me to endeavour to regulate my mind.

Well, these are useless complaints; I shall certainly find no friend on the wide ocean, nor even here in Archangel, among merchants and seamen. Yet some feelings, unallied to the dross of human nature, beat even in these rugged bosoms. My lieutenant, for instance, is a man of wonderful courage and enterprise; he is madly desirous of glory: or rather, to word my phrase more characteristically, of advancement in his profession. He is an Englishman, and in the midst of national and professional prejudices, unsoftened by cultivation, retains some of the noblest endowments of humanity. I first became acquainted with him on board a whale vessel: finding that he was unemployed in this city, I easily engaged him to assist in my enterprise.

The master is a person of an excellent disposition, and is remarkable in the ship for his gentleness and the mildness of his discipline. This circumstance, added to his well known integrity and dauntless courage, made me very desirous to engage him. A youth passed in solitude, my best years spent under your gentle and feminine fosterage, has so refined the groundwork of my character, that I cannot overcome an intense distaste to the usual brutality exercised on board ship: I have never believed it to be necessary; and when I heard of a mariner equally noted for his kindliness of heart, and the respect and obedience paid to him by his crew, I felt myself peculiarly fortunate in being able to secure his services. I heard of him first in rather a romantic manner, from a lady who owes to him the happiness of her life. This, briefly, is his story. Some years ago, he loved a young Russian lady, of moderate fortune; and having amassed a considerable sum in prize-money, the father of the girl consented to the match. He saw his mistress once before the destined ceremony; but she was bathed in tears, and, throwing herself at his feet, entreated him to spare her, confessing at the same time that she loved another, but that he was poor, and that her father would never consent to the union. My generous friend reassured the suppliant, and on being informed of the name of her lover, instantly abandoned his pursuit. He had already bought a farm with his money, on which he had designed to pass the remainder of his life; but he bestowed the whole on his rival, together with the remains of his prize-money to purchase stock, and then himself solicited the young woman's father to consent to her marriage with her lover. But the old man decidedly refused, thinking himself bound in honour to my friend; who, when he found the father inexorable, quitted his country, nor returned until he heard that his former mistress was married according to her inclinations. "What a noble fellow!" you will exclaim. He is so; but then he is wholly uneducated: he is as silent as a Turk, and a kind of ignorant carelessness attends him, which, while it renders his conduct the more astonishing, detracts from the interest and sympathy which otherwise he would command.

Yet do not suppose, because I complain a little, or because I can conceive a consolation for my toils which I may never know, that I am wavering in my resolutions. Those are as fixed as fate; and my voyage is only now delayed until the weather shall permit my embarkation. The winter has been dreadfully severe; but the spring promises well, and it is considered as a remarkably early season; so that perhaps I may sail sooner than I expected. I shall do nothing rashly: you know me sufficiently to confide in my prudence and considerateness, whenever the safety of others is committed to my care.

I cannot describe to you my sensations on the near prospect of my undertaking. It is impossible to communicate to you a conception of the trembling sensation, half pleasurable and half fearful, with which I am preparing to depart. I am going to unexplored regions, to "the land of mist and snow;" but I shall kill no albatross, therefore do not be alarmed for my safety, or if I should come back to you as worn and woful as the "Ancient Mariner?" You will smile at my allusion; but I will disclose a secret. I have often attributed my attachment to, my passionate enthusiasm for, the dangerous mysteries of ocean, to that production of the most imaginative of modern poets. There is something at work in my soul, which I do not understand. I am practically industrious — pains-taking; — a workman to execute with perseverance and labour: — but besides this, there is a love for the marvellous, a belief in the marvellous, intertwined in all my projects, which hurries me out of the common pathways of men, even to the wild sea and unvisited regions I am about to explore.

But to return to dearer considerations. Shall I meet you again, after having traversed immense seas, and returned by the most southern cape of Africa or America? I dare not expect such success, yet I cannot bear to look on the reverse of the picture. Continue for the present to write to me by every opportunity: I may receive your letters on some occasions when I need them most to support my spirits. I love you very tenderly. Remember me with affection, should you never hear from me again.

Your affectionate brother,
Robert Walton.

LETTER III

To Mrs. Saville, England

My dear Sister,   July 7th, 17—.

I write a few lines in haste, to say that I am safe, and well advanced on my voyage. This letter will reach England by a merchantman now on its homeward voyage from Archangel; more fortunate than I, who may not see my native land, perhaps, for many years. I am, however, in good spirits; my men are bold, and apparently firm of purpose; nor do the floating sheets of ice that continually pass us, indicating the dangers of the region towards which we are advancing, appear to dismay them. We have already reached a very high latitude; but it is the height of summer, and although not so warm as in England, the southern gales, which blow us speedily towards those shores which I so ardently desire to attain, breathe a degree of renovating warmth which I had not expected.

No incidents have hitherto befallen us that would make a figure in a letter. One or two stiff gales, and the springing of a leak, are accidents which experienced navigators scarcely remember to record; and I shall be well content if nothing worse happen to us during our voyage.

Adieu, my dear Margaret. Be assured, that for my own sake, as well as yours, I will not rashly encounter danger. I will be cool, persevering, and prudent.

But success *shall* crown my endeavours. Wherefore not? Thus far I have gone, tracing a secure way over the pathless seas: the very stars themselves being witnesses and testimonies of my triumph. Why not still proceed over the untamed yet obedient element? What can stop the determined heart and resolved will of man?

My swelling heart involuntarily pours itself out thus. But I must finish. Heaven bless my beloved sister!

R. W.

LETTER IV

To Mrs. Saville, England

August 5th, 17—.

So strange an accident has happened to us, that I cannot forbear recording it, although it is very probable that you will see me before these papers can come into your possession.

Last Monday (July 31st), we were nearly surrounded by ice, which closed in the ship on all sides, scarcely leaving her the sea-room in which she floated. Our situation was somewhat dangerous, especially as we were compassed round by a very thick fog. We accordingly lay to, hoping that some change would take place in the atmosphere and weather.

About two o'clock the mist cleared away, and we beheld, stretched out in every direction, vast and irregular plains of ice, which seemed to have no end. Some of my comrades groaned, and my own mind began to grow watchful with anxious thoughts, when a strange sight suddenly attracted our attention, and diverted our solicitude from our own situation. We perceived a low carriage, fixed on a sledge and drawn by dogs, pass on towards the north, at the distance of half a mile: a being which had the shape of a man, but apparently of gigantic stature, sat in the sledge, and guided the dogs. We watched the rapid progress of the traveller with our telescopes, until he was lost among the distant inequalities of the ice.

This appearance excited our unqualified wonder. We were, as we believed, many hundred miles from any land; but this apparition seemed to denote that it was not, in reality, so distant as we had supposed. Shut in, however, by ice, it was impossible to follow his track, which we had observed with the greatest attention.

About two hours after this occurrence, we heard the ground sea; and before night the ice broke, and freed our ship. We, however, lay to until the morning, fearing to encounter in the dark those large loose masses which float about after the breaking up of the ice. I profited of this time to rest for a few hours.

In the morning, however, as soon as it was light, I went upon deck, and found all the sailors busy on one side of the vessel, apparently talking to some one in the sea. It was, in fact, a sledge, like that we had seen before, which had drifted towards us in the night, on a large fragment of ice. Only one dog remained alive; but there was a human being within it, whom the sailors were persuading to enter the vessel. He was not, as the other traveller seemed to be, a savage inhabitant of some undiscovered island, but an European. When I appeared on deck, the master said, "Here is our captain, and he will not allow you to perish on the open sea."

On perceiving me, the stranger addressed me in English, although with a foreign accent. "Before I come on board your vessel," said he, "will you have the kindness to inform me whither you are bound?"

You may conceive my astonishment on hearing such a question addressed to me from a man on the brink of destruction, and to whom I should have supposed that my vessel would have been a resource which he would not have exchanged for the most precious wealth the earth can afford. I replied, however, that we were on a voyage of discovery towards the northern pole.

Upon hearing this he appeared satisfied, and consented to come on board. Good God! Margaret, if you had seen the man who thus capitulated for his safety, your surprise would have been boundless. His limbs were nearly frozen, and his body dreadfully emaciated by fatigue and suffering. I never saw a man in so wretched a condition. We attempted to carry him into the cabin; but as soon as he had quitted the fresh air, he fainted. We accordingly brought him back to the deck, and restored him to animation by rubbing him with brandy, and forcing him to swallow a small quantity. As soon as he showed signs of life we wrapped him up in blankets, and placed him near the chimney of the kitchen stove. By slow degrees he recovered, and ate a little soup, which restored him wonderfully.

Two days passed in this manner before he was able to speak; and I often feared that his suffering had deprived him of understanding. When he had in some measure recovered, I removed him to my own cabin, and attended on him as much as my duty would permit. I never saw a more interesting creature: his eyes have generally an expression of wildness, and even madness; but there are moments when, if any one performs an act of kindness towards him, or does him any the most trifling service, his whole countenance is lighted up, as it were, with a beam of benevolence and sweetness that I never saw equalled. But he is generally melancholy and despairing; and sometimes he gnashes his teeth, as if impatient of the weight of woes that oppresses him.

When my guest was a little recovered, I had great trouble to keep off the men, who wished to ask him a thousand questions; but I would not allow him to be tormented by their idle curiosity, in a state of body and mind whose restoration evidently depended upon entire repose. Once, however, the lieutenant asked, Why he had come so far upon the ice in so strange a vehicle?

His countenance instantly assumed an aspect of the deepest gloom; and he replied, "To seek one who fled from me."

"And did the man whom you pursued travel in the same fashion?" "Yes."

"Then I fancy we have seen him; for the day before we picked you up, we saw some dogs drawing a sledge, with a man in it, across the ice."

This aroused the stranger's attention; and he asked a multitude of questions concerning the route which the dæmon, as he called him, had pursued. Soon after, when he was alone with me, he said, — "I have, doubtless, excited your curiosity, as well as that of these good people; but you are too considerate to make enquiries."

"Certainly; it would indeed be very impertinent and inhuman in me to trouble you with any inquisitiveness of mine."

"And yet you rescued me from a strange and perilous situation; you have benevolently restored me to life."

Soon after this he enquired if I thought that the breaking up of the ice had destroyed the other sledge? I replied, that I could not answer with any degree of certainty; for the ice had not broken until near midnight, and the traveller might have arrived at a place of safety before that time; but of this I could not judge.

From this time a new spirit of life animated the decaying frame of the stranger. He manifested the greatest eagerness to be upon deck, to watch for the sledge which had before appeared; but I have persuaded him to remain in the cabin, for he is far too weak to sustain the rawness of the atmosphere. I have promised that some one should watch for him, and give him instant notice if any new object should appear in sight.

Such is my journal of what relates to this strange occurrence up to the present day. The stranger has gradually improved in health, but is very silent, and appears uneasy when any one enters his cabin. Yet his manners are so conciliating and gentle, that the sailors are all interested in him, although they have had very little communication with him. For my own part, I begin to love him as a brother; and his constant and deep grief fills me with sympathy and compassion. He must have been a noble creature in his better days, being even now in wreck so attractive and amiable.

I said in one of my letters, my dear Margaret, that I should find no friend on the wide ocean; yet I have found a man who, before his spirit had been broken by misery, I should have been happy to have possessed as the brother of my heart.

I shall continue my journal concerning the stranger at intervals, should I have any fresh incidents to record.

August 13th, 17—.

My affection for my guest increases every day. He excites at once my admiration and my pity to an astonishing degree. How can I see so noble a creature destroyed by misery, without feeling the most poignant grief? He is so gentle, yet so wise; his mind is so cultivated; and when he speaks, although his words are culled with the choicest art, yet they flow with rapidity and unparalleled eloquence.

He is now much recovered from his illness, and is continually on the deck, apparently watching for the sledge that preceded his own. Yet, although unhappy, he is not so utterly occupied by his own misery, but that he interests himself deeply in the projects of others. He has frequently conversed with me on mine, which I have communicated to him without disguise. He entered attentively into all my arguments in favour of my eventual success, and into every minute detail of the measures I had taken to secure it. I was easily led by the sympathy which he evinced, to use the language of my heart; to give utterance to the burning ardour of my soul; and to say, with all the fervour that warmed me, how gladly I would sacrifice my fortune, my existence, my every hope, to the furtherance of my enterprise. One man's life or death were but a small price to pay for the acquirement of the knowledge which I sought; for the dominion I should acquire and transmit over the elemental foes of our race. As I spoke, a dark gloom spread over my listener's countenance. At first I perceived that he tried to suppress his emotion; he placed his hands before his eyes; and my voice quivered and failed me, as I beheld tears trickle fast from between his fingers, — a groan burst from his heaving breast. I paused; — at length he spoke, in broken accents: — "Unhappy man! Do you share my madness? Have you drank also of the intoxicating draught? Hear me, — let me reveal my tale, and you will dash the cup from your lips!''

Such words, you may imagine, strongly excited my curiosity; but the paroxysm of grief that had seized the stranger overcame his weakened powers, and many hours of repose and tranquil conversation were necessary to restore his composure.

Having conquered the violence of his feelings, he appeared to despise himself for being the slave of passion; and quelling the dark tyranny of despair, he led me again to converse concerning myself personally. He asked me the history of my earlier years. The tale was quickly told: but it awakened various trains of reflection. I spoke of my desire of finding a friend — of my thirst for a more intimate sympathy with a fellow mind than had ever fallen to my lot; and expressed my conviction that a man could boast of little happiness, who did not enjoy this blessing.

"I agree with you," replied the stranger; "we are unfashioned creatures, but half made up, if one wiser, better, dearer than ourselves — such a friend ought to be — do not lend his aid to perfectionate our weak and faulty natures. I once had a friend, the most noble of human creatures, and am entitled, therefore, to judge respecting friendship. You have hope, and the world before you, and have no cause for despair. But I — I have lost every thing, and cannot begin life anew."

As he said this, his countenance became expressive of a calm settled grief, that touched me to the heart. But he was silent, and presently retired to his cabin.

Even broken in spirit as he is, no one can feel more deeply than he does the beauties of nature. The starry sky, the sea, and every sight afforded by these wonderful regions, seems still to have the power of elevating his soul from earth. Such a man has a double existence: he may suffer misery, and be overwhelmed by disappointments; yet, when he has retired into himself, he will be like a celestial spirit, that has a halo around him, within whose circle no grief or folly ventures.

Will you smile at the enthusiasm I express concerning this divine wanderer? You would not, if you saw him. You have been tutored and refined by books and retirement from the world, and you are, therefore, somewhat fastidious; but this only renders you the more fit to appreciate the extraordinary merits of this wonderful man. Sometimes I have endeavoured to discover what quality it is which he possesses, that elevates him so immeasurably above any other person I ever knew. I believe it to be an intuitive discernment; a quick but never-failing power of judgment; a penetration into the causes of things, unequalled for clearness and precision; add to this a facility of expression, and a voice whose varied intonations are soul-subduing music.

August 19, 17—.

Yesterday the stranger said to me, "You may easily perceive, Captain Walton, that I have suffered great and unparalleled misfortunes. I had determined, at one time, that the memory of these evils should die with me; but you have won me to alter my determination. You seek for knowledge and wisdom, as I once did; and I ardently hope that the gratification of your wishes may not be a serpent to sting you, as mine has been. I do not know that the relation of my disasters will be useful to you; yet, when I reflect that you are pursuing the same course, exposing yourself to the same dangers which have rendered me what I am, I imagine that you may deduce an apt moral from my tale; one that may direct you if you succeed in your undertaking, and console you in case of failure. Prepare to hear of occurrences which are usually deemed marvellous. Were we among the tamer scenes of nature, I might fear to encounter your unbelief, perhaps your ridicule; but many things will appear possible in these wild and mysterious regions, which would provoke the laughter of those unacquainted with the ever-varied powers of nature: — nor can I doubt but that my tale conveys in its series internal evidence of the truth of the events of which it is composed."

You may easily imagine that I was much gratified by the offered communication; yet I could not endure that he should renew his grief by a recital of his misfortunes. I felt the greatest eagerness to hear the promised narrative, partly from curiosity, and partly from a strong desire to ameliorate his fate, if it were in my power. I expressed these feelings in my answer.

"I thank you," he replied, "for your sympathy, but it is useless; my fate is nearly fulfilled. I wait but for one event, and then I shall repose in peace. I understand your feeling," continued he, perceiving that I wished to interrupt him; "but you are mistaken, my friend, if thus you will allow me to name you; nothing can alter my destiny: listen to my history, and you will perceive how irrevocably it is determined."

He then told me, that he would commence his narrative the next day when I should be at leisure. This promise drew from me the warmest thanks. I have resolved every night, when I am not imperatively occupied by my duties, to record, as nearly as possible in his own words, what he has related during the day. If I should be engaged, I will at least make notes. This manuscript will doubtless afford you the greatest pleasure: but to me, who know him, and who hear it from his own lips, with what interest and sympathy shall I read it in some future day! Even now, as I commence my task, his full-toned voice swells in my ears; his lustrous eyes dwell on me with all their melancholy sweetness; I see his thin hand raised in animation, while the lineaments of his face are irradiated by the soul within. Strange and harrowing must be his story; frightful the storm which embraced the gallant vessel on its course, and wrecked it — thus!

CHAPTER I

I am by birth a Genevese; and my family is one of the most distinguished of that republic. My ancestors had been for many years counsellors and syndics; and my father had filled several public situations with honour and reputation. He was respected by all who knew him, for his integrity and indefatigable attention to public business. He passed his younger days perpetually occupied by the affairs of his country; a variety of circumstances had prevented his marrying early, nor was it until the decline of life that he became a husband and the father of a family.

As the circumstances of his marriage illustrate his character, I cannot refrain from relating them. One of his most intimate friends was a merchant, who, from a flourishing state, fell, through numerous mischances, into poverty. This man, whose name was Beaufort, was of a proud and unbending disposition, and could not bear to live in poverty and oblivion in the same country where he had formerly been distinguished for his rank and magnificence. Having paid his debts, therefore, in the most honourable manner, he retreated with his daughter to the town of Lucerne, where he lived unknown and in wretchedness. My father loved Beaufort with the truest friendship, and was deeply grieved by his retreat in these unfortunate circumstances. He bitterly deplored the false pride which led his friend to a conduct so little worthy of the affection that united them. He lost no time in endeavouring to seek him out, with the hope of persuading him to begin the world again through his credit and assistance.

Beaufort had taken effectual measures to conceal himself; and it was ten months before my father discovered his abode. Overjoyed at this discovery, he hastened to the house, which was situated in a mean street, near the Reuss. But when he entered, misery and despair alone welcomed him. Beaufort had saved but a very small sum of money from the wreck of his fortunes; but it was sufficient to provide him with sustenance for some months, and in the mean time he hoped to procure some respectable employment in a merchant's house. The interval was, consequently, spent in inaction; his grief only became more deep and rankling, when he had leisure for reflection; and at length it took so fast hold of his mind, that at the end of three months he lay on a bed of sickness, incapable of any exertion.

His daughter attended him with the greatest tenderness; but she saw with despair that their little fund was rapidly decreasing, and that there was no other prospect of support. But Caroline Beaufort possessed a mind of an uncommon mould; and her courage rose to support her in her adversity. She procured plain work; she plaited straw; and by various means contrived to earn a pittance scarcely sufficient to support life.

Several months passed in this manner. Her father grew worse; her time was more entirely occupied in attending him; her means of subsistence decreased; and in the tenth month her father died in her arms, leaving her an orphan and a beggar. This last blow overcame her; and she knelt by Beaufort's coffin, weeping bitterly, when my father entered the chamber. He came like a protecting spirit to the poor girl, who committed herself to his care; and after the interment of his friend, he conducted her to Geneva, and placed her under the protection of a relation. Two years after this event Caroline became his wife.

There was a considerable difference between the ages of my parents, but this circumstance seemed to unite them only closer in bonds of devoted affection. There was a sense of justice in my father's upright mind, which rendered it necessary that he should approve highly to love strongly. Perhaps during former years he had suffered from the late-discovered unworthiness of one beloved, and so was disposed to set a greater value on tried worth. There was a show of gratitude and worship in his attachment to my mother, differing wholly from the doating fondness of age, for it was inspired by reverence for her virtues, and a desire to be the means of, in some degree, recompensing her for the sorrows she had endured, but which gave inexpressible grace to his behaviour to her. Every thing was made to yield to her wishes and her convenience. He strove to shelter her, as a fair exotic is sheltered by the gardener, from every rougher wind, and to surround her with all that could tend to excite pleasurable emotion in her soft and benevolent mind. Her health, and even the tranquillity of her hitherto constant spirit, had been shaken by what she had gone through. During the two years that had elapsed previous to their marriage my father had gradually relinquished all his public functions; and immediately after their union they sought the pleasant climate of Italy, and the change of scene and interest attendant on a tour through that land of wonders, as a restorative for her weakened frame.

From Italy they visited Germany and France. I, their eldest child, was born at Naples, and as an infant accompanied them in their rambles. I remained for several years their only child. Much as they were attached to each other, they seemed to draw inexhaustible stores of affection from a very mine of love to bestow them upon me. My mother's tender caresses, and my father's smile of benevolent pleasure while regarding me, are my first recollections. I was their plaything and their idol, and something better — their child, the innocent and helpless creature bestowed on them by Heaven, whom to bring up to good, and whose future lot it was in their hands to direct to happiness or misery, according as they fulfilled their duties towards me. With this deep consciousness of what they owed towards the being to which they had given life, added to the active spirit of tenderness that animated both, it may be imagined that while during every hour of my infant life I received a lesson of patience, of charity, and of self-control, I was so guided by a silken cord, that all seemed but one train of enjoyment to me.

For a long time I was their only care. My mother had much desired to have a daughter, but I continued their single offspring. When I was about five years old, while making an excursion beyond the frontiers of Italy, they passed a week on the shores of the Lake of Como. Their benevolent disposition often made them enter the cottages of the poor. This, to my mother, was more than a duty; it was a necessity, a passion, — remembering what she had suffered, and how she had been relieved, — for her to act in her turn the guardian angel to the afflicted. During one of their walks a poor cot in the foldings of a vale attracted their notice, as being singularly disconsolate, while the number of half-clothed children gathered about it, spoke of penury in its worst shape. One day, when my father had gone by himself to Milan, my mother, accompanied by me, visited this abode. She found a peasant and his wife, hard working, bent down by care and labour, distributing a scanty meal to five hungry babes. Among these there was one which attracted my mother far above all the rest. She appeared of a different stock. The four others were dark-eyed, hardy little vagrants; this child was thin, and very fair. Her hair was the brightest living gold, and, despite the poverty of her clothing, seemed to set a crown of distinction on her head. Her brow was clear and ample, her blue eyes cloudless, and her lips and the moulding of her face so expressive of sensibility and sweetness, that none could behold her without looking on her as of a distinct species, a being heaven-sent, and bearing a celestial stamp in all her features.

The peasant woman, perceiving that my mother fixed eyes of wonder and admiration on this lovely girl, eagerly communicated her history. She was not her child, but the daughter of a Milanese nobleman. Her mother was a German, and had died on giving her birth. The infant had been placed with these good people to nurse: they were better off then. They had not been long married, and their eldest child was but just born. The father of their charge was one of those Italians nursed in the memory of the antique glory of Italy, — one among the *schiavi ognor f   frementi*, who exerted himself to obtain the liberty of his country. He became the victim of its weakness. Whether he had died, or still lingered in the dungeons of Austria, was not known. His property was confiscated, his child became an orphan and a beggar. She continued with her foster parents, and bloomed in their rude abode, fairer than a garden rose among dark-leaved brambles.

When my father returned from Milan, he found playing with me in the hall of our villa, a child fairer than pictured cherub — a creature who seemed to shed radiance from her looks, and whose form and motions were lighter than the chamois of the hills. The apparition was soon explained. With his permission my mother prevailed on her rustic guardians to yield their charge to her. They were fond of the sweet orphan. Her presence had seemed a blessing to them; but it would be unfair to her to keep her in poverty and want, when Providence afforded her such powerful protection. They consulted their village priest, and the result was, that Elizabeth Lavenza became the inmate of my parents' house — my more than sister — the beautiful and adored companion of all my occupations and my pleasures.

Every one loved Elizabeth. The passionate and almost reverential attachment with which all regarded her became, while I shared it, my pride and my delight. On the evening previous to her being brought to my home, my mother had said playfully, — "I have a pretty present for my Victor — to-morrow he shall have it." And when, on the morrow, she presented Elizabeth to me as her promised gift, I, with childish seriousness, interpreted her words literally, and looked upon Elizabeth as mine — mine to protect, love, and cherish. All praises bestowed on her, I received as made to a possession of my own. We called each other familiarly by the name of cousin. No word, no expression could body forth the kind of relation in which she stood to me — my more than sister, since till death she was to be mine only.

CHAPTER II

We were brought up together; there was not quite a year difference in our ages. I need not say that we were strangers to any species of disunion or dispute. Harmony was the soul of our companionship, and the diversity and contrast that subsisted in our characters drew us nearer together. Elizabeth was of a calmer and more concentrated disposition; but, with all my ardour, I was capable of a more intense application, and was more deeply smitten with the thirst for knowledge. She busied herself with following the aerial creations of the poets; and in the majestic and wondrous scenes which surrounded our Swiss home — the sublime shapes of the mountains; the changes of the seasons; tempest and calm; the silence of winter, and the life and turbulence of our Alpine summers, — she found ample scope for admiration and delight. While my companion contemplated with a serious and satisfied spirit the magnificent appearances of things, I delighted in investigating their causes. The world was to me a secret which I desired to divine. Curiosity, earnest research to learn the hidden laws of nature, gladness akin to rapture, as they were unfolded to me, are among the earliest sensations I can remember.

On the birth of a second son, my junior by seven years, my parents gave up entirely their wandering life, and fixed themselves in their native country. We possessed a house in Geneva, and a *campagne* on Belrive, the eastern shore of the lake, at the distance of rather more than a league from the city. We resided principally in the latter, and the lives of my parents were passed in considerable seclusion. It was my temper to avoid a crowd, and to attach myself fervently to a few. I was indifferent, therefore, to my schoolfellows in general; but I united myself in the bonds of the closest friendship to one among them. Henry Clerval was the son of a merchant of Geneva. He was a boy of singular talent and fancy. He loved enterprise, hardship, and even danger, for its own sake. He was deeply read in books of chivalry and romance. He composed heroic songs, and began to write many a tale of enchantment and knightly adventure. He tried to make us act plays, and to enter into masquerades, in which the characters were drawn from the heroes of Roncesvalles, of the Round Table of King Arthur, and the chivalrous train who shed their blood to redeem the holy sepulchre from the hands of the infidels.

No human being could have passed a happier childhood than myself. My parents were possessed by the very spirit of kindness and indulgence. We felt that they were not the tyrants to rule our lot according to their caprice, but the agents and creators of all the many delights which we enjoyed. When I mingled with other families, I distinctly discerned how peculiarly fortunate my lot was, and gratitude assisted the developement of filial love.

My temper was sometimes violent, and my passions vehement; but by some law in my temperature they were turned, not towards childish pursuits, but to an eager desire to learn, and not to learn all things indiscriminately. I confess that neither the structure of languages, nor the code of governments, nor the politics of various states, possessed attractions for me. It was the secrets of heaven and earth that I desired to learn; and whether it was the outward substance of things, or the inner spirit of nature and the mysterious soul of man that occupied me, still my enquiries were directed to the metaphysical, or, in its highest sense, the physical secrets of the world.

Meanwhile Clerval occupied himself, so to speak, with the moral relations of things. The busy stage of life, the virtues of heroes, and the actions of men, were his theme; and his hope and his dream was to become one among those whose names are recorded in story, as the gallant and adventurous benefactors of our species. The saintly soul of Elizabeth shone like a shrine-dedicated lamp in our peaceful home. Her sympathy was ours; her smile, her soft voice, the sweet glance of her celestial eyes, were ever there to bless and animate us. She was the living spirit of love to soften and attract: I might have become sullen in my study, rough through the ardour of my nature, but that she was there to subdue me to a semblance of her own gentleness. And Clerval — could aught ill entrench on the noble spirit of Clerval? — yet he might not have been so perfectly humane, so thoughtful in his generosity — so full of kindness and tenderness amidst his passion for adventurous exploit, had she not unfolded to him the real loveliness of beneficence, and made the doing good the end and aim of his soaring ambition.

I feel exquisite pleasure in dwelling on the recollections of childhood, before misfortune had tainted my mind, and changed its bright visions of extensive usefulness into gloomy and narrow reflections upon self. Besides, in drawing the picture of my early days, I also record those events which led, by insensible steps, to my after tale of misery: for when I would account to myself for the birth of that passion, which afterwards ruled my destiny, I find it arise, like a mountain river, from ignoble and almost forgotten sources; but, swelling as it proceeded, it became the torrent which, in its course, has swept away all my hopes and joys.

Natural philosophy is the genius that has regulated my fate; I desire, therefore, in this narration, to state those facts which led to my predilection for that science. When I was thirteen years of age, we all went on a party of pleasure to the baths near Thonon; the inclemency of the weather obliged us to remain a day confined to the inn. In this house I chanced to find a volume of the works of Cornelius Agrippa. I opened it with apathy; the theory which he attempts to demonstrate, and the wonderful facts which he relates, soon changed this feeling into enthusiasm. A new light seemed to dawn upon my mind; and, bounding with joy, I communicated my discovery to my father. My father looked carelessly at the titlepage of my book, and said, "Ah! Cornelius Agrippa! My dear Victor, do not waste your time upon this; it is sad trash."

If, instead of this remark, my father had taken the pains to explain to me, that the principles of Agrippa had been entirely exploded, and that a modern system of science had been introduced, which possessed much greater powers than the ancient, because the powers of the latter were chimerical, while those of the former were real and practical; under such circumstances, I should certainly have thrown Agrippa aside, and have contented my imagination, warmed as it was, by returning with greater ardour to my former studies. It is even possible, that the train of my ideas would never have received the fatal impulse that led to my ruin. But the cursory glance my father had taken of my volume by no means assured me that he was acquainted with its contents; and I continued to read with the greatest avidity.

When I returned home, my first care was to procure the whole works of this author, and afterwards of Paracelsus and Albertus Magnus. I read and studied the wild fancies of these writers with delight; they appeared to me treasures known to few beside myself. I have described myself as always having been embued with a fervent longing to penetrate the secrets of nature. In spite of the intense labour and wonderful discoveries of modern philosophers, I always came from my studies discontented and unsatisfied. Sir Isaac Newton is said to have avowed that he felt like a child picking up shells beside the great and unexplored ocean of truth. Those of his successors in each branch of natural philosophy with whom I was acquainted, appeared even to my boy's apprehensions, as tyros engaged in the same pursuit.

The untaught peasant beheld the elements around him, and was acquainted with their practical uses. The most learned philosopher knew little more. He had partially unveiled the face of Nature, but her immortal lineaments were still a wonder and a mystery. He might dissect, anatomise, and give names; but, not to speak of a final cause, causes in their secondary and tertiary grades were utterly unknown to him. I had gazed upon the fortifications and impediments that seemed to keep human beings from entering the citadel of nature, and rashly and ignorantly I had repined.

But here were books, and here were men who had penetrated deeper and knew more. I took their word for all that they averred, and I became their disciple. It may appear strange that such should arise in the eighteenth century; but while I followed the routine of education in the schools of Geneva, I was, to a great degree, self taught with regard to my favourite studies. My father was not scientific, and I was left to struggle with a child's blindness, added to a student's thirst for knowledge. Under the guidance of my new preceptors, I entered with the greatest diligence into the search of the philosopher's stone and the elixir of life; but the latter soon obtained my undivided attention. Wealth was an inferior object; but what glory would attend the discovery, if I could banish disease from the human frame, and render man invulnerable to any but a violent death!

Nor were these my only visions. The raising of ghosts or devils was a promise liberally accorded by my favourite authors, the fulfilment of which I most eagerly sought; and if my incantations were always unsuccessful, I attributed the failure rather to my own inexperience and mistake, than to a want of skill or fidelity in my instructors. And thus for a time I was occupied by exploded systems, mingling, like an unadept, a thousand contradictory theories, and floundering desperately in a very slough of multifarious knowledge, guided by an ardent imagination and childish reasoning, till an accident again changed the current of my ideas.

When I was about fifteen years old we had retired to our house near Belrive, when we witnessed a most violent and terrible thunder-storm. It advanced from behind the mountains of Jura; and the thunder burst at once with frightful loudness from various quarters of the heavens. I remained, while the storm lasted, watching its progress with curiosity and delight. As I stood at the door, on a sudden I beheld a stream of fire issue from an old and beautiful oak, which stood about twenty yards from our house; and so soon as the dazzling light vanished, the oak had disappeared, and nothing remained but a blasted stump. When we visited it the next morning, we found the tree shattered in a singular manner. It was not splintered by the shock, but entirely reduced to thin ribands of wood. I never beheld any thing so utterly destroyed.

Before this I was not unacquainted with the more obvious laws of electricity. On this occasion a man of great research in natural philosophy was with us, and, excited by this catastrophe, he entered on the explanation of a theory which he had formed on the subject of electricity and galvanism, which was at once new and astonishing to me. All that he said threw greatly into the shade Cornelius Agrippa, Albertus Magnus, and Paracelsus, the lords of my imagination; but by some fatality the overthrow of these men disinclined me to pursue my accustomed studies. It seemed to me as if nothing would or could ever be known. All that had so long engaged my attention suddenly grew despicable. By one of those caprices of the mind, which we are perhaps most subject to in early youth, I at once gave up my former occupations; set down natural history and all its progeny as a deformed and abortive creation; and entertained the greatest disdain for a would-be science, which could never even step within the threshold of real knowledge. In this mood of mind I betook myself to the mathematics, and the branches of study appertaining to that science, as being built upon secure foundations, and so worthy of my consideration.

Thus strangely are our souls constructed, and by such slight ligaments are we bound to prosperity or ruin. When I look back, it seems to me as if this almost miraculous change of inclination and will was the immediate suggestion of the guardian angel of my life — the last effort made by the spirit of preservation to avert the storm that was even then hanging in the stars, and ready to envelope me. Her victory was announced by an unusual tranquillity and gladness of soul, which followed the relinquishing of my ancient and latterly tormenting studies. It was thus that I was to be taught to associate evil with their prosecution, happiness with their disregard.

It was a strong effort of the spirit of good; but it was ineffectual. Destiny was too potent, and her immutable laws had decreed my utter and terrible destruction.

CHAPTER III

When I had attained the age of seventeen, my parents resolved that I should become a student at the university of Ingolstadt. I had hitherto attended the schools of Geneva; but my father thought it necessary, for the completion of my education, that I should be made acquainted with other customs than those of my native country. My departure was therefore fixed at an early date; but, before the day resolved upon could arrive, the first misfortune of my life occurred — an omen, as it were, of my future misery.

Elizabeth had caught the scarlet fever; her illness was severe, and she was in the greatest danger. During her illness, many arguments had been urged to persuade my mother to refrain from attending upon her. She had, at first, yielded to our entreaties; but when she heard that the life of her favourite was menaced, she could no longer control her anxiety. She attended her sick bed, — her watchful attentions triumphed over the malignity of the distemper, — Elizabeth was saved, but the consequences of this imprudence were fatal to her preserver. On the third day my mother sickened; her fever was accompanied by the most alarming symptoms, and the looks of her medical attendants prognosticated the worst event. On her death-bed the fortitude and benignity of this best of women did not desert her. She joined the hands of Elizabeth and myself: — "My children," she said, "my firmest hopes of future happiness were placed on the prospect of your union. This expectation will now be the consolation of your father. Elizabeth, my love, you must supply my place to my younger children. Alas! I regret that I am taken from you; and, happy and beloved as I have been, is it not hard to quit you all? But these are not thoughts befitting me; I will endeavour to resign myself cheerfully to death, and will indulge a hope of meeting you in another world."

She died calmly; and her countenance expressed affection even in death. I need not describe the feelings of those whose dearest ties are rent by that most irreparable evil; the void that presents itself to the soul; and the despair that is exhibited on the countenance. It is so long before the mind can persuade itself that she, whom we saw every day, and whose very existence appeared a part of our own, can have departed for ever — that the brightness of a beloved eye can have been extinguished, and the sound of a voice so familiar, and dear to the ear, can be hushed, never more to be heard. These are the reflections of the first days; but when the lapse of time proves the reality of the evil, then the actual bitterness of grief commences. Yet from whom has not that rude hand rent away some dear connection? and why should I describe a sorrow which all have felt, and must feel? The time at length arrives, when grief is rather an indulgence than a necessity; and the smile that plays upon the lips, although it may be deemed a sacrilege, is not banished. My mother was dead, but we had still duties which we ought to perform; we must continue our course with the rest, and learn to think ourselves fortunate, whilst one remains whom the spoiler has not seized.

My departure for Ingolstadt, which had been deferred by these events, was now again determined upon. I obtained from my father a respite of some weeks. It appeared to me sacrilege so soon to leave the repose, akin to death, of the house of mourning, and to rush into the thick of life. I was new to sorrow, but it did not the less alarm me. I was unwilling to quit the sight of those that remained to me; and, above all, I desired to see my sweet Elizabeth in some degree consoled.

She indeed veiled her grief, and strove to act the comforter to us all. She looked steadily on life, and assumed its duties with courage and zeal. She devoted herself to those whom she had been taught to call her uncle and cousins. Never was she so enchanting as at this time, when she recalled the sunshine of her smiles and spent them upon us. She forgot even her own regret in her endeavours to make us forget.

The day of my departure at length arrived. Clerval spent the last evening with us. He had endeavoured to persuade his father to permit him to accompany me, and to become my fellow student; but in vain. His father was a narrow-minded trader, and saw idleness and ruin in the aspirations and ambition of his son. Henry deeply felt the misfortune of being debarred from a liberal education. He said little; but when he spoke, I read in his kindling eye and in his animated glance a restrained but firm resolve, not to be chained to the miserable details of commerce.

We sat late. We could not tear ourselves away from each other, nor persuade ourselves to say the word "Farewell!" It was said; and we retired under the pretence of seeking repose, each fancying that the other was deceived: but when at morning's dawn I descended to the carriage which was to convey me away, they were all there — my father again to bless me, Clerval to press my hand once more, my Elizabeth to renew her entreaties that I would write often, and to bestow the last feminine attentions on her playmate and friend.

I threw myself into the chaise that was to convey me away, and indulged in the most melancholy reflections. I, who had ever been surrounded by amiable companions, continually engaged in endeavouring to bestow mutual pleasure, I was now alone. In the university, whither I was going, I must form my own friends, and be my own protector. My life had hitherto been remarkably secluded and domestic; and this had given me invincible repugnance to new countenances. I loved my brothers, Elizabeth, and Clerval; these were "old familiar faces;" but I believed myself totally unfitted for the company of strangers. Such were

my reflections as I commenced my journey; but as I proceeded, my
spirits and hopes rose. I ardently desired the acquisition of knowledge.
I had often, when at home, thought it hard to remain during my youth
cooped up in one place, and had longed to enter the world, and take
my station among other human beings. Now my desires were complied
with, and it would, indeed, have been folly to repent.

I had sufficient leisure for these and many other reflections during
my journey to Ingolstadt, which was long and fatiguing. At length the
high white steeple of the town met my eyes. I alighted, and was conducted to my solitary apartment, to spend the evening as I pleased.

The next morning I delivered my letters of introduction, and paid
a visit to some of the principal professors. Chance — or rather the evil
influence, the Angel of Destruction, which asserted omnipotent sway
over me from the moment I turned my reluctant steps from my father's
door — led me first to M. Krempe, professor of natural philosophy. He
was an uncouth man, but deeply embued in the secrets of his science.
He asked me several questions concerning my progress in the different
branches of science appertaining to natural philosophy. I replied carelessly; and, partly in contempt, mentioned the names of my alchymists
as the principal authors I had studied. The professor stared: "Have
you," he said, "really spent your time in studying such nonsense?"

I replied in the affirmative. "Every minute," continued M. Krempe
with warmth, "every instant that you have wasted on those books is
utterly and entirely lost. You have burdened your memory with exploded systems and useless names. Good God! in what desert land have
you lived, where no one was kind enough to inform you that these
fancies, which you have so greedily imbibed, are a thousand years old,
and as musty as they are ancient? I little expected, in this enlightened
and scientific age, to find a disciple of Albertus Magnus and Paracelsus.
My dear sir, you must begin your studies entirely anew."

So saying, he stept aside, and wrote down a list of several books
treating of natural philosophy, which he desired me to procure; and
dismissed me, after mentioning that in the beginning of the following week he intended to commence a course of lectures upon natural
philosophy in its general relations, and that M. Waldman, a fellow-
professor, would lecture upon chemistry the alternate days that he
omitted.

I returned home, not disappointed, for I have said that I had long
considered those authors useless whom the professor reprobated; but I
returned, not at all the more inclined to recur to these studies in any
shape. M. Krempe was a little, squat man, with a gruff voice and a

repulsive countenance; the teacher, therefore, did not prepossess me in favour of his pursuits. In rather too philosophical and connected a strain, perhaps, I have given an account of the conclusions I had come to concerning them in my early years. As a child, I had not been content with the results promised by the modern professors of natural science. With a confusion of ideas only to be accounted for by my extreme youth, and my want of a guide on such matters, I had retrod the steps of knowledge along the paths of time, and exchanged the discoveries of recent enquirers for the dreams of forgotten alchymists. Besides, I had a contempt for the uses of modern natural philosophy. It was very different, when the masters of the science sought immortality and power; such views, although futile, were grand: but now the scene was changed. The ambition of the enquirer seemed to limit itself to the annihilation of those visions on which my interest in science was chiefly founded. I was required to exchange chimeras of boundless grandeur for realities of little worth.

Such were my reflections during the first two or three days of my residence at Ingolstadt, which were chiefly spent in becoming acquainted with the localities, and the principal residents in my new abode. But as the ensuing week commenced, I thought of the information which M. Krempe had given me concerning the lectures. And although I could not consent to go and hear that little conceited fellow deliver sentences out of a pulpit, I recollected what he had said of M. Waldman, whom I had never seen, as he had hitherto been out of town.

Partly from curiosity, and partly from idleness, I went into the lecturing room, which M. Waldman entered shortly after. This professor was very unlike his colleague. He appeared about fifty years of age, but with an aspect expressive of the greatest benevolence; a few grey hairs covered his temples, but those at the back of his head were nearly black. His person was short, but remarkably erect; and his voice the sweetest I had ever heard. He began his lecture by a recapitulation of the history of chemistry, and the various improvements made by different men of learning, pronouncing with fervour the names of the most distinguished discoverers. He then took a cursory view of the present state of the science, and explained many of its elementary terms. After having made a few preparatory experiments, he concluded with a panegyric upon modern chemistry, the terms of which I shall never forget: —

"The ancient teachers of this science," said he, "promised impossibilities, and performed nothing. The modern masters promise very little; they know that metals cannot be transmuted, and that the elixir of life is a chimera. But these philosophers, whose hands seem only made to dabble in dirt, and their eyes to pore over the microscope or crucible, have indeed performed miracles. They penetrate into the recesses of nature, and show how she works in her hiding places. They ascend into the heavens: they have discovered how the blood circulates, and the nature of the air we breathe. They have acquired new and almost unlimited powers; they can command the thunders of heaven, mimic the earthquake, and even mock the invisible world with its own shadows."

Such were the professor's words — rather let me say such the words of fate, enounced to destroy me. As he went on, I felt as if my soul were grappling with a palpable enemy; one by one the various keys were touched which formed the mechanism of my being: chord after chord was sounded, and soon my mind was filled with one thought, one conception, one purpose. So much has been done, exclaimed the soul of Frankenstein, — more, far more, will I achieve: treading in the steps already marked, I will pioneer a new way, explore unknown powers, and unfold to the world the deepest mysteries of creation.

I closed not my eyes that night. My internal being was in a state of insurrection and turmoil; I felt that order would thence arise, but I had no power to produce it. By degrees, after the morning's dawn, sleep came. I awoke, and my yesternight's thoughts were as a dream. There only remained a resolution to return to my ancient studies, and to devote myself to a science for which I believed myself to possess a natural talent. On the same day, I paid M. Waldman a visit. His manners in private were even more mild and attractive than in public; for there was a certain dignity in his mien during his lecture, which in his own house was replaced by the greatest affability and kindness. I gave him pretty nearly the same account of my former pursuits as I had given to his fellow-professor. He heard with attention the little narration concerning my studies, and smiled at the names of Cornelius Agrippa and Paracelsus, but without the contempt that M. Krempe had exhibited. He said, that "these were men to whose indefatigable zeal modern philosophers were indebted for most of the foundations of their knowledge. They had left to us, as an easier task, to give new names, and arrange in connected classifications, the facts which they in a great degree had been the instruments of bringing to light. The labours of men of genius, however erroneously directed, scarcely ever fail in ultimately turning to the solid advantage of mankind." I listened to his statement, which was delivered without any presumption or affectation; and then added, that his lecture had removed my prejudices against modern chemists; I expressed myself in measured terms, with the modesty and deference due from a youth to his instructor, without letting escape (inexperience in

life would have made me ashamed) any of the enthusiasm which stimu-
lated my intended labours. I requested his advice concerning the books
I ought to procure.

"I am happy," said M. Waldman, "to have gained a disciple; and
if your application equals your ability, I have no doubt of your success.
Chemistry is that branch of natural philosophy in which the greatest
improvements have been and may be made: it is on that account that
I have made it my peculiar study; but at the same time I have not
neglected the other branches of science. A man would make but a very
sorry chemist if he attended to that department of human knowledge
alone. If your wish is to become really a man of science, and not merely
a petty experimentalist, I should advise you to apply to every branch of
natural philosophy, including mathematics."

He then took me into his laboratory, and explained to me the uses
of his various machines; instructing me as to what I ought to procure,
and promising me the use of his own when I should have advanced far
enough in the science not to derange their mechanism. He also gave
me the list of books which I had requested; and I took my leave.

Thus ended a day memorable to me: it decided my future destiny.

CHAPTER IV

From this day natural philosophy, and particularly chemistry, in the
most comprehensive sense of the term, became nearly my sole occupation. I read with ardour those works, so full of genius and discrimination, which modern enquirers have written on these subjects. I attended the lectures, and cultivated the acquaintance, of the men of
science of the university; and I found even in M. Krempe a great deal of
sound sense and real information, combined, it is true, with a repulsive
physiognomy and manners, but not on that account the less valuable.
In M. Waldman I found a true friend. His gentleness was never tinged
by dogmatism; and his instructions were given with an air of frankness
and good nature, that banished every idea of pedantry. In a thousand
ways he smoothed for me the path of knowledge, and made the most
abstruse enquiries clear and facile to my apprehension. My application
was at first fluctuating and uncertain; it gained strength as I proceeded,
and soon became so ardent and eager, that the stars often disappeared
in the light of morning whilst I was yet engaged in my laboratory.

As I applied so closely, it may be easily conceived that my progress
was rapid. My ardour was indeed the astonishment of the students, and

my proficiency that of the masters. Professor Krempe often asked me, with a sly smile, how Cornelius Agrippa went on? whilst M. Waldman expressed the most heartfelt exultation in my progress. Two years passed in this manner, during which I paid no visit to Geneva, but was engaged, heart and soul, in the pursuit of some discoveries, which I hoped to make. None but those who have experienced them can conceive of the enticements of science. In other studies you go as far as others have gone before you, and there is nothing more to know; but in a scientific pursuit there is continual food for discovery and wonder. A mind of moderate capacity, which closely pursues one study, must infallibly arrive at great proficiency in that study; and I, who continually sought the attainment of one object of pursuit, and was solely wrapt up in this, improved so rapidly, that, at the end of two years, I made some discoveries in the improvement of some chemical instruments, which procured me great esteem and admiration at the university. When I had arrived at this point, and had become as well acquainted with the theory and practice of natural philosophy as depended on the lessons of any of the professors at Ingolstadt, my residence there being no longer conducive to my improvements, I thought of returning to my friends and my native town, when an incident happened that protracted my stay.

One of the phenomena which had peculiarly attracted my attention was the structure of the human frame, and, indeed, any animal endued with life. Whence, I often asked myself, did the principle of life proceed? It was a bold question, and one which has ever been considered as a mystery; yet with how many things are we upon the brink of becoming acquainted, if cowardice or carelessness did not restrain our enquiries. I revolved these circumstances in my mind, and determined thenceforth to apply myself more particularly to those branches of natural philosophy which relate to physiology. Unless I had been animated by an almost supernatural enthusiasm, my application to this study would have been irksome, and almost intolerable. To examine the causes of life, we must first have recourse to death. I became acquainted with the science of anatomy: but this was not sufficient; I must also observe the natural decay and corruption of the human body. In my education my father had taken the greatest precautions that my mind should be impressed with no supernatural horrors. I do not ever remember to have trembled at a tale of superstition, or to have feared the apparition of a spirit. Darkness had no effect upon my fancy; and a churchyard was to me merely the receptacle of bodies deprived of life, which, from being the seat of beauty and strength, had become food for the worm. Now I was led to examine the cause and progress of this decay, and forced to spend days and nights in vaults and charnel-houses. My attention was fixed upon every object the most insupportable to the delicacy of the human feelings. I saw how the fine form of man was degraded and wasted; I beheld the corruption of death succeed to the blooming cheek of life; I saw how the worm inherited the wonders of the eye and brain. I paused, examining and analysing all the minutiæ of causation, as exemplified in the change from life to death, and death to life, until from the midst of this darkness a sudden light broke in upon me — a light so brilliant and wondrous, yet so simple, that while I became dizzy with the immensity of the prospect which it illustrated, I was surprised, that among so many men of genius who had directed their enquiries towards the same science, I alone should be reserved to discover so astonishing a secret.

Remember, I am not recording the vision of a madman. The sun does not more certainly shine in the heavens, than that which I now affirm is true. Some miracle might have produced it, yet the stages of the discovery were distinct and probable. After days and nights of incredible labour and fatigue, I succeeded in discovering the cause of generation and life; nay, more, I became myself capable of bestowing animation upon lifeless matter.

The astonishment which I had at first experienced on this discovery soon gave place to delight and rapture. After so much time spent in painful labour, to arrive at once at the summit of my desires, was the most gratifying consummation of my toils. But this discovery was so great and overwhelming, that all the steps by which I had been progressively led to it were obliterated, and I beheld only the result. What had been the study and desire of the wisest men since the creation of the world was now within my grasp. Not that, like a magic scene, it all opened upon me at once: the information I had obtained was of a nature rather to direct my endeavours so soon as I should point them towards the object of my search, than to exhibit that object already accomplished. I was like the Arabian who had been buried with the dead, and found a passage to life, aided only by one glimmering, and seemingly ineffectual, light.

I see by your eagerness, and the wonder and hope which your eyes express, my friend, that you expect to be informed of the secret with which I am acquainted; that cannot be: listen patiently until the end of my story, and you will easily perceive why I am reserved upon that subject. I will not lead you on, unguarded and ardent as I then was, to your destruction and infallible misery. Learn from me, if not by my precepts, at least by my example, how dangerous is the acquirement of knowledge, and how much happier that man is who believes his native town to be the world, than he who aspires to become greater than his nature will allow.

When I found so astonishing a power placed within my hands, I hesitated a long time concerning the manner in which I should employ it. Although I possessed the capacity of bestowing animation, yet to prepare a frame for the reception of it, with all its intricacies of fibres, muscles, and veins, still remained a work of inconceivable difficulty and labour. I doubted at first whether I should attempt the creation of a being like myself, or one of simpler organization; but my imagination was too much exalted by my first success to permit me to doubt of my ability to give life to an animal as complex and wonderful as man. The materials at present within my command hardly appeared adequate to so arduous an undertaking; but I doubted not that I should ultimately succeed. I prepared myself for a multitude of reverses; my operations might be incessantly baffled, and at last my work be imperfect: yet, when I considered the improvement which every day takes place in science and mechanics, I was encouraged to hope my present attempts would at least lay the foundations of future success. Nor could I consider the magnitude and complexity of my plan as any argument of its impracticability. It was with these feelings that I began the creation of a human being. As the minuteness of the parts formed a great hindrance to my speed, I resolved, contrary to my first intention, to make the being of a gigantic stature; that is to say, about eight feet in height, and proportionably large. After having formed this determination, and having spent some months in successfully collecting and arranging my materials, I began.

No one can conceive the variety of feelings which bore me onwards, like a hurricane, in the first enthusiasm of success. Life and death appeared to me ideal bounds, which I should first break through, and pour a torrent of light into our dark world. A new species would bless me as its creator and source; many happy and excellent natures would owe their being to me. No father could claim the gratitude of his child so completely as I should deserve theirs. Pursuing these reflections, I thought, that if I could bestow animation upon lifeless matter, I might in process of time (although I now found it impossible) renew life where death had apparently devoted the body to corruption.

These thoughts supported my spirits, while I pursued my undertaking with unremitting ardour. My cheek had grown pale with study, and my person had become emaciated with confinement. Sometimes, on the very brink of certainty, I failed; yet still I clung to the hope which the next day or the next hour might realise. One secret which I alone possessed was the hope to which I had dedicated myself; and the moon gazed on my midnight labours, while, with unrelaxed and breathless eagerness, I pursued nature to her hiding-places. Who shall conceive the horrors of my secret toil, as I dabbled among the unhallowed damps of the grave, or tortured the living animal to animate the lifeless clay? My limbs now tremble, and my eyes swim with the remembrance; but then a resistless, and almost frantic, impulse, urged me forward; I seemed to have lost all soul or sensation but for this one pursuit. It was indeed but a passing trance, that only made me feel with renewed acuteness so soon as, the unnatural stimulus ceasing to operate, I had returned to my old habits. I collected bones from charnel-houses; and disturbed, with profane fingers, the tremendous secrets of the human frame. In a solitary chamber, or rather cell, at the top of the house, and separated from all the other apartments by a gallery and staircase, I kept my workshop of filthy creation: my eye-balls were starting from their sockets in attending to the details of my employment. The dissecting room and the slaughter-house furnished many of my materials; and often did my human nature turn with loathing from my occupation, whilst, still urged on by an eagerness which perpetually increased, I brought my work near to a conclusion.

The summer months passed while I was thus engaged, heart and soul, in one pursuit. It was a most beautiful season; never did the fields bestow a more plentiful harvest, or the vines yield a more luxuriant vintage: but my eyes were insensible to the charms of nature. And the same feelings which made me neglect the scenes around me caused me also to forget those friends who were so many miles absent, and whom I had not seen for so long a time. I knew my silence disquieted them; and I well remembered the words of my father: ''I know that while you are pleased with yourself, you will think of us with affection, and we shall hear regularly from you. You must pardon me if I regard any interruption in your correspondence as a proof that your other duties are equally neglected.''

I knew well therefore what would be my father's feelings; but I could not tear my thoughts from my employment, loathsome in itself, but which had taken an irresistible hold of my imagination. I wished, as it were, to procrastinate all that related to my feelings of affection until the great object, which swallowed up every habit of my nature, should be completed.

I then thought that my father would be unjust if he ascribed my neglect to vice, or faultiness on my part; but I am now convinced that he was justified in conceiving that I should not be altogether free from blame. A human being in perfection ought always to preserve a calm and peaceful mind, and never to allow passion or a transitory desire to disturb his tranquillity. I do not think that the pursuit of knowledge is an exception to this rule. If the study to which you apply yourself has a tendency to weaken your affections, and to destroy your taste for those simple pleasures in which no alloy can possibly mix, then that study is certainly unlawful, that is to say, not befitting the human mind. If this rule were always observed; if no man allowed any pursuit whatsoever to interfere with the tranquillity of his domestic affections, Greece had not been enslaved; Cæsar would have spared his country; America would have been discovered more gradually; and the empires of Mexico and Peru had not been destroyed.

But I forget that I am moralising in the most interesting part of my tale; and your looks remind me to proceed.

My father made no reproach in his letters, and only took notice of my silence by enquiring into my occupations more particularly than before. Winter, spring, and summer passed away during my labours; but I did not watch the blossom or the expanding leaves — sights which before always yielded me supreme delight — so deeply was I engrossed in my occupation. The leaves of that year had withered before my work drew near to a close; and now every day showed me more plainly how well I had succeeded. But my enthusiasm was checked by my anxiety, and I appeared rather like one doomed by slavery to toil in the mines, or any other unwholesome trade, than an artist occupied by his favourite employment. Every night I was oppressed by a slow fever, and I became nervous to a most painful degree; the fall of a leaf startled me, and I shunned my fellow-creatures as if I had been guilty of a crime. Sometimes I grew alarmed at the wreck I perceived that I had become; the energy of my purpose alone sustained me: my labours would soon end, and I believed that exercise and amusement would then drive away incipient disease; and I promised myself both of these when my creation should be complete.

CHAPTER V

It was on a dreary night of November, that I beheld the accomplishment of my toils. With an anxiety that almost amounted to agony, I collected the instruments of life around me, that I might infuse a spark of being into the lifeless thing that lay at my feet. It was already one in the morning; the rain pattered dismally against the panes, and my candle was nearly burnt out, when, by the glimmer of the half-extinguished light, I saw the dull yellow eye of the creature open; it breathed hard, and a convulsive motion agitated its limbs.

How can I describe my emotions at this catastrophe, or how delineate the wretch whom with such infinite pains and care I had endeavoured to form? His limbs were in proportion, and I had selected his features as beautiful. Beautiful! — Great God! His yellow skin scarcely covered the work of muscles and arteries beneath; his hair was of a lustrous black, and flowing; his teeth of a pearly whiteness; but these luxuriances only formed a more horrid contrast with his watery eyes, that seemed almost of the same colour as the dun white sockets in which they were set, his shriveled complexion and straight black lips.

The different accidents of life are not so changeable as the feelings of human nature. I had worked hard for nearly two years, for the sole purpose of infusing life into an inanimate body. For this I had deprived myself of rest and health. I had desired it with an ardour that far exceeded moderation; but now that I had finished, the beauty of the dream vanished, and breathless horror and disgust filled my heart. Unable to endure the aspect of the being I had created, I rushed out of the room, and continued a long time traversing my bedchamber, unable to compose my mind to sleep. At length lassitude succeeded to the tumult I had before endured; and I threw myself on the bed in my clothes, endeavouring to seek a few moments of forgetfulness. But it was in vain; I slept, indeed, but I was disturbed by the wildest dreams. I thought I saw Elizabeth, in the bloom of health, walking in the streets of Ingolstadt. Delighted and surprised, I embraced her; but as I imprinted the first kiss on her lips, they became livid with the hue of death; her features appeared to change, and I thought that I held the corpse of my dead mother in my arms; a shroud enveloped her form, and I saw the graveworms crawling in the folds of the flannel. I started from my sleep with horror; a cold dew covered my forehead, my teeth chattered, and every limb became convulsed; when, by the dim and yellow light of the moon, as it forced its way through the window shutters, I beheld the wretch — the miserable monster whom I had created. He held up the curtain of the bed; and his eyes, if eyes they may be called, were fixed on me. His jaws opened, and he muttered some inarticulate sounds, while a grin wrinkled his cheeks. He might have spoken, but I did not hear; one hand was stretched out, seemingly to detain me, but I escaped, and rushed down stairs. I took refuge in the courtyard belonging to the house which I inhabited; where I remained during the rest of the night, walking up and down in the greatest agitation, listening attentively, catching and fearing each sound as if it were to announce the approach of the demoniacal corpse to which I had so miserably given life.

Oh! no mortal could support the horror of that countenance. A mummy again endued with animation could not be so hideous as that wretch. I had gazed on him while unfinished; he was ugly then; but when those muscles and joints were rendered capable of motion, it became a thing such as even Dante could not have conceived.

I passed the night wretchedly. Sometimes my pulse beat so quickly and hardly, that I felt the palpitation of every artery; at others, I nearly sank to the ground through languor and extreme weakness. Mingled with this horror, I felt the bitterness of disappointment; dreams that had been my food and pleasant rest for so long a space were now become a hell to me; and the change was so rapid, the overthrow so complete!

Morning, dismal and wet, at length dawned, and discovered to my sleepless and aching eyes the church of Ingolstadt, its white steeple and clock, which indicated the sixth hour. The porter opened the gates of the court, which had that night been my asylum, and I issued into the streets, pacing them with quick steps, as if I sought to avoid the wretch whom I feared every turning of the street would present to my view. I did not dare return to the apartment which I inhabited, but felt impelled to hurry on, although drenched by the rain which poured from a black and comfortless sky.

I continued walking in this manner for some time, endeavouring, by bodily exercise, to ease the load that weighed upon my mind. I traversed the streets, without any clear conception of where I was, or what I was doing. My heart palpitated in the sickness of fear; and I hurried on with irregular steps, not daring to look about me: —

> Like one who, on a lonely road,
>   Doth walk in fear and dread,
> And, having once turned round, walks on,
>   And turns no more his head;
> Because he knows a frightful fiend
>   Doth close behind him tread.[1]

Continuing thus, I came at length opposite to the inn at which the various diligences and carriages usually stopped. Here I paused, I knew not why; but I remained some minutes with my eyes fixed on a coach

---

[1]From Samuel Taylor Coleridge's "The Rime of Ancient Mariner." — Ed.

that was coming towards me from the other end of the street. As it drew nearer, I observed that it was the Swiss diligence: it stopped just where I was standing; and, on the door being opened, I perceived Henry Clerval, who, on seeing me, instantly sprung out. "My dear Frankenstein," exclaimed he, "how glad I am to see you! how fortunate that you should be here at the very moment of my alighting!"

Nothing could equal my delight on seeing Clerval; his presence brought back to my thoughts my father, Elizabeth, and all those scenes of home so dear to my recollection. I grasped his hand, and in a moment forgot my horror and misfortune; I felt suddenly, and for the first time during many months, calm and serene joy. I welcomed my friend, therefore, in the most cordial manner, and we walked towards my college. Clerval continued talking for some time about our mutual friends, and his own good fortune in being permitted to come to Ingolstadt. "You may easily believe," said he, "how great was the difficulty to persuade my father that all necessary knowledge was not comprised in the noble art of book-keeping; and, indeed, I believe I left him incredulous to the last, for his constant answer to my unwearied entreaties was the same as that of the Dutch schoolmaster in the Vicar of Wakefield: — 'I have ten thousand florins a year without Greek, I eat heartily without Greek.' But his affection for me at length overcame his dislike of learning, and he has permitted me to undertake a voyage of discovery to the land of knowledge."

"It gives me the greatest delight to see you; but tell me how you left my father, brothers, and Elizabeth."

"Very well, and very happy, only a little uneasy that they hear from you so seldom. By the by, I mean to lecture you a little upon their account myself. — But, my dear Frankenstein," continued he, stopping short, and gazing full in my face, "I did not before remark how very ill you appear; so thin and pale; you look as if you had been watching for several nights."

"You have guessed right; I have lately been so deeply engaged in one occupation, that I have not allowed myself sufficient rest, as you see; but I hope, I sincerely hope, that all these employments are now at an end, and that I am at length free."

I trembled excessively; I could not endure to think of, and far less to allude to, the occurrences of the preceding night. I walked with a quick pace, and we soon arrived at my college. I then reflected, and the thought made me shiver, that the creature whom I had left in my apartment might still be there, alive, and walking about. I dreaded to behold this monster; but I feared still more that Henry should see him.

Entreating him, therefore, to remain a few minutes at the bottom of the stairs, I darted up towards my own room. My hand was already on the lock of the door before I recollected myself. I then paused; and a cold shivering came over me. I threw the door forcibly open, as children are accustomed to do when they expect a spectre to stand in waiting for them on the other side; but nothing appeared. I stepped fearfully in: the apartment was empty; and my bedroom was also freed from its hideous guest. I could hardly believe that so great a good fortune could have befallen me; but when I became assured that my enemy had indeed fled, I clapped my hands for joy, and ran down to Clerval.

We ascended into my room, and the servant presently brought breakfast; but I was unable to contain myself. It was not joy only that possessed me; I felt my flesh tingle with excess of sensitiveness, and my pulse beat rapidly. I was unable to remain for a single instant in the same place; I jumped over the chairs, clapped my hands, and laughed aloud. Clerval at first attributed my unusual spirits to joy on his arrival; but when he observed me more attentively, he saw a wildness in my eyes for which he could not account; and my loud, unrestrained, heartless laughter, frightened and astonished him.

"My dear Victor," cried he, "what, for God's sake, is the matter? Do not laugh in that manner. How ill you are! What is the cause of all this?"

"Do not ask me," cried I, putting my hands before my eyes, for I thought I saw the dreaded spectre glide into the room; "*he* can tell. — Oh, save me! save me!" I imagined that the monster seized me; I struggled furiously, and fell down in a fit.

Poor Clerval! what must have been his feelings? A meeting, which he anticipated with such joy, so strangely turned to bitterness. But I was not the witness of his grief; for I was lifeless, and did not recover my senses for a long, long time.

This was the commencement of a nervous fever, which confined me for several months. During all that time Henry was my only nurse. I afterwards learned that, knowing my father's advanced age, and unfitness for so long a journey, and how wretched my sickness would make Elizabeth, he spared them this grief by concealing the extent of my disorder. He knew that I could not have a more kind and attentive nurse than himself; and, firm in the hope he felt of my recovery, he did not doubt that, instead of doing harm, he performed the kindest action that he could towards them.

But I was in reality very ill; and surely nothing but the unbounded and unremitting attentions of my friend could have restored me to life.

The form of the monster on whom I had bestowed existence was for ever before my eyes, and I raved incessantly concerning him. Doubtless my words surprised Henry: he at first believed them to be the wanderings of my disturbed imagination; but the pertinacity with which I continually recurred to the same subject persuaded him that my disorder indeed owed its origin to some uncommon and terrible event.

By very slow degrees, and with frequent relapses, that alarmed and grieved my friend, I recovered. I remember the first time I became capable of observing outward objects with any kind of pleasure, I perceived that the fallen leaves had disappeared, and that the young buds were shooting forth from the trees that shaded my window. It was a divine spring; and the season contributed greatly to my convalescence. I felt also sentiments of joy and affection revive in my bosom; my gloom disappeared, and in a short time I became as cheerful as before I was attacked by the fatal passion.

"Dearest Clerval," exclaimed I, "how kind, how very good you are to me. This whole winter, instead of being spent in study, as you promised yourself, has been consumed in my sick room. How shall I ever repay you? I feel the greatest remorse for the disappointment of which I have been the occasion; but you will forgive me."

"You will repay me entirely, if you do not discompose yourself, but get well as fast as you can; and since you appear in such good spirits, I may speak to you on one subject, may I not?"

I trembled. One subject! what could it be? Could he allude to an object on whom I dared not even think?

"Compose yourself," said Clerval, who observed my change of colour, "I will not mention it, if it agitates you; but your father and cousin would be very happy if they received a letter from you in your own hand-writing. They hardly know how ill you have been, and are uneasy at your long silence."

"Is that all, my dear Henry? How could you suppose that my first thought would not fly towards those dear, dear friends whom I love, and who are so deserving of my love."

"If this is your present temper, my friend, you will perhaps be glad to see a letter that has been lying here some days for you: it is from your cousin, I believe."

CHAPTER VI

Clerval then put the following letter into my hands. It was from my own Elizabeth: —

"My dearest Cousin,

"You have been ill, very ill, and even the constant letters of dear kind Henry are not sufficient to reassure me on your account. You are forbidden to write — to hold a pen; yet one word from you, dear Victor, is necessary to calm our apprehensions. For a long time I have thought that each post would bring this line, and my persuasions have restrained my uncle from undertaking a journey to Ingolstadt. I have prevented his encountering the inconveniences and perhaps dangers of so long a journey; yet how often have I regretted not being able to perform it myself! I figure to myself that the task of attending on your sick bed has devolved on some mercenary old nurse, who could never guess your wishes, nor minister to them with the care and affection of your poor cousin. Yet that is over now: Clerval writes that indeed you are getting better. I eagerly hope that you will confirm this intelligence soon in your own handwriting.

"Get well — and return to us. You will find a happy, cheerful home, and friends who love you dearly. Your father's health is vigorous, and he asks but to see you, — but to be assured that you are well; and not a care will ever cloud his benevolent countenance. How pleased you would be to remark the improvement of our Ernest! He is now sixteen, and full of activity and spirit. He is desirous to be a true Swiss, and to enter into foreign service; but we cannot part with him, at least until his elder brother return to us. My uncle is not pleased with the idea of a military career in a distant country; but Ernest never had your powers of application. He looks upon study as an odious fetter; — his time is spent in the open air, climbing the hills or rowing on the lake. I fear that he will become an idler, unless we yield the point, and permit him to enter on the profession which he has selected.

"Little alteration, except the growth of our dear children, has taken place since you left us. The blue lake, and snow-clad mountains, they never change; — and I think our placid home, and our contented hearts are regulated by the same immutable laws. My trifling occupations take up my time and amuse me, and I am rewarded for any exertions by seeing none but happy, kind faces around me. Since you left us, but one change has taken place in our little household. Do you remember on what occasion Justine Moritz entered our family? Probably you do not; I will relate her history, therefore, in a few words. Madame Moritz, her mother, was a widow with four children, of whom Justine was the third. This girl had always been the favourite of her father; but, through a strange perversity, her mother could not endure her, and, after the death of M. Moritz, treated her very ill. My aunt observed this; and, when Justine was twelve years of age, prevailed on her mother to allow her to live at our house. The republican institutions of our country have produced simpler and happier manners than those which prevail in the great monarchies that surround it. Hence there is less distinction between the several classes of its inhabitants; and the lower orders, being neither so poor nor so despised, their manners are more refined and moral. A servant in Geneva does not mean the same thing as a servant in France and England. Justine, thus received in our family, learned the duties of a servant; a condition which, in our fortunate country, does not include the idea of ignorance, and a sacrifice of the dignity of a human being.

"Justine, you may remember, was a great favourite of yours; and I recollect you once remarked, that if you were in an ill-humour, one glance from Justine could dissipate it, for the same reason that Ariosto gives concerning the beauty of Angelica — she looked so frank-hearted and happy. My aunt conceived a great attachment for her, by which she was induced to give her an education superior to that which she had at first intended. This benefit was fully repaid; Justine was the most grateful little creature in the world; I do not mean that she made any professions; I never heard one pass her lips; but you could see by her eyes that she almost adored her protectress. Although her disposition was gay, and in many respects inconsiderate, yet she paid the greatest attention to every gesture of my aunt. She thought her the model of all excellence, and endeavoured to imitate her phraseology and manners, so that even now she often reminds me of her.

"When my dearest aunt died, every one was too much occupied in their own grief to notice poor Justine, who had attended her during her illness with the most anxious affection. Poor Justine was very ill; but other trials were reserved for her.

"One by one, her brothers and sister died; and her mother, with the exception of her neglected daughter, was left childless. The conscience of the woman was troubled; she began to think that the deaths of her favourites was a judgment from heaven to chastise her partiality. She was a Roman Catholic; and I believe her confessor confirmed the idea which she had conceived. Accordingly, a few months after your departure for Ingolstadt, Justine was called home by her repentant mother. Poor girl! she wept when she quitted our house; she was much altered since the death of my aunt; grief had given softness and a winning mildness to her manners, which had before been remarkable for vivacity. Nor was her residence at her mother's house of a nature to restore her gaiety. The poor woman was very vacillating in her repentance. She sometimes begged Justine to forgive her unkindness, but much oftener accused her of having caused the deaths of her brothers and sister. Perpetual fretting at length threw Madame Moritz into a decline, which at first increased her irritability, but she is now at peace for ever. She died on the first approach of cold weather, at the beginning of this last winter. Justine has returned to us; and I assure you I love her tenderly. She is very clever and gentle, and extremely pretty; as I mentioned before, her mien and her expressions continually remind me of my dear aunt.

"I must say also a few words to you, my dear cousin, of little darling William. I wish you could see him; he is very tall of his age, with sweet laughing blue eyes, dark eyelashes, and curling hair. When he smiles, two little dimples appear on each cheek, which are rosy with health. He has already had one or two little *wives*, but Louisa Biron is his favourite, a pretty little girl of five years of age.

"Now, dear Victor, I dare say you wish to be indulged in a little gossip concerning the good people of Geneva. The pretty Miss Mansfield has already received the congratulatory visits on her approaching marriage with a young Englishman, John Melbourne, Esq. Her ugly sister, Manon, married M. Duvillard, the rich banker, last autumn. Your favourite schoolfellow, Louis Manoir, has suffered several misfortunes since the departure of Clerval from Geneva. But he has already recovered his spirits, and is reported to be on the point of marrying a very lively pretty Frenchwoman, Madame Tavernier. She is a widow, and much older than Manoir; but she is very much admired, and a favourite with everybody.

"I have written myself into better spirits, dear cousin; but my anxiety returns upon me as I conclude. Write, dearest Victor, — one line — one word will be a blessing to us. Ten thousand thanks to Henry for his kindness, his affection, and his many letters: we are sincerely grateful. Adieu! my cousin; take care of your self; and, I entreat you, write!

"ELIZABETH LAVENZA.
"Geneva, March 18th, 17—."

"Dear, dear Elizabeth!" I exclaimed, when I had read her letter: "I will write instantly, and relieve them from the anxiety they must feel." I wrote, and this exertion greatly fatigued me; but my convalescence had commenced, and proceeded regularly. In another fortnight I was able to leave my chamber.

One of my first duties on my recovery was to introduce Clerval to the several professors of the university. In doing this, I underwent a kind of rough usage, ill befitting the wounds that my mind had sustained. Ever since the fatal night, the end of my labours, and the beginning of my misfortunes, I had conceived a violent antipathy even to the name of natural philosophy. When I was otherwise quite restored to health, the sight of a chemical instrument would renew all the agony of my nervous symptoms. Henry saw this, and had removed all my apparatus from my view. He had also changed my apartment; for he perceived that I had acquired a dislike for the room which had previously been my laboratory. But these cares of Clerval were made of no avail when I visited the professors. M. Waldman inflicted torture when he praised, with kindness and warmth, the astonishing progress I had made in the sciences. He soon perceived that I disliked the subject; but not guessing the real cause, he attributed my feelings to modesty, and changed the subject from my improvement, to the science itself, with a desire, as I evidently saw, of drawing me out. What could I do? He meant to please, and he tormented me. I felt as if he had placed carefully, one by one, in my view those instruments which were to be afterwards used in putting me to a slow and cruel death. I writhed under his words, yet dared not exhibit the pain I felt. Clerval, whose eyes and feelings were always quick in discerning the sensations of others, declined the subject, alleging, in excuse, his total ignorance; and the conversation took a more general turn. I thanked my friend from my heart, but I did not speak. I saw plainly that he was surprised, but he never attempted to draw my secret from me; and although I loved him with a mixture of affection and reverence that knew no bounds, yet I could never persuade myself to confide to him that event which was so often present to my recollection, but which I feared to detail to another would only impress more deeply.

M. Krempe was not equally docile; and in my condition at that time, of almost insupportable sensitiveness, his harsh blunt encomiums gave me even more pain than the benevolent approbation of M. Waldman. "D—n the fellow!" cried he; "why, M. Clerval, I assure you he has outstript us all. Ay, stare if you please; but it is nevertheless true. A youngster who, but a few years ago, believed in Cornelius Agrippa as firmly as in the gospel, has now set himself at the head of the university; and if he is not soon pulled down, we shall all be out of countenance. — Ay, ay," continued he, observing my face expressive of suffering, "M. Frankenstein is modest; an excellent quality in a young man. Young men should be diffident of themselves, you know, M. Clerval: I was myself when young; but that wears out in a very short time."

M. Krempe had now commenced an eulogy on himself, which happily turned the conversation from a subject that was so annoying to me.

Clerval had never sympathized in my tastes for natural science; and his literary pursuits differed wholly from those which had occupied me. He came to the university with the design of making himself complete master of the oriental languages, as thus he should open a field for the plan of life he had marked out for himself. Resolved to pursue no inglorious career, he turned his eyes toward the East, as affording scope for his spirit of enterprise. The Persian, Arabic, and Sanscrit languages engaged his attention, and I was easily induced to enter on the same studies. Idleness had ever been irksome to me, and now that I wished to fly from reflection, and hated my former studies, I felt great relief in being the fellow-pupil with my friend, and found not only instruction but consolation in the works of the orientalists. I did not, like him, attempt a critical knowledge of their dialects, for I did not contemplate making any other use of them than temporary amusement. I read merely to understand their meaning, and they well repaid my labours. Their melancholy is soothing, and their joy elevating, to a degree I never experienced in studying the authors of any other country. When you read their writings, life appears to consist in a warm sun and a garden of roses, — in the smiles and frowns of a fair enemy, and the fire that consumes your own heart. How different from the manly and heroical poetry of Greece and Rome!

Summer passed away in these occupations, and my return to Geneva was fixed for the latter end of autumn; but being delayed by several accidents, winter and snow arrived, the roads were deemed impassable, and my journey was retarded until the ensuing spring. I felt this delay very bitterly; for I longed to see my native town and my beloved friends. My return had only been delayed so long, from an unwillingness to leave Clerval in a strange place, before he had become acquainted with any of its inhabitants. The winter, however, was spent cheerfully; and although the spring was uncommonly late, when it came its beauty compensated for its dilatoriness.

The month of May had already commenced, and I expected the letter daily which was to fix the date of my departure, when Henry proposed a pedestrian tour in the environs of Ingolstadt, that I might bid a personal farewell to the country I had so long inhabited. I acceded with pleasure to this proposition: I was fond of exercise, and Clerval had always been my favourite companion in the rambles of this nature that I had taken among the scenes of my native country.

We passed a fortnight in these perambulations: my health and spirits had long been restored, and they gained additional strength from the salubrious air I breathed, the natural incidents of our progress, and the con-

versation of my friend. Study had before secluded me from the intercourse of my fellow-creatures, and rendered me unsocial; but Clerval
called forth the better feelings of my heart; he again taught me to love the
aspect of nature, and the cheerful faces of children. Excellent friend! how
sincerely did you love me, and endeavour to elevate my mind until it was
on a level with your own! A selfish pursuit had cramped and narrowed
me, until your gentleness and affection warmed and opened my senses; I
became the same happy creature who, a few years ago, loved and beloved
by all, had no sorrow or care. When happy, inanimate nature had the
power of bestowing on me the most delightful sensations. A serene sky
and verdant fields filled me with ecstasy. The present season was indeed
divine; the flowers of spring bloomed in the hedges, while those of summer were already in bud. I was undisturbed by thoughts which during the
preceding year had pressed upon me, notwithstanding my endeavours to
throw them off, with an invincible burden.

Henry rejoiced in my gaiety, and sincerely sympathised in my feelings: he exerted himself to amuse me, while he expressed the sensations
that filled his soul. The resources of his mind on this occasion were truly
astonishing: his conversation was full of imagination; and very often, in
imitation of the Persian and Arabic writers, he invented tales of wonderful fancy and passion. At other times he repeated my favourite poems,
or drew me out into arguments, which he supported with great inge-
nuity.

We returned to our college on a Sunday afternoon: the peasants
were dancing, and every one we met appeared gay and happy. My own
spirits were high, and I bounded along with feelings of unbridled joy
and hilarity.

CHAPTER VII

On my return, I found the following letter from my father: —

"My dear Victor,
"You have probably waited impatiently for a letter to fix the date
of your return to us; and I was at first tempted to write only a few lines,
merely mentioning the day on which I should expect you. But that
would be a cruel kindness, and I dare not do it. What would be your
surprise, my son, when you expected a happy and glad welcome, to
behold, on the contrary, tears and wretchedness? And how, Victor, can
I relate our misfortune? Absence cannot have rendered you callous to

our joys and griefs; and how shall I inflict pain on my long absent son? I wish to prepare you for the woful news, but I know it is impossible; even now your eye skims over the page, to seek the words which are to convey to you the horrible tidings.

"William is dead! — that sweet child, whose smiles delighted and warmed my heart, who was so gentle, yet so gay! Victor, he is murdered!

"I will not attempt to console you; but will simply relate the circumstances of the transaction.

"Last Thursday (May 7th), I, my niece, and your two brothers, went to walk in Plainpalais. The evening was warm and serene, and we prolonged our walk farther than usual. It was already dusk before we thought of returning; and then we discovered that William and Ernest, who had gone on before, were not to be found. We accordingly rested on a seat until they should return. Presently Ernest came, and enquired if we had seen his brother: he said, that he had been playing with him, that William had run away to hide himself, and that he vainly sought for him, and afterwards waited for him a long time, but that he did not return.

"This account rather alarmed us, and we continued to search for him until night fell, when Elizabeth conjectured that he might have returned to the house. He was not there. We returned again, with torches; for I could not rest, when I thought that my sweet boy had lost himself, and was exposed to all the damps and dews of night; Elizabeth also suffered extreme anguish. About five in the morning I discovered my lovely boy, whom the night before I had seen blooming and active in health, stretched on the grass livid and motionless: the print of the murderer's finger was on his neck.

"He was conveyed home, and the anguish that was visible in my countenance betrayed the secret to Elizabeth. She was very earnest to see the corpse. At first I attempted to prevent her; but she persisted, and entering the room where it lay, hastily examined the neck of the victim, and clasping her hands exclaimed, 'O God! I have murdered my darling child!'

"She fainted, and was restored with extreme difficulty. When she again lived, it was only to weep and sigh. She told me, that that same evening William had teased her to let him wear a very valuable miniature that she possessed of your mother. This picture is gone, and was doubtless the temptation which urged the murderer to the deed. We have no trace of him at present, although our exertions to discover him are unremitted; but they will not restore my beloved William!

"Come, dearest Victor; you alone can console Elizabeth. She weeps continually, and accuses herself unjustly as the cause of his death; her words pierce my heart. We are all unhappy; but will not that be an additional motive for you, my son, to return and be our comforter? Your dear mother! Alas, Victor! I now say, Thank God she did not live to witness the cruel, miserable death of her youngest darling!

"Come, Victor; not brooding thoughts of vengeance against the assassin, but with feelings of peace and gentleness, that will heal, instead of festering, the wounds of our minds. Enter the house of mourning, my friend, but with kindness and affection for those who love you, and not with hatred for your enemies.

"Your affectionate and afflicted father,
"ALPHONSE FRANKENSTEIN.
"Geneva, May 12th, 17—."

Clerval, who had watched my countenance as I read this letter, was surprised to observe the despair that succeeded to the joy I at first expressed on receiving news from my friends. I threw the letter on the table, and covered my face with my hands.

"My dear Frankenstein," exclaimed Henry, when he perceived me weep with bitterness, "are you always to be unhappy? My dear friend, what has happened?"

I motioned to him to take up the letter, while I walked up and down the room in the extremest agitation. Tears also gushed from the eyes of Clerval, as he read the account of my misfortune.

"I can offer you no consolation, my friend," said he; "your disaster is irreparable. What do you intend to do?"

"To go instantly to Geneva: come with me, Henry, to order the horses."

During our walk, Clerval endeavoured to say a few words of consolation; he could only express his heartfelt sympathy. "Poor William!" said he, "dear lovely child, he now sleeps with his angel mother! Who that had seen him bright and joyous in his young beauty, but must weep over his untimely loss! To die so miserably; to feel the murderer's grasp! How much more a murderer, that could destroy such radiant innocence! Poor little fellow! one only consolation have we; his friends mourn and weep, but he is at rest. The pang is over, his sufferings are at an end for ever. A sod covers his gentle form, and he knows no pain. He can no longer be a subject for pity; we must reserve that for his miserable survivors."

Clerval spoke thus as we hurried through the streets; the words impressed themselves on my mind, and I remembered them afterwards in solitude. But now, as soon as the horses arrived, I hurried into a cabriolet, and bade farewell to my friend.

My journey was very melancholy. At first I wished to hurry on, for I longed to console and sympathise with my loved and sorrowing friends; but when I drew near my native town, I slackened my progress. I could hardly sustain the multitude of feelings that crowded into my mind. I passed through scenes familiar to my youth, but which I had not seen for nearly six years. How altered every thing might be during that time! One sudden and desolating change had taken place; but a thousand little circumstances might have by degrees worked other alterations, which, although they were done more tranquilly, might not be the less decisive. Fear overcame me; I dared not advance, dreading a thousand nameless evils that made me tremble, although I was unable to define them.

I remained two days at Lausanne, in this painful state of mind. I contemplated the lake: the waters were placid; all around was calm; and the snowy mountains, "the palaces of nature," were not changed. By degrees the calm and heavenly scene restored me, and I continued my journey towards Geneva.

The road ran by the side of the lake, which became narrower as I approached my native town. I discovered more distinctly the black sides of Jura, and the bright summit of Mont Blanc. I wept like a child. "Dear mountains! my own beautiful lake! how do you welcome your wanderer? Your summits are clear; the sky and lake are blue and placid. Is this to prognosticate peace, or to mock at my unhappiness?"

I fear, my friend, that I shall render myself tedious by dwelling on these preliminary circumstances; but they were days of comparative happiness, and I think of them with pleasure. My country, my beloved country! who but a native can tell the delight I took in again beholding thy streams, thy mountains, and, more than all, thy lovely lake!

Yet, as I drew nearer home, grief and fear again overcame me. Night also closed around; and when I could hardly see the dark mountains, I felt still more gloomily. The picture appeared a vast and dim scene of evil, and I foresaw obscurely that I was destined to become the most wretched of human beings. Alas! I prophesied truly, and failed only in one single circumstance, that in all the misery I imagined and dreaded, I did not conceive the hundredth part of the anguish I was destined to endure.

It was completely dark when I arrived in the environs of Geneva; the gates of the town were already shut; and I was obliged to pass the night at Secheron, a village at the distance of half a league from the city. The sky was serene; and, as I was unable to rest, I resolved to visit the spot where my poor William had been murdered. As I could not pass through the town, I was obliged to cross the lake in a boat to arrive at Plainpalais. During this short voyage I saw the lightnings playing on the summit of Mont Blanc in the most beautiful figures. The storm appeared to approach rapidly; and, on landing, I ascended a low hill, that I might observe its progress. It advanced; the heavens were clouded, and I soon felt the rain coming slowly in large drops, but its violence quickly increased.

I quitted my seat, and walked on, although the darkness and storm increased every minute, and the thunder burst with a terrific crash over my head. It was echoed from Salêve, the Juras, and the Alps of Savoy; vivid flashes of lightning dazzled my eyes, illuminating the lake, making it appear like a vast sheet of fire; then for an instant every thing seemed of a pitchy darkness, until the eye recovered itself from the preceding flash. The storm, as is often the case in Switzerland, appeared at once in various parts of the heavens. The most violent storm hung exactly north of the town, over that part of the lake which lies between the promontory of Belrive and the village of Copêt. Another storm enlightened Jura with faint flashes; and another darkened and sometimes disclosed the Môle, a peaked mountain to the east of the lake.

While I watched the tempest, so beautiful yet terrific, I wandered on with a hasty step. This noble war in the sky elevated my spirits; I clasped my hands, and exclaimed aloud, "William, dear angel! this is thy funeral, this thy dirge!" As I said these words, I perceived in the gloom a figure which stole from behind a clump of trees near me; I stood fixed, gazing intently; I could not be mistaken. A flash of lightning illuminated the object, and discovered its shape plainly to me: its gigantic stature, and the deformity of its aspect, more hideous than belongs to humanity, instantly informed me that it was the wretch, the filthy dæmon, to whom I had given life. What did he there? Could he be (I shuddered at the conception) the murderer of my brother? No sooner did that idea cross my imagination, than I became convinced of its truth; my teeth chattered, and I was forced to lean against a tree for support. The figure passed me quickly, and I lost it in the gloom. Nothing in human shape could have destroyed that fair child. *He* was the murderer! I could not doubt it. The mere presence of the idea was an irresistible proof of the fact. I thought of pursuing the devil; but it would have been in vain, for another flash discovered him to me hanging among the rocks of the nearly perpendicular ascent of Mont Salêve, a hill that bounds Plainpalais on the south. He soon reached the summit, and disappeared.

I remained motionless. The thunder ceased; but the rain still continued, and the scene was enveloped in an impenetrable darkness. I revolved in my mind the events which I had until now sought to forget: the whole train of my progress towards the creation; the appearance of the work of my own hands alive at my bedside; its departure. Two years had now nearly elapsed since the night on which he first received life; and was this his first crime? Alas! I had turned loose into the world a depraved wretch, whose delight was in carnage and misery; had he not murdered my brother?

No one can conceive the anguish I suffered during the remainder of the night, which I spent, cold and wet, in the open air. But I did not feel the inconvenience of the weather; my imagination was busy in scenes of evil and despair. I considered the being whom I had cast among mankind, and endowed with the will and power to effect purposes of horror, such as the deed which he had now done, nearly in the light of my own vampire, my own spirit let loose from the grave, and forced to destroy all that was dear to me.

Day dawned; and I directed my steps towards the town. The gates were open, and I hastened to my father's house. My first thought was to discover what I knew of the murderer, and cause instant pursuit to be made. But I paused when I reflected on the story that I had to tell. A being whom I myself had formed, and endued with life, had met me at midnight among the precipices of an inaccessible mountain. I remembered also the nervous fever with which I had been seized just at the time that I dated my creation, and which would give an air of delirium to a tale otherwise so utterly improbable. I well knew that if any other had communicated such a relation to me, I should have looked upon it as the ravings of insanity. Besides, the strange nature of the animal would elude all pursuit, even if I were so far credited as to persuade my relatives to commence it. And then of what use would be pursuit? Who could arrest a creature capable of scaling the overhanging sides of Mont Salêve? These reflections determined me, and I resolved to remain silent.

It was about five in the morning when I entered my father's house. I told the servants not to disturb the family, and went into the library to attend their usual hour of rising.

Six years had elapsed, passed as a dream but for one indelible trace, and I stood in the same place where I had last embraced my father before my departure for Ingolstadt. Beloved and venerable parent! He still remained to me. I gazed on the picture of my mother, which stood over the mantel-piece. It was an historical subject, painted at my father's desire, and represented Caroline Beaufort in an agony of despair, kneeling by the coffin of her dead father. Her garb was rustic, and her cheek pale; but there was an air of dignity and beauty, that hardly permitted the sentiment of pity. Below this picture was a miniature of William; and my tears flowed when I looked upon it. While I was thus engaged, Ernest entered; he had heard me arrive, and hastened to welcome me. He expressed a sorrowful delight to see me: "Welcome, my dearest Victor," said he. "Ah! I wish you had come three months ago, and then you would have found us all joyous and delighted. You come to us now to share a misery which nothing can alleviate; yet your presence will, I hope, revive our father, who seems sinking under his misfortune; and your persuasions will induce poor Elizabeth to cease her vain and tormenting self-accusations. — Poor William! he was our darling and our pride!"

Tears, unrestrained, fell from my brother's eyes; a sense of mortal agony crept over my frame. Before, I had only imagined the wretchedness of my desolated home; the reality came on me as a new, and a not less terrible, disaster. I tried to calm Ernest; I enquired more minutely concerning my father, and her I named my cousin.

"She most of all," said Ernest, "requires consolation; she accused herself of having caused the death of my brother, and that made her very wretched. But since the murderer has been discovered — "

"The murderer discovered! Good God! how can that be? who could attempt to pursue him? It is impossible; one might as well try to overtake the winds, or confine a mountain-stream with a straw. I saw him too; he was free last night!"

"I do not know what you mean," replied my brother, in accents of wonder, "but to us the discovery we have made completes our misery. No one would believe it at first; and even now Elizabeth will not be convinced, notwithstanding all the evidence. Indeed, who would credit that Justine Moritz, who was so amiable, and fond of all the family, could suddenly become capable of so frightful, so appalling a crime?"

"Justine Moritz! Poor, poor girl, is she the accused? But it is wrongfully; every one knows that; no one believes it, surely, Ernest?"

"No one did at first; but several circumstances came out, that have almost forced conviction upon us; and her own behaviour has been so confused, as to add to the evidence of facts a weight that, I fear, leaves no hope for doubt. But she will be tried to-day, and you will then hear all."

He related that, the morning on which the murder of poor William had been discovered, Justine had been taken ill, and confined to her bed for several days. During this interval, one of the servants, happening to examine the apparel she had worn on the night of the murder, had discovered in her pocket the picture of my mother, which had been judged to be the temptation of the murderer. The servant instantly showed it to one of the others, who, without saying a word to any of the family, went to a magistrate; and, upon their deposition, Justine was apprehended. On being charged with the fact, the poor girl confirmed the suspicion in a great measure by her extreme confusion of manner.

This was a strange tale, but it did not shake my faith; and I replied earnestly, "You are all mistaken; I know the murderer. Justine, poor, good Justine, is innocent."

At that instant my father entered. I saw unhappiness deeply impressed on his countenance, but he endeavoured to welcome me cheerfully; and, after we had exchanged our mournful greeting, would have introduced some other topic than that of our disaster, had not Ernest exclaimed, "Good God, papa! Victor says that he knows who was the murderer of poor William."

"We do also, unfortunately," replied my father; "for indeed I had rather have been for ever ignorant than have discovered so much depravity and ingratitude in one I valued so highly."

"My dear father, you are mistaken; Justine is innocent."

"If she is, God forbid that she should suffer as guilty. She is to be tried to-day, and I hope, I sincerely hope, that she will be acquitted."

This speech calmed me. I was firmly convinced in my own mind that Justine, and indeed every human being, was guiltless of this murder. I had no fear, therefore, that any circumstantial evidence could be brought forward strong enough to convict her. My tale was not one to announce publicly; its astounding horror would be looked upon as madness by the vulgar. Did any one indeed exist, except I, the creator, who would believe, unless his senses convinced him, in the existence of the living monument of presumption and rash ignorance which I had let loose upon the world?

We were soon joined by Elizabeth. Time had altered her since I last beheld her; it had endowed her with loveliness surpassing the beauty of her childish years. There was the same candour, the same vivacity, but it was allied to an expression more full of sensibility and intellect. She welcomed me with the greatest affection. "Your arrival, my dear cousin," said she, "fills me with hope. You perhaps will find some means to justify my poor guiltless Justine. Alas! who is safe, if she be convicted of crime? I rely on her innocence as certainly as I do upon my own. Our misfortune is doubly hard to us; we have not only lost that lovely darling boy, but this poor girl, whom I sincerely love, is to be torn away by even a worse fate. If she is condemned, I never shall know joy more. But she will not, I am sure she will not; and then I shall be happy again, even after the sad death of my little William."

"She is innocent, my Elizabeth," said I, "and that shall be proved; fear nothing, but let your spirits be cheered by the assurance of her acquittal."

"How kind and generous you are! every one else believes in her guilt, and that made me wretched, for I knew that it was impossible: and to see every one else prejudiced in so deadly a manner rendered me hopeless and despairing." She wept.

"Dearest niece," said my father, "dry your tears. If she is, as you believe, innocent, rely on the justice of our laws, and the activity with which I shall prevent the slightest shadow of partiality."

CHAPTER VIII

We passed a few sad hours, until eleven o'clock, when the trial was to commence. My father and the rest of the family being obliged to attend as witnesses, I accompanied them to the court. During the whole of this wretched mockery of justice I suffered living torture. It was to be decided, whether the result of my curiosity and lawless devices would cause the death of two of my fellow-beings: one a smiling babe, full of innocence and joy; the other far more dreadfully murdered, with every aggravation of infamy that could make the murder memorable in horror. Justine also was a girl of merit, and possessed qualities which promised to render her life happy: now all was to be obliterated in an ignominious grave; and I the cause! A thousand times rather would I have confessed myself guilty of the crime ascribed to Justine; but I was absent when it was committed, and such a declaration would have been considered as the ravings of a madman, and would not have exculpated her who suffered through me.

The appearance of Justine was calm. She was dressed in mourning; and her countenance, always engaging, was rendered, by the solemnity of her feelings, exquisitely beautiful. Yet she appeared confident in innocence, and did not tremble, although gazed on and execrated by thousands; for all the kindness which her beauty might otherwise have excited, was obliterated in the minds of the spectators by the imagination of the enormity she was supposed to have committed. She was tranquil, yet her tranquillity was evidently constrained; and as her confusion had before been adduced as a proof of her guilt, she worked up her mind to an appearance of courage. When she entered the court, she threw her eyes round it, and quickly discovered where we were seated. A tear seemed to dim her eye when she saw us; but she quickly recovered herself, and a look of sorrowful affection seemed to attest her utter guiltlessness.

The trial began; and, after the advocate against her had stated the charge, several witnesses were called. Several strange facts combined against her, which might have staggered any one who had not such proof of her innocence as I had. She had been out the whole of the night on which the murder had been committed, and towards morning had been perceived by a market-woman not far from the spot where the body of the murdered child had been afterwards found. The woman asked her what she did there; but she looked very strangely, and only returned a confused and unintelligible answer. She returned to the house about eight o'clock; and, when one enquired where she had passed the night, she replied that she had been looking for the child, and demanded earnestly if any thing had been heard concerning him. When shown the body, she fell into violent hysterics, and kept her bed for several days. The picture was then produced, which the servant had found in her pocket; and when Elizabeth, in a faltering voice, proved that it was the same which, an hour before the child had been missed, she had placed round his neck, a murmur of horror and indignation filled the court.

Justine was called on for her defence. As the trial had proceeded, her countenance had altered. Surprise, horror, and misery were strongly expressed. Sometimes she struggled with her tears; but, when she was desired to plead, she collected her powers, and spoke, in an audible although variable voice.

"God knows," she said, "how entirely I am innocent. But I do not pretend that my protestations should acquit me: I rest my innocence on a plain and simple explanation of the facts which have been adduced against me; and I hope the character I have always borne will incline my judges to a favourable interpretation, where any circumstance appears doubtful or suspicious."

She then related that, by the permission of Elizabeth, she had passed the evening of the night on which the murder had been committed at the house of an aunt at Chêne, a village situated at about a league from Geneva. On her return, at about nine o'clock, she met a man, who asked her if she had seen any thing of the child who was lost. She was alarmed by this account, and passed several hours in looking for him, when the gates of Geneva were shut, and she was forced to remain several hours of the night in a barn belonging to a cottage, being unwilling to call up the inhabitants, to whom she was well known. Most of the night she spent here watching; towards morning she believed that she slept for a few minutes; some steps disturbed her, and she awoke. It was dawn, and she quitted her asylum, that she might again endeavour to find my brother. If she had gone near the spot where his body lay, it was without her knowledge. That she had been bewildered when questioned by the market-woman was not surprising, since she had passed a sleepless night, and the fate of poor William was yet uncertain. Concerning the picture she could give no account.

"I know," continued the unhappy victim, "how heavily and fatally this one circumstance weighs against me, but I have no power of explaining it; and when I have expressed my utter ignorance, I am only left to conjecture concerning the probabilities by which it might have been placed in my pocket. But here also I am checked. I believe that I have no enemy on earth, and none surely would have been so wicked as to destroy me wantonly. Did the murderer place it there? I know of no opportunity afforded him for so doing; or, if I had, why should he have stolen the jewel, to part with it again so soon?

"I commit my cause to the justice of my judges, yet I see no room for hope. I beg permission to have a few witnesses examined concerning my character; and if their testimony shall not overweigh my supposed guilt, I must be condemned, although I would pledge my salvation on my innocence."

Several witnesses were called, who had known her for many years, and they spoke well of her; but fear, and hatred of the crime of which they supposed her guilty, rendered them timorous, and unwilling to come forward. Elizabeth saw even this last resource, her excellent dispositions and irreproachable conduct, about to fail the accused, when, although violently agitated, she desired permission to address the court.

"I am," said she, "the cousin of the unhappy child who was murdered, or rather his sister, for I was educated by and have lived with his parents ever since and even long before his birth. It may therefore be judged indecent in me to come forward on this occasion; but when I see a fellow-creature about to perish through the cowardice of her pretended friends, I wish to be allowed to speak, that I may say what I know of her character. I am well acquainted with the accused. I have lived in the same house with her, at one time for five, and at another for nearly two years. During all that period she appeared to me the most amiable and benevolent of human creatures. She nursed Madame Frankenstein, my aunt, in her last illness, with the greatest affection and care; and afterwards attended her own mother during a tedious illness, in a manner that excited the admiration of all who knew her; after which she again lived in my uncle's house, where she was beloved by all the family. She was warmly attached to the child who is now dead, and acted towards him like a most affectionate mother. For my own part, I do not hesitate to say, that, notwithstanding all the evidence produced against her, I believe and rely on her perfect innocence. She had no temptation for such an action: as to the bauble on which the chief proof rests, if she had earnestly desired it, I should have willingly given it to her; so much do I esteem and value her.''

A murmur of approbation followed Elizabeth's simple and powerful appeal; but it was excited by her generous interference, and not in favour of poor Justine, on whom the public indignation was turned with renewed violence, charging her with the blackest ingratitude. She herself wept as Elizabeth spoke, but she did not answer. My own agitation and anguish was extreme during the whole trial. I believed in her innocence; I knew it. Could the dæmon, who had (I did not for a minute doubt) murdered my brother, also in his hellish sport have betrayed the innocent to death and ignominy? I could not sustain the horror of my situation; and when I perceived that the popular voice, and the countenances of the judges, had already condemned my unhappy victim, I rushed out of the court in agony. The tortures of the accused did not equal mine; she was sustained by innocence, but the fangs of remorse tore my bosom, and would not forego their hold.

I passed a night of unmingled wretchedness. In the morning I went to the court; my lips and throat were parched. I dared not ask the fatal question; but I was known, and the officer guessed the cause of my visit. The ballots had been thrown; they were all black, and Justine was condemned.

I cannot pretend to describe what I then felt. I had before experienced sensations of horror; and I have endeavoured to bestow upon them adequate expressions, but words cannot convey an idea of the heart-sickening despair that I then endured. The person to whom I addressed myself added, that Justine had already confessed her guilt. "That evidence," he observed, "was hardly required in so glaring a case, but I am glad of it; and, indeed, none of our judges like to condemn a criminal upon circumstantial evidence, be it ever so decisive."

This was strange and unexpected intelligence; what could it mean?

Had my eyes deceived me? and was I really as mad as the whole world
would believe me to be, if I disclosed the object of my suspicions? I
hastened to return home, and Elizabeth eagerly demanded the result.

"My cousin," replied I, "it is decided as you may have expected;
all judges had rather that ten innocent should suffer, than that one
guilty should escape. But she has confessed."

This was a dire blow to poor Elizabeth, who had relied with firmness upon Justine's innocence. "Alas!" said she, "how shall I ever
again believe in human goodness? Justine, whom I loved and esteemed
as my sister, how could she put on those smiles of innocence only to
betray? her mild eyes seemed incapable of any severity or guile, and yet
she has committed a murder."

Soon after we heard that the poor victim had expressed a desire to
see my cousin. My father wished her not to go; but said, that he left it
to her own judgment and feelings to decide. "Yes," said Elizabeth, "I
will go, although she is guilty; and you, Victor, shall accompany me: I
cannot go alone." The idea of this visit was torture to me, yet I could
not refuse.

We entered the gloomy prison-chamber, and beheld Justine sitting
on some straw at the farther end; her hands were manacled, and her
head rested on her knees. She rose on seeing us enter; and when we
were left alone with her, she threw herself at the feet of Elizabeth, weeping bitterly. My cousin wept also.

"Oh, Justine!" said she, "why did you rob me of my last consolation? I relied on your innocence; and although I was then very
wretched, I was not so miserable as I am now."

"And do you also believe that I am so very, very wicked? Do you
also join with my enemies to crush me, to condemn me as a murderer?"
Her voice was suffocated with sobs.

"Rise, my poor girl," said Elizabeth, "why do you kneel, if you
are innocent? I am not one of your enemies; I believed you guiltless,
notwithstanding every evidence, until I heard that you had yourself declared your guilt. That report, you say, is false; and be assured, dear
Justine, that nothing can shake my confidence in you for a moment,
but your own confession."

"I did confess; but I confessed a lie. I confessed, that I might obtain
absolution; but now that falsehood lies heavier at my heart than all my
other sins. The God of heaven forgive me! Ever since I was condemned,
my confessor has besieged me; he threatened and menaced, until I almost began to think that I was the monster that he said I was. He
threatened excommunication and hell fire in my last moments, if I con-

tinued obdurate. Dear lady, I had none to support me; all looked on me as a wretch doomed to ignominy and perdition. What could I do? In an evil hour I subscribed to a lie; and now only am I truly miserable.''

She paused, weeping, and then continued — ''I thought with horror, my sweet lady, that you should believe your Justine, whom your blessed aunt had so highly honoured, and whom you loved, was a creature capable of a crime which none but the devil himself could have perpetrated. Dear William! dearest blessed child! I soon shall see you again in heaven, where we shall all be happy; and that consoles me, going as I am to suffer ignominy and death.''

''Oh, Justine! forgive me for having for one moment distrusted you. Why did you confess? But do not mourn, dear girl. Do not fear. I will proclaim, I will prove your innocence. I will melt the stony hearts of your enemies by my tears and prayers. You shall not die! — You, my play-fellow, my companion, my sister, perish on the scaffold! No! no! I never could survive so horrible a misfortune.''

Justine shook her head mournfully. ''I do not fear to die,'' she said; ''that pang is past. God raises my weakness, and gives me courage to endure the worst. I leave a sad and bitter world; and if you remember me, and think of me as of one unjustly condemned, I am resigned to the fate awaiting me. Learn from me, dear lady, to submit in patience to the will of Heaven!''

During this conversation I had retired to a corner of the prison-room, where I could conceal the horrid anguish that possessed me. Despair! Who dared talk of that? The poor victim, who on the morrow was to pass the awful boundary between life and death, felt not as I did, such deep and bitter agony. I gnashed my teeth, and ground them together, uttering a groan that came from my inmost soul. Justine started. When she saw who it was, she approached me, and said, ''Dear sir, you are very kind to visit me; you, I hope, do not believe that I am guilty?''

I could not answer. ''No, Justine,'' said Elizabeth; ''he is more convinced of your innocence than I was; for even when he heard that you had confessed, he did not credit it.''

''I truly thank him. In these last moments I feel the sincerest gratitude towards those who think of me with kindness. How sweet is the affection of others to such a wretch as I am! It removes more than half my misfortune; and I feel as if I could die in peace, now that my innocence is acknowledged by you, dear lady, and your cousin.''

Thus the poor sufferer tried to comfort others and herself. She indeed gained the resignation she desired. But I, the true murderer, felt the never-dying worm alive in my bosom, which allowed of no hope or consolation. Elizabeth also wept, and was unhappy; but hers also was the misery of innocence, which, like a cloud that passes over the fair moon, for a while hides but cannot tarnish its brightness. Anguish and despair had penetrated into the core of my heart; I bore a hell within me, which nothing could extinguish. We stayed several hours with Justine; and it was with great difficulty that Elizabeth could tear herself away. "I wish," cried she, "that I were to die with you; I cannot live in this world of misery."

Justine assumed an air of cheerfulness, while she with difficulty repressed her bitter tears. She embraced Elizabeth, and said, in a voice of half-suppressed emotion, "Farewell, sweet lady, dearest Elizabeth, my beloved and only friend; may Heaven, in its bounty, bless and preserve you; may this be the last misfortune that you will ever suffer! Live, and be happy, and make others so."

And on the morrow Justine died. Elizabeth's heartrending eloquence failed to move the judges from their settled conviction in the criminality of the saintly sufferer. My passionate and indignant appeals were lost upon them. And when I received their cold answers, and heard the harsh unfeeling reasoning of these men, my purposed avowal died away on my lips. Thus I might proclaim myself a madman, but not revoke the sentence passed upon my wretched victim. She perished on the scaffold as a murderess!

From the tortures of my own heart, I turned to contemplate the deep and voiceless grief of my Elizabeth. This also was my doing! And my father's woe, and the desolation of that late so smiling home — all was the work of my thrice-accursed hands! Ye weep, unhappy ones; but these are not your last tears! Again shall you raise the funeral wail, and the sound of your lamentations shall again and again be heard! Frankenstein, your son, your kinsman, your early, much-loved friend; he who would spend each vital drop of blood for your sakes — who has no thought nor sense of joy, except as it is mirrored also in your dear countenances — who would fill the air with blessings, and spend his life in serving you — he bids you weep — to shed countless tears; happy beyond his hopes, if thus inexorable fate be satisfied, and if the destruction pause before the peace of the grave have succeeded to your sad torments!

Thus spoke my prophetic soul, as, torn by remorse, horror, and despair, I beheld those I loved spend vain sorrow upon the graves of William and Justine, the first hapless victims to my unhallowed arts.

CHAPTER IX

Nothing is more painful to the human mind, than, after the feelings have been worked up by a quick succession of events, the dead calmness of inaction and certainty which follows, and deprives the soul both of hope and fear. Justine died; she rested; and I was alive. The blood flowed freely in my veins, but a weight of despair and remorse pressed on my heart, which nothing could remove. Sleep fled from my eyes; I wandered like an evil spirit, for I had committed deeds of mischief beyond description horrible, and more, much more (I persuaded myself), was yet behind. Yet my heart overflowed with kindness, and the love of virtue. I had begun life with benevolent intentions, and thirsted for the moment when I should put them in practice, and make myself useful to my fellow-beings. Now all was blasted: instead of that serenity of conscience, which allowed me to look back upon the past with self-satisfaction, and from thence to gather promise of new hopes, I was seized by remorse and the sense of guilt, which hurried me away to a hell of intense tortures, such as no language can describe.

This state of mind preyed upon my health, which had perhaps never entirely recovered from the first shock it had sustained. I shunned the face of man; all sound of joy or complacency was torture to me; solitude was my only consolation — deep, dark, deathlike solitude.

My father observed with pain the alteration perceptible in my disposition and habits, and endeavoured by arguments deduced from the feelings of his serene conscience and guiltless life, to inspire me with fortitude, and awaken in me the courage to dispel the dark cloud which brooded over me. "Do you think, Victor," said he, "that I do not suffer also? No one could love a child more than I loved your brother;" (tears came into his eyes as he spoke;) "but is it not a duty to the survivors, that we should refrain from augmenting their unhappiness by an appearance of immoderate grief? It is also a duty owed to yourself; for excessive sorrow prevents improvement or enjoyment, or even the discharge of daily usefulness, without which no man is fit for society."

This advice, although good, was totally inapplicable to my case; I should have been the first to hide my grief, and console my friends, if remorse had not mingled its bitterness, and terror its alarm with my other sensations. Now I could only answer my father with a look of despair, and endeavour to hide myself from his view.

About this time we retired to our house at Belrive. This change was particularly agreeable to me. The shutting of the gates regularly at ten o'clock, and the impossibility of remaining on the lake after that hour, had rendered our residence within the walls of Geneva very irksome to me. I was now free. Often, after the rest of the family had retired for the night, I took the boat, and passed many hours upon the water. Sometimes, with my sails set, I was carried by the wind; and sometimes, after rowing into the middle of the lake, I left the boat to pursue its own course, and gave way to my own miserable reflections. I was often tempted, when all was at peace around me, and I the only unquiet thing that wandered restless in a scene so beautiful and heavenly — if I except some bat, or the frogs, whose harsh and interrupted croaking was heard only when I approached the shore — often, I say, I was tempted to plunge into the silent lake, that the waters might close over me and my calamities for ever. But I was restrained, when I thought of the heroic and suffering Elizabeth, whom I tenderly loved, and whose existence was bound up in mine. I thought also of my father, and surviving brother: should I by my base desertion leave them exposed and unprotected to the malice of the fiend whom I had let loose among them?

At these moments I wept bitterly, and wished that peace would revisit my mind only that I might afford them consolation and happiness. But that could not be. Remorse extinguished every hope. I had been the author of unalterable evils; and I lived in daily fear, lest the monster whom I had created should perpetrate some new wickedness. I had an obscure feeling that all was not over, and that he would still commit some signal crime, which by its enormity should almost efface the recollection of the past. There was always scope for fear, so long as any thing I loved remained behind. My abhorrence of this fiend cannot be conceived. When I thought of him, I gnashed my teeth, my eyes became inflamed, and I ardently wished to extinguish that life which I had so thoughtlessly bestowed. When I reflected on his crimes and malice, my hatred and revenge burst all bounds of moderation. I would have made a pilgrimage to the highest peak of the Andes, could I, when there, have precipitated him to their base. I wished to see him again, that I might wreak the utmost extent of abhorrence on his head, and avenge the deaths of William and Justine.

Our house was the house of mourning. My father's health was deeply shaken by the horror of the recent events. Elizabeth was sad and desponding; she no longer took delight in her ordinary occupations; all pleasure seemed to her sacrilege toward the dead; eternal woe and tears she then thought was the just tribute she should pay to innocence so blasted and destroyed. She was no longer that happy creature, who in earlier youth wandered with me on the banks of the lake, and talked with ecstasy of our future prospects. The first of those sorrows which are sent to wean us from the earth, had visited her, and its dimming influence quenched her dearest smiles. "When I reflect, my dear cousin," said she, "on the miserable death of Justine Moritz, I no longer see the world and its works as they before appeared to me. Before, I looked upon the accounts of vice and injustice, that I read in books or heard from others, as tales of ancient days, or imaginary evils; at least they were remote, and more familiar to reason than to the imagination; but now misery has come home, and men appear to me as monsters thirsting for each other's blood. Yet I am certainly unjust. Every body believed that poor girl to be guilty; and if she could have committed the crime for which she suffered, assuredly she would have been the most depraved of human creatures. For the sake of a few jewels, to have murdered the son of her benefactor and friend, a child whom she had nursed from its birth, and appeared to love as if it had been her own! I could not consent to the death of any human being; but certainly I should have thought such a creature unfit to remain in the society of men. But she was innocent. I know, I feel she was innocent; you are of the same opinion, and that confirms me. Alas! Victor, when falsehood can look so like the truth, who can assure themselves of certain happiness? I feel as if I were walking on the edge of a precipice, towards which thousands are crowding, and endeavouring to plunge me into the abyss. William and Justine were assassinated, and the murderer escapes; he walks about the world free, and perhaps respected. But even if I were condemned to suffer on the scaffold for the same crimes, I would not change places with such a wretch."

I listened to this discourse with the extremest agony. I, not in deed, but in effect, was the true murderer. Elizabeth read my anguish in my countenance, and kindly taking my hand, said, "My dearest friend, you must calm yourself. These events have affected me, God knows how deeply; but I am not so wretched as you are. There is an expression of despair, and sometimes of revenge, in your countenance, that makes me tremble. Dear Victor, banish these dark passions. Remember the friends around you, who centre all their hopes in you. Have we lost the power of rendering you happy? Ah! while we love — while we are true to each other, here in this land of peace and beauty, your native country, we may reap every tranquil blessing, — what can disturb our peace?"

And could not such words from her whom I fondly prized before every other gift of fortune, suffice to chase away the fiend that lurked in my heart? Even as she spoke I drew near to her, as if in terror; lest at that very moment the destroyer had been near to rob me of her.

Thus not the tenderness of friendship, nor the beauty of earth, nor of heaven, could redeem my soul from woe: the very accents of love were ineffectual. I was encompassed by a cloud which no beneficial influence could penetrate. The wounded deer dragging its fainting limbs to some untrodden brake, there to gaze upon the arrow which had pierced it, and to die — was but a type of me.

Sometimes I could cope with the sullen despair that overwhelmed me: but sometimes the whirlwind passions of my soul drove me to seek, by bodily exercise and by change of place, some relief from my intolerable sensations. It was during an access of this kind that I suddenly left my home, and bending my steps towards the near Alpine valleys, sought in the magnificence, the eternity of such scenes, to forget myself and my ephemeral, because human, sorrows. My wanderings were directed towards the valley of Chamounix. I had visited it frequently during my boyhood. Six years had passed since then: *I* was a wreck — but nought had changed in those savage and enduring scenes.

I performed the first part of my journey on horseback. I afterwards hired a mule, as the more sure-footed, and least liable to receive injury on these rugged roads. The weather was fine: it was about the middle of the month of August, nearly two months after the death of Justine; that miserable epoch from which I dated all my woe. The weight upon my spirit was sensibly lightened as I plunged yet deeper in the ravine of Arve. The immense mountains and precipices that overhung me on every side — the sound of the river raging among the rocks, and the dashing of the waterfalls around, spoke of a power mighty as Omnipotence — and I ceased to fear, or to bend before any being less almighty than that which had created and ruled the elements, here displayed in their most terrific guise. Still, as I ascended higher, the valley assumed a more magnificent and astonishing character. Ruined castles hanging on the precipices of piny mountains; the impetuous Arve, and cottages every here and there peeping forth from among the trees, formed a scene of singular beauty. But it was augmented and rendered sublime by the mighty Alps, whose white and shining pyramids and domes towered above all, as belonging to another earth, the habitations of another race of beings.

I passed the bridge of Pélissier, where the ravine, which the river forms, opened before me, and I began to ascend the mountain that overhangs it. Soon after I entered the valley of Chamounix. This valley is more wonderful and sublime, but not so beautiful and picturesque, as that of Servox, through which I had just passed. The high and snowy mountains were its immediate boundaries; but I saw no more ruined castles and fertile fields. Immense glaciers approached the road; I heard the rumbling thunder of the falling avalanche, and marked the smoke of its passage. Mont Blanc, the supreme and magnificent Mont Blanc, raised itself from the surrounding *aiguilles*, and its tremendous *dôme* overlooked the valley.

A tingling long-lost sense of pleasure often came across me during this journey. Some turn in the road, some new object suddenly perceived and recognized, reminded me of days gone by, and were associated with the light-hearted gaiety of boyhood. The very winds whispered in soothing accents, and maternal nature bade me weep no more. Then again the kindly influence ceased to act — I found myself fettered again to grief, and indulging in all the misery of reflection. Then I spurred on my animal, striving so to forget the world, my fears, and, more than all, myself — or, in a more desperate fashion, I alighted, and threw myself on the grass, weighed down by horror and despair.

At length I arrived at the village of Chamounix. Exhaustion succeeded to the extreme fatigue both of body and of mind which I had endured. For a short space of time I remained at the window, watching the pallid lightnings that played above Mont Blanc, and listening to the rushing of the Arve, which pursued its noisy way beneath. The same lulling sounds acted as a lullaby to my too keen sensations: when I placed my head upon my pillow, sleep crept over me; I felt it as it came, and blest the giver of oblivion.

CHAPTER X

I spent the following day roaming through the valley. I stood beside the sources of the Arveiron, which take their rise in a glacier, that with slow pace is advancing down from the summit of the hills, to barricade the valley. The abrupt sides of vast mountains were before me; the icy wall of the glacier overhung me; a few shattered pines were scattered around; and the solemn silence of this glorious presence-chamber of imperial Nature was broken only by the brawling waves, or the fall of some vast fragment, the thunder sound of the avalanche, or the cracking, reverberated along the mountains, of the accumulated ice, which, through the silent working of immutable laws, was ever and anon rent and torn, as if it had been but a plaything in their hands. These sublime and magnificent scenes afforded me the greatest consolation that I was capable of receiving. They elevated me from all littleness of feeling; and although they did not remove my grief, they subdued and tranquillised it. In some degree, also, they diverted my mind from the thoughts over which it had brooded for the last month. I retired to rest at night; my slumbers, as it were, waited on and ministered to by the assemblance of grand shapes which I had contemplated during the day. They congregated round me; the unstained snowy mountain-top, the glittering pinnacle, the pine woods, and ragged bare ravine; the eagle, soaring amidst the clouds — they all gathered round me, and bade me be at peace.

Where had they fled when the next morning I awoke? All of soul-inspiriting fled with sleep, and dark melancholy clouded every thought. The rain was pouring in torrents, and thick mists hid the summits of the mountains, so that I even saw not the faces of those mighty friends. Still I would penetrate their misty veil, and seek them in their cloudy retreats. What were rain and storm to me? My mule was brought to the door, and I resolved to ascend to the summit of Montanvert. I remembered the effect that the view of the tremendous and ever-moving glacier had produced upon my mind when I first saw it. It had then filled me with a sublime ecstasy, that gave wings to the soul, and allowed it to soar from the obscure world to light and joy. The sight of the awful and majestic in nature had indeed always the effect of solemnising my mind, and causing me to forget the passing cares of life. I determined to go without a guide, for I was well acquainted with the path, and the presence of another would destroy the solitary grandeur of the scene.

The ascent is precipitous, but the path is cut into continual and short windings, which enable you to surmount the perpendicularity of the mountain. It is a scene terrifically desolate. In a thousand spots the traces of the winter avalanche may be perceived, where trees lie broken and strewed on the ground; some entirely destroyed, others bent, leaning upon the jutting rocks of the mountain, or transversely upon other trees. The path, as you ascend higher, is intersected by ravines of snow, down which stones continually roll from above; one of them is particularly dangerous, as the slightest sound, such as even speaking in a loud voice, produces a concussion of air sufficient to draw destruction upon the head of the speaker. The pines are not tall or luxuriant, but they are sombre, and add an air of severity to the scene. I looked on the valley beneath; vast mists were rising from the rivers which ran through it, and curling in thick wreaths around the opposite mountains, whose summits were hid in the uniform clouds, while rain poured from the dark sky, and added to the melancholy impression I received from the objects around me. Alas! why does man boast of sensibilities superior to those apparent in the brute; it only renders them more necessary beings. If our impulses were confined to hunger, thirst, and desire, we might be nearly free; but now we are moved by every wind that blows, and a chance word or scene that that word may convey to us.

> We rest; a dream has power to poison sleep.
> We rise; one wand'ring thought pollutes the day.
> We feel, conceive, or reason; laugh or weep,
> Embrace fond woe, or cast our cares away;
> It is the same: for, be it joy or sorrow,
> The path of its departure still is free.
> Man's yesterday may ne'er be like his morrow;
> Nought may endure but mutability![2]

It was nearly noon when I arrived at the top of the ascent. For some time I sat upon the rock that overlooks the sea of ice. A mist covered both that and the surrounding mountains. Presently a breeze dissipated the cloud, and I descended upon the glacier. The surface is very uneven, rising like the waves of a troubled sea, descending low, and interspersed by rifts that sink deep. The field of ice is almost a league in width, but I spent nearly two hours in crossing it. The opposite mountain is a bare perpendicular rock. From the side where I now stood Montanvert was exactly opposite, at the distance of a league; and above it rose Mont Blanc, in awful majesty. I remained in a recess of the rock, gazing on this wonderful and stupendous scene. The sea, or rather the vast river of ice, wound among its dependent mountains, whose aerial summits hung over its recesses. Their icy and glittering peaks shone in the sunlight over the clouds. My heart, which was before sorrowful, now swelled with something like joy; I exclaimed — "Wandering spirits, if indeed ye wander, and do not rest in your narrow beds, allow me this faint happiness, or take me, as your companion, away from the joys of life."

As I said this, I suddenly beheld the figure of a man, at some distance, advancing towards me with superhuman speed. He bounded over the crevices in the ice, among which I had walked with caution; his stature, also, as he approached, seemed to exceed that of man. I was troubled: a mist came over my eyes, and I felt a faintness seize me; but I was quickly restored by the cold gale of the mountains. I perceived, as the shape came nearer (sight tremendous and abhorred!) that it was the wretch whom I had created. I trembled with rage and horror, resolving to wait his approach, and then close with him in mortal combat. He approached; his countenance bespoke bitter anguish, combined with disdain and malig-

---

[2]From Percy Shelley's "Mutability."—Ed.

nity, while its unearthly ugliness rendered it almost too horrible for human eyes. But I scarcely observed this; rage and hatred had at first deprived me of utterance, and I recovered only to overwhelm him with words expressive of furious detestation and contempt.

"Devil," I exclaimed, "do you dare approach me? and do not you fear the fierce vengeance of my arm wreaked on your miserable head? Begone, vile insect! or rather, stay, that I may trample you to dust! and, oh! that I could, with the extinction of your miserable existence, restore those victims whom you have so diabolically murdered!"

"I expected this reception," said the dæmon. "All men hate the wretched; how, then, must I be hated, who am miserable beyond all living things! Yet you, my creator, detest and spurn me, thy creature, to whom thou art bound by ties only dissoluble by the annihilation of one of us. You purpose to kill me. How dare you sport thus with life? Do your duty towards me, and I will do mine towards you and the rest of mankind. If you will comply with my conditions, I will leave them and you at peace; but if you refuse, I will glut the maw of death, until it be satiated with the blood of your remaining friends."

"Abhorred monster! fiend that thou art! the tortures of hell are too mild a vengeance for thy crimes. Wretched devil! you reproach me with your creation; come on, then, that I may extinguish the spark which I so negligently bestowed."

My rage was without bounds; I sprang on him, impelled by all the feelings which can arm one being against the existence of another.

He easily eluded me, and said —

"Be calm! I entreat you to hear me, before you give vent to your hatred on my devoted head. Have I not suffered enough, that you seek to increase my misery? Life, although it may only be an accumulation of anguish, is dear to me, and I will defend it. Remember, thou hast made me more powerful than thyself; my height is superior to thine; my joints more supple. But I will not be tempted to set myself in opposition to thee. I am thy creature, and I will be even mild and docile to my natural lord and king, if thou wilt also perform thy part, the which thou owest me. Oh, Frankenstein, be not equitable to every other, and trample upon me alone, to whom thy justice, and even thy clemency and affection, is most due. Remember, that I am thy creature; I ought to be thy Adam; but I am rather the fallen angel, whom thou drivest from joy for no misdeed. Every where I see bliss, from which I alone am irrevocably excluded. I was benevolent and good; misery made me a fiend. Make me happy, and I shall again be virtuous."

"Begone! I will not hear you. There can be no community between you and me; we are enemies. Begone, or let us try our strength in a fight, in which one must fall.''

"How can I move thee? Will no entreaties cause thee to turn a favourable eye upon thy creature, who implores thy goodness and compassion? Believe me, Frankenstein: I was benevolent; my soul glowed with love and humanity: but am I not alone, miserably alone? You, my creator, abhor me; what hope can I gather from your fellow-creatures, who owe me nothing? they spurn and hate me. The desert mountains and dreary glaciers are my refuge. I have wandered here many days; the caves of ice, which I only do not fear, are a dwelling to me, and the only one which man does not grudge. These bleak skies I hail, for they are kinder to me than your fellow-beings. If the multitude of mankind knew of my existence, they would do as you do, and arm themselves for my destruction. Shall I not then hate them who abhor me? I will keep no terms with my enemies. I am miserable, and they shall share my wretchedness. Yet it is in your power to recompense me, and deliver them from an evil which it only remains for you to make so great, that not only you and your family, but thousands of others, shall be swallowed up in the whirlwinds of its rage. Let your compassion be moved, and do not disdain me. Listen to my tale: when you have heard that, abandon or commiserate me, as you shall judge that I deserve. But hear me. The guilty are allowed, by human laws, bloody as they are, to speak in their own defence before they are condemned. Listen to me, Frankenstein. You accuse me of murder; and yet you would, with a satisfied conscience, destroy your own creature. Oh, praise the eternal justice of man! Yet I ask you not to spare me: listen to me; and then, if you can, and if you will, destroy the work of your hands.''

"Why do you call to my remembrance,'' I rejoined, "circumstances, of which I shudder to reflect, that I have been the miserable origin and author? Cursed be the day, abhorred devil, in which you first saw light! Cursed (although I curse myself) be the hands that formed you! You have made me wretched beyond expression. You have left me no power to consider whether I am just to you, or not. Begone! relieve me from the sight of your detested form.''

"Thus I relieve thee, my creator,'' he said, and placed his hated hands before my eyes, which I flung from me with violence; "thus I take from thee a sight which you abhor. Still thou canst listen to me, and grant me thy compassion. By the virtues that I once possessed, I demand this from you. Hear my tale; it is long and strange, and the temperature of this place is not fitting to your fine sensations; come to the hut upon the mountain. The sun is yet high in the heavens; before it descends to hide itself behind yon snowy precipices, and illuminate another world, you will have heard my story, and can decide. On you it rests, whether I quit for ever the neighbourhood of man, and lead a harmless life, or become the scourge of your fellow-creatures, and the author of your own speedy ruin.''

As he said this, he led the way across the ice: I followed. My heart was full, and I did not answer him; but, as I proceeded, I weighed the various arguments that he had used, and determined at least to listen to his tale. I was partly urged by curiosity, and compassion confirmed my resolution. I had hitherto supposed him to be the murderer of my brother, and I eagerly sought a confirmation or denial of this opinion. For the first time, also, I felt what the duties of a creator towards his creature were, and that I ought to render him happy before I complained of his wickedness. These motives urged me to comply with his demand. We crossed the ice, therefore, and ascended the opposite rock. The air was cold, and the rain again began to descend: we entered the hut, the fiend with an air of exultation, I with a heavy heart, and depressed spirits. But I consented to listen; and, seating myself by the fire which my odious companion had lighted, he thus began his tale.

CHAPTER XI

"It is with considerable difficulty that I remember the original era of my being: all the events of that period appear confused and indistinct. A strange multiplicity of sensations seized me, and I saw, felt, heard, and smelt, at the same time; and it was, indeed, a long time before I learned to distinguish between the operations of my various senses. By degrees, I remember, a stronger light pressed upon my nerves, so that I was obliged to shut my eyes. Darkness then came over me, and troubled me; but hardly had I felt this, when, by opening my eyes, as I now suppose, the light poured in upon me again. I walked, and, I believe, descended; but I presently found a great alteration in my sensations. Before, dark and opaque bodies had surrounded me, impervious to my touch or sight; but I now found that I could wander on at liberty, with no obstacles which I could not either surmount or avoid. The light became more and more oppressive to me; and, the heat wearying me as I walked, I sought a place where I could receive shade. This was the forest near Ingolstadt, and here I lay by the side of a brook resting from my fatigue, until I felt tormented by hunger and thirst. This roused me from my nearly dormant state, and I ate some berries which I found hanging on the trees, or lying on the ground. I slaked my thirst at the brook; and then lying down, was overcome by sleep.

"It was dark when I awoke; I felt cold also, and half-frightened, as it were instinctively, finding myself so desolate. Before I had quitted your apartment, on a sensation of cold, I had covered myself with some clothes; but these were insufficient to secure me from the dews of night. I was a poor, helpless, miserable wretch; I knew, and could distinguish, nothing; but feeling pain invade me on all sides, I sat down and wept.

"Soon a gentle light stole over the heavens, and gave me a sensation of pleasure. I started up, and beheld a radiant form rise from among the trees. I gazed with a kind of wonder. It moved slowly, but it enlightened my path; and I again went out in search of berries. I was still cold, when under one of the trees I found a huge cloak, with which I covered myself, and sat down upon the ground. No distinct ideas occupied my mind; all was confused. I felt light, and hunger, and thirst, and darkness; innumerable sounds rung in my ears, and on all sides various scents saluted me: the only object that I could distinguish was the bright moon, and I fixed my eyes on that with pleasure.

"Several changes of day and night passed, and the orb of night had greatly lessened, when I began to distinguish my sensations from each other. I gradually saw plainly the clear stream that supplied me with drink, and the trees that shaded me with their foliage. I was delighted when I first discovered that a pleasant sound, which often saluted my ears, proceeded from the throats of the little winged animals who had often intercepted the light from my eyes. I began also to observe, with greater accuracy, the forms that surrounded me, and to perceive the boundaries of the radiant roof of light which canopied me. Sometimes I tried to imitate the pleasant songs of the birds, but was unable. Sometimes I wished to express my sensations in my own mode, but the uncouth and inarticulate sounds which broke from me frightened me into silence again.

"The moon had disappeared from the night, and again, with a lessened form, showed itself, while I still remained in the forest. My sensations had, by this time, become distinct, and my mind received every day additional ideas. My eyes became accustomed to the light, and to perceive objects in their right forms; I distinguished the insect from the herb, and, by degrees, one herb from another. I found that the sparrow uttered none but harsh notes, whilst those of the blackbird and thrush were sweet and enticing.

"One day, when I was oppressed by cold, I found a fire which had been left by some wandering beggars, and was overcome with delight at the warmth I experienced from it. In my joy I thrust my hand into the live embers, but quickly drew it out again with a cry of pain. How strange, I thought, that the same cause should produce such opposite effects! I examined the materials of the fire, and to my joy found it to be composed of wood. I quickly collected some branches; but they were wet, and would not burn. I was pained at this, and sat still watching the operation of the fire. The wet wood which I had placed near the heat dried, and itself became inflamed. I reflected on this; and, by touching the various branches, I discovered the cause, and busied myself in collecting a great quantity of wood, that I might dry it, and have a plentiful supply of fire. When night came on, and brought sleep with it, I was in the greatest fear lest my fire should be extinguished. I covered it carefully with dry wood and leaves, and placed wet branches upon it; and then, spreading my cloak, I lay on the ground, and sunk into sleep.

"It was morning when I awoke, and my first care was to visit the fire. I uncovered it, and a gentle breeze quickly fanned it into a flame. I observed this also, and contrived a fan of branches, which roused the embers when they were nearly extinguished. When night came again, I found, with pleasure, that the fire gave light as well as heat; and that the discovery of this element was useful to me in my food; for I found some of the offals that the travellers had left had been roasted, and tasted much more savoury than the berries I gathered from the trees. I tried, therefore, to dress my food in the same manner, placing it on the live embers. I found that the berries were spoiled by this operation, and the nuts and roots much improved.

"Food, however, became scarce; and I often spent the whole day searching in vain for a few acorns to assuage the pangs of hunger. When I found this, I resolved to quit the place that I had hitherto inhabited, to seek for one where the few wants I experienced would be more easily satisfied. In this emigration, I exceedingly lamented the loss of the fire which I had obtained through accident, and knew not how to reproduce it. I gave several hours to the serious consideration of this difficulty; but I was obliged to relinquish all attempt to supply it; and, wrapping myself up in my cloak, I struck across the wood towards the setting sun. I passed three days in these rambles, and at length discovered the open country. A great fall of snow had taken place the night before, and the fields were of one uniform white; the appearance was disconsolate, and I found my feet chilled by the cold damp substance that covered the ground.

"It was about seven in the morning, and I longed to obtain food and shelter; at length I perceived a small hut, on a rising ground, which had doubtless been built for the convenience of some shepherd. This was a new sight to me; and I examined the structure with great curiosity. Finding the door open, I entered. An old man sat in it, near a fire, over which he was preparing his breakfast. He turned on hearing a noise; and, perceiving me, shrieked loudly, and, quitting the hut, ran across the fields with a speed of which his debilitated form hardly appeared capable. His appearance, different from any I had ever before seen, and his flight, somewhat surprised me. But I was enchanted by the appearance of the hut: here the snow and rain could not penetrate; the ground was dry; and it presented to me then as exquisite and divine a retreat as Pandæmonium appeared to the dæmons of hell after their sufferings in the lake of fire. I greedily devoured the remnants of the shepherd's breakfast, which consisted of bread, cheese, milk, and wine; the latter, however, I did not like. Then, overcome by fatigue, I lay down among some straw, and fell asleep.

"It was noon when I awoke; and, allured by the warmth of the sun, which shone brightly on the white ground, I determined to recommence my travels; and, depositing the remains of the peasant's breakfast in a wallet I found, I proceeded across the fields for several hours, until at sunset I arrived at a village. How miraculous did this appear! the huts, the neater cottages, and stately houses, engaged my admiration by turns. The vegetables in the gardens, the milk and cheese that I saw placed at the windows of some of the cottages, allured my appetite. One of the best of these I entered; but I had hardly placed my foot within the door, before the children shrieked, and one of the women fainted. The whole village was roused; some fled, some attacked me, until, grievously bruised by stones and many other kinds of missile weapons, I escaped to the open country, and fearfully took refuge in a low hovel, quite bare, and making a wretched appearance after the palaces I had beheld in the village. This hovel, however, joined a cottage of a neat and pleasant appearance; but, after my late dearly bought experience, I dared not enter it. My place of refuge was constructed of wood, but so low, that I could with difficulty sit upright in it. No wood, however, was placed on the earth, which formed the floor, but it was dry; and although the wind entered it by innumerable chinks, I found it an agreeable asylum from the snow and rain.

"Here then I retreated, and lay down happy to have found a shelter, however miserable, from the inclemency of the season, and still more from the barbarity of man.

"As soon as morning dawned, I crept from my kennel, that I might view the adjacent cottage, and discover if I could remain in the habitation I had found. It was situated against the back of the cottage, and surrounded on the sides which were exposed by a pig-sty and a clear pool of water. One part was open, and by that I had crept in; but now I covered every crevice by which I might be perceived with stones and wood, yet in such a manner that I might move them on occasion to pass out: all the light I enjoyed came through the sty, and that was sufficient for me.

"Having thus arranged my dwelling, and carpeted it with clean straw, I retired; for I saw the figure of a man at a distance, and I remembered too well my treatment the night before, to trust myself in his power. I had first, however, provided for my sustenance for that day, by a loaf of coarse bread, which I purloined, and a cup with which I could drink, more conveniently than from my hand, of the pure water which flowed by my retreat. The floor was a little raised, so that it was kept perfectly dry, and by its vicinity to the chimney of the cottage it was tolerably warm.

"Being thus provided, I resolved to reside in this hovel, until something should occur which might alter my determination. It was indeed a paradise, compared to the bleak forest, my former residence, the rain-dropping branches, and dank earth. I ate my breakfast with pleasure, and was about to remove a plank to procure myself a little water, when I heard a step, and looking through a small chink, I beheld a young creature, with a pail on her head, passing before my hovel. The girl was young, and of gentle demeanour, unlike what I have since found cottagers and farm-house servants to be. Yet she was meanly dressed, a coarse blue petticoat and a linen jacket being her only garb; her fair hair was plaited, but not adorned: she looked patient, yet sad. I lost sight of her; and in about a quarter of an hour she returned, bearing the pail, which was now partly filled with milk. As she walked along, seemingly incommoded by the burden, a young man met her, whose countenance expressed a deeper despondence. Uttering a few sounds with an air of melancholy, he took the pail from her head, and bore it to the cottage himself. She followed, and they disappeared. Presently I saw the young man again, with some tools in his hand, cross the field behind the cottage; and the girl was also busied, sometimes in the house, and sometimes in the yard.

"On examining my dwelling, I found that one of the windows of the cottage had formerly occupied a part of it, but the panes had been filled up with wood. In one of these was a small and almost imperceptible chink, through which the eye could just penetrate. Through this crevice a small room was visible, whitewashed and clean, but very bare of furniture. In one corner, near a small fire, sat an old man, leaning his head on his hands in a disconsolate attitude. The young girl was occupied in arranging the cottage; but presently she took something out of a drawer, which employed her hands, and she sat down beside the old man, who, taking up an instrument, began to play, and to produce sounds sweeter than the voice of the thrush or the nightingale. It was a lovely sight, even to me, poor wretch! who had never beheld aught beautiful before. The silver hair and benevolent countenance of the aged cottager won my reverence, while the gentle manners of the girl enticed my love. He played a sweet mournful air, which I perceived drew tears from the eyes of his amiable companion, of which the old man took no notice, until she sobbed audibly; he then pronounced a few sounds, and the fair creature, leaving her work, knelt at his feet. He raised her, and smiled with such kindness and affection, that I felt sensations of a peculiar and overpowering nature: they were a mixture of pain and pleasure, such as I had never before experienced, either from hunger or cold, warmth or food; and I withdrew from the window, unable to bear these emotions.

"Soon after this the young man returned, bearing on his shoulders a load of wood. The girl met him at the door, helped to relieve him of his burden, and, taking some of the fuel into the cottage, placed it on the fire; then she and the youth went apart into a nook of the cottage, and he showed her a large loaf and a piece of cheese. She seemed pleased, and went into the garden for some roots and plants, which she placed in water, and then upon the fire. She afterwards continued her work, whilst the young man went into the garden, and appeared busily employed in digging and pulling up roots. After he had been employed thus about an hour, the young woman joined him, and they entered the cottage together.

"The old man had, in the mean time, been pensive; but, on the appearance of his companions, he assumed a more cheerful air, and they sat down to eat. The meal was quickly despatched. The young woman was again occupied in arranging the cottage; the old man walked before the cottage in the sun for a few minutes, leaning on the arm of the youth. Nothing could exceed in beauty the contrast between these two excellent creatures. One was old, with silver hairs and a countenance beaming with benevolence and love: the younger was slight and graceful in his figure, and his features were moulded with the finest symmetry; yet his eyes and attitude expressed the utmost sadness and despondency. The old man returned to the cottage; and the youth, with tools different from those he had used in the morning, directed his steps across the fields.

"Night quickly shut in; but, to my extreme wonder, I found that the cottagers had a means of prolonging light by the use of tapers, and was delighted to find that the setting of the sun did not put an end to the pleasure I experienced in watching my human neighbours. In the evening, the young girl and her companion were employed in various occupations which I did not understand; and the old man again took up the instrument which produced the divine sounds that had enchanted me in the morning. So soon as he had finished, the youth began, not to play, but to utter sounds that were monotonous, and neither resembling the harmony of the old man's instrument nor the songs of the birds: I since found that he read aloud, but at that time I knew nothing of the science of words or letters.

"The family, after having been thus occupied for a short time, extinguished their lights, and retired, as I conjectured, to rest.

CHAPTER XII

"I lay on my straw, but I could not sleep. I thought of the occurrences of the day. What chiefly struck me was the gentle manners of these people; and I longed to join them, but dared not. I remembered too well the treatment I had suffered the night before from the barbarous villagers, and resolved, whatever course of conduct I might hereafter think it right to pursue, that for the present I would remain quietly in my hovel, watching, and endeavouring to discover the motives which influenced their actions.

"The cottagers arose the next morning before the sun. The young woman arranged the cottage, and prepared the food; and the youth departed after the first meal.

"This day was passed in the same routine as that which preceded it. The young man was constantly employed out of doors, and the girl in various laborious occupations within. The old man, whom I soon perceived to be blind, employed his leisure hours on his instrument or in contemplation. Nothing could exceed the love and respect which the younger cottagers exhibited towards their venerable companion. They performed towards him every little office of affection and duty with gentleness; and he rewarded them by his benevolent smiles.

"They were not entirely happy. The young man and his companion often went apart, and appeared to weep. I saw no cause for their unhappiness; but I was deeply affected by it. If such lovely creatures were miserable, it was less strange that I, an imperfect and solitary being, should be wretched. Yet why were these gentle beings unhappy? They possessed a delightful house (for such it was in my eyes) and every luxury; they had a fire to warm them when chill, and delicious viands when hungry; they were dressed in excellent clothes; and, still more, they enjoyed one another's company and speech, interchanging each day looks of affection and kindness. What did their tears imply? Did they really express pain? I was at first unable to solve these questions; but perpetual attention and time explained to me many appearances which were at first enigmatic.

"A considerable period elapsed before I discovered one of the causes of the uneasiness of this amiable family: it was poverty; and they suffered that evil in a very distressing degree. Their nourishment consisted entirely of the vegetables of their garden, and the milk of one cow, which gave very little during the winter, when its masters could scarcely procure food to support it. They often, I believe, suffered the pangs of hunger very poignantly, especially the two younger cottagers; for several times they placed food before the old man, when they reserved none for themselves.

"This trait of kindness moved me sensibly. I had been accustomed, during the night, to steal a part of their store for my own consumption; but when I found that in doing this I inflicted pain on the cottagers, I abstained, and satisfied myself with berries, nuts, and roots, which I gathered from a neighbouring wood.

"I discovered also another means through which I was enabled to assist their labours. I found that the youth spent a great part of each day in collecting wood for the family fire; and, during the night, I often took his tools, the use of which I quickly discovered, and brought home firing sufficient for the consumption of several days.

"I remember, the first time that I did this, the young woman, when she opened the door in the morning, appeared greatly astonished on seeing a great pile of wood on the outside. She uttered some words in a loud voice, and the youth joined her, who also expressed surprise. I observed, with pleasure, that he did not go to the forest that day, but spent it in repairing the cottage, and cultivating the garden.

"By degrees I made a discovery of still greater moment. I found that these people possessed a method of communicating their experience and feelings to one another by articulate sounds. I perceived that the words they spoke sometimes, produced pleasure or pain, smiles or sadness, in the minds and countenances of the hearers. This was indeed a godlike science, and I ardently desired to become acquainted with it. But I was baffled in every attempt I made for this purpose. Their pronunciation was quick; and the words they uttered, not having any apparent connection with visible objects, I was unable to discover any clue by which I could unravel the mystery of their reference. By great application, however, and after having remained during the space of several revolutions of the moon in my hovel, I discovered the names that were given to some of the most familiar objects of discourse; I learned and applied the words, *fire, milk, bread,* and *wood*. I learned also the names of the cottagers themselves. The youth and his companion had each of them several names, but the old man had only one, which was *father*. The girl was called *sister*, or *Agatha;* and the youth *Felix, brother*, or *son*. I cannot describe the delight I felt when I learned the ideas appropriated to each of these sounds, and was able to pronounce them. I distinguished several other words, without being able as yet to understand or apply them; such as *good, dearest, unhappy*.

"I spent the winter in this manner. The gentle manners and beauty of the cottagers greatly endeared them to me: when they were unhappy, I felt depressed; when they rejoiced, I sympathised in their joys. I saw few human beings beside them; and if any other happened to enter the cottage, their harsh manners and rude gait only enhanced to me the superior accomplishments of my friends. The old man, I could perceive, often endeavoured to encourage his children, as sometimes I found that he called them, to cast off their melancholy. He would talk in a cheerful accent, with an expression of goodness that bestowed pleasure even upon me. Agatha listened with respect, her eyes sometimes filled with tears, which she endeavoured to wipe away unperceived; but I generally found that her countenance and tone were more cheerful after having listened to the exhortations of her father. It was not thus with Felix. He was always the saddest of the group; and, even to my unpractised senses, he appeared to have suffered more deeply than his friends. But if his countenance was more sorrowful, his voice was more cheerful than that of his sister, especially when he addressed the old man.

"I could mention innumerable instances, which, although slight, marked the dispositions of these amiable cottagers. In the midst of poverty and want, Felix carried with pleasure to his sister the first little white flower that peeped out from beneath the snowy ground. Early in the morning, before she had risen, he cleared away the snow that obstructed her path to the milk-house, drew water from the well, and brought the wood from the out-house, where, to his perpetual astonishment, he found his store always replenished by an invisible hand. In the day, I believe, he worked sometimes for a neighbouring farmer, because he often went forth, and did not return until dinner, yet brought no wood with him. At other times he worked in the garden; but, as there was little to do in the frosty season, he read to the old man and Agatha.

"This reading had puzzled me extremely at first; but, by degrees, I discovered that he uttered many of the same sounds when he read, as when he talked. I conjectured, therefore, that he found on the paper signs for speech which he understood, and I ardently longed to comprehend these also; but how was that possible, when I did not even understand the sounds for which they stood as signs? I improved, however, sensibly in this science, but not sufficiently to follow up any kind of conversation, although I applied my whole mind to the endeavour: for I easily perceived that, although I eagerly longed to discover myself to the cottagers, I ought not to make the attempt until I had first become master of their language; which knowledge might enable me to make them overlook the deformity of my figure; for with this also the contrast perpetually presented to my eyes had made me acquainted.

"I had admired the perfect forms of my cottagers — their grace, beauty, and delicate complexions: but how was I terrified, when I viewed myself in a transparent pool! At first I started back, unable to believe that it was indeed I who was reflected in the mirror; and when I became fully convinced that I was in reality the monster that I am, I was filled with the bitterest sensations of despondence and mortification. Alas! I did not yet entirely know the fatal effects of this miserable deformity.

"As the sun became warmer, and the light of day longer, the snow vanished, and I beheld the bare trees and the black earth. From this time Felix was more employed; and the heart-moving indications of impending famine disappeared. Their food, as I afterwards found, was coarse, but it was wholesome; and they procured a sufficiency of it. Several new kinds of plants sprung up in the garden, which they dressed; and these signs of comfort increased daily as the season advanced.

"The old man, leaning on his son, walked each day at noon, when it did not rain, as I found it was called when the heavens poured forth its waters. This frequently took place; but a high wind quickly dried the earth, and the season became far more pleasant than it had been.

"My mode of life in my hovel was uniform. During the morning, I attended the motions of the cottagers; and when they were dispersed in various occupations, I slept: the remainder of the day was spent in observing my friends. When they had retired to rest, if there was any moon, or the night was star-light, I went into the woods, and collected my own food and fuel for the cottage. When I returned, as often as it was necessary, I cleared their path from the snow, and performed those offices that I had seen done by Felix. I afterwards found that these labours, performed by an invisible hand, greatly astonished them; and once or twice I heard them, on these occasions, utter the words *good spirit, wonderful;* but I did not then understand the signification of these terms.

"My thoughts now became more active, and I longed to discover the motives and feelings of these lovely creatures; I was inquisitive to know why Felix appeared so miserable, and Agatha so sad. I thought (foolish wretch!) that it might be in my power to restore happiness to these deserving people. When I slept, or was absent, the forms of the venerable blind father, the gentle Agatha, and the excellent Felix, flitted before me. I looked upon them as superior beings, who would be the arbiters of my future destiny. I formed in my imagination a thousand pictures of presenting myself to them, and their reception of me. I imagined that they would be disgusted, until, by my gentle demeanour and conciliating words, I should first win their favour, and afterwards their love.

"These thoughts exhilarated me, and led me to apply with fresh ardour to the acquiring the art of language. My organs were indeed harsh, but supple; and although my voice was very unlike the soft music of their tones, yet I pronounced such words as I understood with tolerable ease. It was as the ass and the lap-dog; yet surely the gentle ass whose intentions were affectionate, although his manners were rude, deserved better treatment than blows and execration.

"The pleasant showers and genial warmth of spring greatly altered the aspect of the earth. Men, who before this change seemed to have been hid in caves, dispersed themselves, and were employed in various arts of cultivation. The birds sang in more cheerful notes, and the leaves began to bud forth on the trees. Happy, happy earth! fit habitation for gods, which, so short a time before, was bleak, damp, and unwholesome. My spirits were elevated by the enchanting appearance of nature; the past was blotted from my memory, the present was tranquil, and the future gilded by bright rays of hope, and anticipations of joy.

CHAPTER XIII

"I now hasten to the more moving part of my story. I shall relate events, that impressed me with feelings which, from what I had been, have made me what I am.

"Spring advanced rapidly; the weather became fine, and the skies cloudless. It surprised me, that what before was desert and gloomy should now bloom with the most beautiful flowers and verdure. My senses were gratified and refreshed by a thousand scents of delight, and a thousand sights of beauty.

"It was on one of these days, when my cottagers periodically rested from labour — the old man played on his guitar, and the children listened to him — that I observed the countenance of Felix was melancholy beyond expression; he sighed frequently; and once his father paused in his music, and I conjectured by his manner that he enquired the cause of his son's sorrow. Felix replied in a cheerful accent, and the old man was recommencing his music, when some one tapped at the door.

"It was a lady on horseback, accompanied by a countryman as a guide. The lady was dressed in a dark suit, and covered with a thick black veil. Agatha asked a question; to which the stranger only replied by pronouncing, in a sweet accent, the name of Felix. Her voice was musical, but unlike that of either of my friends. On hearing this word, Felix came up hastily to the lady; who, when she saw him, threw up her veil, and I beheld a countenance of angelic beauty and expression. Her hair of a shining raven black, and curiously braided; her eyes were dark, but gentle, although animated; her features of a regular proportion, and her complexion wondrously fair, each cheek tinged with a lovely pink.

"Felix seemed ravished with delight when he saw her, every trait of sorrow vanished from his face, and it instantly expressed a degree of ecstatic joy, of which I could hardly have believed it capable; his eyes sparkled, as his cheek flushed with pleasure; and at that moment I thought him as beautiful as the stranger. She appeared affected by different feelings; wiping a few tears from her lovely eyes, she held out her hand to Felix, who kissed it rapturously, and called her, as well as I could distinguish, his sweet Arabian. She did not appear to understand him, but smiled. He assisted her to dismount, and dismissing her guide, conducted her into the cottage. Some conversation took place between him and his father; and the young stranger knelt at the old man's feet, and would have kissed his hand, but he raised her, and embraced her affectionately.

"I soon perceived, that although the stranger uttered articulate sounds, and appeared to have a language of her own, she was neither understood by, nor herself understood, the cottagers. They made many signs which I did not comprehend; but I saw that her presence diffused gladness through the cottage, dispelling their sorrow as the sun dissipates the morning mists. Felix seemed peculiarly happy, and with smiles of delight welcomed his Arabian. Agatha, the ever-gentle Agatha, kissed the hands of the lovely stranger; and, pointing to her brother, made signs which appeared to me to mean that he had been sorrowful until she came. Some hours passed thus, while they, by their countenances, expressed joy, the cause of which I did not comprehend. Presently I found, by the frequent recurrence of some sound which the stranger repeated after them, that she was endeavouring to learn their language; and the idea instantly occurred to me, that I should make use of the same instructions to the same end. The stranger learned about twenty words at the first lesson, most of them, indeed, were those which I had before understood, but I profited by the others.

"As night came on, Agatha and the Arabian retired early. When they separated, Felix kissed the hand of the stranger, and said, 'Good night, sweet Safie.' He sat up much longer, conversing with his father; and, by the frequent repetition of her name, I conjectured that their lovely guest was the subject of their conversation. I ardently desired to understand them, and bent every faculty towards that purpose, but found it utterly impossible.

"The next morning Felix went out to his work; and, after the usual occupations of Agatha were finished, the Arabian sat at the feet of the old man, and, taking his guitar, played some airs so entrancingly beautiful, that they at once drew tears of sorrow and delight from my eyes. She sang, and her voice flowed in a rich cadence, swelling or dying away, like a nightingale of the woods.

"When she had finished, she gave the guitar to Agatha, who at first declined it. She played a simple air, and her voice accompanied it in sweet accents, but unlike the wondrous strain of the stranger. The old man appeared enraptured, and said some words, which Agatha endeavoured to explain to Safie, and by which he appeared to wish to express that she bestowed on him the greatest delight by her music.

"The days now passed as peaceably as before, with the sole alteration, that joy had taken place of sadness in the countenances of my friends. Safie was always gay and happy; she and I improved rapidly in the knowledge of language, so that in two months I began to comprehend most of the words uttered by my protectors.

"In the meanwhile also the black ground was covered with herbage, and the green banks interspersed with innumerable flowers, sweet to the scent and the eyes, stars of pale radiance among the moonlight woods; the sun became warmer, the nights clear and balmy; and my nocturnal rambles were an extreme pleasure to me, although they were considerably shortened by the late setting and early rising of the sun; for I never ventured abroad during daylight, fearful of meeting with the same treatment I had formerly endured in the first village which I entered.

"My days were spent in close attention, that I might more speedily master the language; and I may boast that I improved more rapidly than the Arabian, who understood very little, and conversed in broken accents, whilst I comprehended and could imitate almost every word that was spoken.

"While I improved in speech, I also learned the science of letters, as it was taught to the stranger; and this opened before me a wide field for wonder and delight.

"The book from which Felix instructed Safie was Volney's 'Ruins of Empires.' I should not have understood the purport of this book, had not Felix, in reading it, given very minute explanations. He had chosen this work, he said, because the declamatory style was framed in imitation of the eastern authors. Through this work I obtained a cursory knowledge of history, and a view of the several empires at present existing in the world; it gave me an insight into the manners, governments, and religions of the different nations of the earth. I heard of the slothful Asiatics; of the stupendous genius and mental activity of the Grecians; of the wars and wonderful virtue of the early Romans — of their subsequent degenerating — of the decline of that mighty empire; of chivalry, Christianity, and kings. I heard of the discovery of the American hemisphere, and wept with Safie over the hapless fate of its original inhabitants.

"These wonderful narrations inspired me with strange feelings. Was man, indeed, at once so powerful, so virtuous, and magnificent, yet so vicious and base? He appeared at one time a mere scion of the evil principle, and at another, as all that can be conceived of noble and godlike. To be a great and virtuous man appeared the highest honour that can befall a sensitive being; to be base and vicious, as many on record have been, appeared the lowest degradation, a condition more abject than that of the blind mole or harmless worm. For a long time I could not conceive how one man could go forth to murder his fellow, or even why there were laws and governments; but when I heard details of vice and bloodshed, my wonder ceased, and I turned away with disgust and loathing.

"Every conversation of the cottagers now opened new wonders to me. While I listened to the instructions which Felix bestowed upon the

Arabian, the strange system of human society was explained to me. I heard of the division of property, of immense wealth and squalid poverty; of rank, descent, and noble blood.

"The words induced me to turn towards myself. I learned that the possessions most esteemed by your fellow-creatures were high and unsullied descent united with riches. A man might be respected with only one of these advantages; but, without either, he was considered, except in very rare instances, as a vagabond and a slave, doomed to waste his powers for the profits of the chosen few! And what was I? Of my creation and creator I was absolutely ignorant; but I knew that I possessed no money, no friends, no kind of property. I was, besides, endued with a figure hideously deformed and loathsome; I was not even of the same nature as man. I was more agile than they, and could subsist upon coarser diet; I bore the extremes of heat and cold with less injury to my frame; my stature far exceeded theirs. When I looked around, I saw and heard of none like me. Was I then a monster, a blot upon the earth, from which all men fled, and whom all men disowned?

"I cannot describe to you the agony that these reflections inflicted upon me: I tried to dispel them, but sorrow only increased with knowledge. Oh, that I had for ever remained in my native wood, nor known nor felt beyond the sensations of hunger, thirst, and heat!

"Of what a strange nature is knowledge! It clings to the mind, when it has once seized on it, like a lichen on the rock. I wished sometimes to shake off all thought and feeling; but I learned that there was but one means to overcome the sensation of pain, and that was death — a state which I feared yet did not understand. I admired virtue and good feelings, and loved the gentle manners and amiable qualities of my cottagers; but I was shut out from intercourse with them, except through means which I obtained by stealth, when I was unseen and unknown, and which rather increased than satisfied the desire I had of becoming one among my fellows. The gentle words of Agatha, and the animated smiles of the charming Arabian, were not for me. The mild exhortations of the old man, and the lively conversation of the loved Felix, were not for me. Miserable, unhappy wretch!

"Other lessons were impressed upon me even more deeply. I heard of the difference of sexes; and the birth and growth of children; how the father doated on the smiles of the infant, and the lively sallies of the older child; how all the life and cares of the mother were wrapped up in the precious charge; how the mind of youth expanded and gained knowledge; of brother, sister, and all the various relationships which bind one human being to another in mutual bonds.

"But where were my friends and relations? No father had watched my infant days, no mother had blessed me with smiles and caresses; or if they had, all my past life was now a blot, a blind vacancy in which I distinguished nothing. From my earliest remembrance I had been as I then was in height and proportion. I had never yet seen a being resembling me, or who claimed any intercourse with me. What was I? The question again recurred, to be answered only with groans.

"I will soon explain to what these feelings tended; but allow me now to return to the cottagers, whose story excited in me such various feelings of indignation, delight, and wonder, but which all terminated in additional love and reverence for my protectors (for so I loved, in an innocent, half painful self-deceit, to call them).

CHAPTER XIV

"Some time elapsed before I learned the history of my friends. It was one which could not fail to impress itself deeply on my mind, unfolding as it did a number of circumstances, each interesting and wonderful to one so utterly inexperienced as I was.

"The name of the old man was De Lacey. He was descended from a good family in France, where he had lived for many years in affluence, respected by his superiors, and beloved by his equals. His son was bred in the service of his country; and Agatha had ranked with ladies of the highest distinction. A few months before my arrival, they had lived in a large and luxurious city, called Paris, surrounded by friends, and possessed of every enjoyment which virtue, refinement of intellect, or taste, accompanied by a moderate fortune, could afford.

"The father of Safie had been the cause of their ruin. He was a Turkish merchant, and had inhabited Paris for many years, when, for some reason which I could not learn, he became obnoxious to the government. He was seized and cast into prison the very day that Safie arrived from Constantinople to join him. He was tried, and condemned to death. The injustice of his sentence was very flagrant; all Paris was indignant; and it was judged that his religion and wealth, rather than the crime alleged against him, had been the cause of his condemnation.

"Felix had accidentally been present at the trial; his horror and indignation were uncontrollable, when he heard the decision of the court. He made, at that moment, a solemn vow to deliver him, and then looked around for the means. After many fruitless attempts to gain admittance to the prison, he found a strongly grated window in an un-guarded part of the building, which lighted the dungeon of the unfortu-nate Mahometan; who, loaded with chains, waited in despair the execution of the barbarous sentence. Felix visited the grate at night, and made known to the prisoner his intentions in his favour. The Turk, amazed and delighted, endeavoured to kindle the zeal of his deliverer by promises of reward and wealth. Felix rejected his offers with con-tempt; yet when he saw the lovely Safie, who was allowed to visit her father, and who, by her gestures, expressed her lively gratitude, the youth could not help owning to his own mind, that the captive pos-sessed a treasure which would fully reward his toil and hazard.

"The Turk quickly perceived the impression that his daughter had made on the heart of Felix, and endeavoured to secure him more en-tirely in his interests by the promise of her hand in marriage, so soon as he should be conveyed to a place of safety. Felix was too delicate to accept this offer; yet he looked forward to the probability of the event as to the consummation of his happiness.

"During the ensuing days, while the preparations were going for-ward for the escape of the merchant, the zeal of Felix was warmed by several letters that he received from this lovely girl, who found means to express her thoughts in the language of her lover by the aid of an old man, a servant of her father, who understood French. She thanked him in the most ardent terms for his intended services towards her parent; and at the same time she gently deplored her own fate.

"I have copies of these letters; for I found means, during my resi-dence in the hovel, to procure the implements of writing; and the let-ters were often in the hands of Felix or Agatha. Before I depart, I will give them to you, they will prove the truth of my tale; but at present, as the sun is already far declined, I shall only have time to repeat the substance of them to you.

"Safie related, that her mother was a Christian Arab, seized and made a slave by the Turks; recommended by her beauty, she had won the heart of the father of Safie, who married her. The young girl spoke in high and enthusiastic terms of her mother, who, born in freedom, spurned the bondage to which she was now reduced. She instructed her daughter in the tenets of her religion, and taught her to aspire to higher powers of intellect, and an independence of spirit, forbidden to the female followers of Mahomet. This lady died; but her lessons were indelibly impressed on the mind of Safie, who sickened at the prospect of again returning to Asia, and being immured within the walls of a haram, allowed only to occupy herself with infantile amusements, ill suited to the temper of her soul, now accustomed to grand ideas and a noble emulation for virtue. The prospect of marrying a Christian, and remaining in a country where women were allowed to take a rank in society, was enchanting to her.

"The day for the execution of the Turk was fixed; but, on the night previous to it, he quitted his prison, and before morning was distant many leagues from Paris. Felix had procured passports in the name of his father, sister, and himself. He had previously communicated his plan to the former, who aided the deceit by quitting his house, under the pretence of a journey, and concealed himself, with his daughter, in an obscure part of Paris.

"Felix conducted the fugitives through France to Lyons, and across Mont Cenis to Leghorn, where the merchant had decided to wait a favourable opportunity of passing into some part of the Turkish dominions.

"Safie resolved to remain with her father until the moment of his departure, before which time the Turk renewed his promise that she should be united to his deliverer; and Felix remained with them in expectation of that event; and in the mean time he enjoyed the society of the Arabian, who exhibited towards him the simplest and tenderest affection. They conversed with one another through the means of an interpreter, and sometimes with the interpretation of looks; and Safie sang to him the divine airs of her native country.

"The Turk allowed this intimacy to take place, and encouraged the hopes of the youthful lovers, while in his heart he had formed far other plans. He loathed the idea that his daughter should be united to a Christian; but he feared the resentment of Felix, if he should appear lukewarm; for he knew that he was still in the power of his deliverer, if he should choose to betray him to the Italian state which they inhabited. He revolved a thousand plans by which he should be enabled to prolong the deceit until it might be no longer necessary, and secretly to take his daughter with him when he departed. His plans were facilitated by the news which arrived from Paris.

"The government of France were greatly enraged at the escape of their victim, and spared no pains to detect and punish his deliverer. The plot of Felix was quickly discovered, and De Lacey and Agatha were thrown into prison. The news reached Felix, and roused him from his dream of pleasure. His blind and aged father, and his gentle sister, lay in a noisome dungeon, while he enjoyed the free air, and the society of her whom he loved. This idea was torture to him. He quickly arranged with the Turk, that if the latter should find a favourable opportunity for escape before Felix could return to Italy, Safie should remain as a boarder at a convent at Leghorn; and then, quitting the lovely Arabian, he hastened to Paris, and delivered himself up to the vengeance of the law, hoping to free De Lacey and Agatha by this proceeding.

"He did not succeed. They remained confined for five months before the trial took place; the result of which deprived them of their fortune, and condemned them to a perpetual exile from their native country.

"They found a miserable asylum in the cottage in Germany, where I discovered them. Felix soon learned that the treacherous Turk, for whom he and his family endured such unheard-of oppression, on discovering that his deliverer was thus reduced to poverty and ruin, became a traitor to good feeling and honour, and had quitted Italy with his daughter, insultingly sending Felix a pittance of money, to aid him, as he said, in some plan of future maintenance.

"Such were the events that preyed on the heart of Felix, and rendered him, when I first saw him, the most miserable of his family. He could have endured poverty; and while this distress had been the meed of his virtue, he gloried in it: but the ingratitude of the Turk, and the loss of his beloved Safie, were misfortunes more bitter and irreparable. The arrival of the Arabian now infused new life into his soul.

"When the news reached Leghorn, that Felix was deprived of his wealth and rank, the merchant commanded his daughter to think no more of her lover, but to prepare to return to her native country. The generous nature of Safie was outraged by this command; she attempted to expostulate with her father, but he left her angrily, reiterating his tyrannical mandate.

"A few days after, the Turk entered his daughter's apartment, and told her hastily, that he had reason to believe that his residence at Leghorn had been divulged, and that he should speedily be delivered up to the French government; he had, consequently, hired a vessel to convey him to Constantinople, for which city he should sail in a few hours. He intended to leave his daughter under the care of a confidential servant, to follow at her leisure with the greater part of his property, which had not yet arrived at Leghorn.

"When alone, Safie resolved in her own mind the plan of conduct that it would become her to pursue in this emergency. A residence in Turkey was abhorrent to her; her religion and her feelings were alike adverse to it. By some papers of her father, which fell into her hands, she heard of the exile of her lover, and learnt the name of the spot where he then resided. She hesitated some time, but at length she formed her determination. Taking with her some jewels that belonged to her, and a sum of money, she quitted Italy with an attendant, a native of Leghorn, but who understood the common language of Turkey, and departed for Germany.

"She arrived in safety at a town about twenty leagues from the cottage of De Lacey, when her attendant fell dangerously ill. Safie nursed her with the most devoted affection; but the poor girl died, and the Arabian was left alone, unacquainted with the language of the country, and utterly ignorant of the customs of the world. She fell, however, into good hands. The Italian had mentioned the name of the spot for which they were bound; and, after her death, the woman of the house in which they had lived took care that Safie should arrive in safety at the cottage of her lover.

CHAPTER XV

"Such was the history of my beloved cottagers. It impressed me deeply. I learned, from the views of social life which it developed, to admire their virtues, and to deprecate the vices of mankind.

"As yet I looked upon crime as a distant evil; benevolence and generosity were ever present before me, inciting within me a desire to become an actor in the busy scene where so many admirable qualities were called forth and displayed. But, in giving an account of the progress of my intellect, I must not omit a circumstance which occurred in the beginning of the month of August of the same year.

"One night, during my accustomed visit to the neighbouring wood, where I collected my own food, and brought home firing for my protectors, I found on the ground a leathern portmanteau, containing several articles of dress and some books. I eagerly seized the prize, and returned with it to my hovel. Fortunately the books were written in the language, the elements of which I had acquired at the cottage; they consisted of 'Paradise Lost,' a volume of 'Plutarch's Lives,' and the 'Sorrows of Werter.' The possession of these treasures gave me extreme delight; I now continually studied and exercised my mind upon these histories, whilst my friends were employed in their ordinary occupations.

"I can hardly describe to you the effect of these books. They produced in me an infinity of new images and feelings, that sometimes raised me to ecstasy, but more frequently sunk me into the lowest dejection. In the 'Sorrows of Werter,' besides the interest of its simple and affecting story, so many opinions are canvassed, and so many lights thrown upon what had hitherto been to me obscure subjects, that I found in it a never-ending source of speculation and astonishment. The gentle and domestic manners it described, combined with lofty senti-ments and feelings, which had for their object something out of self, accorded well with my experience among my protectors, and with the wants which were for ever alive in my own bosom. But I thought Wer-ter himself a more divine being than I had ever beheld or imagined; his character contained no pretension, but it sunk deep. The disquisitions upon death and suicide were calculated to fill me with wonder. I did not pretend to enter into the merits of the case, yet I inclined towards the opinions of the hero, whose extinction I wept, without precisely understanding it.

"As I read, however, I applied much personally to my own feelings and condition. I found myself similar, yet at the same time strangely unlike to the beings concerning whom I read, and to whose conversa-tion I was a listener. I sympathised with, and partly understood them, but I was unformed in mind; I was dependent on none, and related to none. 'The path of my departure was free;' and there was none to la-ment my annihilation. My person was hideous, and my stature gigantic: what did this mean? Who was I? What was I? Whence did I come? What was my destination? These questions continually recurred, but I was unable to solve them.

"The volume of 'Plutarch's Lives,' which I possessed, contained the histories of the first founders of the ancient republics. This book had a far different effect upon me from the 'Sorrows of Werter.' I learned from Werter's imaginations despondency and gloom: but Plu-tarch taught me high thoughts; he elevated me above the wretched sphere of my own reflections, to admire and love the heroes of past ages. Many things I read surpassed my understanding and experience. I had a very confused knowledge of kingdoms, wide extents of country, mighty rivers, and boundless seas. But I was perfectly unacquainted with towns, and large assemblages of men. The cottage of my protectors had been the only school in which I had studied human nature; but this book developed new and mightier scenes of action. I read of men concerned in public affairs, governing or massacring their species. I felt the greatest ardour for virtue rise within me, and abhorrence for vice, as far as I understood the significance of those terms, relative as they were, as I applied them, to pleasure and pain alone. Induced by these feelings, I was of course led to admire peaceable lawgivers, Numa, So-lon, and Lycurgus, in preference to Romulus and Theseus. The patriar-

chal lives of my protectors caused these impressions to take a firm hold
on my mind; perhaps, if my first introduction to humanity had been
made by a young soldier, burning for glory and slaughter, I should have
been imbued with different sensations.

"But 'Paradise Lost' excited different and far deeper emotions. I
read it, as I had read the other volumes which had fallen into my hands,
as a true history. It moved every feeling of wonder and awe, that the
picture of an omnipotent God warring with his creatures was capable
of exciting. I often referred the several situations, as their similarity
struck me, to my own. Like Adam, I was apparently united by no link
to any other being in existence; but his state was far different from mine
in every other respect. He had come forth from the hands of God a
perfect creature, happy and prosperous, guarded by the especial care of
his Creator; he was allowed to converse with, and acquire knowledge
from, beings of a superior nature: but I was wretched, helpless, and
alone. Many times I considered Satan as the fitter emblem of my condition; for often, like him, when I viewed the bliss of my protectors, the
bitter gall of envy rose within me.

"Another circumstance strengthened and confirmed these feelings.
Soon after my arrival in the hovel, I discovered some papers in the
pocket of the dress which I had taken from your laboratory. At first I
had neglected them; but now that I was able to decipher the characters
in which they were written, I began to study them with diligence. It
was your journal of the four months that preceded my creation. You
minutely described in these papers every step you took in the progress
of your work; this history was mingled with accounts of domestic occurrences. You, doubtless, recollect these papers. Here they are. Every
thing is related in them which bears reference to my accursed origin;
the whole detail of that series of disgusting circumstances which produced it, is set in view; the minutest description of my odious and
loathsome person is given, in language which painted your own horrors, and rendered mine indelible. I sickened as I read. 'Hateful day
when I received life!' I exclaimed in agony. 'Accursed creator! Why did
you form a monster so hideous that even *you* turned from me in disgust?
God, in pity, made man beautiful and alluring, after his own image;
but my form is a filthy type of yours, more horrid even from the very
resemblance. Satan had his companions, fellow-devils, to admire and
encourage him; but I am solitary and abhorred.'

"These were the reflections of my hours of despondency and solitude; but when I contemplated the virtues of the cottagers, their amiable and benevolent dispositions, I persuaded myself that when they

should become acquainted with my admiration of their virtues, they would compassionate me, and overlook my personal deformity. Could they turn from their door one, however monstrous, who solicited their compassion and friendship? I resolved, at least, not to despair, but in every way to fit myself for an interview with them which would decide my fate. I postponed this attempt for some months longer; for the importance attached to its success inspired me with a dread lest I should fail. Besides, I found that my understanding improved so much with every day's experience, that I was unwilling to commence this undertaking until a few more months should have added to my sagacity.

"Several changes, in the mean time, took place in the cottage. The presence of Safie diffused happiness among its inhabitants; and I also found that a greater degree of plenty reigned there. Felix and Agatha spent more time in amusement and conversation, and were assisted in their labours by servants. They did not appear rich, but they were contented and happy; their feelings were serene and peaceful, while mine became every day more tumultuous. Increase of knowledge only discovered to me more clearly what a wretched outcast I was. I cherished hope, it is true; but it vanished, when I beheld my person reflected in water, or my shadow in the moonshine, even as that frail image and that inconstant shade.

"I endeavoured to crush these fears, and to fortify myself for the trial which in a few months I resolved to undergo; and some times I allowed my thoughts, unchecked by reason, to ramble in the fields of Paradise, and dared to fancy amiable and lovely creatures sympathising with my feelings, and cheering my gloom; their angelic countenances breathed smiles of consolation. But it was all a dream; no Eve soothed my sorrows, nor shared my thoughts; I was alone. I remembered Adam's supplication to his Creator. But where was mine? He had abandoned me; and, in the bitterness of my heart, I cursed him.

"Autumn passed thus. I saw, with surprise and grief, the leaves decay and fall, and nature again assume the barren and bleak appearance it had worn when I first beheld the woods and the lovely moon. Yet I did not heed the bleakness of the weather; I was better fitted by my conformation for the endurance of cold than heat. But my chief delights were the sight of the flowers, the birds, and all the gay apparel of summer; when those deserted me, I turned with more attention towards the cottagers. Their happiness was not decreased by the absence of summer. They loved, and sympathised with one another; and their joys, depending on each other, were not interrupted by the casualties that took place around them. The more I saw of them, the greater became my desire to claim their protection and kindness; my heart yearned to be known and loved by these amiable creatures: to see their sweet looks directed towards me with affection, was the utmost limit of my ambition. I dared not think that they would turn them from me with disdain and horror. The poor that stopped at their door were never driven away. I asked, it is true, for greater treasures than a little food or rest: I required kindness and sympathy; but I did not believe myself utterly unworthy of it.

"The winter advanced, and an entire revolution of the seasons had taken place since I awoke into life. My attention, at this time, was solely directed towards my plan of introducing myself into the cottage of my protectors. I revolved many projects; but that on which I finally fixed was, to enter the dwelling when the blind old man should be alone. I had sagacity enough to discover, that the unnatural hideousness of my person was the chief object of horror with those who had formerly beheld me. My voice, although harsh, had nothing terrible in it; I thought, therefore, that if, in the absence of his children, I could gain the good-will and mediation of the old De Lacey, I might, by his means, be tolerated by my younger protectors.

"One day, when the sun shone on the red leaves that strewed the ground, and diffused cheerfulness, although it denied warmth, Safie, Agatha, and Felix departed on a long country walk, and the old man, at his own desire, was left alone in the cottage. When his children had departed, he took up his guitar, and played several mournful but sweet airs, more sweet and mournful than I had ever heard him play before. At first his countenance was illuminated with pleasure, but, as he continued, thoughtfulness and sadness succeeded; at length, laying aside the instrument, he sat absorbed in reflection.

"My heart beat quick; this was the hour and moment of trial, which would decide my hopes, or realise my fears. The servants were gone to a neighbouring fair. All was silent in and around the cottage: it was an excellent opportunity; yet, when I proceeded to execute my plan, my limbs failed me, and I sank to the ground. Again I rose; and, exerting all the firmness of which I was master, removed the planks which I had placed before my hovel to conceal my retreat. The fresh air revived me, and, with renewed determination, I approached the door of their cottage.

"I knocked. 'Who is there?' said the old man — 'Come in.'

"I entered; 'Pardon this intrusion,' said I: 'I am a traveller in want of a little rest; you would greatly oblige me, if you would allow me to remain a few minutes before the fire.'

" 'Enter,' said De Lacey; 'and I will try in what manner I can relieve your wants; but, unfortunately, my children are from home, and, as I am blind, I am afraid I shall find it difficult to procure food for you.'

" 'Do not trouble yourself, my kind host, I have food; it is warmth and rest only that I need.'

"I sat down, and a silence ensued. I knew that every minute was precious to me, yet I remained irresolute in what manner to commence the interview; when the old man addressed me —

" 'By your language, stranger, I suppose you are my countryman; — are you French?'

" 'No; but I was educated by a French family, and understand that language only. I am now going to claim the protection of some friends, whom I sincerely love, and of whose favour I have some hopes.'

" 'Are they Germans?'

" 'No, they are French. But let us change the subject. I am an unfortunate and deserted creature; I look around, and I have no relation or friend upon earth. These amiable people to whom I go have never seen me, and know little of me. I am full of fears; for if I fail there, I am an outcast in the world for ever.'

" 'Do not despair. To be friendless is indeed to be unfortunate; but the hearts of men, when unprejudiced by any obvious self-interest, are full of brotherly love and charity. Rely, therefore, on your hopes; and if these friends are good and amiable, do not despair.'

" 'They are kind — they are the most excellent creatures in the world; but, unfortunately, they are prejudiced against me. I have good dispositions; my life has been hitherto harmless, and in some degree beneficial; but a fatal prejudice clouds their eyes, and where they ought to see a feeling and kind friend, they behold only a detestable monster.'

" 'That is indeed unfortunate; but if you are really blameless, cannot you undeceive them?'

" 'I am about to undertake that task; and it is on that account that I feel so many overwhelming terrors. I tenderly love these friends; I have, unknown to them, been for many months in the habits of daily kindness towards them; but they believe that I wish to injure them, and it is that prejudice which I wish to overcome.'

" 'Where do these friends reside?'

" 'Near this spot.'

"The old man paused, and then continued, 'If you will unreservedly confide to me the particulars of your tale, I perhaps may be of use in undeceiving them. I am blind, and cannot judge of your countenance, but there is something in your words, which persuades me that you are sincere. I am poor, and an exile; but it will afford me true plea-sure to be in any way serviceable to a human creature.'

"'Excellent man! I thank you, and accept your generous offer. You raise me from the dust by this kindness; and I trust that, by your aid, I shall not be driven from the society and sympathy of your fellow-creatures.'

"'Heaven forbid! even if you were really criminal; for that can only drive you to desperation, and not instigate you to virtue. I also am unfortunate; I and my family have been condemned, although inno-cent: judge, therefore, if I do not feel for your misfortunes.'

"'How can I thank you, my best and only benefactor? From your lips first have I heard the voice of kindness directed towards me; I shall be for ever grateful; and your present humanity assures me of success with those friends whom I am on the point of meeting.'

"'May I know the names and residence of those friends?'

"I paused. This, I thought, was the moment of decision, which was to rob me of, or bestow happiness on me for ever. I struggled vainly for firmness sufficient to answer him, but the effort destroyed all my remaining strength; I sank on the chair, and sobbed aloud. At that mo-ment I heard the steps of my younger protectors. I had not a moment to lose; but, seizing the hand of the old man I cried, 'Now is the time! — save and protect me! You and your family are the friends whom I seek. Do not you desert me in the hour of trial!'

"'Great God!' exclaimed the old man, 'who are you?'

"At that instant the cottage door was opened, and Felix, Safie, and Agatha entered. Who can describe their horror and consternation on beholding me? Agatha fainted; and Safie, unable to attend to her friend, rushed out of the cottage. Felix darted forward, and with supernatural force tore me from his father, to whose knees I clung: in a transport of fury, he dashed me to the ground, and struck me violently with a stick. I could have torn him limb from limb, as the lion rends the antelope. But my heart sunk within me as with bitter sickness, and I refrained. I saw him on the point of repeating his blow, when, overcome by pain and anguish, I quitted the cottage, and in the general tumult escaped unperceived to my hovel.

CHAPTER XVI

"Cursed, cursed creator! Why did I live? Why, in that instant, did I not extinguish the spark of existence which you had so wantonly bestowed? I know not; despair had not yet taken possession of me; my feelings were those of rage and revenge. I could with pleasure have destroyed the cottage and its inhabitants, and have glutted myself with their shrieks and misery.

"When night came, I quitted my retreat, and wandered in the wood; and now, no longer restrained by the fear of discovery, I gave vent to my anguish in fearful howlings. I was like a wild beast that had broken the toils; destroying the objects that obstructed me, and ranging through the wood with a stag-like swiftness. O! what a miserable night I passed! the cold stars shone in mockery, and the bare trees waved their branches above me: now and then the sweet voice of a bird burst forth amidst the universal stillness. All, save I, were at rest or in enjoyment: I, like the arch-fiend, bore a hell within me; and, finding myself unsympathised with, wished to tear up the trees, spread havoc and destruction around me, and then to have sat down and enjoyed the ruin.

"But this was a luxury of sensation that could not endure; I became fatigued with excess of bodily exertion, and sank on the damp grass in the sick impotence of despair. There was none among the myriads of men that existed who would pity or assist me; and should I feel kindness towards my enemies? No: from that moment I declared everlasting war against the species, and, more than all, against him who had formed me, and sent me forth to this insupportable misery.

"The sun rose; I heard the voices of men, and knew that it was impossible to return to my retreat during that day. Accordingly I hid myself in some thick underwood, determining to devote the ensuing hours to reflection on my situation.

"The pleasant sunshine, and the pure air of day, restored me to some degree of tranquillity; and when I considered what had passed at the cottage, I could not help believing that I had been too hasty in my conclusions. I had certainly acted imprudently. It was apparent that my conversation had interested the father in my behalf, and I was a fool in having exposed my person to the horror of his children. I ought to have familiarised the old De Lacey to me, and by degrees to have discovered myself to the rest of his family, when they should have been prepared for my approach. But I did not believe my errors to be irretrievable; and, after much consideration, I resolved to return to the cottage, seek the old man, and by my representations win him to my party.

"These thoughts calmed me, and in the afternoon I sank into a profound sleep; but the fever of my blood did not allow me to be visited by peaceful dreams. The horrible scene of the preceding day was for ever acting before my eyes; the females were flying, and the enraged

Felix tearing me from his father's feet. I awoke exhausted; and, finding that it was already night, I crept forth from my hiding-place, and went in search of food.

"When my hunger was appeased, I directed my steps towards the well-known path that conducted to the cottage. All there was at peace. I crept into my hovel, and remained in silent expectation of the accustomed hour when the family arose. That hour passed, the sun mounted high in the heavens, but the cottagers did not appear. I trembled violently, apprehending some dreadful misfortune. The inside of the cottage was dark, and I heard no motion; I cannot describe the agony of this suspense.

"Presently two countrymen passed by; but, pausing near the cottage, they entered into conversation, using violent gesticulations; but I did not understand what they said, as they spoke the language of the country, which differed from that of my protectors. Soon after, however, Felix approached with another man: I was surprised, as I knew that he had not quitted the cottage that morning, and waited anxiously to discover, from his discourse, the meaning of these unusual appearances.

"'Do you consider,' said his companion to him, 'that you will be obliged to pay three months' rent, and to lose the produce of your garden? I do not wish to take any unfair advantage, and I beg therefore that you will take some days to consider of your determination.'

"'It is utterly useless,' replied Felix; 'we can never again inhabit your cottage. The life of my father is in the greatest danger, owing to the dreadful circumstance that I have related. My wife and my sister will never recover their horror. I entreat you not to reason with me any more. Take possession of your tenement, and let me fly from this place.'

"Felix trembled violently as he said this. He and his companion entered the cottage, in which they remained for a few minutes, and then departed. I never saw any of the family of De Lacey more.

"I continued for the remainder of the day in my hovel in a state of utter and stupid despair. My protectors had departed, and had broken the only link that held me to the world. For the first time the feelings of revenge and hatred filled my bosom, and I did not strive to control them; but, allowing myself to be borne away by the stream, I bent my mind towards injury and death. When I thought of my friends, of the mild voice of De Lacey, the gentle eyes of Agatha, and the exquisite beauty of the Arabian, these thoughts vanished, and a gush of tears somewhat soothed me. But again, when I reflected that they had spurned and deserted me, anger returned, a rage of anger; and, unable to injure any thing human, I turned my fury towards inanimate objects. As night advanced, I placed a variety of combustibles around the cottage; and, after having destroyed every vestige of cultivation in the garden, I waited with forced impatience until the moon had sunk to commence my operations.

"As the night advanced, a fierce wind arose from the woods, and quickly dispersed the clouds that had loitered in the heavens: the blast tore along like a mighty avalanche, and produced a kind of insanity in my spirits, that burst all bounds of reason and reflection. I lighted the dry branch of a tree, and danced with fury around the devoted cottage, my eyes still fixed on the western horizon, the edge of which the moon nearly touched. A part of its orb was at length hid, and I waved my brand; it sunk, and, with a loud scream, I fired the straw, and heath, and bushes, which I had collected. The wind fanned the fire, and the cottage was quickly enveloped by the flames, which clung to it, and licked it with their forked and destroying tongues.

"As soon as I was convinced that no assistance could save any part of the habitation, I quitted the scene, and sought for refuge in the woods.

"And now, with the world before me, whither should I bend my steps? I resolved to fly far from the scene of my misfortunes; but to me, hated and despised, every country must be equally horrible. At length the thought of you crossed my mind. I learned from your papers that you were my father, my creator; and to whom could I apply with more fitness than to him who had given me life? Among the lessons that Felix had bestowed upon Safie, geography had not been omitted: I had learned from these the relative situations of the different countries of the earth. You had mentioned Geneva as the name of your native town; and towards this place I resolved to proceed.

"But how was I to direct myself? I knew that I must travel in a south-westerly direction to reach my destination; but the sun was my only guide. I did not know the names of the towns that I was to pass through, nor could I ask information from a single human being; but I did not despair. From you only could I hope for succour, although towards you I felt no sentiment but that of hatred. Unfeeling, heartless creator! you had endowed me with perceptions and passions, and then cast me abroad an object for the scorn and horror of mankind. But on you only had I any claim for pity and redress, and from you I determined to seek that justice which I vainly attempted to gain from any other being that wore the human form.

"My travels were long, and the sufferings I endured intense. It was late in autumn when I quitted the district where I had so long resided. I travelled only at night, fearful of encountering the visage of a human being. Nature decayed around me, and the sun became heatless; rain and snow poured around me; mighty rivers were frozen; the surface of the earth was hard and chill, and bare, and I found no shelter. Oh, earth! how often did I imprecate curses on the cause of my being! The mildness of my nature had fled, and all within me was turned to gall and bitterness. The nearer I approached to your habitation, the more deeply did I feel the spirit of revenge enkindled in my heart. Snow fell, and the waters were hardened; but I rested not. A few incidents now and then directed me, and I possessed a map of the country; but I often wandered wide from my path. The agony of my feelings allowed me no respite: no incident occurred from which my rage and misery could not extract its food; but a circumstance that happened when I arrived on the confines of Switzerland, when the sun had recovered its warmth, and the earth again began to look green, confirmed in an especial manner the bitterness and horror of my feelings.

"I generally rested during the day, and travelled only when I was secured by night from the view of man. One morning, however, finding that my path lay through a deep wood, I ventured to continue my journey after the sun had risen; the day, which was one of the first of spring, cheered even me by the loveliness of its sunshine and the balminess of the air. I felt emotions of gentleness and pleasure, that had long appeared dead, revive within me. Half surprised by the novelty of these sensations, I allowed myself to be borne away by them; and, forgetting my solitude and deformity, dared to be happy. Soft tears again bedewed my cheeks, and I even raised my humid eyes with thankfulness towards the blessed sun which bestowed such joy upon me.

"I continued to wind among the paths of the wood, until I came to its boundary, which was skirted by a deep and rapid river, into which many of the trees bent their branches, now budding with the fresh spring. Here I paused, not exactly knowing what path to pursue, when I heard the sound of voices, that induced me to conceal myself under the shade of a cypress. I was scarcely hid, when a young girl came running towards the spot where I was concealed, laughing, as if she ran from some one in sport. She continued her course along the precipitous sides of the river, when suddenly her foot slipt, and she fell into the rapid stream. I rushed from my hiding-place; and, with extreme labour from the force of the current, saved her, and dragged her to shore. She was senseless; and I endeavoured, by every means in my power, to restore animation, when I was suddenly interrupted by the approach of a rustic, who was probably the person from whom she had playfully fled. On seeing me, he darted towards me, and tearing the girl from my arms, hastened towards the deeper parts of the wood. I followed speedily, I hardly knew why; but when the man saw me draw near, he aimed a gun, which he carried, at my body, and fired. I sunk to the ground, and my injurer, with increased swiftness, escaped into the wood.

"This was then the reward of my benevolence! I had saved a human being from destruction, and, as a recompense, I now writhed under the miserable pain of a wound, which shattered the flesh and bone. The feelings of kindness and gentleness, which I had entertained but a few moments before, gave place to hellish rage and gnashing of teeth. Inflamed by pain, I vowed eternal hatred and vengeance to all mankind. But the agony of my wound overcame me; my pulses paused, and I fainted.

"For some weeks I led a miserable life in the woods, endeavouring to cure the wound which I had received. The ball had entered my shoulder, and I knew not whether it had remained there or passed through; at any rate I had no means of extracting it. My sufferings were augmented also by the oppressive sense of the injustice and ingratitude of their infliction. My daily vows rose for revenge — a deep and deadly revenge, such as would alone compensate for the outrages and anguish I had endured.

"After some weeks my wound healed, and I continued my journey. The labours I endured were no longer to be alleviated by the bright sun or gentle breezes of spring; all joy was but a mockery, which insulted my desolate state, and made me feel more painfully that I was not made for the enjoyment of pleasure.

"But my toils now drew near a close; and, in two months from this time, I reached the environs of Geneva.

"It was evening when I arrived, and I retired to a hiding-place among the fields that surround it, to meditate in what manner I should apply to you. I was oppressed by fatigue and hunger, and far too unhappy to enjoy the gentle breezes of evening, or the prospect of the sun setting behind the stupendous mountains of Jura.

"At this time a slight sleep relieved me from the pain of reflection, which was disturbed by the approach of a beautiful child, who came running into the recess I had chosen, with all the sportiveness of infancy. Suddenly, as I gazed on him, an idea seized me, that this little creature was unprejudiced, and had lived too short a time to have imbibed a horror of deformity. If, therefore, I could seize him, and educate him as my companion and friend, I should not be so desolate in this peopled earth.

"Urged by this impulse, I seized on the boy as he passed, and drew him towards me. As soon as he beheld my form, he placed his hands before his eyes, and uttered a shrill scream: I drew his hand forcibly from his face, and said, 'Child, what is the meaning of this? I do not intend to hurt you; listen to me.'

"He struggled violently. 'Let me go,' he cried; 'monster! ugly wretch! you wish to eat me, and tear me to pieces — You are an ogre — Let me go, or I will tell my papa.'

"'Boy, you will never see your father again; you must come with me.'

"'Hideous monster! let me go. My papa is a Syndic — he is M. Frankenstein — he will punish you. You dare not keep me.'

"'Frankenstein! you belong then to my enemy — to him towards whom I have sworn eternal revenge; you shall be my first victim.'

"The child still struggled, and loaded me with epithets which carried despair to my heart; I grasped his throat to silence him, and in a moment he lay dead at my feet.

"I gazed on my victim, and my heart swelled with exultation and hellish triumph: clapping my hands, I exclaimed, 'I, too, can create desolation; my enemy is not invulnerable; this death will carry despair to him, and a thousand other miseries shall torment and destroy him.'

"As I fixed my eyes on the child, I saw something glittering on his breast. I took it; it was a portrait of a most lovely woman. In spite of my malignity, it softened and attracted me. For a few moments I gazed with delight on her dark eyes, fringed by deep lashes, and her lovely lips; but presently my rage returned: I remembered that I was for ever deprived of the delights that such beautiful creatures could bestow; and that she whose resemblance I contemplated would, in regarding me, have changed that air of divine benignity to one expressive of disgust and affright.

"Can you wonder that such thoughts transported me with rage? I only wonder that at that moment, instead of venting my sensations in exclamations and agony, I did not rush among mankind, and perish in the attempt to destroy them.

"While I was overcome by these feelings, I left the spot where I had committed the murder, and seeking a more secluded hiding-place, I entered a barn which had appeared to me to be empty. A woman was sleeping on some straw; she was young: not indeed so beautiful as her whose portrait I held; but of an agreeable aspect, and blooming in the loveliness of youth and health. Here, I thought, is one of those whose joy-imparting smiles are bestowed on all but me. And then I bent over her, and whispered, 'Awake, fairest, thy lover is near — he who would give his life but to obtain one look of affection from thine eyes: my beloved, awake!'

"The sleeper stirred; a thrill of terror ran through me. Should she indeed awake, and see me, and curse me, and denounce the murderer? Thus would she assuredly act, if her darkened eyes opened, and she beheld me. The thought was madness; it stirred the fiend within me — not I, but she shall suffer: the murder I have committed because I am for ever robbed of all that she could give me, she shall atone. The crime had its source in her: be hers the punishment! Thanks to the lessons of Felix and the sanguinary laws of man, I had learned now to work mischief. I bent over her, and placed the portrait securely in one of the folds of her dress. She moved again, and I fled.

"For some days I haunted the spot where these scenes had taken place; sometimes wishing to see you, sometimes resolved to quit the world and its miseries for ever. At length I wandered towards these mountains, and have ranged through their immense recesses, consumed by a burning passion which you alone can gratify. We may not part until you have promised to comply with my requisition. I am alone, and miserable; man will not associate with me; but one as deformed and horrible as myself would not deny herself to me. My companion must be of the same species, and have the same defects. This being you must create.''

CHAPTER XVII

The being finished speaking, and fixed his looks upon me in expectation of a reply. But I was bewildered, perplexed, and unable to arrange my ideas sufficiently to understand the full extent of his proposition. He continued —

"You must create a female for me, with whom I can live in the interchange of those sympathies necessary for my being. This you alone can do; and I demand it of you as a right which you must not refuse to concede.''

The latter part of his tale had kindled anew in me the anger that had died away while he narrated his peaceful life among the cottagers, and, as he said this, I could no longer suppress the rage that burned within me.

"I do refuse it,'' I replied; "and no torture shall ever extort a consent from me. You may render me the most miserable of men, but you shall never make me base in my own eyes. Shall I create another like yourself, whose joint wickedness might desolate the world? Begone! I have answered you; you may torture me, but I will never consent.''

"You are in the wrong," replied the fiend; "and, instead of threatening, I am content to reason with you. I am malicious because I am miserable. Am I not shunned and hated by all mankind? You, my creator, would tear me to pieces, and triumph; remember that, and tell me why I should pity man more than he pities me? You would not call it murder, if you could precipitate me into one of those ice-rifts, and destroy my frame, the work of your own hands. Shall I respect man, when he contemns me? Let him live with me in the interchange of kindness; and, instead of injury, I would bestow every benefit upon him with tears of gratitude at his acceptance. But that cannot be; the human senses are insurmountable barriers to our union. Yet mine shall not be the submission of abject slavery. I will revenge my injuries: if I cannot inspire love, I will cause fear; and chiefly towards you my arch-enemy, because my creator, do I swear inextinguishable hatred. Have a care: I will work at your destruction, nor finish until I desolate your heart, so that you shall curse the hour of your birth."

A fiendish rage animated him as he said this; his face was wrinkled into contortions too horrible for human eyes to behold; but presently he calmed himself and proceeded —

"I intended to reason. This passion is detrimental to me; for you do not reflect that *you* are the cause of its excess. If any being felt emotions of benevolence towards me, I should return them an hundred and an hundred fold; for that one creature's sake, I would make peace with the whole kind! But I now indulge in dreams of bliss that cannot be realised. What I ask of you is reasonable and moderate; I demand a creature of another sex, but as hideous as myself; the gratification is small, but it is all that I can receive, and it shall content me. It is true, we shall be monsters, cut off from all the world; but on that account we shall be more attached to one another. Our lives will not be happy, but they will be harmless, and free from the misery I now feel. Oh! my creator, make me happy; let me feel gratitude towards you for one benefit! Let me see that I excite the sympathy of some existing thing; do not deny me my request!"

I was moved. I shuddered when I thought of the possible consequences of my consent; but I felt that there was some justice in his argument. His tale, and the feelings he now expressed, proved him to be a creature of fine sensations; and did I not, as his maker, owe him all the portion of happiness that it was in my power to bestow? He saw my change of feeling, and continued —

"If you consent, neither you nor any other human being shall ever see us again: I will go to the vast wilds of South America. My food is

not that of man; I do not destroy the lamb and the kid to glut my
appetite; acorns and berries afford me sufficient nourishment. My companion will be of the same nature as myself, and will be content with
the same fare. We shall make our bed of dried leaves; the sun will shine
on us as on man, and will ripen our food. The picture I present to you
is peaceful and human, and you must feel that you could deny it only
in the wantonness of power and cruelty. Pitiless as you have been towards me, I now see compassion in your eyes; let me seize the favourable moment, and persuade you to promise what I so ardently desire.''

"You propose," replied I, "to fly from the habitations of man, to
dwell in those wilds where the beasts of the field will be your only
companions. How can you, who long for the love and sympathy of
man, persevere in this exile? You will return, and again seek their kindness, and you will meet with their detestation; your evil passions will
be renewed, and you will then have a companion to aid you in the task
of destruction. This may not be: cease to argue the point, for I cannot
consent."

"How inconstant are your feelings! but a moment ago you were
moved by my representations, and why do you again harden yourself
to my complaints? I swear to you, by the earth which I inhabit, and by
you that made me, that, with the companion you bestow, I will quit
the neighbourhood of man, and dwell as it may chance, in the most
savage of places. My evil passions will have fled, for I shall meet with
sympathy! my life will flow quietly away, and, in my dying moments,
I shall not curse my maker."

His words had a strange effect upon me. I compassioned him, and
sometimes felt a wish to console him; but when I looked upon him,
when I saw the filthy mass that moved and talked, my heart sickened,
and my feelings were altered to those of horror and hatred. I tried to
stifle these sensations; I thought, that as I could not sympathise with
him, I had no right to withhold from him the small portion of happiness which was yet in my power to bestow.

"You swear," I said, "to be harmless; but have you not already
shown a degree of malice that should reasonably make me distrust you?
May not even this be a feint that will increase your triumph by affording
a wider scope for your revenge?"

"How is this? I must not be trifled with: and I demand an answer.
If I have no ties and no affections, hatred and vice must be my portion;
the love of another will destroy the cause of my crimes, and I shall
become a thing, of whose existence every one will be ignorant. My vices
are the children of a forced solitude that I abhor; and my virtues will

necessarily arise when I live in communion with an equal. I shall feel the affections of a sensitive being, and become linked to the chain of existence and events, from which I am now excluded."

I paused some time to reflect on all he had related, and the various arguments which he had employed. I thought of the promise of virtues which he had displayed on the opening of his existence, and the subsequent blight of all kindly feeling by the loathing and scorn which his protectors had manifested towards him. His power and threats were not omitted in my calculations: a creature who could exist in the ice-caves of the glaciers, and hide himself from pursuit among the ridges of inaccessible precipices, was a being possessing faculties it would be vain to cope with. After a long pause of reflection, I concluded that the justice due both to him and my fellow-creatures demanded of me that I should comply with his request. Turning to him, therefore, I said —

"I consent to your demand, on your solemn oath to quit Europe for ever, and every other place in the neighbourhood of man, as soon as I shall deliver into your hands a female who will accompany you in your exile."

"I swear," he cried, "by the sun, and by the blue sky of Heaven, and by the fire of love that burns my heart, that if you grant my prayer, while they exist you shall never behold me again. Depart to your home, and commence your labours: I shall watch their progress with unutterable anxiety; and fear not but that when you are ready I shall appear."

Saying this, he suddenly quitted me, fearful, perhaps, of any change in my sentiments. I saw him descend the mountain with greater speed than the flight of an eagle, and quickly lost him among the undulations of the sea of ice.

His tale had occupied the whole day; and the sun was upon the verge of the horizon when he departed. I knew that I ought to hasten my descent towards the valley, as I should soon be encompassed in darkness; but my heart was heavy, and my steps slow. The labour of winding among the little paths of the mountains, and fixing my feet firmly as I advanced, perplexed me, occupied as I was by the emotions which the occurrences of the day had produced. Night was far advanced, when I came to the half-way resting-place, and seated myself beside the fountain. The stars shone at intervals, as the clouds passed from over them; the dark pines rose before me, and every here and there a broken tree lay on the ground: it was a scene of wonderful solemnity, and stirred strange thoughts within me. I wept bitterly; and clasping my hands in agony, I exclaimed, "Oh! stars and clouds, and winds, ye are all about to mock me: if ye really pity me, crush sensation and memory; let me become as nought; but if not, depart, depart, and leave me in darkness.''

These were wild and miserable thoughts; but I cannot describe to you how the eternal twinkling of the stars weighed upon me, and how I listened to every blast of wind, as if it were a dull, ugly siroc on its way to consume me.

Morning dawned before I arrived at the village of Chamounix; I took no rest, but returned immediately to Geneva. Even in my own heart I could give no expression to my sensations — they weighed on me with a mountain's weight, and their excess destroyed my agony beneath them. Thus I returned home, and entering the house, presented myself to the family. My haggard and wild appearance awoke intense alarm; but I answered no question, scarcely did I speak. I felt as if I were placed under a ban — as if I had no right to claim their sympathies — as if never more might I enjoy companionship with them. Yet even thus I loved them to adoration; and to save them, I resolved to dedicate myself to my most abhorred task. The prospect of such an occupation made every other circumstance of existence pass before me like a dream; and that thought only had to me the reality of life.

CHAPTER XVIII

Day after day, week after week, passed away on my return to Geneva; and I could not collect the courage to recommence my work. I feared the vengeance of the disappointed fiend, yet I was unable to overcome my repugnance to the task which was enjoined me. I found that I could not compose a female without again devoting several months to profound study and laborious disquisition. I had heard of some discoveries having been made by an English philosopher, the knowledge of which was material to my success, and I sometimes thought of obtaining my father's consent to visit England for this purpose; but I clung to every pretence of delay, and shrunk from taking the first step in an undertaking whose immediate necessity began to appear less absolute to me. A change indeed had taken place in me: my health, which had hitherto declined, was now much restored; and my spirits, when unchecked by the memory of my unhappy promise, rose proportionably. My father saw this change with pleasure, and he turned his thoughts towards the best method of eradicating the remains of my melancholy, which every now and then would return by fits, and with a devouring blackness overcast the approaching sunshine. At these moments I took refuge in the most perfect solitude. I passed whole days on the lake alone in a little boat, watching the clouds, and listening to the rippling of the waves, silent and listless. But the fresh air and bright sun seldom failed to restore me to some degree of composure; and, on my return, I met the salutations of my friends with a readier smile and a more cheerful heart.

It was after my return from one of these rambles, that my father, calling me aside, thus addressed me: —

"I am happy to remark, my dear son, that you have resumed your former pleasures, and seem to be returning to yourself. And yet you are still unhappy, and still avoid our society. For some time I was lost in conjecture as to the cause of this; but yesterday an idea struck me, and if it is well founded, I conjure you to avow it. Reserve on such a point would be not only useless, but draw down treble misery on us all."

I trembled violently at his exordium, and my father continued —

"I confess, my son, that I have always looked forward to your marriage with our dear Elizabeth as the tie of our domestic comfort, and the stay of my declining years. You were attached to each other from your earliest infancy; you studied together, and appeared, in dispositions and tastes, entirely suited to one another. But so blind is the experience of man, that what I conceived to be the best assistants to my plan, may have entirely destroyed it. You, perhaps, regard her as your sister, without any wish that she might become your wife. Nay, you may have met with another whom you may love; and, considering yourself as bound in honour to Elizabeth, this struggle may occasion the poignant misery which you appear to feel."

"My dear father, re-assure yourself. I love my cousin tenderly and sincerely. I never saw any woman who excited, as Elizabeth does, my warmest admiration and affection. My future hopes and prospects are entirely bound up in the expectation of our union."

"The expression of your sentiments on this subject, my dear Victor, gives me more pleasure than I have for some time experienced. If you feel thus, we shall assuredly be happy, however present events may cast a gloom over us. But it is this gloom which appears to have taken so strong a hold of your mind, that I wish to dissipate. Tell me, therefore, whether you object to an immediate solemnisation of the marriage. We have been unfortunate, and recent events have drawn us from that every-day tranquillity befitting my years and infirmities. You are younger; yet I do not suppose, possessed as you are of a competent fortune, that an early marriage would at all interfere with any future plans of honour and utility that you may have formed. Do not suppose,

however, that I wish to dictate happiness to you, or that a delay on
your part would cause me any serious uneasiness. Interpret my words
with candour, and answer me, I conjure you, with confidence and sin-
cerity.''

I listened to my father in silence, and remained for some time incapable of offering any reply. I revolved rapidly in my mind a multitude
of thoughts, and endeavoured to arrive at some conclusion. Alas! to me
the idea of an immediate union with my Elizabeth was one of horror
and dismay. I was bound by a solemn promise, which I had not yet
fulfilled, and dared not break; or, if I did, what manifold miseries might
not impend over me and my devoted family! Could I enter into a festi-
val with this deadly weight yet hanging round my neck, and bowing
me to the ground? I must perform my engagement, and let the monster
depart with his mate, before I allowed myself to enjoy the delight of an
union from which I expected peace.

I remembered also the necessity imposed upon me of either journeying to England, or entering into a long correspondence with those
philosophers of that country, whose knowledge and discoveries were of
indispensable use to me in my present undertaking. The latter method
of obtaining the desired intelligence was dilatory and unsatisfactory: besides, I had an insurmountable aversion to the idea of engaging myself
in my loathsome task in my father's house, while in habits of familiar
intercourse with those I loved. I knew that a thousand fearful accidents
might occur, the slightest of which would disclose a tale to thrill all
connected with me with horror. I was aware also that I should often
lose all self-command, all capacity of hiding the harrowing sensations
that would possess me during the progress of my unearthly occupation.
I must absent myself from all I loved while thus employed. Once commenced, it would quickly be achieved, and I might be restored to my
family in peace and happiness. My promise fulfilled, the monster would
depart for ever. Or (so my fond fancy imaged) some accident might
meanwhile occur to destroy him, and put an end to my slavery for ever.

These feelings dictated my answer to my father. I expressed a wish
to visit England; but, concealing the true reasons of this request, I
clothed my desires under a guise which excited no suspicion, while
I urged my desire with an earnestness that easily induced my father
to comply. After so long a period of an absorbing melancholy, that
resembled madness in its intensity and effects, he was glad to find that
I was capable of taking pleasure in the idea of such a journey, and he
hoped that change of scene and varied amusement would, before my
return, have restored me entirely to myself.

The duration of my absence was left to my own choice; a few months, or at most a year, was the period contemplated. One paternal kind precaution he had taken to ensure my having a companion. Without previously communicating with me, he had, in concert with Elizabeth, arranged that Clerval should join me at Strasburgh. This interfered with the solitude I coveted for the prosecution of my task; yet at the commencement of my journey the presence of my friend could in no way be an impediment, and truly I rejoiced that thus I should be saved many hours of lonely, maddening reflection. Nay, Henry might stand between me and the intrusion of my foe. If I were alone, would he not at times force his abhorred presence on me, to remind me of my task, or to contemplate its progress?

To England, therefore, I was bound, and it was understood that my union with Elizabeth should take place immediately on my return. My father's age rendered him extremely averse to delay. For myself, there was one reward I promised myself from my detested toils — one consolation for my unparalleled sufferings; it was the prospect of that day when, enfranchised from my miserable slavery, I might claim Elizabeth, and forget the past in my union with her.

I now made arrangements for my journey; but one feeling haunted me, which filled me with fear and agitation. During my absence I should leave my friends unconscious of the existence of their enemy, and unprotected from his attacks, exasperated as he might be by my departure. But he had promised to follow me wherever I might go; and would he not accompany me to England? This imagination was dreadful in itself, but soothing, inasmuch as it supposed the safety of my friends. I was agonised with the idea of the possibility that the reverse of this might happen. But through the whole period during which I was the slave of my creature, I allowed myself to be governed by the impulses of the moment; and my present sensations strongly intimated that the fiend would follow me, and exempt my family from the danger of his machinations.

It was in the latter end of September that I again quitted my native country. My journey had been my own suggestion, and Elizabeth, therefore, acquiesced: but she was filled with disquiet at the idea of my suffering, away from her, the inroads of misery and grief. It had been her care which provided me a companion in Clerval — and yet a man is blind to a thousand minute circumstances, which call forth a woman's sedulous attention. She longed to bid me hasten my return, — a thousand conflicting emotions rendered her mute, as she bade me a tearful silent farewell.

I threw myself into the carriage that was to convey me away, hardly knowing whither I was going, and careless of what was passing around. I remembered only, and it was with a bitter anguish that I reflected on it, to order that my chemical instruments should be packed to go with me. Filled with dreary imaginations, I passed through many beautiful and majestic scenes; but my eyes were fixed and unobserving. I could only think of the bourne of my travels, and the work which was to occupy me whilst they endured.

After some days spent in listless indolence, during which I traversed many leagues, I arrived at Strasburgh, where I waited two days for Clerval. He came. Alas, how great was the contrast between us! He was alive to every new scene; joyful when he saw the beauties of the setting sun, and more happy when he beheld it rise, and recommence a new day. He pointed out to me the shifting colours of the landscape, and the appearances of the sky. "This is what it is to live," he cried, "now I enjoy existence! But you, my dear Frankenstein, wherefore are you desponding and sorrowful?" In truth, I was occupied by gloomy thoughts, and neither saw the descent of the evening star, nor the golden sunrise reflected in the Rhine. — And you, my friend, would be far more amused with the journal of Clerval, who observed the scenery with an eye of feeling and delight, than in listening to my reflections. I, a miserable wretch, haunted by a curse that shut up every avenue to enjoyment.

We had agreed to descend the Rhine in a boat from Strasburgh to Rotterdam, whence we might take shipping for London. During this voyage, we passed many willowy islands, and saw several beautiful towns. We stayed a day at Manheim, and, on the fifth from our departure from Strasburgh, arrived at Mayence. The course of the Rhine below Mayence becomes much more picturesque. The river descends rapidly, and winds between hills, not high, but steep, and of beautiful forms. We saw many ruined castles standing on the edges of precipices, surrounded by black woods, high and inaccessible. This part of the Rhine, indeed, presents a singularly variegated landscape. In one spot you view rugged hills, ruined castles overlooking tremendous precipices, with the dark Rhine rushing beneath; and, on the sudden turn of a promontory, flourishing vineyards, with green sloping banks, and a meandering river, and populous towns occupy the scene.

We travelled at the time of the vintage, and heard the song of the labourers, as we glided down the stream. Even I, depressed in mind, and my spirits continually agitated by gloomy feelings, even I was pleased. I lay at the bottom of the boat, and, as I gazed on the cloudless blue sky, I seemed to drink in a tranquillity to which I had long been a stranger. And if these were my sensations, who can describe those of

Henry? He felt as if he had been transported to Fairy-land, and enjoyed a happiness seldom tasted by man. "I have seen," he said, "the most beautiful scenes of my own country; I have visited the lakes of Lucerne and Uri, where the snowy mountains descend almost perpendicularly to the water, casting black and impenetrable shades, which would cause a gloomy and mournful appearance, were it not for the most verdant islands that relieve the eye by their gay appearance; I have seen this lake agitated by a tempest, when the wind tore up whirlwinds of water, and gave you an idea of what the water-spout must be on the great ocean, and the waves dash with fury the base of the mountain, where the priest and his mistress were overwhelmed by an avalanche, and where their dying voices are still said to be heard amid the pauses of the nightly wind; I have seen the mountains of La Valais, and the Pays de Vaud: but this country, Victor, pleases me more than all those wonders. The mountains of Switzerland are more majestic and strange; but there is a charm in the banks of this divine river, that I never before saw equalled. Look at that castle which overhangs yon precipice; and that also on the island, almost concealed amongst the foliage of those lovely trees; and now that group of labourers coming from among their vines; and that village half hid in the recess of the mountain. Oh, surely, the spirit that inhabits and guards this place has a soul more in harmony with man, than those who pile the glacier, or retire to the inaccessible peaks of the mountains of our own country."

Clerval! beloved friend! even now it delights me to record your words, and to dwell on the praise of which you are so eminently deserving. He was a being formed in the "very poetry of nature." His wild and enthusiastic imagination was chastened by the sensibility of his heart. His soul overflowed with ardent affections, and his friendship was of that devoted and wondrous nature that the worldly-minded teach us to look for only in the imagination. But even human sympathies were not sufficient to satisfy his eager mind. The scenery of external nature, which others regard only with admiration, he loved with ardour: —

> ———— The sounding cataract
> Haunted him like a passion: the tall rock,
> The mountain, and the deep and gloomy wood,
> Their colours and their forms, were then to him
> An appetite; a feeling, and a love,
> That had no need of a remoter charm,
> By thought supplied, or any interest
> Unborrow'd from the eye.[3]

[3]From William Wordsworth's "Tintern Abbey."—Ed.

And where does he now exist? Is this gentle and lovely being lost for ever? Has this mind, so replete with ideas, imaginations fanciful and magnificent, which formed a world, whose existence depended on the life of its creator; — has this mind perished? Does it now only exist in my memory? No, it is not thus; your form so divinely wrought, and beaming with beauty, has decayed, but your spirit still visits and consoles your unhappy friend.

Pardon this gush of sorrow; these ineffectual words are but a slight tribute to the unexampled worth of Henry, but they soothe my heart, overflowing with the anguish which his remembrance creates. I will proceed with my tale.

Beyond Cologne we descended to the plains of Holland; and we resolved to post the remainder of our way; for the wind was contrary, and the stream of the river was too gentle to aid us.

Our journey here lost the interest arising from beautiful scenery; but we arrived in a few days at Rotterdam, whence we proceeded by sea to England. It was on a clear morning, in the latter days of December, that I first saw the white cliffs of Britain. The banks of the Thames presented a new scene; they were flat, but fertile, and almost every town was marked by the remembrance of some story. We saw Tilbury Fort, and remembered the Spanish armada; Gravesend, Woolwich, and Greenwich, places which I had heard of even in my country.

At length we saw the numerous steeples of London, St. Paul's towering above all, and the Tower famed in English history.

CHAPTER XIX

London was our present point of rest; we determined to remain several months in this wonderful and celebrated city. Clerval desired the intercourse of the men of genius and talent who flourished at this time; but this was with me a secondary object; I was principally occupied with the means of obtaining the information necessary for the completion of my promise, and quickly availed myself of the letters of introduction that I had brought with me, addressed to the most distinguished natural philosophers.

If this journey had taken place during my days of study and happiness, it would have afforded me inexpressible pleasure. But a blight had come over my existence, and I only visited these people for the sake of the information they might give me on the subject in which my interest was so terribly profound. Company was irksome to me; when alone, I could fill my mind with the sights of heaven and earth; the voice of Henry soothed me, and I could thus cheat myself into a transitory peace. But busy, uninteresting, joyous faces brought back despair to my heart. I saw an insurmountable barrier placed between me and my fellow-men; this barrier was sealed with the blood of William and Justine; and to reflect on the events connected with those names filled my soul with anguish.

But in Clerval I saw the image of my former self; he was inquisitive, and anxious to gain experience and instruction. The difference of manners which he observed was to him an inexhaustible source of instruction and amusement. He was also pursuing an object he had long had in view. His design was to visit India, in the belief that he had in his knowledge of its various languages, and in the views he had taken of its society, the means of materially assisting the progress of European colonisation and trade. In Britain only could he further the execution of his plan. He was for ever busy; and the only check to his enjoyments was my sorrowful and dejected mind. I tried to conceal this as much as possible, that I might not debar him from the pleasures natural to one, who was entering on a new scene of life, undisturbed by any care or bitter recollection. I often refused to accompany him, alleging another engagement, that I might remain alone. I now also began to collect the materials necessary for my new creation, and this was to me like the torture of single drops of water continually falling on the head. Every thought that was devoted to it was an extreme anguish, and every word that I spoke in allusion to it caused my lips to quiver, and my heart to palpitate.

After passing some months in London, we received a letter from a person in Scotland, who had formerly been our visiter at Geneva. He mentioned the beauties of his native country, and asked us if those were not sufficient allurements to induce us to prolong our journey as far north as Perth, where he resided. Clerval eagerly desired to accept this invitation; and I, although I abhorred society, wished to view again mountains and streams, and all the wondrous works with which Nature adorns her chosen dwelling-places.

We had arrived in England at the beginning of October, and it was now February. We accordingly determined to commence our journey towards the north at the expiration of another month. In this expedition we did not intend to follow the great road to Edinburgh, but to visit Windsor, Oxford, Matlock, and the Cumberland lakes, resolving to arrive at the completion of this tour about the end of July. I packed up my chemical instruments, and the materials I had collected, resolving to finish my labours in some obscure nook in the northern highlands of Scotland.

We quitted London on the 27th of March, and remained a few days at Windsor, rambling in its beautiful forest. This was a new scene to us mountaineers; the majestic oaks, the quantity of game, and the herds of stately deer, were all novelties to us.

From thence we proceeded to Oxford. As we entered this city, our minds were filled with the remembrance of the events that had been transacted there more than a century and a half before. It was here that Charles I. had collected his forces. This city had remained faithful to him, after the whole nation had forsaken his cause to join the standard of parliament and liberty. The memory of that unfortunate king, and his companions, the amiable Falkland, the insolent Goring, his queen, and son, gave a peculiar interest to every part of the city, which they might be supposed to have inhabited. The spirit of elder days found a dwelling here, and we delighted to trace its footsteps. If these feelings had not found an imaginary gratification, the appearance of the city had yet in itself sufficient beauty to obtain our admiration. The colleges are ancient and picturesque; the streets are almost magnificent; and the lovely Isis, which flows beside it through meadows of exquisite verdure, is spread forth into a placid expanse of waters, which reflects its majestic assemblage of towers, and spires, and domes, embosomed among aged trees.

I enjoyed this scene; and yet my enjoyment was embittered both by the memory of the past, and the anticipation of the future. I was formed for peaceful happiness. During my youthful days discontent never visited my mind; and if I was ever overcome by *ennui*, the sight of what is beautiful in nature, or the study of what is excellent and sublime in the productions of man, could always interest my heart, and communicate elasticity to my spirits. But I am a blasted tree; the bolt has entered my soul; and I felt then that I should survive to exhibit, what I shall soon cease to be — a miserable spectacle of wrecked humanity, pitiable to others, and intolerable to myself.

We passed a considerable period at Oxford, rambling among its environs, and endeavouring to identify every spot which might relate to the most animating epoch of English history. Our little voyages of discovery were often prolonged by the successive objects that presented themselves. We visited the tomb of the illustrious Hampden, and the field on which that patriot fell. For a moment my soul was elevated from its debasing and miserable fears, to contemplate the divine ideas of liberty and self-sacrifice, of which these sights were the monuments and the remembrancers. For an instant I dared to shake off my chains, and look around me with a free and lofty spirit; but the iron had eaten into my flesh, and I sank again, trembling and hopeless, into my miserable self.

We left Oxford with regret, and proceeded to Matlock, which was our next place of rest. The country in the neighbourhood of this village resembled, to a greater degree, the scenery of Switzerland; but every thing is on a lower scale, and the green hills want the crown of distant white Alps, which always attend on the piny mountains of my native country. We visited the wondrous cave, and the little cabinets of natural history, where the curiosities are disposed in the same manner as in the collections at Servox and Chamounix. The latter name made me tremble, when pronounced by Henry; and I hastened to quit Matlock, with which that terrible scene was thus associated.

From Derby, still journeying northward, we passed two months in Cumberland and Westmorland. I could now almost fancy myself among the Swiss mountains. The little patches of snow which yet lingered on the northern sides of the mountains, the lakes, and the dashing of the rocky streams, were all familiar and dear sights to me. Here also we made some acquaintances, who almost contrived to cheat me into happiness. The delight of Clerval was proportionably greater than mine; his mind expanded in the company of men of talent, and he found in his own nature greater capacities and resources than he could have imagined himself to have possessed while he associated with his inferiors. "I could pass my life here," said he to me; "and among these mountains I should scarcely regret Switzerland and the Rhine."

But he found that a traveller's life is one that includes much pain amidst its enjoyments. His feelings are for ever on the stretch; and when he begins to sink into repose, he finds himself obliged to quit that on which he rests in pleasure for something new, which again engages his attention, and which also he forsakes for other novelties.

We had scarcely visited the various lakes of Cumberland and Westmorland, and conceived an affection for some of the inhabitants, when the period of our appointment with our Scotch friend approached, and we left them to travel on. For my own part I was not sorry. I had now neglected my promise for some time, and I feared the effects of the dæmon's disappointment. He might remain in Switzerland, and wreak his vengeance on my relatives. This idea pursued me, and tormented me at every moment from which I might otherwise have snatched repose and peace. I waited for my letters with feverish impatience: if they were delayed, I was miserable, and overcome by a thousand fears; and when they arrived, and I saw the superscription of Elizabeth or my father, I hardly dared to read and ascertain my fate. Sometimes I thought that the fiend followed me, and might expedite my remissness by murdering my companion. When these thoughts possessed me, I would not quit Henry for a moment, but followed him as his shadow, to protect him from the fancied rage of his destroyer. I felt as if I had committed some great crime, the consciousness of which haunted me. I was guiltless, but I had indeed drawn down a horrible curse upon my head, as mortal as that of crime.

I visited Edinburgh with languid eyes and mind; and yet that city might have interested the most unfortunate being. Clerval did not like it so well as Oxford: for the antiquity of the latter city was more pleasing to him. But the beauty and regularity of the new town of Edinburgh, its romantic castle and its environs, the most delightful in the world, Arthur's Seat, St. Bernard's Well, and the Pentland Hills, compensated him for the change, and filled him with cheerfulness and admiration. But I was impatient to arrive at the termination of my journey.

We left Edinburgh in a week, passing through Coupar, St. Andrew's, and along the banks of the Tay, to Perth, where our friend expected us. But I was in no mood to laugh and talk with strangers, or enter into their feelings or plans with the good humour expected from a guest; and accordingly I told Clerval that I wished to make the tour of Scotland alone. "Do you," said I, "enjoy yourself, and let this be our rendezvous. I may be absent a month or two; but do not interfere with my motions, I entreat you: leave me to peace and solitude for a short time; and when I return, I hope it will be with a lighter heart, more congenial to your own temper."

Henry wished to dissuade me; but, seeing me bent on this plan, ceased to remonstrate. He entreated me to write often. "I had rather be with you," he said, "in your solitary rambles, than with these Scotch people, whom I do not know: hasten then, my friend, to return, that I may again feel myself somewhat at home, which I cannot do in your absence."

Having parted from my friend, I determined to visit some remote spot of Scotland, and finish my work in solitude. I did not doubt but that the monster followed me, and would discover himself to me when I should have finished, that he might receive his companion.

With this resolution I traversed the northern highlands, and fixed on one of the remotest of the Orkneys as the scene of my labours. It was a place fitted for such a work, being hardly more than a rock, whose high sides were continually beaten upon by the waves. The soil was barren, scarcely affording pasture for a few miserable cows, and oatmeal for its inhabitants, which consisted of five persons, whose gaunt and scraggy limbs gave tokens of their miserable fare. Vegetables and bread, when they indulged in such luxuries, and even fresh water, was to be procured from the main land, which was about five miles distant.

On the whole island there were but three miserable huts, and one of these was vacant when I arrived. This I hired. It contained but two rooms, and these exhibited all the squalidness of the most miserable penury. The thatch had fallen in, the walls were unplastered, and the door was off its hinges. I ordered it to be repaired, bought some furniture, and took possession; an incident which would, doubtless, have occasioned some surprise, had not all the senses of the cottagers been benumbed by want and squalid poverty. As it was, I lived ungazed at and unmolested, hardly thanked for the pittance of food and clothes which I gave; so much does suffering blunt even the coarsest sensations of men.

In this retreat I devoted the morning to labour; but in the evening, when the weather permitted, I walked on the stony beach of the sea, to listen to the waves as they roared and dashed at my feet. It was a monotonous yet ever-changing scene. I thought of Switzerland; it was far different from this desolate and appalling landscape. Its hills are covered with vines, and its cottages are scattered thickly in the plains. Its fair lakes reflect a blue and gentle sky; and, when troubled by the winds, their tumult is but as the play of a lively infant, when compared to the roarings of the giant ocean.

In this manner I distributed my occupations when I first arrived; but, as I proceeded in my labour, it became every day more horrible and irksome to me. Sometimes I could not prevail on myself to enter my laboratory for several days; and at other times I toiled day and night in order to complete my work. It was, indeed, a filthy process in which I was engaged. During my first experiment, a kind of enthusiastic frenzy had blinded me to the horror of my employment; my mind was intently fixed on the consummation of my labour, and my eyes were shut to the horror of my proceedings. But now I went to it in cold blood, and my heart often sickened at the work of my hands.

Thus situated, employed in the most detestable occupation, immersed in a solitude where nothing could for an instant call my attention from the actual scene in which I was engaged, my spirits became unequal; I grew restless and nervous. Every moment I feared to meet my persecutor. Sometimes I sat with my eyes fixed on the ground, fear-

ing to raise them, lest they should encounter the object which I
so much dreaded to behold. I feared to wander from the sight of my
fellow-creatures, lest when alone he should come to claim his companion.

In the mean time I worked on, and my labour was already considerably advanced. I looked towards its completion with a tremulous and
eager hope, which I dared not trust myself to question, but which was
intermixed with obscure forebodings of evil, that made my heart sicken
in my bosom.

CHAPTER XX

I sat one evening in my laboratory; the sun had set, and the moon
was just rising from the sea; I had not sufficient light for my employment, and I remained idle, in a pause of consideration of whether I
should leave my labour for the night, or hasten its conclusion by an
unremitting attention to it. As I sat, a train of reflection occurred to
me, which led me to consider the effects of what I was now doing.
Three years before I was engaged in the same manner, and had created
a fiend whose unparalleled barbarity had desolated my heart, and filled
it for ever with the bitterest remorse. I was now about to form another
being, of whose dispositions I was alike ignorant; she might become
ten thousand times more malignant than her mate, and delight, for
its own sake, in murder and wretchedness. He had sworn to quit the
neighbourhood of man, and hide himself in deserts; but she had not;
and she, who in all probability was to become a thinking and reasoning
animal, might refuse to comply with a compact made before her creation. They might even hate each other; the creature who already lived
loathed his own deformity, and might he not conceive a greater abhorrence for it when it came before his eyes in the female form? She also
might turn with disgust from him to the superior beauty of man; she
might quit him, and he be again alone, exasperated by the fresh provo-
cation of being deserted by one of his own species.

Even if they were to leave Europe, and inhabit the deserts of the
new world, yet one of the first results of those sympathies for which
the dæmon thirsted would be children, and a race of devils would be
propagated upon the earth, who might make the very existence of the
species of man a condition precarious and full of terror. Had I a right,
for my own benefit, to inflict this curse upon everlasting generations? I
had before been moved by the sophisms of the being I had created; I

had been struck senseless by his fiendish threats: but now, for the first time, the wickedness of my promise burst upon me; I shuddered to think that future ages might curse me as their pest, whose selfishness had not hesitated to buy its own peace at the price, perhaps, of the existence of the whole human race.

I trembled, and my heart failed within me; when, on looking up, I saw, by the light of the moon, the dæmon at the casement. A ghastly grin wrinkled his lips as he gazed on me, where I sat fulfilling the task which he had allotted to me. Yes, he had followed me in my travels; he had loitered in forests, hid himself in caves, or taken refuge in wide and desert heaths; and he now came to mark my progress, and claim the fulfillment of my promise.

As I looked on him, his countenance expressed the utmost extent of malice and treachery. I thought with a sensation of madness on my promise of creating another like to him, and trembling with passion, tore to pieces the thing on which I was engaged. The wretch saw me destroy the creature on whose future existence he depended for happiness, and, with a howl of devilish despair and revenge, withdrew.

I left the room, and, locking the door, made a solemn vow in my own heart never to resume my labours; and then, with trembling steps, I sought my own apartment. I was alone; none were near me to dissipate the gloom, and relieve me from the sickening oppression of the most terrible reveries.

Several hours passed, and I remained near my window gazing on the sea; it was almost motionless, for the winds were hushed, and all nature reposed under the eye of the quiet moon. A few fishing vessels alone specked the water, and now and then the gentle breeze wafted the sound of voices, as the fishermen called to one another. I felt the silence, although I was hardly conscious of its extreme profundity, until my ear was suddenly arrested by the paddling of oars near the shore, and a person landed close to my house.

In a few minutes after, I heard the creaking of my door, as if some one endeavoured to open it softly. I trembled from head to foot; I felt a presentiment of who it was, and wished to rouse one of the peasants who dwelt in a cottage not far from mine; but I was overcome by the sensation of helplessness, so often felt in frightful dreams, when you in vain endeavour to fly from an impending danger, and was rooted to the spot.

Presently I heard the sound of footsteps along the passage; the door opened, and the wretch whom I dreaded appeared. Shutting the door, he approached me, and said, in a smothered voice —

"You have destroyed the work which you began; what is it that you intend? Do you dare to break your promise? I have endured toil and misery: I left Switzerland with you; I crept along the shores of the Rhine, among its willow islands, and over the summits of its hills. I have dwelt many months in the heaths of England, and among the deserts of Scotland. I have endured incalculable fatigue, and cold, and hunger; do you dare destroy my hopes?"

"Begone! I do break my promise; never will I create another like yourself, equal in deformity and wickedness."

"Slave, I have reasoned with you, but you have proved yourself unworthy of my condescension. Remember that I have power; you believe yourself miserable, but I can make you so wretched that the light of day will be hateful to you. You are my creator, but I am your master; — obey!"

"The hour of my irresolution is past, and the period of your power is arrived. Your threats cannot move me to do an act of wickedness; but they confirm me in a determination of not creating you a companion in vice. Shall I, in cool blood, set loose upon the earth a dæmon, whose delight is in death and wretchedness? Begone! I am firm, and your words will only exasperate my rage."

The monster saw my determination in my face, and gnashed his teeth in the impotence of anger. "Shall each man," cried he, "find a wife for his bosom, and each beast have his mate, and I be alone? I had feelings of affection, and they were requited by detestation and scorn. Man! you may hate; but beware! your hours will pass in dread and misery, and soon the bolt will fall which must ravish from you your happiness for ever. Are you to be happy, while I grovel in the intensity of my wretchedness? You can blast my other passions; but revenge remains — revenge, henceforth dearer than light or food! I may die; but first you, my tyrant and tormentor, shall curse the sun that gazes on your misery. Beware; for I am fearless, and therefore powerful. I will watch with the wiliness of a snake, that I may sting with its venom. Man, you shall repent of the injuries you inflict."

"Devil, cease; and do not poison the air with these sounds of malice. I have declared my resolution to you, and I am no coward to bend beneath words. Leave me; I am inexorable."

"It is well. I go; but remember, I shall be with you on your wedding-night."

I started forward, and exclaimed, "Villain! before you sign my death-warrant, be sure that you are yourself safe."

I would have seized him; but he eluded me, and quitted the house with precipitation. In a few moments I saw him in his boat, which shot across the waters with an arrowy swiftness, and was soon lost amidst the waves.

All was again silent; but his words rung in my ears. I burned with rage to pursue the murderer of my peace, and precipitate him into the ocean. I walked up and down my room hastily and perturbed, while my imagination conjured up a thousand images to torment and sting me. Why had I not followed him, and closed with him in mortal strife? But I had suffered him to depart, and he had directed his course towards the main land. I shuddered to think who might be the next victim sacrificed to his insatiate revenge. And then I thought again of his words — *"I will be with you on your wedding-night."* That then was the period fixed for the fulfilment of my destiny. In that hour I should die, and at once satisfy and extinguish his malice. The prospect did not move me to fear; yet when I thought of my beloved Elizabeth, — of her tears and endless sorrow, when she should find her lover so barbarously snatched from her, — tears, the first I had shed for many months, streamed from my eyes, and I resolved not to fall before my enemy without a bitter struggle.

The night passed away, and the sun rose from the ocean; my feelings became calmer, if it may be called calmness, when the violence of rage sinks into the depths of despair. I left the house, the horrid scene of the last night's contention, and walked on the beach of the sea, which I almost regarded as an insuperable barrier between me and my fellow-creatures; nay, a wish that such should prove the fact stole across me. I desired that I might pass my life on that barren rock, wearily, it is true, but uninterrupted by any sudden shock of misery. If I returned, it was to be sacrificed, or to see those whom I most loved die under the grasp of a dæmon whom I had myself created.

I walked about the isle like a restless spectre, separated from all it loved, and miserable in the separation. When it became noon, and the sun rose higher, I lay down on the grass, and was overpowered by a deep sleep. I had been awake the whole of the preceding night, my nerves were agitated, and my eyes inflamed by watching and misery. The sleep into which I now sunk refreshed me; and when I awoke, I again felt as if I belonged to a race of human beings like myself, and I began to reflect upon what had passed with greater composure; yet still the words of the fiend rung in my ears like a death-knell, they appeared like a dream, yet distinct and oppressive as a reality.

The sun had far descended, and I still sat on the shore, satisfying my appetite, which had become ravenous, with an oaten cake, when I saw a fishing-boat land close to me, and one of the men brought me a packet; it contained letters from Geneva, and one from Clerval, entreating me to join him. He said that he was wearing away his time fruitlessly where he was; that letters from the friends he had formed in London desired his return to complete the negotiation they had entered into for his Indian enterprise. He could not any longer delay his departure; but as his journey to London might be followed, even sooner than he now conjectured, by his longer voyage, he entreated me to bestow as much of my society on him as I could spare. He besought me, therefore, to leave my solitary isle, and to meet him at Perth, that we might proceed southwards together. This letter in a degree recalled me to life, and I determined to quit my island at the expiration of two days.

Yet, before I departed, there was a task to perform, on which I shuddered to reflect: I must pack up my chemical instruments; and for that purpose I must enter the room which had been the scene of my odious work, and I must handle those utensils, the sight of which was sickening to me. The next morning, at daybreak, I summoned sufficient courage, and unlocked the door of my laboratory. The remains of the half-finished creature, whom I had destroyed, lay scattered on the floor, and I almost felt as if I had mangled the living flesh of a human being. I paused to collect myself, and then entered the chamber. With trembling hand I conveyed the instruments out of the room; but I reflected that I ought not to leave the relics of my work to excite the horror and suspicion of the peasants; and I accordingly put them into a basket, with a great quantity of stones, and, laying them up, determined to throw them into the sea that very night; and in the mean time I sat upon the beach, employed in cleaning and arranging my chemical apparatus.

Nothing could be more complete than the alteration that had taken place in my feelings since the night of the appearance of the dæmon. I had before regarded my promise with a gloomy despair, as a thing that, with whatever consequences, must be fulfilled; but I now felt as if a film had been taken from before my eyes, and that I, for the first time, saw clearly. The idea of renewing my labours did not for one instant occur to me; the threat I had heard weighed on my thoughts, but I did not reflect that a voluntary act of mine could avert it. I had resolved in my own mind, that to create another like the fiend I had first made would be an act of the basest and most atrocious selfishness; and I banished from my mind every thought that could lead to a different conclusion.

Between two and three in the morning the moon rose; and I then, putting my basket aboard a little skiff, sailed out about four miles from the shore. The scene was perfectly solitary: a few boats were returning towards land, but I sailed away from them. I felt as if I was about the commission of a dreadful crime, and avoided with shuddering anxiety any encounter with my fellow-creatures. At one time the moon, which had before been clear, was suddenly overspread by a thick cloud, and I took advantage of the moment of darkness, and cast my basket into the sea: I listened to the gurgling sound as it sunk, and then sailed away from the spot. The sky became clouded; but the air was pure, although chilled by the north-east breeze that was then rising. But it refreshed me, and filled me with such agreeable sensations, that I resolved to prolong my stay on the water; and, fixing the rudder in a direct position, stretched myself at the bottom of the boat. Clouds hid the moon, every thing was obscure, and I heard only the sound of the boat, as its keel cut through the waves; the murmur lulled me, and in a short time I slept soundly.

I do not know how long I remained in this situation, but when I awoke I found that the sun had already mounted considerably. The wind was high, and the waves continually threatened the safety of my little skiff. I found that the wind was north-east, and must have driven me far from the coast from which I had embarked. I endeavoured to change my course, but quickly found that, if I again made the attempt, the boat would be instantly filled with water. Thus situated, my only resource was to drive before the wind. I confess that I felt a few sensations of terror. I had no compass with me, and was so slenderly acquainted with the geography of this part of the world, that the sun was of little benefit to me. I might be driven into the wide Atlantic, and feel all the tortures of starvation, or be swallowed up in the immeasurable waters that roared and buffeted around me. I had already been out many hours, and felt the torment of a burning thirst, a prelude to my other sufferings. I looked on the heavens, which were covered by clouds that flew the wind, only to be replaced by others: I looked upon the sea, it was to be my grave. "Fiend," I exclaimed, "your task is already fulfilled!" I thought of Elizabeth, of my father, and of Clerval; all left behind, on whom the monster might satisfy his sanguinary and merciless passions. This idea plunged me into a reverie, so despairing and frightful, that even now, when the scene is on the point of closing before me for ever, I shudder to reflect on it.

Some hours passed thus; but by degrees, as the sun declined towards the horizon, the wind died away into a gentle breeze, and the sea became free from breakers. But these gave place to a heavy swell: I felt sick, and hardly able to hold the rudder, when suddenly I saw a line of high land towards the south.

Almost spent, as I was, by fatigue, and the dreadful suspense I endured for several hours, this sudden certainty of life rushed like a flood of warm joy to my heart, and tears gushed from my eyes.

How mutable are our feelings, and how strange is that clinging love we have of life even in the excess of misery! I constructed another sail with a part of my dress, and eagerly steered my course towards the land. It had a wild and rocky appearance; but, as I approached nearer, I easily perceived the traces of cultivation. I saw vessels near the shore, and found myself suddenly transported back to the neighbourhood of civilised man. I carefully traced the windings of the land, and hailed a steeple which I at length saw issuing from behind a small promontory. As I was in a state of extreme debility, I resolved to sail directly towards the town, as a place where I could most easily procure nourishment. Fortunately, I had money with me. As I turned the promontory, I perceived a small, neat town and a good harbour, which I entered, my heart bounding with joy at my unexpected escape.

As I was occupied in fixing the boat and arranging the sails, several people crowded towards the spot. They seemed much surprised at my appearance; but, instead of offering me any assistance, whispered together with gestures that at any other time might have produced in me a slight sensation of alarm. As it was, I merely remarked that they spoke English; and I therefore addressed them in that language: "My good friends," said I, "will you be so kind as to tell me the name of this town, and inform me where I am?"

"You will know that soon enough," replied a man with a hoarse voice. "May be you are come to a place that will not prove much to your taste; but you will not be consulted as to your quarters, I promise you."

I was exceedingly surprised on receiving so rude an answer from a stranger; and I was also disconcerted on perceiving the frowning and angry countenances of his companions. "Why do you answer me so roughly?" I replied; "surely it is not the custom of Englishmen to receive strangers so inhospitably."

"I do not know," said the man, "what the custom of the English may be; but it is the custom of the Irish to hate villains."

While this strange dialogue continued, I perceived the crowd rapidly increase. Their faces expressed a mixture of curiosity and anger, which annoyed, and in some degree alarmed me. I enquired the way to the inn; but no one replied. I then moved forward, and a murmuring sound arose from the crowd as they followed and surrounded me; when an ill-looking man approached, tapped me on the shoulder, and said, "Come, sir, you must follow me to Mr. Kirwin's, to give an account of yourself."

"Who is Mr. Kirwin? Why am I to give an account of myself? Is not this a free country?"

"Ay, sir, free enough for honest folks. Mr. Kirwin is a magistrate; and you are to give an account of the death of a gentleman who was found murdered here last night."

This answer startled me; but I presently recovered myself. I was innocent; that could easily be proved: accordingly I followed my conductor in silence, and was led to one of the best houses in the town. I was ready to sink from fatigue and hunger; but, being surrounded by a crowd, I thought it politic to rouse all my strength, that no physical debility might be construed into apprehension or conscious guilt. Little did I then expect the calamity that was in a few moments to overwhelm me, and extinguish in horror and despair all fear of ignominy or death.

I must pause here; for it requires all my fortitude to recall the memory of the frightful events which I am about to relate, in proper detail, to my recollection.

CHAPTER XXI

I was soon introduced into the presence of the magistrate, an old benevolent man, with calm and mild manners. He looked upon me, however, with some degree of severity: and then, turning towards my conductors, he asked who appeared as witnesses on this occasion.

About half a dozen men came forward; and, one being selected by the magistrate, he deposed, that he had been out fishing the night before with his son and brother-in-law, Daniel Nugent, when, about ten o'clock, they observed a strong northerly blast rising, and they accordingly put in for port. It was a very dark night, as the moon had not yet risen; they did not land at the harbour, but, as they had been accustomed, at a creek about two miles below. He walked on first, carrying a part of the fishing tackle, and his companions followed him at some distance. As he was proceeding along the sands, he struck his foot against something, and fell at his length on the ground. His companions came up to assist him; and, by the light of their lantern, they found that he had fallen on the body of a man, who was to all appearance dead. Their first supposition was, that it was the corpse of some person who had been drowned, and was thrown on shore by the waves; but, on examination, they found that the clothes were not wet, and even that the body was not then cold. They instantly carried it to the cottage of an old woman near the spot, and endeavoured, but in vain, to restore it to life. It appeared to be a handsome young man, about five and twenty years of age. He had apparently been strangled; for there was no sign of any violence, except the black mark of fingers on his neck.

The first part of this deposition did not in the least interest me; but when the mark of the fingers was mentioned, I remembered the murder of my brother, and felt myself extremely agitated; my limbs trembled, and a mist came over my eyes, which obliged me to lean on a chair for support. The magistrate observed me with a keen eye, and of course drew an unfavourable augury from my manner.

The son confirmed his father's account: but when Daniel Nugent was called, he swore positively that, just before the fall of his companion, he saw a boat, with a single man in it, at a short distance from the shore; and, as far as he could judge by the light of a few stars, it was the same boat in which I had just landed.

A woman deposed, that she lived near the beach, and was standing at the door of her cottage, waiting for the return of the fishermen, about an hour before she heard of the discovery of the body, when she saw a boat, with only one man in it, push off from that part of the shore where the corpse was afterwards found.

Another woman confirmed the account of the fishermen having brought the body into her house; it was not cold. They put it into a bed, and rubbed it; and Daniel went to the town for an apothecary, but life was quite gone.

Several other men were examined concerning my landing; and they agreed, that, with the strong north wind that had arisen during the night, it was very probable that I had beaten about for many hours, and had been obliged to return nearly to the same spot from which I had departed. Besides, they observed that it appeared that I had brought the body from another place, and it was likely, that as I did not appear to know the shore, I might have put into the harbour ignorant of the distance of the town of * * * from the place where I had deposited the corpse.

Mr. Kirwin, on hearing this evidence, desired that I should be taken into the room where the body lay for interment, that it might be observed what effect the sight of it would produce upon me. This idea was probably suggested by the extreme agitation I had exhibited when the mode of the murder had been described. I was accordingly conducted, by the magistrate and several other persons, to the inn. I could not help being struck by the strange coincidences that had taken place during this eventful night; but, knowing that I had been conversing with several persons in the island I had inhabited about the time that the body had been found, I was perfectly tranquil as to the consequences of the affair.

I entered the room where the corpse lay, and was led up to the coffin. How can I describe my sensations on beholding it? I feel yet parched with horror, nor can I reflect on that terrible moment without shuddering and agony. The examination, the presence of the magistrate and witnesses, passed like a dream from my memory, when I saw the lifeless form of Henry Clerval stretched before me. I gasped for breath; and, throwing myself on the body, I exclaimed, "Have my murderous machinations deprived you also, my dearest Henry, of life? Two I have already destroyed; other victims await their destiny: but you, Clerval, my friend, my benefactor — "

The human frame could no longer support the agonies that I endured, and I was carried out of the room in strong convulsions.

A fever succeeded to this. I lay for two months on the point of death: my ravings, as I afterwards heard, were frightful; I called myself the murderer of William, of Justine, and of Clerval. Sometimes I entreated my attendants to assist me in the destruction of the fiend by whom I was tormented; and at others, I felt the fingers of the monster already grasping my neck, and screamed aloud with agony and terror. Fortunately, as I spoke my native language, Mr. Kirwin alone understood me; but my gestures and bitter cries were sufficient to affright the other witnesses.

Why did I not die? More miserable than man ever was before, why did I not sink into forgetfulness and rest? Death snatches away many blooming children, the only hopes of their doating parents: how many brides and youthful lovers have been one day in the bloom of health and hope, and the next a prey for worms and the decay of the tomb! Of what materials was I made, that I could thus resist so many shocks, which, like the turning of the wheel, continually renewed the torture?

But I was doomed to live; and, in two months, found myself as awaking from a dream, in a prison, stretched on a wretched bed, surrounded by gaolers, turnkeys, bolts, and all the miserable apparatus of a dungeon. It was morning, I remember, when I thus awoke to understanding: I had forgotten the particulars of what had happened, and only felt as if some great misfortune had suddenly overwhelmed me; but when I looked around, and saw the barred windows, and the squalidness of the room in which I was, all flashed across my memory, and I groaned bitterly.

This sound disturbed an old woman who was sleeping in a chair beside me. She was a hired nurse, the wife of one of the turnkeys, and her countenance expressed all those bad qualities which often characterise that class. The lines of her face were hard and rude, like that of persons accustomed to see without sympathising in sights of misery. Her tone expressed her entire indifference; she addressed me in English, and the voice struck me as one that I had heard during my sufferings: —

"Are you better now, sir?" said she.

I replied in the same language, with a feeble voice, "I believe I am; but if it be all true, if indeed I did not dream, I am sorry that I am still alive to feel this misery and horror."

"For that matter," replied the old woman, "if you mean about the gentleman you murdered, I believe that it were better for you if you were dead, for I fancy it will go hard with you! However, that's none of my business; I am sent to nurse you, and get you well; I do my duty with a safe conscience; it were well if every body did the same."

I turned with loathing from the woman who could utter so unfeeling a speech to a person just saved, on the very edge of death; but I felt languid, and unable to reflect on all that had passed. The whole series of my life appeared to me as a dream; I sometimes doubted if indeed it were all true, for it never presented itself to my mind with the force of reality.

As the images that floated before me became more distinct, I grew feverish; a darkness pressed around me: no one was near me who soothed me with the gentle voice of love; no dear hand supported me. The physician came and prescribed medicines, and the old woman prepared them for me; but utter carelessness was visible in the first, and the expression of brutality was strongly marked in the visage of the second. Who could be interested in the fate of a murderer, but the hangman who would gain his fee?

These were my first reflections; but I soon learned that Mr. Kirwin had shown me extreme kindness. He had caused the best room in the prison to be prepared for me (wretched indeed was the best); and it was he who had provided a physician and a nurse. It is true, he seldom came to see me; for, although he ardently desired to relieve the sufferings of every human creature, he did not wish to be present at the agonies and miserable ravings of a murderer. He came, therefore, sometimes, to see that I was not neglected; but his visits were short, and with long intervals.

One day, while I was gradually recovering, I was seated in a chair, my eyes half open, and my cheeks livid like those in death. I was overcome by gloom and misery, and often reflected I had better seek death than desire to remain in a world which to me was replete with wretchedness. At one time I considered whether I should not declare myself guilty, and suffer the penalty of the law, less innocent than poor Justine had been. Such were my thoughts, when the door of my apartment was opened, and Mr. Kirwin entered. His countenance expressed sympathy and compassion; he drew a chair close to mine, and addressed me in French —

"I fear that this place is very shocking to you; can I do any thing to make you more comfortable?"

"I thank you; but all that you mention is nothing to me: on the whole earth there is no comfort which I am capable of receiving."

"I know that the sympathy of a stranger can be but of little relief to one borne down as you are by so strange a misfortune. But you will, I hope, soon quit this melancholy abode; for, doubtless, evidence can easily be brought to free you from the criminal charge."

"That is my least concern: I am, by a course of strange events, become the most miserable of mortals. Persecuted and tortured as I am and have been, can death be any evil to me?"

"Nothing indeed could be more unfortunate and agonising than the strange chances that have lately occurred. You were thrown, by some surprising accident, on this shore, renowned for its hospitality; seized immediately, and charged with murder. The first sight that was presented to your eyes was the body of your friend, murdered in so unaccountable a manner, and placed, as it were, by some fiend across your path."

As Mr. Kirwin said this, notwithstanding the agitation I endured on this retrospect of my sufferings, I also felt considerable surprise at the knowledge he seemed to possess concerning me. I suppose some astonishment was exhibited in my countenance; for Mr. Kirwin hastened to say —

"Immediately upon your being taken ill, all the papers that were on your person were brought to me, and I examined them that I might discover some trace by which I could send to your relations an account of your misfortune and illness. I found several letters, and, among others, one which I discovered from its commencement to be from your father. I instantly wrote to Geneva: nearly two months have elapsed since the departure of my letter. — But you are ill; even now you tremble: you are unfit for agitation of any kind."

"This suspense is a thousand times worse than the most horrible event: tell me what new scene of death has been acted, and whose murder I am now to lament?"

"Your family is perfectly well," said Mr. Kirwin, with gentleness; "and some one, a friend, is come to visit you."

I know not by what chain of thought the idea presented itself, but it instantly darted into my mind that the murderer had come to mock at my misery, and taunt me with the death of Clerval, as a new incitement for me to comply with his hellish desires. I put my hand before my eyes, and cried out in agony —

"Oh! take him away! I cannot see him; for God's sake, do not let him enter!"

Mr. Kirwin regarded me with a troubled countenance. He could not help regarding my exclamation as a presumption of my guilt, and said, in rather a severe tone —

"I should have thought, young man, that the presence of your father would have been welcome, instead of inspiring such violent repugnance."

"My father!" cried I, while every feature and every muscle was relaxed from anguish to pleasure: "is my father indeed come? How kind, how very kind! But where is he, why does he not hasten to me?"

My change of manner surprised and pleased the magistrate; perhaps he thought that my former exclamation was a momentary return of delirium, and now he instantly resumed his former benevolence. He rose, and quitted the room with my nurse, and in a moment my father entered it.

Nothing, at this moment, could have given me greater pleasure than the arrival of my father. I stretched out my hand to him, and cried —

"Are you then safe — and Elizabeth — and Ernest?"

My father calmed me with assurances of their welfare, and endeavoured, by dwelling on these subjects so interesting to my heart, to raise my desponding spirits; but he soon felt that a prison cannot be the abode of cheerfulness. "What a place is this that you inhabit, my son!" said he, looking mournfully at the barred windows, and wretched appearance of the room. "You travelled to seek happiness, but a fatality seems to pursue you. And poor Clerval — "

The name of my unfortunate and murdered friend was an agitation too great to be endured in my weak state; I shed tears.

"Alas! yes, my father," replied I; "some destiny of the most horrible kind hangs over me, and I must live to fulfil it, or surely I should have died on the coffin of Henry."

We were not allowed to converse for any length of time, for the precarious state of my health rendered every precaution necessary that could ensure tranquillity. Mr. Kirwin came in, and insisted that my strength should not be exhausted by too much exertion. But the appearance of my father was to me like that of my good angel, and I gradually recovered my health.

As my sickness quitted me, I was absorbed by a gloomy and black melancholy, that nothing could dissipate. The image of Clerval was for ever before me, ghastly and murdered. More than once the agitation into which these reflections threw me made my friends dread a dangerous relapse. Alas! why did they preserve so miserable and detested a life? It was surely that I might fulfil my destiny, which is now drawing to a close. Soon, oh! very soon, will death extinguish these throbbings, and relieve me from the mighty weight of anguish that bears me to the dust; and, in executing the award of justice, I shall also sink to rest. Then the appearance of death was distant, although the wish was ever present to my thoughts; and I often sat for hours motionless and speechless, wishing for some mighty revolution that might bury me and my destroyer in its ruins.

The season of the assizes approached. I had already been three months in prison; and although I was still weak, and in continual danger of a relapse, I was obliged to travel nearly a hundred miles to the county-town, where the court was held. Mr. Kirwin charged himself with every care of collecting witnesses, and arranging my defence. I was spared the disgrace of appearing publicly as a criminal, as the case was not brought before the court that decides on life and death. The grand jury rejected the bill, on its being proved that I was on the Orkney Islands at the hour the body of my friend was found; and a fortnight after my removal I was liberated from prison.

My father was enraptured on finding me freed from the vexations of a criminal charge, that I was again allowed to breathe the fresh atmosphere, and permitted to return to my native country. I did not participate in these feelings; for to me the walls of a dungeon or a palace were alike hateful. The cup of life was poisoned for ever; and although the sun shone upon me, as upon the happy and gay of heart, I saw around me nothing but a dense and frightful darkness, penetrated by no light but the glimmer of two eyes that glared upon me. Sometimes they were the expressive eyes of Henry, languishing in death, the dark orbs nearly covered by the lids, and the long black lashes that fringed them; sometimes it was the watery, clouded eyes of the monster, as I first saw them in my chamber at Ingolstadt.

My father tried to awaken in me the feelings of affection. He talked of Geneva, which I should soon visit — of Elizabeth and Ernest; but these words only drew deep groans from me. Sometimes, indeed, I felt a wish for happiness; and thought, with melancholy delight, of my beloved cousin; or longed, with a devouring *maladie du pays,* to see once more the blue lake and rapid Rhone, that had been so dear to me in early childhood: but my general state of feeling was a torpor, in which a prison was as welcome a residence as the divinest scene in nature; and these fits were seldom interrupted but by paroxysms of anguish and despair. At these moments I often endeavoured to put an end to the existence I loathed; and it required unceasing attendance and vigilance to restrain me from committing some dreadful act of violence.

Yet one duty remained to me, the recollection of which finally triumphed over my selfish despair. It was necessary that I should return without delay to Geneva, there to watch over the lives of those I so fondly loved; and to lie in wait for the murderer, that if any chance led me to the place of his concealment, or if he dared again to blast me by his presence, I might, with unfailing aim, put an end to the existence of the monstrous Image which I had endued with the mockery of a soul still more monstrous. My father still desired to delay our departure, fearful that I could not sustain the fatigues of a journey: for I was a shattered wreck, — the shadow of a human being. My strength was gone. I was a mere skeleton; and fever night and day preyed upon my wasted frame.

Still, as I urged our leaving Ireland with such inquietude and impatience, my father thought it best to yield. We took our passage on board a vessel bound for Havre-de-Grace, and sailed with a fair wind from the Irish shores. It was midnight. I lay on the deck, looking at the stars, and listening to the dashing of the waves. I hailed the darkness that shut Ireland from my sight; and my pulse beat with a feverish joy when I reflected that I should soon see Geneva. The past appeared to me in the light of a frightful dream; yet the vessel in which I was, the wind that blew me from the detested shore of Ireland, and the sea which surrounded me, told me too forcibly that I was deceived by no vision, and that Clerval, my friend and dearest companion, had fallen a victim to me and the monster of my creation. I repassed, in my memory, my whole life; my quiet happiness while residing with my family in Geneva, the death of my mother, and my departure for Ingolstadt. I remembered, shuddering, the mad enthusiasm that hurried me on to the creation of my hideous enemy, and I called to mind the night in which he first lived. I was unable to pursue the train of thought; a thousand feelings pressed upon me, and I wept bitterly.

Ever since my recovery from the fever, I had been in the custom of taking every night a small quantity of laudanum; for it was by means of this drug only that I was enabled to gain the rest necessary for the preservation of life. Oppressed by the recollection of my various misfortunes, I now swallowed double my usual quantity, and soon slept profoundly. But sleep did not afford me respite from thought and misery; my dreams presented a thousand objects that scared me. Towards morning I was possessed by a kind of night-mare; I felt the fiend's grasp in my neck, and could not free myself from it; groans and cries rung in my ears. My father, who was watching over me, perceiving my restlessness, awoke me; the dashing waves were around: the cloudy sky above; the fiend was not here: a sense of security, a feeling that a truce was established between the present hour and the irresistible, disastrous future, imparted to me a kind of calm forgetfulness, of which the human mind is by its structure peculiarly susceptible.

CHAPTER XXII

The voyage came to an end. We landed, and proceeded to Paris. I soon found that I had overtaxed my strength, and that I must repose before I could continue my journey. My father's care and attentions were indefatigable; but he did not know the origin of my sufferings, and sought erroneous methods to remedy the incurable ill. He wished me to seek amusement in society. I abhorred the face of man. Oh, not abhorred! they were my brethren, my fellow beings, and I felt attracted even to the most repulsive among them, as to creatures of an angelic nature and celestial mechanism. But I felt that I had no right to share their intercourse. I had unchained an enemy among them, whose joy it was to shed their blood, and to revel in their groans. How they would, each and all, abhor me, and hunt me from the world, did they know my unhallowed acts, and the crimes which had their source in me!

My father yielded at length to my desire to avoid society, and strove by various arguments to banish my despair. Sometimes he thought that I felt deeply the degradation of being obliged to answer a charge of murder, and he endeavoured to prove to me the futility of pride.

"Alas! my father," said I, "how little do you know me. Human beings, their feelings and passions, would indeed be degraded if such a wretch as I felt pride. Justine, poor unhappy Justine, was as innocent as I, and she suffered the same charge; she died for it; and I am the cause of this — I murdered her. William, Justine, and Henry — they all died by my hands."

My father had often, during my imprisonment, heard me make the same assertion; when I thus accused myself, he sometimes seemed to desire an explanation, and at others he appeared to consider it as the offspring of delirium, and that, during my illness, some idea of this kind had presented itself to my imagination, the remembrance of which I preserved in my convalescence. I avoided explanation, and maintained a continual silence concerning the wretch I had created. I had a persuasion that I should be supposed mad; and this in itself would for ever have chained my tongue. But, besides, I could not bring myself to disclose a secret which would fill my hearer with consternation, and make fear and unnatural horror the inmates of his breast. I checked, therefore, my impatient thirst for sympathy, and was silent when I would have given the world to have confided the fatal secret. Yet still words like those I have recorded, would burst uncontrollably from me. I could offer no explanation of them; but their truth in part relieved the burden of my mysterious woe.

Upon this occasion my father said, with an expression of unbounded wonder, "My dearest Victor, what infatuation is this? My dear son, I entreat you never to make such an assertion again."

"I am not mad," I cried energetically; "the sun and the heavens, who have viewed my operations, can bear witness of my truth. I am the assassin of those most innocent victims; they died by my machinations. A thousand times would I have shed my own blood, drop by drop, to have saved their lives; but I could not, my father, indeed I could not sacrifice the whole human race."

The conclusion of this speech convinced my father that my ideas were deranged, and he instantly changed the subject of our conversation, and endeavoured to alter the course of my thoughts. He wished as much as possible to obliterate the memory of the scenes that had taken place in Ireland, and never alluded to them, or suffered me to speak of my misfortunes.

As time passed away I became more calm: misery had her dwelling in my heart, but I no longer talked in the same incoherent manner of my own crimes; sufficient for me was the consciousness of them. By the utmost self-violence, I curbed the imperious voice of wretchedness, which sometimes desired to declare itself to the whole world; and my manners were calmer and more composed than they had ever been since my journey to the sea of ice.

A few days before we left Paris on our way to Switzerland, I received the following letter from Elizabeth: —

"My dear Friend,

"It gave me the greatest pleasure to receive a letter from my uncle dated at Paris; you are no longer at a formidable distance, and I may hope to see you in less than a fortnight. My poor cousin, how much you must have suffered! I expect to see you looking even more ill than when you quitted Geneva. This winter has been passed most miserably, tortured as I have been by anxious suspense; yet I hope to see peace in your countenance, and to find that your heart is not totally void of comfort and tranquillity.

"Yet I fear that the same feelings now exist that made you so miserable a year ago, even perhaps augmented by time. I would not disturb you at this period, when so many misfortunes weigh upon you; but a conversation that I had with my uncle previous to his departure renders some explanation necessary before we meet.

"Explanation! you may possibly say; what can Elizabeth have to explain? If you really say this, my questions are answered, and all my doubts satisfied. But you are distant from me, and it is possible that you may dread, and yet be pleased with this explanation; and, in a probability of this being the case, I dare not any longer postpone writing what, during your absence, I have often wished to express to you, but have never had the courage to begin.

"You well know, Victor, that our union had been the favourite plan of your parents ever since our infancy. We were told this when young, and taught to look forward to it as an event that would certainly take place. We were affectionate playfellows during childhood, and, I believe, dear and valued friends to one another as we grew older. But as brother and sister often entertain a lively affection towards each other, without desiring a more intimate union, may not such also be our case? Tell me, dearest Victor. Answer me, I conjure you, by our mutual happiness, with simple truth — Do you not love another?

"You have travelled; you have spent several years of your life at Ingolstadt; and I confess to you, my friend, that when I saw you last autumn so unhappy, flying to solitude, from the society of every creature, I could not help supposing that you might regret our connection, and believe yourself bound in honour to fulfil the wishes of your parents, although they opposed themselves to your inclinations. But this is false reasoning. I confess to you, my friend, that I love you, and that in my airy dreams of futurity you have been my constant friend and companion. But it is your happiness I desire as well as my own, when I declare to you, that our marriage would render me eternally miserable, unless it were the dictate of your own free choice. Even now I weep to think, that, borne down as you are by the cruellest misfortunes, you may stifle, by the word *honour*, all hope of that love and happiness which would alone restore you to yourself. I, who have so disinterested an affection for you, may increase your miseries tenfold, by being an obstacle to your wishes. Ah! Victor, be assured that your cousin and playmate has too sincere a love for you not to be made miserable by this supposition. Be happy, my friend; and if you obey me in this one request, remain satisfied that nothing on earth will have the power to interrupt my tranquillity.

"Do not let this letter disturb you; do not answer tomorrow, or the next day, or even until you come, if it will give you pain. My uncle will send me news of your health; and if I see but one smile on your lips when we meet, occasioned by this or any other exertion of mine, I shall need no other happiness.

"Geneva, May 18th, 17—."
"Elizabeth Lavenza.

This letter revived in my memory what I had before forgotten, the threat of the fiend — *"I will be with you on your wedding-night!"* Such was my sentence, and on that night would the dæmon employ every art to destroy me, and tear me from the glimpse of happiness which promised partly to console my sufferings. On that night he had determined to consummate his crimes by my death. Well, be it so; a deadly struggle would then assuredly take place, in which if he were victorious I should be at peace, and his power over me be at an end. If he were vanquished, I should be a free man. Alas! what freedom? such as the peasant enjoys when his family have been massacred before his eyes, his cottage burnt, his lands laid waste, and he is turned adrift, homeless, penniless, and alone, but free. Such would be my liberty, except that in my Elizabeth I possessed a treasure; alas! balanced by those horrors of remorse and guilt, which would pursue me until death.

Sweet and beloved Elizabeth! I read and re-read her letter, and some softened feelings stole into my heart, and dared to whisper paradisiacal dreams of love and joy; but the apple was already eaten, and the angel's arm bared to drive me from all hope. Yet I would die to make her happy. If the monster executed his threat, death was inevitable; yet, again, I considered whether my marriage would hasten my fate. My destruction might indeed arrive a few months sooner; but if my torturer should suspect that I postponed it, influenced by his menaces, he would surely find other, and perhaps more dreadful means of revenge. He had vowed *to be with me on my wedding-night*, yet he did not consider that threat as binding him to peace in the mean time; for, as if to show me that he was not yet satiated with blood, he had murdered Clerval immediately after the enunciation of his threats. I resolved, therefore, that if my immediate union with my cousin would conduce either to hers or my father's happiness, my adversary's designs against my life should not retard it a single hour.

In this state of mind I wrote to Elizabeth. My letter was calm and affectionate. "I fear, my beloved girl," I said, "little happiness remains for us on earth; yet all that I may one day enjoy is centred in you. Chase away your idle fears; to you alone do I consecrate my life, and my endeavours for contentment. I have one secret, Elizabeth, a dreadful one; when revealed to you, it will chill your frame with horror, and then, far from being surprised at my misery, you will only wonder that I survive what I have endured. I will confide this tale of misery and terror to you the day after our marriage shall take place; for, my sweet cousin, there must be perfect confidence between us. But until then, I conjure you, do not mention or allude to it. This I most earnestly entreat, and I know you will comply."

In about a week after the arrival of Elizabeth's letter, we returned to Geneva. The sweet girl welcomed me with warm affection; yet tears were in her eyes, as she beheld my emaciated frame and feverish cheeks. I saw a change in her also. She was thinner, and had lost much of that heavenly vivacity that had before charmed me; but her gentleness, and soft looks of compassion, made her a more fit companion for one blasted and miserable as I was.

The tranquillity which I now enjoyed did not endure. Memory brought madness with it; and when I thought of what had passed, a real insanity possessed me; sometimes I was furious, and burnt with rage, sometimes low and despondent. I neither spoke, nor looked at any one, but sat motionless, bewildered by the multitude of miseries that overcame me.

Elizabeth alone had the power to draw me from these fits; her gentle voice would soothe me when transported by passion, and inspire me with human feelings when sunk in torpor. She wept with me, and for me. When reason returned, she would remonstrate, and endeavour to inspire me with resignation. Ah! it is well for the unfortunate to be resigned, but for the guilty there is no peace. The agonies of remorse poison the luxury there is otherwise sometimes found in indulging the excess of grief.

Soon after my arrival, my father spoke of my immediate marriage with Elizabeth. I remained silent.

"Have you, then, some other attachment?"

"None on earth. I love Elizabeth, and look forward to our union with delight. Let the day therefore be fixed; and on it I will consecrate myself, in life or death, to the happiness of my cousin."

"My dear Victor, do not speak thus. Heavy misfortunes have befallen us; but let us only cling closer to what remains, and transfer our love for those whom we have lost, to those who yet live. Our circle will be small, but bound close by the ties of affection and mutual misfortune. And when time shall have softened your despair, new and dear objects of care will be born to replace those of whom we have been so cruelly deprived."

Such were the lessons of my father. But to me the remembrance of the threat returned: nor can you wonder, that, omnipotent as the fiend had yet been in his deeds of blood, I should almost regard him as invincible; and that when he had pronounced the words, "I shall be with you on your wedding-night," I should regard the threatened fate as unavoidable. But death was no evil to me, if the loss of Elizabeth were balanced with it; and I therefore, with a contented and even cheerful countenance, agreed with my father, that if my cousin would consent, the ceremony should take place in ten days, and thus put, as I imagined, the seal to my fate.

Great God! if for one instant I had thought what might be the hellish intention of my fiendish adversary, I would rather have banished myself for ever from my native country, and wandered a friendless outcast over the earth, than have consented to this miserable marriage. But, as if possessed of magic powers, the monster had blinded me to his real intentions; and when I thought that I had prepared only my own death, I hastened that of a far dearer victim.

As the period fixed for our marriage drew nearer, whether from cowardice or a prophetic feeling, I felt my heart sink within me. But I concealed my feelings by an appearance of hilarity, that brought smiles and joy to the countenance of my father, but hardly deceived the ever-watchful and nicer eye of Elizabeth. She looked forward to our union with placid contentment, not unmingled with a little fear, which past misfortunes had impressed, that what now appeared certain and tangible happiness, might soon dissipate into an airy dream, and leave no trace but deep and everlasting regret.

Preparations were made for the event; congratulatory visits were received; and all wore a smiling appearance. I shut up, as well as I could, in my own heart the anxiety that preyed there, and entered with seeming earnestness into the plans of my father, although they might only serve as the decorations of my tragedy. Through my father's exertions, a part of the inheritance of Elizabeth had been restored to her by the Austrian government. A small possession on the shores of Como belonged to her. It was agreed that, immediately after our union, we should proceed to Villa Lavenza, and spend our first days of happiness beside the beautiful lake near which it stood.

In the mean time I took every precaution to defend my person, in case the fiend should openly attack me. I carried pistols and a dagger constantly about me, and was ever on the watch to prevent artifice; and by these means gained a greater degree of tranquillity. Indeed, as the period approached, the threat appeared more as a delusion, not to be regarded as worthy to disturb my peace, while the happiness I hoped for in my marriage wore a greater appearance of certainty, as the day fixed for its solemnisation drew nearer, and I heard it continually spoken of as an occurrence which no accident could possibly prevent.

Elizabeth seemed happy; my tranquil demeanour contributed greatly to calm her mind. But on the day that was to fulfil my wishes and my destiny, she was melancholy, and a presentiment of evil pervaded her; and perhaps also she thought of the dreadful secret which I had promised to reveal to her on the following day. My father was in the mean time overjoyed, and, in the bustle of preparation, only recognised in the melancholy of his niece the diffidence of a bride.

After the ceremony was performed, a large party assembled at my father's; but it was agreed that Elizabeth and I should commence our journey by water, sleeping that night at Evian, and continuing our voyage on the following day. The day was fair, the wind favourable, all smiled on our nuptial embarkation.

Those were the last moments of my life during which I enjoyed the feeling of happiness. We passed rapidly along: the sun was hot, but we were sheltered from its rays by a kind of canopy, while we enjoyed the beauty of the scene, sometimes on one side of the lake, where we saw Mont Salêve, the pleasant banks of Montalègre, and at a distance, surmounting all, the beautiful Mont Blanc, and the assemblage of snowy mountains that in vain endeavour to emulate her; sometimes coasting the opposite banks, we saw the mighty Jura opposing its dark side to the ambition that would quit its native country, and an almost insurmountable barrier to the invader who should wish to enslave it.

I took the hand of Elizabeth: "You are sorrowful, my love. Ah! if you knew what I have suffered, and what I may yet endure, you would endeavour to let me taste the quiet and freedom from despair, that this one day at least permits me to enjoy."

"Be happy, my dear Victor," replied Elizabeth; "there is, I hope, nothing to distress you; and be assured that if a lively joy is not painted in my face, my heart is contented. Something whispers to me not to depend too much on the prospect that is opened before us; but I will not listen to such a sinister voice. Observe how fast we move along, and how the clouds, which sometimes obscure and sometimes rise above the dome of Mont Blanc, render this scene of beauty still more interesting. Look also at the innumerable fish that are swimming in the clear waters, where we can distinguish every pebble that lies at the bottom. What a divine day! how happy and serene all nature appears!"

Thus Elizabeth endeavoured to divert her thoughts and mine from all reflection upon melancholy subjects. But her temper was fluctuating; joy for a few instants shone in her eyes, but it continually gave place to distraction and reverie.

The sun sunk lower in the heavens; we passed the river Drance, and observed its path through the chasms of the higher, and the glens of the lower hills. The Alps here come closer to the lake, and we approached the amphitheatre of mountains which forms its eastern boundary. The spire of Evian shone under the woods that surrounded it, and the range of mountain above mountain by which it was overhung.

The wind, which had hitherto carried us along with amazing rapidity, sunk at sunset to a light breeze; the soft air just ruffled the water, and caused a pleasant motion among the trees as we approached the shore, from which it wafted the most delightful scent of flowers and hay. The sun sunk beneath the horizon as we landed; and as I touched the shore, I felt those cares and fears revive, which soon were to clasp me, and cling to me for ever.

CHAPTER XXIII

It was eight o'clock when we landed; we walked for a short time on the shore, enjoying the transitory light, and then retired to the inn, and contemplated the lovely scene of waters, woods, and mountains, obscured in darkness, yet still displaying their black outlines.

The wind, which had fallen in the south, now rose with great violence in the west. The moon had reached her summit in the heavens, and was beginning to descend; the clouds swept across it swifter than the flight of the vulture, and dimmed her rays, while the lake reflected the scene of the busy heavens, rendered still busier by the restless waves that were beginning to rise. Suddenly a heavy storm of rain descended.

I had been calm during the day; but so soon as night obscured the shapes of objects, a thousand fears arose in my mind. I was anxious and watchful, while my right hand grasped a pistol which was hidden in my bosom; every sound terrified me; but I resolved that I would sell my life dearly, and not shrink from the conflict until my own life, or that of my adversary, was extinguished.

Elizabeth observed my agitation for some time in timid and fearful silence; but there was something in my glance which communicated terror to her, and trembling she asked, "What is it that agitates you, my dear Victor? What is it you fear?"

"Oh! peace, peace, my love," replied I; "this night, and all will be safe: but this night is dreadful, very dreadful."

I passed an hour in this state of mind, when suddenly I reflected how fearful the combat which I momentarily expected would be to my wife, and I earnestly entreated her to retire, resolving not to join her until I had obtained some knowledge as to the situation of my enemy.

She left me, and I continued some time walking up and down the passages of the house, and inspecting every corner that might afford a retreat to my adversary. But I discovered no trace of him, and was beginning to conjecture that some fortunate chance had intervened to prevent the execution of his menaces; when suddenly I heard a shrill and dreadful scream. It came from the room into which Elizabeth had retired. As I heard it, the whole truth rushed into my mind, my arms dropped, the motion of every muscle and fibre was suspended; I could feel the blood trickling in my veins, and tingling in the extremities of my limbs. This state lasted but for an instant; the scream was repeated, and I rushed into the room.

Great God! why did I not then expire! Why am I here to relate the destruction of the best hope, and the purest creature of earth? She was there, lifeless and inanimate, thrown across the bed, her head hanging down, and her pale and distorted features half covered by her hair. Every where I turn I see the same figure — her bloodless arms and relaxed form flung by the murderer on its bridal bier. Could I behold this, and live? Alas! life is obstinate, and clings closest where it is most hated. For a moment only did I lose recollection; I fell senseless on the ground.

When I recovered, I found myself surrounded by the people of the inn; their countenances expressed a breathless terror: but the horror of others appeared only as a mockery, a shadow of the feelings that oppressed me. I escaped from them to the room where lay the body of Elizabeth, my love, my wife, so lately living, so dear, so worthy. She had been moved from the posture in which I had first beheld her; and now, as she lay, her head upon her arm, and a handkerchief thrown across her face and neck, I might have supposed her asleep. I rushed towards her, and embraced her with ardour; but the deadly languor and coldness of the limbs told me, that what I now held in my arms had ceased to be the Elizabeth whom I had loved and cherished. The murderous mark of the fiend's grasp was on her neck, and the breath had ceased to issue from her lips.

While I still hung over her in the agony of despair, I happened to look up. The windows of the room had before been darkened, and I felt a kind of panic on seeing the pale yellow light of the moon illuminate the chamber. The shutters had been thrown back; and, with a sensation of horror not to be described, I saw at the open window a figure the most hideous and abhorred. A grin was on the face of the monster; he seemed to jeer, as with his fiendish finger he pointed towards the corpse of my wife. I rushed towards the window, and drawing a pistol from my bosom, fired; but he eluded me, leaped from his station, and, running with the swiftness of lightning, plunged into the lake.

The report of the pistol brought a crowd into the room. I pointed to the spot where he had disappeared, and we followed the track with boats; nets were cast, but in vain. After passing several hours, we returned hopeless, most of my companions believing it to have been a form conjured up by my fancy. After having landed, they proceeded to search the country, parties going in different directions among the woods and vines.

I attempted to accompany them, and proceeded a short distance from the house; but my head whirled round, my steps were like those of a drunken man, I fell at last in a state of utter exhaustion; a film covered my eyes, and my skin was parched with the heat of fever. In this state I was carried back, and placed on a bed, hardly conscious of what had happened; my eyes wandered around the room, as if to seek something that I had lost.

After an interval, I arose, and, as if by instinct, crawled into the room where the corpse of my beloved lay. There were women weeping around — I hung over it, and joined my sad tears to theirs — all this time no distinct idea presented itself to my mind; but my thoughts rambled to various subjects, reflecting confusedly on my misfortunes, and their cause. I was bewildered in a cloud of wonder and horror. The death of William, the execution of Justine, the murder of Clerval, and lastly of my wife; even at that moment I knew not that my only remaining friends were safe from the malignity of the fiend; my father even now might be writhing under his grasp, and Ernest might be dead at his feet. This idea made me shudder, and recalled me to action. I started up, and resolved to return to Geneva with all possible speed.

There were no horses to be procured, and I must return by the lake; but the wind was unfavourable, and the rain fell in torrents. However, it was hardly morning, and I might reasonably hope to arrive by night. I hired men to row, and took an oar myself; for I had always experienced relief from mental torment in bodily exercise. But the overflowing misery I now felt, and the excess of agitation that I endured, rendered me incapable of any exertion. I threw down the oar; and leaning my head upon my hands, gave way to every gloomy idea that arose. If I looked up, I saw the scenes which were familiar to me in my happier time, and which I had contemplated but the day before in the company of her who was now but a shadow and a recollection. Tears streamed from my eyes. The rain had ceased for a moment, and I saw the fish play in the waters as they had done a few hours before; they had then been observed by Elizabeth. Nothing is so painful to the human mind as a great and sudden change. The sun might shine, or the clouds might lower: but nothing could appear to me as it had done the day before. A fiend had snatched from me every hope of future happiness: no creature had ever been so miserable as I was; so frightful an event is single in the history of man.

But why should I dwell upon the incidents that followed this last overwhelming event? Mine has been a tale of horrors; I have reached their *acme*, and what I must now relate can but be tedious to you. Know that, one by one, my friends were snatched away; I was left desolate. My own strength is exhausted; and I must tell, in a few words, what remains of my hideous narration.

I arrived at Geneva. My father and Ernest yet lived; but the former sunk under the tidings that I bore. I see him now, excellent and venerable old man! his eyes wandered in vacancy, for they had lost their charm and their delight — his Elizabeth, his more than daughter, whom he doated on with all that affection which a man feels, who in the decline of life, having few affections, clings more earnestly to those that remain. Cursed, cursed be the fiend that brought misery on his grey hairs, and

doomed him to waste in wretchedness! He could not live under the
horrors that were accumulated around him; the springs of existence
suddenly gave way: he was unable to rise from his bed, and in a few
days he died in my arms.

What then became of me? I know not; I lost sensation, and chains
and darkness were the only objects that pressed upon me. Sometimes,
indeed, I dreamt that I wandered in flowery meadows and pleasant vales
with the friends of my youth; but I awoke, and found myself in a dungeon. Melancholy followed, but by degrees I gained a clear conception
of my miseries and situation, and was then released from my prison.
For they had called me mad; and during many months, as I understood,
a solitary cell had been my habitation.

Liberty, however, had been an useless gift to me, had I not, as I
awakened to reason, at the same time awakened to revenge. As the
memory of past misfortunes pressed upon me, I began to reflect on
their cause — the monster whom I had created, the miserable dæmon
whom I had sent abroad into the world for my destruction. I was possessed by a maddening rage when I thought of him, and desired and
ardently prayed that I might have him within my grasp to wreak a great
and signal revenge on his cursed head.

Nor did my hate long confine itself to useless wishes; I began to
reflect on the best means of securing him; and for this purpose, about
a month after my release, I repaired to a criminal judge in the town, and
told him that I had an accusation to make; that I knew the destroyer of
my family; and that I required him to exert his whole authority for the
apprehension of the murderer.

The magistrate listened to me with attention and kindness: — "Be
assured, sir," said he, "no pains or exertions on my part shall be spared
to discover the villain."

"I thank you," replied I; "listen, therefore, to the deposition that
I have to make. It is indeed a tale so strange, that I should fear you
would not credit it, were there not something in truth which, however
wonderful, forces conviction. The story is too connected to be mistaken
for a dream, and I have no motive for falsehood." My manner, as I
thus addressed him, was impressive, but calm; I had formed in my own
heart a resolution to pursue my destroyer to death; and this purpose
quieted my agony, and for an interval reconciled me to life. I now related my history, briefly, but with firmness and precision, marking the
dates with accuracy, and never deviating into invective or exclamation.

The magistrate appeared at first perfectly incredulous, but as I continued he became more attentive and interested; I saw him sometimes

shudder with horror, at others a lively surprise, unmingled with disbelief, was painted on his countenance.

When I had concluded my narration, I said, "This is the being whom I accuse, and for whose seizure and punishment I call upon you to exert your whole power. It is your duty as a magistrate, and I believe and hope that your feelings as a man will not revolt from the execution of those functions on this occasion."

This address caused a considerable change in the physiognomy of my own auditor. He had heard my story with that half kind of belief that is given to a tale of spirits and supernatural events; but when he was called upon to act officially in consequence, the whole tide of his incredulity returned. He, however, answered mildly, "I would willingly afford you every aid in your pursuit; but the creature of whom you speak appears to have powers which would put all my exertions to defiance. Who can follow an animal which can traverse the sea of ice, and inhabit caves and dens where no man would venture to intrude? Besides, some months have elapsed since the commission of his crimes, and no one can conjecture to what place he has wandered, or what region he may now inhabit."

"I do not doubt that he hovers near the spot which I inhabit; and if he has indeed taken refuge in the Alps, he may be hunted like the chamois, and destroyed as a beast of prey. But I perceive your thoughts: you do not credit my narrative, and do not intend to pursue my enemy with the punishment which is his desert."

As I spoke, rage sparkled in my eyes; the magistrate was intimidated: — "You are mistaken," said he, "I will exert myself; and if it is in my power to seize the monster, be assured that he shall suffer punishment proportionate to his crimes. But I fear, from what you have yourself described to be his properties, that this will prove impracticable; and thus, while every proper measure is pursued, you should make up your mind to disappointment."

"That cannot be; but all that I can say will be of little avail. My revenge is of no moment to you; yet, while I allow it to be a vice, I confess that it is the devouring and only passion of my soul. My rage is unspeakable, when I reflect that the murderer, whom I have turned loose upon society, still exists. You refuse my just demand: I have but one resource; and I devote myself, either in my life or death, to his destruction."

I trembled with excess of agitation as I said this; there was a frenzy in my manner, and something, I doubt not, of that haughty fierceness which the martyrs of old are said to have possessed. But to a Genevan magistrate, whose mind was occupied by far other ideas than those of devotion and heroism, this elevation of mind had much the appearance of madness. He endeavoured to soothe me as a nurse does a child, and reverted to my tale as the effects of delirium.

"Man," I cried, "how ignorant art thou in thy pride of wisdom! Cease; you know not what it is you say."

I broke from the house angry and disturbed, and retired to meditate on some other mode of action.

CHAPTER XXIV

My present situation was one in which all voluntary thought was swallowed up and lost. I was hurried away by fury; revenge alone endowed me with strength and composure; it moulded my feelings, and allowed me to be calculating and calm, at periods when otherwise delirium or death would have been my portion.

My first resolution was to quit Geneva for ever; my country, which, when I was happy and beloved, was dear to me, now, in my adversity, became hateful. I provided myself with a sum of money, together with a few jewels which had belonged to my mother, and departed.

And now my wanderings began, which are to cease but with life. I have traversed a vast portion of the earth, and have endured all the hardships which travellers, in deserts and barbarous countries, are wont to meet. How I have lived I hardly know; many times have I stretched my failing limbs upon the sandy plain, and prayed for death. But revenge kept me alive; I dared not die, and leave my adversary in being.

When I quitted Geneva, my first labour was to gain some clue by which I might trace the steps of my fiendish enemy. But my plan was unsettled; and I wandered many hours round the confines of the town, uncertain what path I should pursue. As night approached, I found myself at the entrance of the cemetery where William, Elizabeth, and my father reposed. I entered it, and approached the tomb which marked their graves. Every thing was silent, except the leaves of the trees, which were gently agitated by the wind; the night was nearly dark; and the scene would have been solemn and affecting even to an uninterested observer. The spirits of the departed seemed to flit around, and to cast a shadow, which was felt but not seen, around the head of the mourner.

The deep grief which this scene had at first excited quickly gave way to rage and despair. They were dead, and I lived; their murderer also lived, and to destroy him I must drag out my weary existence. I knelt on the grass, and kissed the earth, and with quivering lips exclaimed, "By the sacred earth on which I kneel, by the shades that wander near me, by the deep and eternal grief that I feel, I swear; and by thee, O Night, and the spirits that preside over thee, to pursue the dæmon, who caused this misery, until he or I shall perish in mortal conflict. For this purpose I will preserve my life: to execute this dear revenge, will I again behold the sun, and tread the green herbage of earth, which otherwise should vanish from my eyes for ever. And I call on you, spirits of the dead; and on you, wandering ministers of vengeance, to aid and conduct me in my work. Let the cursed and hellish monster drink deep of agony; let him feel the despair that now torments me."

I had begun my adjuration with solemnity, and an awe which almost assured me that the shades of my murdered friends heard and approved my devotion; but the furies possessed me as I concluded, and rage choked my utterance.

I was answered through the stillness of night by a loud and fiendish laugh. It rung on my ears long and heavily; the mountains re-echoed it, and I felt as if all hell surrounded me with mockery and laughter. Surely in that moment I should have been possessed by frenzy, and have destroyed my miserable existence, but that my vow was heard, and that I was reserved for vengeance. The laughter died away; when a well-known and abhorred voice, apparently close to my ear, addressed me in an audible whisper — "I am satisfied: miserable wretch! you have determined to live, and I am satisfied."

I darted towards the spot from which the sound proceeded; but the devil eluded my grasp. Suddenly the broad disk of the moon arose, and shone full upon his ghastly and distorted shape, as he fled with more than mortal speed.

I pursued him; and for many months this has been my task. Guided by a slight clue, I followed the windings of the Rhone, but vainly. The blue Mediterranean appeared; and, by a strange chance, I saw the fiend enter by night, and hide himself in a vessel bound for the Black Sea. I took my passage in the same ship; but he escaped, I know not how.

Amidst the wilds of Tartary and Russia, although he still evaded me, I have ever followed in his track. Sometimes the peasants, scared by this horrid apparition, informed me of his path; sometimes he himself, who feared that if I lost all trace of him, I should despair and die, left some mark to guide me. The snows descended on my head, and I saw the print of his huge step on the white plain. To you first entering on life, to whom care is new, and agony unknown, how can you understand what I have felt, and still feel? Cold, want, and fatigue, were the least pains which I was destined to endure; I was cursed by some devil, and carried about with me my eternal hell; yet still a spirit of good followed and directed my steps; and, when I most murmured, would suddenly extricate me from seemingly insurmountable difficulties. Sometimes, when nature, overcome by hunger, sunk under the exhaustion, a repast was prepared for me in the desert, that restored and inspirited me. The fare was, indeed, coarse, such as the peasants of the country ate; but I will not doubt that it was set there by the spirits that I had invoked to aid me. Often, when all was dry, the heavens cloudless, and I was parched by thirst, a slight cloud would bedim the sky, shed the few drops that revived me, and vanish.

I followed, when I could, the courses of the rivers; but the dæmon generally avoided these, as it was here that the population of the country chiefly collected. In other places human beings were seldom seen; and I generally subsisted on the wild animals that crossed my path. I had money with me, and gained the friendship of the villagers by distributing it; or I brought with me some food that I had killed, which, after taking a small part, I always presented to those who had provided me with fire and utensils for cooking.

My life, as it passed thus, was indeed hateful to me, and it was during sleep alone that I could taste joy. O blessed sleep! often, when most miserable, I sank to repose, and my dreams lulled me even to rapture. The spirits that guarded me had provided these moments, or rather hours, of happiness, that I might retain strength to fulfill my pilgrimage. Deprived of this respite, I should have sunk under my hardships. During the day I was sustained and inspirited by the hope of night: for in sleep I saw my friends, my wife, and my beloved country; again I saw the benevolent countenance of my father, heard the silver tones of my Elizabeth's voice, and beheld Clerval enjoying health and youth. Often, when wearied by a toilsome march, I persuaded myself that I was dreaming until night should come, and that I should then enjoy reality in the arms of my dearest friends. What agonising fondness did I feel for them! how did I cling to their dear forms, as sometimes they haunted even my waking hours, and persuade myself that they still lived! At such moments vengeance, that burned within me, died in my heart, and I pursued my path towards the destruction of the dæmon, more as a task enjoined by heaven, as the mechanical impulse of some power of which I was unconscious, than as the ardent desire of my soul.

What his feelings were whom I pursued I cannot know. Sometimes, indeed, he left marks in writing on the barks of the trees, or cut in stone, that guided me, and instigated my fury. "My reign is not yet over," (these words were legible in one of these inscriptions;) "you live, and my power is complete. Follow me; I seek the everlasting ices of the north, where you will feel the misery of cold and frost, to which I am impassive. You will find near this place, if you follow not too tardily, a dead hare; eat, and be refreshed. Come on, my enemy; we have yet to wrestle for our lives; but many hard and miserable hours must you endure until that period shall arrive."

Scoffing devil! Again do I vow vengeance; again do I devote thee, miserable fiend, to torture and death. Never will I give up my search, until he or I perish; and then with what ecstasy shall I join my Elizabeth, and my departed friends, who even now prepare for me the reward of my tedious toil and horrible pilgrimage!

As I still pursued my journey to the northward, the snows thickened, and the cold increased in a degree almost too severe to support. The peasants were shut up in their hovels, and only a few of the most hardy ventured forth to seize the animals whom starvation had forced from their hiding-places to seek for prey. The rivers were covered with ice, and no fish could be procured; and thus I was cut off from my chief article of maintenance.

The triumph of my enemy increased with the difficulty of my labours. One inscription that he left was in these words: — "Prepare! your toils only begin: wrap yourself in furs, and provide food; for we shall soon enter upon a journey where your sufferings will satisfy my everlasting hatred."

My courage and perseverance were invigorated by these scoffing words; I resolved not to fail in my purpose; and, calling on Heaven to support me, I continued with unabated fervour to traverse immense deserts, until the ocean appeared at a distance, and formed the utmost boundary of the horizon. Oh! how unlike it was to the blue seas of the south! Covered with ice, it was only to be distinguished from land by its superior wildness and ruggedness. The Greeks wept for joy when they beheld the Mediterranean from the hills of Asia, and hailed with rapture the boundary of their toils. I did not weep; but I knelt down, and, with a full heart, thanked my guiding spirit for conducting me in safety to the place where I hoped, notwithstanding my adversary's gibe, to meet and grapple with him.

Some weeks before this period I had procured a sledge and dogs, and thus traversed the snows with inconceivable speed. I know not whether the fiend possessed the same advantages; but I found that, as before I had daily lost ground in the pursuit, I now gained on him: so much so, that when I first saw the ocean, he was but one day's journey in advance, and I hoped to intercept him before he should reach the beach. With new courage, therefore, I pressed on, and in two days arrived at a wretched hamlet on the sea-shore. I enquired of the inhabitants concerning the fiend, and gained accurate information. A gigantic monster, they said, had arrived the night before, armed with a gun and many pistols; putting to flight the inhabitants of a solitary cottage, through fear of his terrific appearance. He had carried off their store of winter food, and, placing it in a sledge, to draw which he had seized on a numerous drove of trained dogs, he had harnessed them, and the same night, to the joy of the horror-struck villagers, had pursued his journey across the sea in a direction that led to no land; and they conjectured that he must speedily be destroyed by the breaking of the ice, or frozen by the eternal frosts.

On hearing this information, I suffered a temporary access of despair. He had escaped me; and I must commence a destructive and almost endless journey across the mountainous ices of the ocean, — amidst cold that few of the inhabitants could long endure, and which I, the native of a genial and sunny climate, could not hope to survive. Yet at the idea that the fiend should live and be triumphant, my rage and vengeance returned, and, like a mighty tide, overwhelmed every other feeling. After a slight repose, during which the spirits of the dead hovered round, and instigated me to toil and revenge, I prepared for my journey.

I exchanged my land-sledge for one fashioned for the inequalities of the Frozen Ocean; and purchasing a plentiful stock of provisions, I departed from land.

I cannot guess how many days have passed since then; but I have endured misery, which nothing but the eternal sentiment of a just retribution burning within my heart could have enabled me to support. Immense and rugged mountains of ice often barred up my passage, and I often heard the thunder of the ground sea, which threatened my destruction. But again the frost came, and made the paths of the sea secure.

By the quantity of provision which I had consumed, I should guess that I had passed three weeks in this journey; and the continual protraction of hope, returning back upon the heart, often wrung bitter drops of despondency and grief from my eyes. Despair had indeed almost secured her prey, and I should soon have sunk beneath this misery. Once, after the poor animals that conveyed me had with incredible toil gained the summit of a sloping ice-mountain, and one, sinking under his fatigue, died, I viewed the expanse before me with anguish, when suddenly my eye caught a dark speck upon the dusky plain. I strained my sight to discover what it could be, and uttered a wild cry of ecstasy when I distinguished a sledge, and the distorted proportions of a well-known form within. Oh! with what a burning gush did hope revisit my heart! warm tears filled my eyes, which I hastily wiped away, that they might not intercept the view I had of the dæmon; but still my sight was dimmed by the burning drops, until, giving way to the emotions that oppressed me, I wept aloud.

But this was not the time for delay: I disencumbered the dogs of their dead companion, gave them a plentiful portion of food; and, after an hour's rest, which was absolutely necessary, and yet which was bitterly irksome to me, I continued my route. The sledge was still visible; nor did I again lose sight of it, except at the moments when for a short time some ice-rock concealed it with its intervening crags. I indeed perceptibly gained on it; and when, after nearly two days' journey, I beheld my enemy at no more than a mile distant, my heart bounded within me.

But now, when I appeared almost within grasp of my foe, my hopes were suddenly extinguished, and I lost all traces of him more utterly than I had ever done before. A ground sea was heard; the thunder of its progress, as the waters rolled and swelled beneath me, became every moment more ominous and terrific. I pressed on, but in vain. The wind arose; the sea roared; and, as with the mighty shock of an earthquake, it split, and cracked with a tremendous and overwhelming sound. The work was soon finished: in a few minutes a tumultuous sea rolled between me and my enemy, and I was left drifting on a scattered piece of ice, that was continually lessening, and thus preparing for me a hideous death.

In this manner many appalling hours passed; several of my dogs died; and I myself was about to sink under the accumulation of distress, when I saw your vessel riding at anchor, and holding forth to me hopes of succour and life. I had no conception that vessels ever came so far north, and was astounded at the sight. I quickly destroyed part of my sledge to construct oars; and by these means was enabled, with infinite fatigue, to move my ice-raft in the direction of your ship. I had determined, if you were going southward, still to trust myself to the mercy of the seas rather than abandon my purpose. I hoped to induce you to grant me a boat with which I could pursue my enemy. But your direction was northward. You took me on board when my vigour was exhausted, and I should soon have sunk under my multiplied hardships into a death which I still dread — for my task is unfulfilled.

Oh! when will my guiding spirit, in conducting me to the dæmon, allow me the rest I so much desire; or must I die, and he yet live? If I do, swear to me, Walton, that he shall not escape; that you will seek him, and satisfy my vengeance in his death. And do I dare to ask of you to undertake my pilgrimage, to endure the hardships that I have undergone? No; I am not so selfish. Yet, when I am dead, if he should appear; if the ministers of vengeance should conduct him to you, swear that he shall not live — swear that he shall not triumph over my accumulated woes, and survive to add to the list of his dark crimes. He is eloquent and persuasive; and once his words had even power over my heart; but trust him not. His soul is as hellish as his form, full of treachery and fiendlike malice. Hear him not; call on the manes of William, Justine, Clerval, Elizabeth, my father, and of the wretched Victor, and thrust your sword into his heart. I will hover near, and direct the steel aright.

Walton, *in continuation*.

August 26th, 17—.

You have read this strange and terrific story, Margaret; and do you not feel your blood congeal with horror, like that which even now curdles mine? Sometimes, seized with sudden agony, he could not continue his tale; at others, his voice broken, yet piercing, uttered with difficulty the words so replete with anguish. His fine and lovely eyes were now lighted up with indignation, now subdued to downcast sorrow, and quenched in infinite wretchedness. Sometimes he commanded his countenance and tones, and related the most horrible incidents with a tranquil voice, suppressing every mark of agitation; then, like a volcano bursting forth, his face would suddenly change to an expression of the wildest rage, as he shrieked out imprecations on his persecutor.

His tale is connected, and told with an appearance of the simplest truth, yet I own to you that the letters of Felix and Safie, which he showed me, and the apparition of the monster seen from our ship, brought to me a greater conviction of the truth of his narrative than his asseverations, however earnest and connected. Such a monster has then really existence! I cannot doubt it; yet I am lost in surprise and admiration. Sometimes I endeavoured to gain from Frankenstein the particulars of his creature's formation: but on this point he was impenetrable.

"Are you mad, my friend?" said he; "or whither does your senseless curiosity lead you? Would you also create for yourself and the world a demoniacal enemy? Peace, peace! learn my miseries, and do not seek to increase your own."

Frankenstein discovered that I made notes concerning his history: he asked to see them, and then himself corrected and augmented them in many places; but principally in giving the life and spirit to the conversations he held with his enemy. "Since you have preserved my narration," said he, "I would not that a mutilated one should go down to posterity."

Thus has a week passed away, while I have listened to the strangest tale that ever imagination formed. My thoughts, and every feeling of my soul, have been drunk up by the interest for my guest, which this tale, and his own elevated and gentle manners, have created. I wish to soothe him; yet can I counsel one so infinitely miserable, so destitute of every hope of consolation, to live? Oh, no! the only joy that he can now know will be when he composes his shattered spirit to peace and death. Yet he enjoys one comfort, the offspring of solitude and delirium: he believes, that, when in dreams he holds converse with his friends, and derives from that communion consolation for his miseries, or excitements to his vengeance, they are not the creations of his fancy, but the beings themselves who visit him from the regions of a remote world. This faith gives a solemnity to his reveries that render them to me almost as imposing and interesting as truth.

Our conversations are not always confined to his own history and misfortunes. On every point of general literature he displays unbounded knowledge, and a quick and piercing apprehension. His eloquence is forcible and touching; nor can I hear him, when he relates a pathetic incident, or endeavours to move the passions of pity or love, without tears. What a glorious creature must he have been in the days of his prosperity, when he is thus noble and godlike in ruin! He seems to feel his own worth, and the greatness of his fall.

"When younger," said he, "I believed myself destined for some great enterprise. My feelings are profound; but I possessed a coolness of judgment that fitted me for illustrious achievements. This sentiment of the worth of my nature supported me, when others would have been oppressed; for I deemed it criminal to throw away in useless grief those talents that might be useful to my fellow-creatures. When I reflected on the work I had completed, no less a one than the creation of a sensitive and rational animal, I could not rank myself with the herd of common projectors. But this thought, which supported me in the commencement of my career, now serves only to plunge me lower in the dust. All my speculations and hopes are as nothing; and, like the archangel who aspired to omnipotence, I am chained in an eternal hell. My imagination was vivid, yet my powers of analysis and application were intense; by the union of these qualities I conceived the idea, and executed the creation of a man. Even now I cannot recollect, without passion, my reveries while the work was incomplete. I trod heaven in my thoughts, now exulting in my powers, now burning with the idea of their effects. From my infancy I was imbued with high hopes and a lofty ambition; but how am I sunk! Oh! my friend, if you had known me as I once was, you would not recognise me in this state of degradation. Despondency rarely visited my heart; a high destiny seemed to bear me on, until I fell, never, never again to rise."

Must I then lose this admirable being? I have longed for a friend; I have sought one who would sympathise with and love me. Behold, on these desert seas I have found such a one; but, I fear, I have gained him only to know his value, and lose him. I would reconcile him to life, but he repulses the idea.

"I thank you, Walton," he said, "for your kind intentions towards so miserable a wretch; but when you speak of new ties, and fresh affections, think you that any can replace those who are gone? Can any man be to me as Clerval was; or any woman another Elizabeth? Even where the affections are not strongly moved by any superior excellence, the companions of our childhood always possess a certain power over our minds, which hardly any later friend can obtain. They know our infantine dispositions, which, however they may be afterwards modified, are never eradicated; and they can judge of our actions with more certain conclusions as to the integrity of our motives. A sister or a brother can never, unless indeed such symptoms have been shown early, suspect the other of fraud or false dealing, when another friend, however strongly he may be attached, may, in spite of himself, be contemplated with suspicion. But I enjoyed friends, dear not only through habit and association, but from their own merits; and wherever I am, the soothing voice of my Elizabeth, and the conversation of Clerval, will be ever whispered in my ear. They are dead; and but one feeling in such a solitude can persuade me to preserve my life. If I were engaged in any high undertaking or design, fraught with extensive utility to my fellow-creatures, then could I live to fulfil it. But such is not my destiny; I must pursue and destroy the being to whom I gave existence; then my lot on earth will be fulfilled, and I may die."

My beloved Sister,   September 2d.
  I write to you, encompassed by peril, and ignorant whether I am

ever doomed to see again dear England, and the dearer friends that inhabit it. I am surrounded by mountains of ice, which admit of no escape, and threaten every moment to crush my vessel. The brave fellows, whom I have persuaded to be my companions, look towards me for aid; but I have none to bestow. There is something terribly appalling in our situation, yet my courage and hopes do not desert me. Yet it is terrible to reflect that the lives of all these men are endangered through me. If we are lost, my mad schemes are the cause.

And what, Margaret, will be the state of your mind? You will not hear of my destruction, and you will anxiously await my return. Years will pass, and you will have visitings of despair, and yet be tortured by hope. Oh! my beloved sister, the sickening failing of your heart-felt expectations is, in prospect, more terrible to me than my own death. But you have a husband, and lovely children; you may be happy: Heaven bless you, and make you so!

My unfortunate guest regards me with the tenderest compassion. He endeavours to fill me with hope; and talks as if life were a possession which he valued. He reminds me how often the same accidents have happened to other navigators, who have attempted this sea, and, in spite of myself, he fills me with cheerful auguries. Even the sailors feel the power of his eloquence: when he speaks, they no longer despair; he rouses their energies, and, while they hear his voice, they believe these vast mountains of ice are mole-hills, which will vanish before the resolutions of man. These feelings are transitory; each day of expectation delayed fills them with fear, and I almost dread a mutiny caused by this despair.

September 5th.

A scene has just passed of such uncommon interest, that although it is highly probable that these papers may never reach you, yet I cannot forbear recording it.

We are still surrounded by mountains of ice, still in imminent danger of being crushed in their conflict. The cold is excessive, and many of my unfortunate comrades have already found a grave amidst this scene of desolation. Frankenstein has daily declined in health: a feverish fire still glimmers in his eyes; but he is exhausted, and, when suddenly roused to any exertion, he speedily sinks again into apparent lifelessness.

I mentioned in my last letter the fears I entertained of a mutiny. This morning, as I sat watching the wan countenance of my friend — his eyes half closed, and his limbs hanging listlessly, — I was roused by half a dozen of the sailors, who demanded admission into the cabin.

They entered, and their leader addressed me. He told me that he and his companions had been chosen by the other sailors to come in deputation to me, to make me a requisition, which, in justice, I could not refuse. We were immured in ice, and should probably never escape; but they feared that if, as was possible, the ice should dissipate, and a free passage be opened, I should be rash enough to continue my voyage, and lead them into fresh dangers, after they might happily have surmounted this. They insisted, therefore, that I should engage with a solemn promise, that if the vessel should be freed I would instantly direct my course southward.

This speech troubled me. I had not despaired; nor had I yet conceived the idea of returning, if set free. Yet could I, in justice, or even in possibility, refuse this demand? I hesitated before I answered; when Frankenstein, who had at first been silent, and, indeed, appeared hardly to have force enough to attend, now roused himself; his eyes sparkled, and his cheeks flushed with momentary vigour. Turning towards the men, he said —

"What do you mean? What do you demand of your captain? Are you then so easily turned from your design? Did you not call this a glorious expedition? And wherefore was it glorious? Not because the way was smooth and placid as a southern sea, but because it was full of dangers and terror; because, at every new incident, your fortitude was to be called forth, and your courage exhibited; because danger and death surrounded it, and these you were to brave and overcome. For this was it a glorious, for this was it an honourable undertaking. You were hereafter to be hailed as the benefactors of your species; your names adored, as belonging to brave men who encountered death for honour, and the benefit of mankind. And now, behold, with the first imagination of danger, or, if you will, the first mighty and terrific trial of your courage, you shrink away, and are content to be handed down as men who had not strength enough to endure cold and peril; and so, poor souls, they were chilly, and returned to their warm firesides. Why, that requires not this preparation; ye need not have come thus far, and dragged your captain to the shame of a defeat, merely to prove yourselves cowards. Oh! be men, or be more than men. Be steady to your purposes, and firm as a rock. This ice is not made of such stuff as your hearts may be; it is mutable, and cannot withstand you, if you say that it shall not. Do not return to your families with the stigma of disgrace marked on your brows. Return as heroes who have fought and conquered, and who know not what it is to turn their backs on the foe."

He spoke this with a voice so modulated to the different feelings expressed in his speech, with an eye so full of lofty design and heroism, that can you wonder that these men were moved? They looked at one another, and were unable to reply. I spoke; I told them to retire, and consider of what had been said: that I would not lead them farther north, if they strenuously desired the contrary; but that I hoped that, with reflection, their courage would return.

They retired, and I turned towards my friend; but he was sunk in languor, and almost deprived of life.

How all this will terminate, I know not; but I had rather die than return shamefully, — my purpose unfulfilled. Yet I fear such will be my fate; the men, unsupported by ideas of glory and honour, can never willingly continue to endure their present hardships.

September 7th.

The die is cast; I have consented to return, if we are not destroyed. Thus are my hopes blasted by cowardice and indecision; I come back ignorant and disappointed. It requires more philosophy than I possess, to bear this injustice with patience.

September 12th.

It is past; I am returning to England. I have lost my hopes of utility and glory; — I have lost my friend. But I will endeavour to detail these bitter circumstances to you, my dear sister; and, while I am wafted towards England, and towards you, I will not despond.

September 9th, the ice began to move, and roarings like thunder were heard at a distance, as the islands split and cracked in every direction. We were in the most imminent peril; but, as we could only remain passive, my chief attention was occupied by my unfortunate guest, whose illness increased in such a degree, that he was entirely confined to his bed. The ice cracked behind us, and was driven with force towards the north; a breeze sprung from the west, and on the 11th the passage towards the south became perfectly free. When the sailors saw this, and that their return to their native country was apparently assured, a shout of tumultuous joy broke from them, loud and long-continued. Frankenstein, who was dozing, awoke, and asked the cause of the tumult. "They shout," I said, "because they will soon return to England."

"Do you then really return?"

"Alas! yes; I cannot withstand their demands. I cannot lead them unwillingly to danger, and I must return."

"Do so, if you will; but I will not. You may give up your purpose, but mine is assigned to me by Heaven, and I dare not. I am weak; but surely the spirits who assist my vengeance will endow me with sufficient strength." Saying this, he endeavoured to spring from the bed, but the exertion was too great for him; he fell back, and fainted.

It was long before he was restored; and I often thought that life was entirely extinct. At length he opened his eyes; he breathed with difficulty, and was unable to speak. The surgeon gave him a composing draught, and ordered us to leave him undisturbed. In the mean time he told me, that my friend had certainly not many hours to live.

His sentence was pronounced; and I could only grieve, and be patient. I sat by his bed, watching him; his eyes were closed, and I thought he slept; but presently he called to me in a feeble voice, and, bidding me come near, said — "Alas! the strength I relied on is gone; I feel that I shall soon die, and he, my enemy and persecutor, may still be in being. Think not, Walton, that in the last moments of my existence I feel that burning hatred, and ardent desire of revenge, I once expressed; but I feel myself justified in desiring the death of my adversary. During these last days I have been occupied in examining my past conduct; nor do I find it blameable. In a fit of enthusiastic madness I created a rational creature, and was bound towards him, to assure, as far as was in my power, his happiness and well-being. This was my duty; but there was another still paramount to that. My duties towards the beings of my own species had greater claims to my attention, because they included a greater proportion of happiness or misery. Urged by this view, I refused, and I did right in refusing, to create a companion for the first creature. He showed unparalleled malignity and selfishness, in evil: he destroyed my friends; he devoted to destruction beings who possessed exquisite sensations, happiness, and wisdom; nor do I know where this thirst for vengeance may end. Miserable himself, that he may render no other wretched, he ought to die. The task of his destruction was mine, but I have failed. When actuated by selfishness and vicious motives, I asked you to undertake my unfinished work; and I renew this request now, when I am only induced by reason and virtue.

"Yet I cannot ask you to renounce your country and friends, to fulfil this task; and now, that you are returning to England, you will have little chance of meeting with him. But the consideration of these points, and the well balancing of what you may esteem your duties, I leave to you; my judgment and ideas are already disturbed by the near approach of death. I dare not ask you to do what I think right, for I may still be misled by passion.

"That he should live to be an instrument of mischief disturbs me; in other respects, this hour, when I momentarily expect my release, is the only happy one which I have enjoyed for several years. The forms of the beloved dead flit before me, and I hasten to their arms. Farewell, Walton! Seek happiness in tranquillity, and avoid ambition, even if it be only the apparently innocent one of distinguishing yourself in science and discoveries. Yet why do I say this? I have myself been blasted in these hopes, yet another may succeed."

His voice became fainter as he spoke; and at length, exhausted by his effort, he sunk into silence. About half an hour afterwards he attempted again to speak, but was unable; he pressed my hand feebly, and his eyes closed for ever, while the irradiation of a gentle smile passed away from his lips.

Margaret, what comment can I make on the untimely extinction of this glorious spirit? What can I say, that will enable you to understand the depth of my sorrow? All that I should express would be inadequate and feeble. My tears flow; my mind is overshadowed by a cloud of disappointment. But I journey towards England, and I may there find consolation.

I am interrupted. What do these sounds portend? It is midnight; the breeze blows fairly, and the watch on deck scarcely stir. Again; there is a sound as of a human voice, but hoarser; it comes from the cabin where the remains of Frankenstein still lie. I must arise, and examine. Good night, my sister.

Great God! what a scene has just taken place! I am yet dizzy with the remembrance of it. I hardly know whether I shall have the power to detail it; yet the tale which I have recorded would be incomplete without this final and wonderful catastrophe.

I entered the cabin, where lay the remains of my ill-fated and admirable friend. Over him hung a form which I cannot find words to describe; gigantic in stature, yet uncouth and distorted in its proportions. As he hung over the coffin, his face was concealed by long locks of ragged hair; but one vast hand was extended, in colour and apparent texture like that of a mummy. When he heard the sound of my approach, he ceased to utter exclamations of grief and horror, and sprung towards the window. Never did I behold a vision so horrible as his face, of such loathsome yet appalling hideousness. I shut my eyes involuntarily, and endeavoured to recollect what were my duties with regard to this destroyer. I called on him to stay.

He paused, looking on me with wonder; and, again turning towards the lifeless form of his creator, he seemed to forget my presence, and every feature and gesture seemed instigated by the wildest rage of some uncontrollable passion.

"That is also my victim!" he exclaimed: "in his murder my crimes are consummated; the miserable series of my being is wound to its close! Oh, Frankenstein! generous and self-devoted being! what does it avail that I now ask thee to pardon me? I, who irretrievably destroyed thee by destroying all thou lovedst. Alas! he is cold, he cannot answer me."

His voice seemed suffocated; and my first impulses, which had suggested to me the duty of obeying the dying request of my friend, in destroying his enemy, were now suspended by a mixture of curiosity and compassion. I approached this tremendous being; I dared not again raise my eyes to his face, there was something so scaring and unearthly in his ugliness. I attempted to speak, but the words died away on my lips. The monster continued to utter wild and incoherent self-reproaches. At length I gathered resolution to address him in a pause of the tempest of his passion: "Your repentance," I said, "is now superfluous. If you had listened to the voice of conscience, and heeded the stings of remorse, before you had urged your diabolical vengeance to this extremity, Frankenstein would yet have lived."

"And do you dream?" said the dæmon; "do you think that I was then dead to agony and remorse? — He," he continued, pointing to the corpse, "he suffered not in the consummation of the deed — oh! not the ten-thousandth portion of the anguish that was mine during the lingering detail of its execution. A frightful selfishness hurried me on, while my heart was poisoned with remorse. Think you that the groans of Clerval were music to my ears? My heart was fashioned to be susceptible of love and sympathy; and, when wrenched by misery to vice and hatred, it did not endure the violence of the change, without torture such as you cannot even imagine.

"After the murder of Clerval, I returned to Switzerland, heart-broken and overcome. I pitied Frankenstein; my pity amounted to horror: I abhorred myself. But when I discovered that he, the author at once of my existence and of its unspeakable torments, dared to hope for happiness; that while he accumulated wretchedness and despair upon me, he sought his own enjoyment in feelings and passions from the indulgence of which I was for ever barred, then impotent envy and bitter indignation filled me with an insatiable thirst for vengeance. I recollected my threat, and resolved that it should be accomplished. I knew that I was preparing for myself a deadly torture; but I was the slave, not the master, of an impulse, which I detested, yet could not disobey. Yet when she died! — nay, then I was not miserable. I had cast off all feeling, subdued all anguish, to riot in the excess of my despair. Evil thenceforth became my good. Urged thus far, I had no choice but to adapt my nature to an element which I had willingly chosen. The completion of my demoniacal design became an insatiable passion. And now it is ended; there is my last victim!''

I was first touched by the expressions of his misery; yet, when I called to mind what Frankenstein had said of his powers of eloquence and persuasion, and when I again cast my eyes on the lifeless form of my friend, indignation was rekindled within me. "Wretch!" I said, "it is well that you come here to whine over the desolation that you have made. You throw a torch into a pile of buildings; and, when they are consumed, you sit among the ruins, and lament the fall. Hypocritical fiend! if he whom you mourn still lived, still would he be the object, again would he become the prey, of your accursed vengeance. It is not pity that you feel; you lament only because the victim of your malignity is withdrawn from your power.''

"Oh, it is not thus — not thus,'' interrupted the being; "yet such must be the impression conveyed to you by what appears to be the purport of my actions. Yet I seek not a fellow-feeling in my misery. No sympathy may I ever find. When I first sought it, it was the love of virtue, the feelings of happiness and affection with which my whole being overflowed, that I wished to be participated. But now, that virtue has become to me a shadow, and that happiness and affection are turned into bitter and loathing despair, in what should I seek for sympathy? I am content to suffer alone, while my sufferings shall endure: when I die, I am well satisfied that abhorrence and opprobrium should load my memory. Once my fancy was soothed with dreams of virtue, of fame, and of enjoyment. Once I falsely hoped to meet with beings, who, pardoning my outward form, would love me for the excellent qualities which I was capable of unfolding. I was nourished with high thoughts of honour and devotion. But now crime has degraded me beneath the meanest animal. No guilt, no mischief, no malignity, no misery, can be found comparable to mine. When I run over the frightful catalogue of my sins, I cannot believe that I am the same creature whose thoughts were once filled with sublime and transcendent visions of the beauty and the majesty of goodness. But it is even so; the fallen angel becomes a malignant devil. Yet even that enemy of God and man had friends and associates in his desolation; I am alone.

"You, who call Frankenstein your friend, seem to have a knowledge of my crimes and his misfortunes. But, in the detail which he gave you of them, he could not sum up the hours and months of misery which I endured, wasting in impotent passions. For while I destroyed his hopes, I did not satisfy my own desires. They were for ever ardent and craving; still I desired love and fellowship, and I was still spurned. Was there no injustice in this? Am I to be thought the only criminal, when all human kind sinned against me? Why do you not hate Felix, who drove his friend from his door with contumely? Why do you not execrate the rustic who sought to destroy the saviour of his child? Nay, these are virtuous and immaculate beings! I, the miserable and the abandoned, am an abortion, to be spurned at, and kicked, and trampled on. Even now my blood boils at the recollection of this injustice.

"But it is true that I am a wretch. I have murdered the lovely and the helpless; I have strangled the innocent as they slept, and grasped to death his throat who never injured me or any other living thing. I have devoted my creator, the select specimen of all that is worthy of love and admiration among men, to misery; I have pursued him even to that irremediable ruin. There he lies, white and cold in death. You hate me; but your abhorrence cannot equal that with which I regard myself. I look on the hands which executed the deed; I think on the heart in which the imagination of it was conceived, and long for the moment when these hands will meet my eyes, when that imagination will haunt my thoughts no more.

"Fear not that I shall be the instrument of future mischief. My work is nearly complete. Neither yours nor any man's death is needed to consummate the series of my being, and accomplish that which must be done; but it requires my own. Do not think that I shall be slow to perform this sacrifice. I shall quit your vessel on the ice-raft which brought me thither, and shall seek the most northern extremity of the globe; I shall collect my funeral pile, and consume to ashes this miserable frame, that its remains may afford no light to any curious and unhallowed wretch, who would create such another as I have been. I shall die. I shall no longer feel the agonies which now consume me, or be the prey of feelings unsatisfied, yet unquenched. He is dead who called me into being; and when I shall be no more, the very remembrance of us both will speedily vanish. I shall no longer see the sun or stars, or feel the winds play on my cheeks. Light, feeling, and sense will pass away; and in this condition must I find my happiness. Some years ago, when the images which this world affords first opened upon me, when I felt the cheering warmth of summer, and heard the rustling of the leaves and the warbling of the birds, and these were all to me, I should have wept to die; now it is my only consolation. Polluted by crimes, and torn by the bitterest remorse, where can I find rest but in death?

"Farewell! I leave you, and in you the last of human kind whom these eyes will ever behold. Farewell, Frankenstein! If thou wert yet alive, and yet cherished a desire of revenge against me, it would be better satiated in my life than in my destruction. But it was not so; thou didst seek my extinction, that I might not cause greater wretchedness; and if yet, in some mode unknown to me, thou hadst not ceased to think and feel, thou wouldst not desire against me a vengeance greater than that which I feel. Blasted as thou wert, my agony was still superior to thine; for the bitter sting of remorse will not cease to rankle in my wounds until death shall close them for ever.

"But soon," he cried, with sad and solemn enthusiasm, "I shall die, and what I now feel be no longer felt. Soon these burning miseries will be extinct. I shall ascend my funeral pile triumphantly, and exult in the agony of the torturing flames. The light of that conflagration will fade away; my ashes will be swept into the sea by the winds. My spirit will sleep in peace; or if it thinks, it will not surely think thus. Farewell."

He sprung from the cabin-window, as he said this, upon the ice-raft which lay close to the vessel. He was soon borne away by the waves, and lost in darkness and distance.

THE END

PART TWO

Frankenstein:
A Case Study in
Contemporary Criticism

A Critical History of *Frankenstein*

Until the last twenty years or so, academic criticism of Mary Shelley's *Frankenstein* has been thin on the ground. The novel did receive several reviews on its publication and reissues, and it is often mentioned in nineteenth-century histories of literature. Until recently, however, most commentators focused on author rather than novel. Biographical studies appended remarks on *Frankenstein* to discussions of Mary's life as Percy Shelley's wife. Nonbiographical criticism was infrequent and tended to discuss Mary Shelley's work either in relation to Percy's and that of other Romantics, or more generally as a minor incident in other predominantly masculine literary traditions. One aspect of *Frankenstein*'s critical history, then, is this tendency not to examine the novel in its own right.

Another and related aspect of this tendency has been to focus on *Frankenstein*'s popularity and its effects on its audience. The novel's popularity has indeed been prodigious. It has been reprinted in dozens of English-language editions and translated into Japanese, Arabic, Urdu, Malayam, and most European languages; the 1942 Armed Services and Overseas editions were clearly aimed at a popular audience, as were the 1945 comic book and the many "simplified" versions designed for children; and the story's appeal is further evidenced in the number of nineteenth-century melodramas and twentieth-century horror movies based (however loosely) on the novel. Many commentators have been uneasy with this popular appeal. Early- and late-nineteenth-century reviewers were often troubled by the novel's potentially delete-rious effects on its large and low-brow audience, while academic criti-cism has found it difficult to come to terms with *Frankenstein*'s status as a noncanonical text. A collection of academic criticism on the novel, *The Endurance of "Frankenstein,"* did not appear until 1979, and even it seemed uneasy with taking the book seriously. The editors' history of the collection — first discovering "closet aficionados" of *Frankenstein* and then imagining "half-jokingly" how they might write about it — is itself half-joking, but it does evince their discomfort at applying to *Frankenstein* "the 'high seriousness' of the Arnoldian literary critic" (Le-vine and Knoepflmacher, "Preface" xi–xii). While the editors hoped to account for *Frankenstein*'s "persistent hold" on the popular imagination (xii), they also attempted to establish the novel's high seriousness so as to "rescue" it from the abyss of popular culture. More recent critics have revised this dismissive idea of low culture, in part by relocating *Frankenstein* in traditions of popular literature and taking those tradi-tions seriously.

By tracing a history of *Frankenstein* criticism, we can chart such shifts in judgments. We will see the novel taken quite seriously for its possible effect on a popular audience, revaluated and admitted to the high-culture pantheon of Romanticism, and revaluated again as a text of popular culture. We will also see a revision in views of Mary Shelley: from Percy Shelley's wife and William Godwin's daughter, to Mary Wollstonecraft's daughter, to Mary Wollstonecraft Shelley. In addition, I have attempted to prepare for Part Two of this book, its detailed intro-ductions to and exemplars of five critical methodologies, by suggesting how each of the methods arises from earlier criticism. Finally, we can begin to see why certain judgments of value get made, how and why texts fall from and return to critical favor — how, in short, a critical his-tory is constructed.

Mary Shelley's first critic was her husband Percy. Although his essay "On Frankenstein" was not published until 1832, ten years after his death, it was written in 1817 and apparently intended to counter poten-tially hostile reviews. Now, this intention is somewhat disingenuous — Percy Shelley's feigned ignorance of *Frankenstein*'s author masks his own contributions to the novel; nonetheless the review raises two issues that persist in later criticism. The first is a question: Who is finally responsi-ble for the monster's monstrosity? In Percy's view, "you" — us, soci-ety — have created the monster. He sums up the novel's "direct moral"

(12) as "Treat a person ill, and he will become wicked": "divide him, a social being, from society, and you impose upon him the irresistible obligations [of] malevolence and selfishness." But Percy also suggests that no one can finally be held responsible. The creature's crimes are not "the offspring of an unaccountable propensity to evil," so they are not his fault, but neither are they Victor Frankenstein's: rather they are "the children, as it were, of Necessity and Human Nature." Applied to a novel that conspicuously bypasses the usual reproductive process, this language of "offspring" and "children" is striking: as it suggests that "necessity" and "human nature" produced the monster, it exonerates the father-creator Victor. But as early as 1824 one commentator insisted that "justice is indisputably" on the monster's side, for "Frankenstein ought to have reflected on the means of giving happiness to the being of his creation, before he *did* create him" ("Anniversary" 198–99), and many later critics saw Victor as the source of the monster's misdeeds.

Criticism has also pursued the second issue raised in Percy Shelley's review, namely how sensational fiction might (mis)educate its readers. Praising the novel as "a source of powerful and profound emotion" (12), Percy distinguishes between serious and frivolous responses to this emotion. The reader interested in "anything beside[s] a new love-story" will "feel a responsive string touched" by the "elementary feelings" which are the novel's subject; however, only the reader "accustomed to reason deeply" on the "origin and tendency" of such feelings can "sympathize, to the full extent," with the events they produce. Here we have three levels of readers: those that read only love-stories, who are clearly below the salt if not beyond the pale; those capable of vibrating in sympathy with emotions other than the romantic; and those, fit audience though few, capable of full (because reasoned) sympathy with all the emotions represented. Percy's moral seems addressed directly to the last category, to the "you" whose reason and sympathies are to be educated through reading; the reader who does not learn this lesson could thus be as guilty of producing monsters as the novel's characters.

Others among *Frankenstein*'s first reviewers, however, feared the reader's emotions would lead to far different moral effects. Walter Scott admired the novel's "harsh and savage delineations of passion, relieved . . . by the gentler features of domestic and simple feelings," but he also faulted its "dark and gloomy views of nature and of man, bordering too closely on impiety" (249), and he criticized the "shock" (253) that "the expression, 'Creator,' applied to a mere human being" gave "some of our highest and most reverential feelings." Less evenhanded, the aptly named John Croker ridiculed the plot, sputtered over the novel's "tissue of horrible and disgusting absurdity" (382), and concluded that it would please only readers with "deplorably vitiated" tastes (385), since it "fatigues the feelings without interesting the understanding" and "inculcates no lesson of conduct, manners, or morality." Such concerns persisted. In his introduction to the 1886 edition, the Reverend Hugh Haweis admitted to "some degree of hesitation" over reissuing the novel (5). Not only did he fear that its "moral thrust — if there is any — is vague and indeterminate" (6), he compared horror stories to vivisection: "In cases where neither physical nor moral interests are furthered, many people think that such things had best be left alone." This analogy between *Frankenstein* and vivisection, which many contemporaries considered a misuse of scientific method, indicates Haweis's fear that tales of terror might provoke a similar misuse of readers' emotions. As these reviews emphasize the novel's effect on the reader, they show the importance nineteenth-century high culture attached to the formation of popular taste. This is why the popular appeal of *Frankenstein*'s Gothic terror and horror struck early critics as significant: like the monster's, the reader's moral sense might be deformed by undisciplined indulgence in sensation.

Some reviewers agreed with Percy Shelley that the novel's emphasis on sensation could be a force for good. In 1844 Richard Horne felt that *Frankenstein* "teaches the tragic results of attainment when an impetuous irresistible passion hurries on the soul to its doom"; through the novel the reader learns both "the sacrificial fires out of which humanity rises purified" and "one form of the great ministry of Pain" (228). M. A. Goldberg's 1952 article was among the first modern interpretations to recover this sense of the novel's moral purpose; in fact, she found the horror-tale elements that troubled Haweis to be integral to this purpose. In her view *Frankenstein*'s "moral context" was the eighteenth-century aesthetic that taking "pleasure in terror bears ethical and social implications" (28–29), and so the terror *Frankenstein* inspires was meant to instill its moral lesson. By relocating the novel in its social context, Goldberg's critical method reconciled its popular elements with its high moral seriousness, closed the gap between low and high culture.

Other modern critical approaches, however, kept this gap open by locating the novel not in a popular lineage of horror fiction but in more canonical traditions. One branch of such criticism established an impeccable high-culture pedigree for *Frankenstein* by taking Mary Shelley's philosophical ideas seriously. Burton Pollin claimed the novel's "respectable philosophical intent" (108) by analyzing the monster's education in terms of Locke's *Essay Concerning Human Understanding* (1689) and Condillac's *Treatise on Sensations* (1754). Other scholars found in Mary Shelley's novel the educational and political ideas of her father, philosopher William Godwin. Katherine Powers and Christopher Small saw significant parallels between her ideas and Godwin's; in contrast, Lee Sterrenburg saw *Frankenstein* as a critique of Godwin's *Enquiry concerning Political Justice*. Despite disagreements and differing emphases, all these critics assumed that *Frankenstein* was a respectable novel of ideas.

Other scholars based their claims for *Frankenstein*'s high-culture status on its literary rather than philosophical lineage. Taking their cue from the novel's subtitle, some critics read Victor as a Promethean overreacher attempting to usurp divine power; in so doing they inserted *Frankenstein* in a masculine literary tradition of Marlowe's *Dr. Faustus*, Milton's *Paradise Lost*, Byron's *Manfred*, and Percy Shelley's *Prometheus Unbound*. L. J. Swingle located Mary Shelley in the Romantic tradition via her concern with the problem of knowledge, and Harold Bloom called *Frankenstein* an examination of "the Romantic mythology of the self" (9). Such strategies for asserting the novel's merit often amounted to hooking a popular novel by a woman to a train of literary classics by men. However, P. D. Fleck contended that Mary Shelley was in fact criticizing the idealism of much Romantic literature, and Elsie B. Michie has recently stressed her "resistance to Romanticism" (32). Similarly, where some critics had seen Rousseau's *Confessions* as an unproblematic influence on Mary's novel, James O'Rourke argued that *Frankenstein* worked out a challenge to Rousseauian Romanticism.

Analyses of *Frankenstein*'s scientific ideas have followed a similar revisionist course that mirrors changes in our culture's view of science itself. One of the novel's first reviewers clearly disapproved of "the pride of Science" by which Victor "presumes to take upon himself the structure of a human being" (*Gentleman's Magazine* 334). Equating science with truth, however, later scholars often pooh-poohed *Frankenstein*'s science as inaccurate; in this view, vague descriptions of Victor's laboratory work and the monster's animation marked the novel as pseudoscience. Although Samuel Holmes Vasbinder then defended Mary Shelley's knowledge of contemporary science, other critics shifted the terms of this debate: less than enamored of science's claims to absolute knowledge and benevolent power, they saw these flawed claims as central to *Frankenstein*'s meaning. John A. Dussinger related Victor's failed experiments in alchemical science to modern civilization's rigorously econom-

ical thinking and its obsessive desire for mastery over nature. Theodore
Ziolkowski and Ray Hammond emphasized Mary Shelley's representation of scientific irresponsibility and its consequences, and Anne K.
Mellor read the novel as a feminist critique of masculine science. Laura
Kranzler recently argued that Victor Frankenstein's bypassing the female reproductive role parallels modern science's creation of sperm
banks and artificial wombs: both show a "masculine desire to claim
female (re)productivity for themselves" (45).

For some critics, taking *Frankenstein*'s science seriously has also
meant inserting the novel in a new lineage of popular literature — the
tradition of science fiction. In this revisionist literary history Judith
Spector claimed Mary Shelley as the mother of science fiction, and John
Rieder has traced the figure of "the fantastic alien" (26) from *Frankenstein* to *Star Wars*. It seems fitting that this genre, itself undergoing a
revaluation (once seen as escapist trash, it is now perceived as serious
commentary on contemporary runaway science) should find a precursor
in *Frankenstein*. This shifting critical response to the novel's science is
an especially instructive example of how one text can be accommodated
to many critical agendas.

Critics who continued to defend *Frankenstein*'s claim to high-litera-
ture status argued that, although the first novel of an inexperienced
writer, it is no simple tale of schlock horror but instead reveals a complex narrative technique and a sophisticated understanding of the problems of reading and interpretation. Richard Dunn viewed the three narratives as failed searches for a sympathetic audience; thus *Frankenstein*'s
narrative form "structurally dramatizes the failure of human community" and of more conventional novels' overly pat portrayals of such
community (408). Gay Clifford argued that *Frankenstein*'s first-person
narration avoids the "self-regarding Romantic cliché" of lonely alienation and in fact dramatizes the solipsism of its self-absorbed narrators
(604). Similarly, for John Reed the likenesses between Walton's and
Frankenstein's narratives — both men desire to benefit humanity, both
boldly go where no man has gone before — highlight thematic parallels
between the narrators' quests for Romantic transcendence. For Beth
Newman, *Frankenstein*'s frame structure and such embedded stories as
Justine's show the inadequacy of conventional modes of interpretation.
Many deconstructive critics have also pointed to the novel's concerns
about reading and the difficulties of interpretation. Henriette Lazardis
Power saw in its "nested narratives" (85) several problematics of a
writer's narrative authority. Peter Brooks suggested that Walton's letters
are addressed to readers but do not define monstrosity for them; rather

the novel "contaminates us with a residue of meaning that cannot be explained or rationalized" (220).

A set of critical methods adapted from psychoanalytic theory has been concerned less with *Frankenstein*'s literary merit than with the psychology of its characters. Morton Kaplan's Freudian reading saw in Victor the son's classic oedipal desire to displace the father in the mother's affections; furthermore, the monster's accusation against Justine enacts Victor's irrational anger against a too seductive mother. In these terms the monster is the return of Victor's repressed desire *and* hatred for the mother; as Victor's *doppelgänger* or double, the monster is the id (instinctual self) repressed by the ego (conscious self) but escaping to act out the ego's subconscious desires. For Paul Sherwin, however, seeing the monster as Victor's double replicates Victor's misreading; he argued that as readers we must reject such "overhasty recourse[s] designed to mediate or neutralize a puzzling discontinuity" (44) and instead "abide with the [novel's] discontinuities" (52).

Other psychoanalytic critics have read *Frankenstein* through Mary Shelley's psychology. U. C. Knoepflmacher called the novel "a fantasy designed to relieve deep personal anxieties" about her relation to her parents (92). Peter Dale Scott argued that Mary transferred these ambivalent emotions from her father to her husband, and that she extended these personal feelings about men into a political critique of her culture's "patriarchal despotism" (193). Other psychoanalytic readings focused on Mary's relation to her mother, Mary Wollstonecraft. Ellen Moers read *Frankenstein* through Mary Shelley's experience both *of* her mother (who died giving birth to her) and *as* a mother (several of whose children died); in this interpretation the novel is a "birth myth" (79) dramatizing the author's sense that birth and death are "hideously intermixed" (84). J. M. Hill interpreted *Frankenstein* as a Freudian "family romance" of Victor's incestuous desire for a mother's exclusive love, and thus as Mary Shelley's attempt to detach herself by "authorial otherness" from her own obsessive desire for a mother's love (339–40). In contrast, Marc Rubinstein saw the author as searching for an origin in her mother; because Wollstonecraft was criticized for both sexual license and feminist writing, however, her dual legacy created difficulties that the daughter attempts to work out through *Frankenstein*.

Some critics have applied psychoanalytic concepts not to an individual psychology but to the novel's structure. Kaplan compared *Frankenstein*'s Gothic horror form to a nightmare: both follow a structural logic in which readers/dreamers can gratify forbidden desires as long as terror disguises this gratification. Daniel Cottom saw the narrative's careful organizing structure as a Freudian displacement of repressed disorder. For Joseph Kestner, the novel's tale-within-a-tale structure is a kind of narcissism. Like this pathological egoism that turns the outer world of Others into a mirror of the self, each tale and narrator narcissistically reflects the others; hence they reveal Walton's and especially Victor's isolation and self-absorption.

Other readings of *Frankenstein* have borrowed from Lacanian psychoanalysis. Jacques Lacan postulated that when an infant enters "the Imaginary order" it begins to conceive of its self *as* a self and to form an ego, but it also retains an anxious sense of its now lost undifferentiation, of its lost union with the mother. Gradually, however, as it enters "the Symbolic order" the infant comes to accept the dominion of what Lacan calls the Law of the Father; now the infant learns to bring its ego into synch with the whole complex of social constructs that structure our relations with each other and our culture. One of these constructs is language, and Peter Brooks used this idea of "language as relation" (208) to analyze the novel's failures of communication. Elissa Marder applied Lacanian theories of women's exclusion from language to interpret *Frankenstein*'s ubiquitous dead mothers. Rosemary Jackson read the novel's fantasies of dualism as an effort to escape the Law of the Father, to regain a sense of "undifferentiated existence" by being "at one with the mother again" (48).

Jackson related the monster's disappearance at the novel's end to the suppressions enforced by masculine culture, and so her psychoanalytic reading had a feminist component. Such feminist readings of *Frankenstein* have provided instructive re-visions of many sites of earlier criticism: Mary's relations with her parents and husband; her position in the literary traditions of Romanticism and the Gothic novel; the significance of *Frankenstein*'s mothers and other women; most generally, all the ramifications of the fact that it was written by a woman.

Frankenstein was published anonymously, and most early reviews assumed it was written by a man; when "the name of Shelley was whispered," as *Blackwood's* noted in 1823, the Shelley in question was assumed to be Percy. This reviewer also recorded his surprise at finding the author to be Mary: "For a man [the novel] was excellent, but for a woman it was wonderful" (qtd. in Grylls 319). Some seventy years later, Richard Garnett's introduction to his edition of Mary Shelley's works took the same patronizing tone: *Frankenstein* is superior to anything she wrote after Percy Shelley's death, he explained, because "her brain, magnetized by his companionship, was capable of an effort never to be repeated" (v). In contrast, a woman contemporary of Garnett reversed the magnetic poles: Florence Marshall found Mary Shelley's "sustaining and refining influence" (2.325) to be "in great measure" (1.2) responsible for Percy Shelley's achievements. To a point this was a feminist statement, but it exemplified the limited or "domestic" feminism in which women's roles and qualities are highly valued but severely restricted to home and family. At times Marshall herself was uneasy with this limitation: although she claimed that "to love [Percy] Shelley adequately and worthily" was "a vocation, a career — enough for a lifetime" (2.317), she also admitted that Mary Shelley's "free growth" as a writer was "checked" by her marriage, for "two original geniuses can rarely develop side by side, certainly not in marriage, least of all in a happy marriage" (2.315). Written at a time when women's domestic roles and marriage itself were being revaluated, these comments prefigure some of the preoccupations of feminist criticism of *Frankenstein* during another period of such revaluation, the 1970s.

With the construction in the 1970s of a tradition of women's literature, many feminist critics revised earlier views of *Frankenstein*'s sources, its place in literary history, and its structure. Sandra Gilbert and Susan Gubar acknowledged *Paradise Lost*'s influence on *Frankenstein* but used it to argue that the novel dramatizes "the blind rejection of women by misogynistic/Miltonic patriarchy" (243). Earlier critics had postulated that Percy Shelley's revisions and additions to the novel made him a "minor collaborator" (Rieger xviii), "though always in keeping with Mary's conception" (Murray 67); against this view Mellor assembled a body of evidence from the early manuscript versions to suggest that Percy often seriously misrepresented Mary's intentions. Where earlier critics such as Paulson placed *Frankenstein* in a masculine tradition of the Gothic novel, Moers called it a female Gothic and Marcia Tillotson explored some implications of this new alignment. Other critics saw the novel's narrative structure as specifically feminist. Mary Poovey read the three narratives as a network of relations that allows Mary to both express and efface her unladylike wish for literary fame and in the process draws the reader into sympathy with this ambivalence; she also argued that in the 1831 revisions Mary attempted to align her novel and her younger self with standards of feminine propriety. For Devon Hodges, *Frankenstein* challenges a masculine narrative pattern of sequence and closure intended to master the text; as the novel's several narratives disrupt sequence and evade closure, this masculine pattern comes to "seem unnatural, inadequate" (158). Similarly, James B. Carson interpreted *Frankenstein*'s male-voiced narratives as a woman's commentary on "the male expropriation of the voice of the conventionally passive female" (435).

Another area of feminist interest was *Frankenstein*'s self-contradictory approval and critique of the "separate-spheres" ideology of domesticity. This nineteenth-century idea strictly distinguished the man's public sphere of business from the woman's private sphere of domestic duties; shoring up this distinction was the identification of certain traits (such as aggression) as naturally "masculine" and complementary traits (such as nurturance) as naturally "feminine." Kate Ellis argued that the novel's three concentric stories critique this social order "that separates 'outer' and 'inner,' the masculine sphere of discovery and the feminine sphere of domesticity" (124); as each tale moves out of its protected domesticity, narrative movement dramatizes the deficiencies of the bourgeois family sphere. For Barbara Johnson the novel conveys "the unresolvable contradictions inherent in being female" (9), the conflicting demands of a domestic ideology of nurturant femininity and Mary Shelley's desire to write.

Some critics found another critique of separate spheres in the novel's suggestion that men too have important domestic roles. Such arguments often incorporated late 1970s' feminist revisions of psychoanalysis that shifted away from the Freudian emphasis on father–son relations to a new emphasis on the mother–daughter bond and on the importance of such "feminine" traits as nurturance. But such theories risk simply replicating the separate-spheres assumption of naturally "feminine" qualities, and some *Frankenstein* criticism has tended to accept traditional gender categories. In contrast, Margaret Homans saw in *Frankenstein* "a woman's knowledge of the irrefutable independence of the [female] body" from the "projective male fantasy" (114) that constructs a "femininity" to complement "masculine" traits.

A related revaluation was the effort to rethink women's "natural" role as mother, that is, the domestic-feminism view of motherhood as women's natural right and power. In line with this view, Robert Kiely argued that Victor's presumption was not a Promethean usurpation of divine power but rather his unnatural "attempt to usurp the power of woman" to create life (165). But such an ideal of woman as "naturally" maternal raises a problem: women whose experience does not measure up to this ideology may perceive themselves as unnatural, indeed monstrous. Moers addressed this problem when she focused on Mary's experiences of childbirth as a "horror story of maternity" (85); *Franken-*

stein is thus "most feminine" — and least ideal — when it expresses a mother's "revulsion against newborn life" (81).

Alan Bewell's analysis of maternity in *Frankenstein* exemplified another revisionist critical method, that of cultural criticism. Unlike approaches that would simply locate *Frankenstein* in a historical period, Bewell's essay showed that literature and other forms of writing not only reflect their culture but also create and shape it. He interpreted Mary's maternal experience as not only biological "but also a social and discursive event" (106); that is, by comparing *Frankenstein*'s language of obstetrics with that of eighteenth-century manuals on midwifery, Bewell examined the social construction through language of such apparently "natural" events as childbirth. Similarly emphasizing literature's role in "the production of cultural representation" (243), Gayatri Spivak read the novel as a text of "English cultural identity" (254) to show how *Frankenstein* problematizes imperialism and feminist individualism. Other cultural criticism has rethought the distinction between high and low culture often used to denigrate *Frankenstein*'s popular-culture progeny. From a high-culture perspective, the novel was seen as "infinitely more complicated and suggestive" than the movies based on it (Levine and Knoepflmacher, "Preface" xiii). In contrast, Albert J. LaValley and John Rieder took such movies seriously, and Chris Baldick's recent book examined the many forms in which the idea of a Frankenstein-monster has entered high as well as low culture's discourses.

Marxist criticism too has provided a parallax view of several aspects of *Frankenstein*. Where psychoanalytic critics identified the novel's family relations as Freudian incest fantasies, Anca Vlasopolos called Victor's tendency toward incest a form of "aristocratic protectionism" (126) that "erects an aesthetics of exclusion to perpetuate its ascendancy" (133); she argued that the novel indicts this form of class selection. Where feminist critics discussed *Frankenstein*'s women in terms of domestic ideology, Vlasopolos and Daniel Cottom analyzed the class-specific traits that mark certain women as worthy of elevation into the Frankenstein family. Where other feminist critics found a critique of patriarchy in *Frankenstein*, Burton Hatlen saw the "revolutionary thrust" (42) of this critique as directed against patriarchal categories of class and gender Other; for him the novel participates in the struggle toward a classless society free of all such categories.

Two additional concepts Marxist critics have examined in *Frankenstein* are the alienation of labor and the class struggle. Where psychoanalytic theory explained the monster as Victor's *doppelgänger*, the Marxist concept of alienation gives an *economic* explanation of this relation between Victor (the creator/worker) and the monster (his creation/product). Under capitalism the workers' labor belongs not to them but to their employer, and it satisfies not their own needs but those of capital; thus the laborers become alienated from their own labor. This alienation produces what Marx calls "misshapen" workers, and Franco Moretti argued that the monster represents this deformed proletariat. For Elsie B. Michie, the creation of both the monster and the novel shows that "works of art are objective products which alienate the artist/worker" (32). The second Marxist concept, class struggle, describes the situation of capitalism: in Marx's words, "the whole of society must split into the two classes of *property owners* and propertyless *workers*" (qtd. in Moretti 83), which are antagonistic to each other. Paul O'Flinn argued that *Frankenstein* is "a straightforward allegory" of this class struggle: just as Victor's creation hounds him to death, "so too a class called into being by the bourgeoisie and yet rejected and frustrated by it will in the end turn on that class in fury and vengeance and destroy it" (199). Where other criticism explained conflicting strands in the novel through Mary's own conflicts or a Freudian model of id versus ego, O'Flinn's Marxist analysis located these conflicts not in the individual but in capitalist culture.

   With one exception, each of the pieces in this collection follows from the critical history I have been sketching. Mary Lowe-Evans's field-study essay builds on a hitherto neglected site, reader-response criticism of *Frankenstein*. David Collings's Lacanian reading discusses the Imaginary and the Symbolic realms in *Frankenstein* and thereby suggests new interactions between psychoanalytic theory and literature. In my feminist essay I join biographical data with analyses of the novel's representation of domesticity to explore the creation and constraints of gender roles. Warren Montag's Marxist essay first locates *Frankenstein* in history and then shows how history operates as a force within the text. Finally, Lee E. Heller's cultural-criticism reading connects *Frankenstein* with both contemporary issues and its popular-culture successors, so as to close the gap between high and low culture. Like the earlier collection with which this history began, all these readings testify to the endurance of critical interest in *Frankenstein*.

WORKS CITED

"The Anniversary." *Knight's Quarterly Magazine* 3 (Aug.–Nov. 1824): 195–99.

Baldick, Chris. *In Frankenstein's Shadow: Myth, Monstrosity, and Nineteenth-Century Writing.* Oxford: Clarendon, 1987.

Bewell, Alan. "An Issue of Monstrous Desire: *Frankenstein* and Obstetrics." *Yale Journal of Criticism* 2.1 (Fall 1988): 105–28.

Bloom, Harold, ed. *Mary Shelley's "Frankenstein."* New York: Chelsea, 1987.

———. Introduction. *Mary Shelley's "Frankenstein."* By Bloom. 1–11.

Brooks, Peter. "'Godlike Science/Unhallowed Arts': Language, Nature, and Monstrosity." Levine and Knoepflmacher 205–20.

Carson, James B. "Bringing the Author Forward: *Frankenstein* through Mary Shelley's Letters." *Criticism* 30.4 (Fall 1988): 431–53.

Clifford, Gay. "*Caleb Williams* and *Frankenstein*: First-Person Narratives and 'Things as They Are'." *Genre* 10 (Winter 1977): 601–17.

Cottom, Daniel. "*Frankenstein* and the Monster of Representation." *Sub-Stance* 28 (1980): 60–71.

[Croker, John.] Review of *Frankenstein; or, The Modern Prometheus. Quarterly Review* 18 (Jan. 1818): 379–85.

Dunn, Richard J. "Narrative Distance in *Frankenstein.*" *Studies in the Novel* 6.4 (Winter 1974): 408–17.

Dussinger, John A. "Kinship and Guilt in Mary Shelley's *Frankenstein.*" *Studies in the Novel* 8 (1976): 38–55.

Ellis, Kate. "Monsters in the Garden: Mary Shelley and the Bourgeois Family." Levine and Knoepflmacher 123–42.

Fleck, P. D. "Mary Shelley's Notes to Shelley's Poems and *Frankenstein.*" *Studies in Romanticism* 6 (1966–67): 226–54.

Garnett, Richard. Introduction. *Tales and Stories by Mary Wollstonecraft Shelley.* London: William Paterson, 1891. i–xi.

Gentleman's Magazine NS 88 (Apr. 1818): 334–35. Review of *Frankenstein; or, The Modern Prometheus.*

Gilbert, Sandra M., and Susan Gubar. *The Madwoman in the Attic: The Woman Writer and the Nineteenth-Century Literary Imagination.* New Haven: Yale UP, 1979. 213–47.

Goldberg, M. A. "Moral and Myth in Mrs. Shelley's *Frankenstein.*" *Keats–Shelley Journal* 8.1 (Winter 1959): 27–38.

Grylls, R. Glynn. *Mary Shelley: A Biography*. London: Oxford UP, 1938.

Hammond, Ray. *The Modern Frankenstein: Fiction Becomes Fact*. Poole: Blandford, 1986.

Hatlen, Burton. "Milton, Mary Shelley, and Patriarchy." *Bucknell Review* 28.2 (1983): 19–47.

Haweis, Hugh Reginald. Introduction. *Frankenstein, or the Modern Prometheus*. By Mrs. Shelley. London: George Routledge, 1886. 5–9.

Hill, J. M. "*Frankenstein* and the Physiognomy of Desire." *American Imago* 32.4 (1975): 335–58.

Hodges, Devon. "*Frankenstein* and the Feminine Subversion of the Novel." *Tulsa Studies in Women's Literature* 2.2 (Fall 1983): 155–64.

Homans, Margaret. *Bearing the Word: Language and Female Experience in Nineteenth-Century Women's Writing*. Chicago: U of Chicago P, 1986. 100–19.

Horne, Richard. *The Spirit of the Age*. 2 vols. London: Smith and Elder, 1844. 1:223–33.

Jackson, Rosemary. "Narcissism and Beyond: A Psychoanalytic Reading of *Frankenstein* and Fantasies of the Double." In *Aspects of Fantasy: Selected Essays from the Second International Conference on the Fantastic in Literature and Film*. Ed. William Coyle. Contributions to the Study of Science Fiction & Fantasy 19. Westport: Greenwood, 1986. 45–53.

Johnson, Barbara. "My Monster/My Self." *Diacritics* 12.2 (Summer 1982): 2–10.

Kaplan, Morton. "Fantasy of Paternity and the Doppelgänger: Mary Shelley's *Frankenstein*." In *The Unspoken Motive: A Guide to Psychoanalytic Literary Criticism*. By Kaplan and Robert Kloss. New York: Free, 1973. 119–45.

Kestner, Joseph. "Narcissism as Symptom and Structure: The Case of Mary Shelley's *Frankenstein*." In *The Nature of Identity: Essays Presented to Donald E. Haydon by the Graduate Faculty of Modern Letters, University of Tulsa*. Ed. William Weathers. Tulsa: U of Tulsa P, 1981. 15–25.

Kiely, Robert. *The Romantic Novel in England*. Cambridge: Harvard UP, 1972. 155–73.

Knoepflmacher, U. C. "Thoughts on the Aggression of Daughters." Levine and Knoepflmacher 88–119.

Kranzler, Laura. "Frankenstein and the Technological Future." *Foundation* 44 (Winter 1988–89): 42–49.

LaValley, Albert J. "The Stage and Film Children of *Frankenstein*: A Survey." Levine and Knoepflmacher 243–89.

Levine, George, and U. C. Knoepflmacher, eds. *The Endurance of Frankenstein: Essays on Mary Shelley's Novel*. Berkeley: U of California P, 1979.

——. Preface, *The Endurance of Frankenstein*. By Levine and Knoepflmacher xi–xvi.

Marder, Elissa. "The Mother Tongue in *Phèdre* and *Frankenstein*." *Yale French Studies* 76 (1989): 59–77.

Marshall, Florence. *The Life and Letters of Mary Wollstonecraft Shelley*. London: Bentley, 1889. 2 vols.

Mellor, Anne K. *Mary Shelley: Her Life, Her Fiction, Her Monsters*. New York: Routledge, 1988.

Michie, Elsie B. "Production Replaces Creation: Market Forces and *Frankenstein* as Critique of Romanticism." *Nineteenth-Century Contexts* 12.1 (1988): 27–33.

Moers, Ellen. "Female Gothic." Levine and Knoepflmacher 77–87.

Moretti, Franco. *Signs Taken for Wonders: Essays in the Sociology of Literary Forms*. Trans. Susan Fischer, David Forgacs, and David Miller. London: Verso, 1983. 83–90.

Murray, E. B. "Shelley's Contribution to Mary's *Frankenstein*." *Keats–Shelley Memorial Bulletin* 29 (1978): 50–68.

Newman, Beth. "Narratives of Seduction and the Seductions of Narrative: The Frame Structure of *Frankenstein*." *ELH* 53.1 (Spring 1986): 141–63.

O'Flinn, Paul. "Production and Reproduction: The Case of *Frankenstein*." *Literature and History* 9.2 (Autumn 1983): 194–213.

O'Rourke, James. "'Nothing More Unnatural': Mary Shelley's Revision of Rousseau." *ELH* 56.3 (Fall 1989): 543–69.

Paulson, Ronald. "Gothic Fiction and the French Revolution." *ELH* 48.3 (Fall 1981): 532–54.

Pollin, Burton R. "Philosophical and Literary Sources of *Frankenstein*." *Comparative Literature* 17.2 (Spring 1965): 97–108.

Poovey, Mary. *The Proper Lady and the Woman Writer: Ideology as Style in the Works of Mary Wollstonecraft, Mary Shelley, and Jane Austen*. Chicago: U of Chicago P, 1984. 114–42.

Power, Henriette Lazardis. "The Text as Trap: The Problem of Difference in Mary Shelley's *Frankenstein*." *Nineteenth-Century Contexts* 12.1 (1988): 85–103.

Powers, Katherine Richardson. *The Influence of William Godwin on the Novels of Mary Shelley*. New York: Arno, 1980.

Reed, John R. "Will and Fate in *Frankenstein*." *Bulletin of Research in the Humanities* 83 (1980): 319–38.

Rieder, John. "Embracing the Alien: Science Fiction in Mass Culture." *Science-Fiction Studies* 9.1 (March 1982): 26–37.

Rieger, James. Introduction. *Frankenstein; or, the Modern Prometheus* (The 1818 Text). By Mary Shelley. Ed. James Rieger. 1974; Chicago: U of Chicago P, 1982. xi–xxxvii.

Rubinstein, Marc A. "'My Accursed Origin': The Search for the Mother in *Frankenstein*." *Studies in Romanticism* 15 (Spring 1976): 165–94.

Scott, Peter Dale. "Vital Artifice: Mary, Percy, and the Psychopolitical Integrity of *Frankenstein*." Levine and Knoepflmacher 172–202.

[Scott, Walter.] Review of *Frankenstein; or, The Modern Prometheus*. *Edinburgh Magazine* NS 2 (Mar. 1818): 249–53.

Shelley, Percy Bysshe. "On Frankenstein." In *The Works of Percy Bysshe Shelley in Verse and Prose*. 8 vols. Ed. Harry Buxton Forman. London: Reeves and Turner, 1880. 7:11–14.

Sherwin, Paul. "*Frankenstein*: Creation as Catastrophe." Bloom 27–54.

Small, Christopher. *Ariel like a Harpy: Shelley, Mary, and "Frankenstein."* London: Gollancz, 1972.

Spector, Judith A. "Science Fiction and the Sex War: A Womb of One's Own." *Literature and Psychology* 31.1 (1981): 21–32.

Spivak, Gayatri Chakravorty. "Three Women's Texts and a Critique of Imperialism." *Critical Inquiry* 12.1 (1985): 243–61.

Sterrenburg, Lee. "Mary Shelley's Monster: Politics and Psyche in *Frankenstein*." Levine and Knoepflmacher 143–71.

Swingle, L. J. "Frankenstein's Monster and Its Romantic Relatives: Problems of Knowledge in English Romanticism." *Texas Studies in Literature and Language* 15.1 (Spring 1973): 51–65.

Tillotson, Marcia. "'A Forced Solitude': Mary Shelley and the Creation of Frankenstein's Monster." *The Female Gothic*. Ed. Juliann E. Fleenor. Montreal: Eden, 1983. 167–75.

Vasbinder, Samuel Holmes. *Scientific Attitudes in Mary Shelley's "Frankenstein."* Studies in Speculative Fiction 8. Ann Arbor: UMI, 1984.

Vlasopolos, Anca. "*Frankenstein*'s Hidden Skeleton: The Psycho-Politics of Oppression." *Science-Fiction Studies* 10.2 (July 1983): 125–36.

Ziolkowski, Theodore. "Science, Frankenstein, and Myth." *Sewanee Review* 89.1 (Winter 1981): 34–56.

Reader-Response Criticism
and
Frankenstein

WHAT IS READER-RESPONSE CRITICISM?

Students are routinely asked in English courses for their reactions to texts they are reading. Sometimes there are so many different reactions that we may wonder whether everyone has read the same text. And some students respond so idiosyncratically to what they read that we say their responses are "totally off the wall."

Reader-response critics are interested in the variety of our responses. Reader-response criticism raises theoretical questions about whether our responses to a work are the same as its meanings, whether a work can have as many meanings as we have responses to it, and whether some responses are more valid than, or superior to, others. It asks us to pose the following questions: What have we internalized that helps us determine what is and what isn't "off the wall"? In other words, what is the wall, and what standards help us to define it?

Reader-response criticism also provides models that are useful in answering such questions. Adena Rosmarin has suggested that a work can be likened to an incomplete work of sculpture: to see it fully, we *must* complete it imaginatively, taking care to do so in a way that responsibly takes into account what is there. An introduction to several other models of reader-response theory will allow you to understand better the reader-oriented essay that follows as well as to see a variety of ways in which, as a reader-response critic, you might respond to *Frankenstein*.

Reader-response criticism, which emerged during the 1970s, focuses on what texts do to, or in, the mind of the reader, rather than regarding a text as something with properties exclusively its own. A poem, Louise M. Rosenblatt wrote as early as 1969, "is what the reader lives through under the guidance of the text and experiences as relevant to the text." Rosenblatt knew her definition would be difficult for many to accept: "The idea that a *poem* presupposes a *reader* actively involved with a *text*," she wrote, "is particularly shocking to those seeking to emphasize the objectivity of their interpretations" (127).

Rosenblatt is implicitly referring to the formalists, the old "New Critics," when she speaks of supposedly objective interpreters shocked by the notion that readers help make poems. Formalists preferred to discuss "the poem itself," the "concrete work of art," the "real poem." And they refused to describe what a work of literature makes a reader "live through." In fact, in *The Verbal Icon* (1954), William K. Wimsatt and Monroe C. Beardsley defined as fallacious the very notion that a reader's response is part of the meaning of a literary work:

> The Affective Fallacy is a confusion between the poem and its *results* (what it *is* and what it *does*). . . . It begins by trying to derive the standards of criticism from the psychological effects of a poem and ends in impressionism and relativism. The outcome . . . is that the poem itself, as an object of specifically critical judgment, tends to disappear. (21)

Reader-response critics take issue with their formalist predecessors. Stanley Fish, author of a highly influential article entitled "Literature in the Reader: Affective Stylistics" (1970), argues that any school of criticism that would see a work of literature as an object, that would claim to describe what it *is* and never what it *does*, is guilty of misconstruing what literature and reading really are. Literature exists when it is read, Fish suggests, and its force is an affective force. Furthermore, reading is a temporal process. Formalists assume it is a spatial one as they step back and survey the literary work as if it were an object spread out before them. They may find elegant patterns in the texts they examine and reexamine, but they fail to take into account that the work is quite different to a reader who is turning the pages and being moved, or affected, by lines that appear and disappear as the reader reads.

In a discussion of the effect that a sentence penned by the seven-teenth-century physician Thomas Browne has on a reader reading, Fish pauses to say this about his analysis and also, by extension, about the overall critical strategy he has largely developed: "Whatever is persuasive and illuminating about [it] . . . is the result of my substituting for one question — what does this sentence mean? — another, more operational question — what does this sentence do?" He then quotes a line from John Milton's *Paradise Lost,* a line that refers to Satan and the other fallen angels: "Nor did they not perceive their evil plight." Whereas more traditional critics might say that the "meaning" of the line is "They did perceive their evil plight," Fish relates the uncertain move-ment of the reader's mind *to* that half-satisfying interpretation. Further-more, he declares that "the reader's inability to tell whether or not 'they' do perceive and his involuntary question . . . are part of the line's *meaning,* even though they take place in the mind, not on the page" (*Text* 26).

This stress on what pages *do* to minds pervades the writings of most, if not all, reader-response critics. Wolfgang Iser, author of *The Implied Reader* (1974) and *The Act of Reading: A Theory of Aesthetic Response* (1976), finds texts to be full of "gaps," and these gaps, or "blanks," as he sometimes calls them, powerfully affect the reader. The reader is forced to explain them, to connect what the gaps separate, literally to create in his or her mind a poem or novel or play that isn't *in* the text but that the text incites. Stephen Booth, who greatly influenced Fish, equally emphasizes what words, sentences, and passages "do." He stresses in his analyses the "reading experience that results" from a "multiplicity of organizations" in, say, a Shakespeare sonnet (*Essay* ix). Sometimes these organizations don't make complete sense, and some-times they even seem curiously contradictory. But that is precisely what interests reader-response critics, who, unlike formalists, are at least as interested in fragmentary, inconclusive, and even unfinished texts as in polished, unified works. For it is the reader's struggle to *make sense* of a challenging work that reader-response critics seek to describe.

In *Self-Consuming Artifacts: The Experience of Seventeenth-Century Lit-erature* (1972), Fish reveals his preference for literature that makes read-ers work at making meaning. He contrasts two kinds of literary presen-tation. By the phrase "rhetorical presentation," he describes literature that reflects and reinforces opinions that readers already hold; by "dia-lectical presentation," he refers to works that prod and provoke. A dia-lectical text, rather than presenting an opinion as if it were truth, chal-lenges readers to discover truths on their own. Such a text may not even have the kind of symmetry that formalist critics seek. Instead of offering a "single, sustained argument," a dialectical text, or self-consuming artifact, may be "so arranged that to enter into the spirit and assumptions of any one of [its] . . . units is implicitly to reject the spirit and assumptions of the unit immediately preceding" (*Artifacts* 9). Such a text needs a reader-response critic to elucidate its workings. Another kind of critic is likely to try to explain why the units are unified and coherent, not why such units are contradicting and "consuming" their predecessors. The reader-response critic proceeds by describing the reader's way of dealing with the sudden twists and turns that characterize the dialectical text, making the reader return to earlier passages and see them in an entirely new light.

"The value of such a procedure," Fish has written, "is predicated on the idea of meaning as *an event*," not as something "located (presumed to be embedded) *in* the utterance" or "verbal object as a thing in itself" (*Text* 28). By redefining meaning as an event, the reader-response critic once again locates meaning in time: the reader's time. A text exists and signifies while it is being read, and what it signifies or means will depend, to no small extent, on *when* it is read. (*Paradise Lost* had some meanings for a seventeenth-century Puritan that it would not have for a twentieth-century atheist.)

With the redefinition of literature as something that only exists meaningfully in the mind of the reader, with the redefinition of the literary work as a catalyst of mental events, comes a concurrent redefinition of the reader. No longer is the reader the passive recipient of those ideas that an author has planted in a text. "The reader is *active*," Rosenblatt insists (123). Fish begins "Literature in the Reader" with a similar observation: "If at this moment someone were to ask, 'what are you doing,' you might reply, 'I am reading,' and thereby acknowledge that reading is . . . something *you do*" (*Text* 22). In "How to Recognize a Poem When You See One," he is even more provocative: "Interpreters do not decode poems: they make them" (*Text* 327). Iser, in focusing critical interest on the gaps in texts, on what is not expressed, similarly redefines the reader as an active maker. In an essay entitled "Interaction between Text and Reader," he argues that what is missing from a narrative causes the reader to fill in the blanks creatively.

Iser's title implies a cooperation between reader and text that is also implied by Rosenblatt's definition of a poem as "what the reader lives through under the guidance of the text." Indeed, Rosenblatt borrowed the term "transactional" to describe the dynamics of the reading process, which in her view involves interdependent texts and readers inter-acting. The view that texts and readers make poems together, though, is not shared by *all* interpreters generally thought of as reader-response critics. Steven Mailloux has divided reader-response critics into several categories, one of which he labels "subjective." Subjective critics, like David Bleich (or Norman Holland after his conversion by Bleich), as-sume what Mailloux calls the "absolute priority of individual selves as creators of texts" (*Conventions* 31). In other words, these critics do not see the reader's response as one "guided" by the text but rather as one motivated by deep-seated, personal, psychological needs. What they find in texts is, in Holland's phrase, their own "identity theme." Hol-land has argued that as readers we use "the literary work to symbolize and finally to replicate ourselves. We work out through the text our own characteristic patterns of desire" ("UNITY" 816).

Subjective critics, as you may already have guessed, often find them-selves confronted with the following question: If all interpretation is a function of private, psychological identity, then why have so many read-ers interpreted, say, Shakespeare's *Hamlet* in the same way? Different subjective critics have answered the question differently. Holland simply has said that common identity themes exist, such as that involving an oedipal fantasy. Fish, who went through a subjectivist stage, has pro-vided a different answer. In "Interpreting the *Variorum*," he argues that the "stability of interpretation among readers" is a function of shared "interpretive strategies." These strategies, which "exist prior to the act of reading and therefore determine the shape of what is read," are held in common by "interpretive communities" such as the one comprised by American college students reading *Frankenstein* (*Text* 167, 171).

As I have suggested in the paragraph above, reader-response criti-cism is not a monolithic school of thought, as is assumed by some de-tractors who like to talk about the "School of Fish." Several of the critics mentioned thus far have, over time, adopted different versions of reader-response criticism. I have hinted at Holland's growing subjec-tivism as well as the evolution of Fish's own thought. Fish, having at first viewed meaning as the cooperative production of readers and texts, went on to become a subjectivist, and very nearly a "deconstructor" ready to suggest that all criticism is imaginative creation, fiction about literature, or *metafiction*. In developing the notion of interpretive com-munities, however, Fish has become more of a social, structuralist, reader-response critic; currently, he is engaged in studying reading com-munities and their interpretive conventions in order to understand the conditions that give rise to a work's intelligibility.

In spite of the gaps between reader-response critics and even between the assumptions that they have held at various stages of their
respective careers, all try to answer similar questions and to use similar
strategies to describe the reader's response to a given text. One question
these critics are commonly asked has already been discussed: Why do
individual readers come up with such similar interpretations if meaning
is not embedded *in* the work itself? Other recurring, troubling questions
include the following interrelated ones: Just who *is* the reader? (or, to
place the emphasis differently, Just who is *the* reader?) Aren't you
reader-response critics just talking about your own idiosyncratic responses when you describe what a line from *Paradise Lost* "does" in and
to "the reader's" mind? What about my responses? What if they're
different? Will you be willing to say that all responses are equally valid?

Fish defines "the reader" in this way: "*the* reader is the *informed*
reader." The informed reader is someone who is "sufficiently experienced as a reader to have internalized the properties of literary discourses, including everything from the most local of devices (figures of
speech, etc.) to whole genres." And, of course, the informed reader is
in full possession of the "semantic knowledge" (knowledge of idioms,
for instance) assumed by the text (*Artifacts* 406).

Other reader-response critics use terms besides "the *informed*
reader" to define "*the* reader," and these other terms mean slightly
different things. Wayne Booth uses the phrase "the implied reader" to
mean the reader "created by the work." (Only "by agreeing to play the
role of this created audience," Susan Suleiman explains, "can an actual
reader correctly understand and appreciate the work" [8].) Gerard Gen-
ette and Gerald Prince prefer to speak of "the narratee, . . . the necessary counterpart of a given narrator, that is, the person or figure who
receives a narrative" (Suleiman 13). Like Booth, Iser employs the term
"the implied reader," but he also uses "the educated reader" when he
refers to what Fish calls the "informed" or "intended" reader. Thus,
with different terms, each critic denies the claim that reader-response
criticism might lead people to think that there are as many correct interpretations of a work as there are readers to read it.

As Mailloux has shown, reader-response critics share not only questions, answers, concepts, and terms for those concepts but also strategies of reading. Two of the basic "moves," as he calls them, are to show
that a work gives readers something to do, and to describe what the
reader does by way of response. And there are more complex moves as
well. For instance, a reader-response critic might typically (1) cite direct
references to reading in the text, in order to justify the focus on reading

and show that the inside of the text is continuous with what the reader is doing; (2) show how other nonreading situations in the text nonetheless mirror the situation the reader is in ("Fish shows how in *Paradise Lost* Michael's teaching of Adam in Book XI resembles Milton's teaching of the reader throughout the poem"); and (3) show, therefore, that the reader's response is, or is perfectly analogous to, the topic of the story. For Stephen Booth, *Hamlet* is the tragic story of "an audience that cannot make up its mind." In the view of Roger Easson, Blake's *Jerusalem* "may be read as a poem about the experience of reading *Jerusalem*" (Mailloux, "Learning" 103).

In the essay that follows, Mary Lowe-Evans, like reader-response critics going all the way back to Rosenblatt, focuses on readers and what they *do*. In her own words, she analyzes "the way modern students *form* attitudes to a particular literary work, attitudes that *determine* for them what the work means" (emphasis added; 215). Following the theoretical promptings of Stanley Fish, Lowe-Evans treats reading as an experiential and experimental *process;* indeed, her essay is based on a kind of experiment that uses actual college students' experiences of reading *Frankenstein* as the grounds for her emerging interpretation of the novel. The class of students was, in Fish's terms, an "interpretive community"; their responses to the text, presumably, would turn out to be a more-or-less uniform response to what Iser would call gaps in the text — places where the text calls upon the audience to make sense of it according to associations they bring to it from their community.

One powerful set of associations shared by modern American readers, associations shared both with the text of *Frankenstein* and with one another, would of course be the several film "versions" of Mary Shelley's story. But in these films, "Frankenstein" refers mainly to the monster, and the story line revolves around the anxieties of the ghoul's victims — rather than around the fears of the human creator and his less-than-human creation. Lowe-Evans argues that the associations that modern audiences have with these popular film versions "frustrate" the process of *reading* Mary Shelley's original.

Lowe-Evans shows how modern readers respond to these frustrations, in the process treating the text as something that, though it was written in the nineteenth century, presently involves the reader in thinking about twentieth-century horror movies. The result of her approach is a fascinatingly fresh reading of *Frankenstein*, one that throws its opening and its epistolary structure (both of which have been made confusing, even off-putting, by twentieth-century versions of the story) into a new, contemporary light. The correspondence between Walton and his sister becomes a kind of metaphor for the reader's position vis-à-vis the text, for reader and text respond to each other (and thus are "co-respondents") as meaning emerges from that interaction we call reading. Because Walton's sister Margaret is or is cast by the letters in the traditional feminine role of the "encouraging, understanding, and sympathetic" person, the reader is shown to be one whose responses to the text are, from the beginning, guided by that implied or suggested role.

Like all masterful essays taking a particular, theoretical approach, Lowe-Evans's argument inevitably shades into other approaches; the fact that twentieth-century male as well as female readers are cast in the role of eighteenth-century sisters elicits a feminist awareness of the resistances inevitable in those reader-text relationships. Lowe-Evans subtly provides that awareness, in the form of a provocative suggestion about the role of education (of men and women) in Mary Shelley's day and, by extension, in our own.

READER-RESPONSE CRITICISM: A SELECTED BIBLIOGRAPHY

Some Introductions to Reader-Response Criticism

Fish, Stanley E. "Literature in the Reader: Affective Stylistics." *New Literary History* 2 (1970): 123–61. Rpt. in Fish 21–67 and in Primeau 154–79.

Freund, Elizabeth. *The Return of the Reader: Reader-Response Criticism.* London: Methuen, 1987.

Holland, Norman N. "UNITY IDENTITY TEXT SELF." *PMLA* 90 (1975): 813–22.

Holub, Robert C. *Reception Theory: A Critical Introduction.* New York: Methuen, 1984.

Mailloux, Steven. "Learning to Read: Interpretation and Reader-Response Criticism." *Studies in the Literary Imagination* 12 (1979): 93–108.

———. "Reader-Response Criticism?" *Genre* 10 (1977): 413–31.

Rosenblatt, Louise M. "Towards a Transactional Theory of Reading." *Journal of Reading Behavior* 1 (1969): 31–47. Rpt. in Primeau 121–46.

Suleiman, Susan R. "Introduction: Varieties of Audience-Oriented Criticism." Suleiman and Crossman 3–45.

Tompkins, Jane P. "An Introduction to Reader-Response Criticism." Tompkins ix–xxiv.

Reader-Response Criticism in Anthologies and Collections

Fish, Stanley Eugene. *Is There a Text in This Class? The Authority of Interpretive Communities.* Cambridge: Harvard UP, 1980. In this volume are collected most of Fish's most influential essays, including "Literature in the Reader: Affective Stylistics," "What It's Like to Read *L'Allegro* and *Il Penseroso*," "Interpreting the *Variorum*," "Is There a Text in This Class?" "How to Recognize a Poem When You See One," and "What Makes an Interpretation Acceptable?"

Garvin, Harry R., ed. *Theories of Reading, Looking, and Listening.* Lewisburg: Bucknell UP, 1981. See the essays by Cain and Rosenblatt.

Leitch, Vincent B. *American Literary Criticism from the Thirties to the Eighties.* New York: Columbia UP, 1988.

Primeau, Ronald, ed. *Influx: Essays on Literary Influence.* Port Washington: Kennikat, 1977. See the essays by Fish, Holland, and Rosenblatt.

Suleiman, Susan R., and Inge Crossman, eds. *The Reader in the Text: Essays on Audience and Interpretation.* Princeton: Princeton UP, 1980. See especially the essays by Culler, Iser, and Todorov.

Tompkins, Jane P., ed. *Reader-Response Criticism: From Formalism to Post-Structuralism.* Baltimore: Johns Hopkins UP, 1980. See especially the essays by Bleich, Fish, Holland, Prince, and Tompkins.

Reader-Response Criticism: Some Major Works

Bleich, David. *Subjective Criticism.* Baltimore: Johns Hopkins UP, 1978.

Booth, Stephen. *An Essay on Shakespeare's Sonnets.* New Haven: Yale UP, 1969.

Eco, Umberto. *The Role of the Reader.* Bloomington: Indiana UP, 1979.

Fish, Stanley Eugene. *Self-Consuming Artifacts: The Experience of Seventeenth-Century Literature.* Berkeley: U of California P, 1972.

———. *Surprised by Sin: The Reader in Paradise Lost.* 2nd ed. Berkeley: U of California P, 1971.

Holland, Norman N. *5 Readers Reading.* New Haven: Yale UP, 1975.

Iser, Wolfgang. *The Act of Reading: A Theory of Aesthetic Response.* Baltimore: Johns Hopkins UP, 1978.

———. *The Implied Reader: Patterns of Communication in Prose Fiction from Bunyan to Beckett.* Baltimore: Johns Hopkins UP, 1974.

Jauss, Hans Robert. *Toward an Aesthetic of Reception.* Trans. Timothy Bahti. Intro. Paul de Man. Brighton, Eng.: Harvester, 1982.

Mailloux, Steven. *Interpretive Conventions: The Reader in the Study of American Fiction.* Ithaca: Cornell UP, 1982.

Prince, Gerald. *Narratology.* New York: Mouton, 1982.

Exemplary Short Readings of Major Texts

Anderson, Howard. "*Tristram Shandy* and the Reader's Imagination." *PMLA* 86 (1971): 966–73.

Berger, Carole. "The Rake and the Reader in Jane Austen's Novels." *Studies in English Literature, 1500–1900* 15 (1975): 531–44.

Booth, Stephen. "On the Value of *Hamlet*." *Reinterpretations of English Drama: Selected Papers from the English Institute.* Ed. Norman Rabkin. New York: Columbia UP, 1969. 137–76.

Easson, Robert R. "William Blake and His Reader in *Jerusalem*." *Blake's Sublime Allegory.* Ed. Stuart Curran and Joseph A. Wittreich. Madison: U of Wisconsin P, 1973. 309–28.

Kirk, Carey H. "*Moby Dick:* The Challenge of Response." *Papers on Language and Literature* 13 (1977): 383–90.

Leverenz, David. "Mrs. Hawthorne's Headache: Reading *The Scarlet Letter.*" *The Scarlet Letter: A Case Study in Contemporary Criticism.* Ed. Ross C Murfin. Boston: Bedford–St. Martin's, 1991. 263–74.

Rosmarin, Adena. "Darkening the Reader: Reader-Response Criticism and *Heart of Darkness*." *Heart of Darkness: A Case Study in Contemporary Criticism.* Ed. Ross C Murfin. Boston: Bedford–St. Martin's, 1989. 148–69.

Other Works Referred to in "What Is Reader-Response Criticism?"

Wimsatt, William K., and Monroe C. Beardsley. *The Verbal Icon.* Lexington: U of Kentucky P, 1954. See especially the discussion of

"The Affective Fallacy," with which reader-response critics have so sharply disagreed.

A READER-RESPONSE PERSPECTIVE ON *FRANKENSTEIN*

MARY LOWE-EVANS

Reading with a "Nicer Eye": Responding to *Frankenstein*

In 1929 appeared a work entitled *Practical Criticism* that has influenced the way literature is taught to this day. In that work, I. A. Richards showed that recording and examining readers' responses to literature is necessary for understanding how readers and texts work together to produce meaning. Although Richards certainly would not have called himself a reader-response critic, his methods and conclusions demonstrate that readers inevitably bring to literary works preconceptions (he called them "irrelevant associations" and "stock responses") that the language of the texts may either reinforce or resist. The process whereby the preconceptions of the reader combine with the language of the work coincides with the process of making sense of the text. Having recorded a number of his students' reactions to a set of poems, Richards derived a list of barriers to literary appreciation. In his view, recognizing the barriers would make overcoming them, and thereby enhancing understanding, an easier task for students and teachers.

This essay results from a project very loosely based on Richards's methods. It shares Richards's aim of introducing a "kind of documentation [of] the contemporary state of culture" (3). My larger purpose, however, is not to examine "barriers" to literary appreciation but to analyze the way modern students form attitudes to a particular literary work, attitudes that determine for them what the work means. This account of how a group of modern students is influenced by media-inspired preconceptions, by my own interpretive prompts, and by the text of *Frankenstein* itself to derive certain meanings from the novel is based on the actual responses of college juniors and seniors. In a college literature course, I assigned *Frankenstein* and asked my students to answer in writing the questions: Whose story is this? What does the novel mean? and Is the narrator reliable?

My strategy for interpreting *Frankenstein*, and providing the students a way of interpreting it, incorporates the methods and philosophies not only of I. A. Richards, but also of Wolfgang Iser and Stanley Fish, two reader-response critics who to some extent argue against a belief, like Richards's, in the objective reality of the text. As Iser does, I presume that a literary text has an "implied reader," a term that "incorporates both the prestructuring of meaning by the text, and the reader's actualization of this potential through the reading process. It refers to the active nature of this process — which will vary historically from one age to another" (xii). *Frankenstein*, it seems to me, employs conventions described by Iser as typical of both eighteenth- and nineteenth-century novels:

> While the eighteenth-century novel reader was cast by the author in a specific role, so that he could be guided — directly, or indirectly, through affirmation or through negation — toward a conception of human nature and of reality, in the nineteenth century the reader was not told what part he was to play. Instead, he had to discover the fact that society had imposed a part on him, the object being for him eventually to take up a critical attitude toward this imposition. (xiii)

To test Iser's and my own beliefs about the implied reader, I asked my students to note, as they read *Frankenstein*, any pressure from the language of the text to assume a particular role requiring certain attitudes to the events and characters being described. And if a role is imposed, I asked, does it remain consistent throughout the work?

In order to track possible changes in their own attitudes, I directed students to jot down examples of "rhetorical signposts": words, phrases, plot configurations, and associations that "pushed" them toward their responses. Those jottings, the results of roughly two hours of class discussion, and excerpts from my class lectures are worked into this essay. To keep student reaction to *Frankenstein* as fresh as possible, I gave the customary lecture on its biographical and historical contexts only after all responses were in. During class discussions, even when conflicting interpretations had been expressed, students most often reached consensus about the meanings of various events, motifs, and characters in the novel. Not surprisingly, that consensus often (but not always) took shape under the influence of interpretations I had suggested.

Every student in the class recalled having seen some film version of *Frankenstein* prior to the course and most had seen several. None had previously read the novel. Because my class of readers all brought to the work similar preconceptions about the story of Frankenstein based on film versions but were ignorant of the novel itself, I also used the opportunity to test, albeit in a radically limited format, the theory set forth by Stanley Fish in *Is There a Text in This Class?* In contrast to I. A. Richards, Fish would argue that there is no such thing as an "irrelevant association," since all associations contribute to meaning, and that all responses are in some sense "stock," for they can be taken only from an inventory of reactions already available to a community of readers. Fish would agree, though, that the individual's response may change when that reader becomes convinced that an alternative interpretation, unavailable in his or her own "interpretive community," is superior to one that is. Using Fish's terms, I tracked the changes in "interpretive strategies," or attitudes, of the class, which I treated as an interpretive community, toward a work they were preconditioned to view as frivolous, but came to see as serious. I acted as far more than the disinterested transcriber of a process, however. Representing an interpretive community of my own — one that views *Frankenstein* as a complex treatise on situational ethics — I attempted to dislodge and even replace the students' perceptions of *Frankenstein* by persuading them to consider rhetorical signposts and gaps within the text in ways they might not otherwise have considered.

"The reader" I refer to in this essay, then, represents a composite of the most commonly expressed student responses. But when the variety of responses seems irresolvable into a single one, I refer to "the students," or to the response of an individual. I also indicate where I have consciously attempted to influence the students' attitudes. Since, under my guidance, students developed one of their most pervasive interpretive strategies in the preliminary pages of *Frankenstein* (from the Preface up to Chapter I) I focus on their developing responses to that section.

The modern consumer of film media comes to the novel *Frankenstein* conditioned to expect, first and foremost, a monster story, an entertainment. Such a tale plays on predictable human reaction to the terrifying behavior of a manlike but disproportionately powerful creature. The reader conditioned by movies mistakenly assigns the name "Frankenstein" primarily to the monster and only secondarily to the monster's creator, the mad scientist. Yet, in this contemporary perception, *Frankenstein* is not in any serious sense the monster's or the scientist's story — not an attempt, that is, to investigate the monster's

feelings, challenge the philosophy of his maker, or analyze the relationship between the two. Rather, the story is "about" the fear and anguish
the horrid creature elicits from his victims. Even those emotions, however, are not often closely examined and evaluated by the modern
viewer.

Beginning with the Preface, the preliminary pages of *Frankenstein*
provide means for the reader to break away from this conventional
monster-story bias and even from reliance on the name "Frankenstein"
to identify the novel's subject. The Preface asks that the reader exempt
the text from "the disadvantages of a mere tale of spectres or enchantment" and attend to the "*novelty* of the situations" and the way in
which the author "*innovate[s]* upon [the] combinations" of "elementary principles of human nature" (24) (emphasis mine). This is not to
be a typical monster story, then, I point out to my students, but some
new genre that represents human nature responding to unusual stimuli
in unfamiliar and complex situations. For the modern reader, the
rhetorical style of the Preface, typical of late eighteenth- and early
nineteenth-century addresses to the reader, and therefore more apparently formal than the language in modern novels, contributes to the
impression that the story to follow is likely to be more serious than
frivolous. Further on, however, the Preface seems to put *Frankenstein*
back into the tradition of monster tales and thus undercuts the seriousness of the work. For instance, one student noted the passage in the
Preface that "German stories of ghosts . . . excited . . . a playful desire
of imitation" (25) in the author. The reader, having begun to clear out
previous notions of what *Frankenstein* is about, thus again anticipates an
entertaining monster story.

But the opening pages of *Frankenstein* proper frustrate both these
tendencies established in the Preface. The reader discovers not the traditional beginning of either moral or monster tale, the straightforward
introduction of setting and characters, but a letter. Clearly marked as
the first in a series, that letter is directed to a married woman in England. The reader's confusion at apparently having been denied any
grounds for judging the novel is increased by the fact that no mention
is made either of monster or mad scientist. Instead, an unidentified
correspondent reveals to an absent sister — in whose place the reader
now sits — his fears, hopes, and ambitions about an imminent voyage
into unexplored arctic territory.

The very word "correspondent," I point out, referring to both the
sender and the recipient of the letter, encapsulates the project that *Frankenstein* now undertakes. "Co-" suggests the cooperative nature of read-

ing, the sympathy that must arise between reader and text if the reading is to continue. "Respondent" insists on a reply, an active giving back of both meaning and moral to the story. Furthermore, the epistolary form, placing the reader in the position of recipient, requires the reader to subordinate his or her usual identity and assume the role of "Mrs. Saville," a woman living in eighteenth-century London. The fact that Mrs. Saville is the first character to be named and placed in the novel, as one student noted, insinuates her importance as reader–role model. Nor is the reader left without clues about how to play this part. We learn immediately that Mrs. Saville is a beloved sister named Margaret, so concerned about her brother's plans that the brother is anxious to eliminate her "evil forebodings" by insisting on his "increasing confidence" (25–26) of success. In such ways, as Iser has noted eighteenth-century novels tend to do, *Frankenstein* provides rather obvious clues about the precise nature of the reader's role.

Even as the unnamed correspondent reassures his sister, I observe, he seeks her encouragement, understanding, and sympathy. "Do you understand this feeling?" (26) he asks, as he justifies his high ambitions, recalling his early disappointments and failures (already known to her), while congratulating himself for his perseverance. "And now, dear Margaret, do I not deserve to accomplish some great purpose? . . . Oh, that some encouraging voice would answer in the affirmative!" (27). The voice from which he urgently seeks a response, it seems, is Margaret's. The ardent correspondent signs himself, "Your affectionate brother, R. Walton" (28), disappointing the reader, who, conditioned by films, and primed by the writer's self-proclaimed ambition, half expects him to be Dr. Frankenstein.

In both form and content, I tell my students, this first letter implies a contract between reader and text. The reader, man or woman, is invited to assume an eighteenth-century, sisterly attitude toward the words on the page: loving, kind, and generally affirming. This feminine affirmation seems to encourage the text to go on. Even my male students were willing, as far as possible, to assume a sisterly role, seeing their compliance as comparable to taking the feminine point of view in a novel whose narrator is a girl or protagonist a woman.

The next five letters establish more firmly, but somewhat modify, the quality of the reader's response. Not only is Margaret's relationship to Walton and to the text clarified, but Walton's ambitions, insecurities, and virtues, especially as they affect his relationships with other characters, are further revealed. And the reader is primed to respond to *Frankenstein* according to the values Walton holds. Prominent in these letters is the notion of sympathy that, because of the various contexts in which it appears, I suggest, can be taken to include all of its connotations: affinity, association, relationship, understanding, love, and forgiveness.

In the second letter, Walton expresses his need for a friend, "a man who could sympathise with me; whose eyes would reply to mine." Furthermore, this friend should be "cultivated" (28). Walton's longing for a sympathetic, cultivated friend seems somehow connected with a fear of his own inadequate cultivation, for he repeats here a concern mentioned in the first letter, and noted by several students, about the fact that he is "self-educated" (27, 29). Indeed, he even calls his self-education an "evil" (29). The reader now begins to notice a pattern emerging in Walton's discourse that involves the interrelationship of sympathy and education. Embedded in this second letter, too, is the first of many stories within the story of Walton that reinforces the link between sympathy and education. Recounting a tale that highlights the generosity of the ship's master, Walton notes that "he is wholly uneducated [which] detracts from the interest and sympathy" he commands (30). Surprisingly, none of my students called Walton to account for his own lack of sympathy in this letter. When I asked how they felt about Walton's assessment of the uneducated (though clearly admirable) ship's master and the friendly, courageous merchants and seamen of the town, most agreed that his feeling of "difference" from them was understandable. Education, one student proposed, has a way of distancing one from those who are not so educated.

The reader learns in this second letter, too, that Walton owes his upbringing to Margaret. Accounting for his own aversion to violence, he reminds her that "my best years [were] spent under your gentle and feminine fosterage" (29). By addressing this account of his momentous and dangerous undertaking to Margaret, he solicits her continuing gentle fosterage, I contend, while including her in the adventure. Identifying with Margaret, the reader is further disposed to gently foster the text at hand.

Walton's third, and quite brief, letter reveals that he has embarked on his voyage. It is meant to reassure Margaret, but his mentioning "floating sheets of ice that continually pass us" and "stiff gales" contradicts Walton's pledge that he will not "rashly encounter danger [but] will be cool, persevering, and prudent" (31). Not only does the riskiness of Walton's business become clear in this passage but another textual pattern, of his contradictory behaviors and speeches, emerges. Responding in the established role of concerned sister, the reader is here

disappointed at the brevity of the letter, uneasy about the hazards surrounding Walton's ship, and only moderately comforted by his reassur-
ances. Still, somewhat overriding those responses is Walton's exhilarat-
ing and inspiring question: "What can stop the determined heart and
resolved will of man?" (32).

The reader who felt somewhat disappointed at the brevity of Letter
III is even more disappointed to find no salutation opening Letter IV.
By now, we await those direct and indirect calls for sympathy Walton
has transcribed in his earlier correspondence. But the detailed events
Walton presently recounts soon engross the reader and recall the conventions of the horror story that, for the most part, have been set aside
until now. Surely, the "being which had the shape of a man . . . of
gigantic stature" (32) that passes Walton's currently ice-bound ship is
the monster the reader has been waiting for. But, the reader is surprised
to find, the monster does not remain the focus of attention for long,
because another ice-traveler approaches and eventually boards Walton's
ship.

This man "was not, as the other traveller seemed to be, a savage
inhabitant of some undiscovered island, but an European" (33). Walton is so impressed by the European that he sees him as not only the
friend he had hoped for, but, possibly, the "brother of [his] heart"
(35). Walton's interest in the traveler, my students suggested, may arise
from the contradictions in the man's moods, since Walton himself is
full of contradictions. There is a "wildness, and even madness" in the
newcomer's eyes, belied by an occasional "benevolence and sweetness"
in his countenance. "Melancholy and despairing" about his failure to
capture the "dæmon" he has been pursuing across the ice (34), the
stranger strikes the reader's as well as Walton's fancy.

By now convinced that the stranger must be the mad scientist himself, the reader at first resists but later succumbs to Walton's implicit
invitation to view this man as a brother worthy of sympathy and compassion. Undoubtedly influenced by the monster film tradition, the
reader suspects what Walton does not: that this refined stranger created
the very monster he pursues. The modern reader also finds Walton's
enthusiasm for the stranger almost "too much to be believed." Several
of the young men in my class argued that "men don't talk that way
about each other." But, a majority of students finally agreed, because
this is an "old-fashioned" story, that Walton's effusions are convincing.
His enthusiasm is also more acceptable than it might otherwise have
been, the class conceded to my suggestion, because it reinforces the
sympathy–education link forged earlier. Viewing the stranger as Walton

does, then, I suggest that Margaret (and the reader) are expected also to see the stranger as a brother. The bond of kinship established between Walton and his sister-reader now begins to stretch so as to accommodate this interesting new "sibling."

The next letter, preceded by a date but without a salutation, resembles a diary entry where Walton explains to himself his intense and growing interest in his "guest." The sympathetic, sisterly reader feels with Walton, though, according to several students, the lack of a salutation has a distancing effect that somewhat modifies that sympathy. As Walton describes his increasing affection for the stranger, the pattern that began emerging in the first letter reappears: Walton reveals that his affection for this man stems in part from the man's cultivation. Furthermore, Walton finds to his great pleasure, the stranger is sympathetic in turn; as a result

> I was easily led by the sympathy which he evinced, to use the language of my heart; to give utterance to the burning ardour of my soul; and to say, with all the fervour that warmed me, how gladly I would sacrifice my fortune, my existence, my every hope, to the furtherance of my enterprise. One man's life or death were but a small price to pay for the acquirement of the knowledge which I sought; for the dominion I should acquire and transmit over the elemental foes of our race. (35)

Although already aware of Walton's enthusiasm for his own ambitious undertaking, the reader was surprised, as no doubt Margaret is, by the vehemence of Walton's "utterance." Even allowing for the florid style of writing, to which the modern reader is unaccustomed, Walton's determination to risk everything for the sake of some vague sort of knowledge seems excessive. Earlier, when soliciting approval for his journey from Margaret, Walton's commitment to his project seemed more tentative to most students. The question suggested to one of the students by this passionate confession is, Why does Walton more readily reveal the extent of his ambition to this cultivated European stranger than to his devoted sister? Walton says that he was led by the sympathy that the stranger evinced. Some students were helped to account for Walton's openness with the stranger by the similarity in their temperaments and the fact that they are both men. Other students offered that perhaps because she is content to stay home, and apparently has no such urges, Margaret would have been unsympathetic toward Walton's unbridled ambition had she been told of it directly. In any case, several students pointed out, Walton *now* reveals his excessive ambition to Margaret, even if indirectly, by transcribing his conversation with the stranger in her letter.

Thus, what I called this confession within a confession further involves Walton, the stranger, Margaret, and the reader in a community of attitudes; yet the students generally sensed a qualitative difference in the kind of sympathy each member of this community is expected to bring to Walton's story. I suggested that as the degree of sympathy owed the various participants in this tale becomes more and more problematic, the readers move toward the role cast by the nineteenth-century novelist as defined by Iser. The readers must "take up a critical attitude" (Iser xiii) toward the roles imposed on them. I attempted to give force to my suggestion by having students focus on the following passage:

> I beheld tears trickle fast from between his fingers, — a groan burst from his heaving breast. I paused; — at length he spoke, in broken accents: — "Unhappy man! Do you share my madness? Have you drank also of the intoxicating draught? Hear me, — let me reveal my tale, and you will dash the cup from your lips!" (35–36)

Despite its reproachful tone, I proposed, this outburst clearly highlights the stranger's kinship with Walton. For the first time, Walton's ambition is characterized as a type of madness, a madness the stranger shares. As he calms down, the stranger leads Walton back into a conversation during which Walton reveals his "desire of finding a friend [and his] thirst for a more intimate sympathy with a fellow mind" (36). Recalling a valued friend of his own, now "lost," the stranger agrees that friendship is invaluable but immediately retires to his cabin, leaving Walton and the reader to reflect on the "celestial" merits of his guest (36).

Rather abruptly, when the sister-reader is directly addressed, we are now reminded that the text at hand is meant to be a letter:

> Will you smile at the enthusiasm I express concerning this divine wanderer? You would not, if you saw him. You have been tutored and refined by books and retirement from the world, and you are, therefore, somewhat fastidious; but this only renders you the more fit to appreciate the extraordinary merits of this wonderful man. (36)

The exceptional and complex perspective Margaret (and therefore the reader) is asked to assume seems specifically addressed in this passage. Indulgent — for she is expected to smile at Walton's enthusiasm — yet refined and fastidious, Margaret is uniquely qualified "to appreciate the extraordinary merits of this wonderful man" (36). I suggest that not only counting on her indulgence but also complimenting her fastidiousness and refinement, Walton encourages Margaret to share his enthusiasm for his alter ego, but at the same time to check and control it. Each of the attitudes implied in Margaret's fastidious and refined indulgence is equally important to her role as reader and evaluator of the tale Walton will soon record. I point out that later on, as he tells his own story, the stranger will refer to his fiancée's "ever-watchful and nicer eye." Like "fastidious," the term "nice" implies a delicate tendency to make fine distinctions. But nice also means gentle and kind. It is through the fusion of these two sensibilities, I suggest, that the reader is meant to view *Frankenstein* with the nicer eye of an eighteenth-century woman like Margaret or Elizabeth.

The last of Walton's preliminary letters to his sister, another diary-like entry, records the stranger's purpose in relating his disastrous story: "I imagine that you may deduce an apt moral from my tale" (37). In the pages that follow, the bond that has been established among reader, Margaret, Walton, and the stranger will hold; but the tension on it will vary. The recurring and overlapping themes of sympathy and education become one with the stories of madman and monster, and apparently one with the ambiguous moral Victor Frankenstein means to convey, for those stories are themselves an education in the uses and abuses of sympathy.

In class discussion, my students interpreted the sympathy–education theme that runs through the novel in a variety of ways, but eventually they agreed on some general implications of these frequently juxtaposed concepts. Some of their interpretive strategies originated in film-induced preconceptions, others were influenced by my suggestions, and still others by pressures I cannot pin down. For example, one student noted that the monster's education influenced our sympathy by making him intelligible to us; by contrast, the monster in the film version the students saw, incapable of verbally expressing emotion, gets no sympathy. In spite of his moving tale, however, the monster in the novel cannot be allowed to survive, for, accepting Frankenstein's reasoning, most students believed the monster would be likely to terrorize the earth.

The students were especially intrigued by my suggestion that the quality of education the major characters had received seemed directly related to the quality of sympathy they could give and expect. For example, I noted that the qualities assigned most of the female characters —

cultivation, long-sufferance, inexperience in the ways of the world — remind the reader to keep a "nicer eye" on the tale, suggesting that only with the aid of such an eye, not through Walton's eye alone, can an apt moral be perceived. Furthermore, as one student observed, the novel depicts the most broadly educated and cultivated of its characters, Frankenstein himself, getting the most sympathy and indulgence from the other characters.

At this point, various students asked whether the novel therefore "means" that as we become more educated, we become less human, or at least less sympathetic — or that scientific education, in particular, is dehumanizing whereas the type of education an eighteenth-century woman received is not. It seemed to some students that experience in combination with education tended to be dehumanizing since it was the monster's experiences, contradicting what he was led to expect by his education, that inspired his violence. Furthermore, the women in the novel, educated but inexperienced, were the most unquestioningly sympathetic to other characters. But, other students noted, those women did not receive the sympathy they deserved in return. Finally, in the same discussion, the students agreed that at least one meaning of the novel might be that sympathy is necessary in all relationships, but that determining "how far to go with it" is difficult. The evidence of the novel leads to the conclusion that education can either strengthen sympathetic bonds or erect barriers between classes, sexes, and individuals. At this point, the dominant theme of the novel for the majority of students was summed up by one as "Being able to 'control' one's sympathy, to keep it in balance so that you're not hurting, and may even be helping, others, depending on what you owe them, and are fulfilling your own potential." This notion of controlled, hierarchically arranged sympathy for others, tempered by self-interest, influenced all further responses to the novel.

Because sympathy had thus far been so highly valued in the text, and because Frankenstein had described his family and friends with affectionate detail, the students were surprised when Frankenstein, away at school, so thoughtlessly neglected to correspond with his relatives. The modern reader finds it especially difficult to understand how he could put aside, for months at a time, his beautiful and adored companion, Elizabeth. Additional barriers to sympathizing with Frankenstein soon arise. When Frankenstein receives his father's letter telling of his young brother's murder, the reader knows, as Frankenstein soon will, that the monster is guilty. The reader whose sympathetic sensibilities have been aroused therefore expects Frankenstein to take this opportunity to confess. He owes his community of family and friends, clearly in danger from the monster, such a confession.

The case of Justine Moritz, the young girl accused, tried, convicted, and executed for the murder, taxes the reader's sympathy for Frankenstein almost to the limit. No argument of Frankenstein's for not revealing his own guilt in the situation seems strong enough to exonerate him. And the contrast of Elizabeth's willingness to defend the girl in the face of overwhelming condemning evidence makes Frankenstein's behavior even more reprehensible. Sympathy for Walton as champion of Frankenstein, for Frankenstein himself, and even for the text has reached its nadir. Because of Frankenstein's apparently irreparable breaking of sympathetic bonds, it is actually difficult for many students to go on reading.

Nonetheless, some students accepted Frankenstein's argument that his story would have been too bizarre to be believed. Furthermore, sympathy *is* the operative attitude for this text; realizing that, through Walton, Frankenstein in a sense confesses his sins and thus implicitly begs sympathetic forgiveness, the reader continues. This tendency to accept confession as retribution or as cause for exoneration becomes an influential interpretive strategy in the remainder of the reading process.

Next to Justine's story, the monster's tale is the most affecting passage in the novel. Nothing in most film versions of *Frankenstein* has prepared the modern reader for the monster's intelligence and sensitivity. When, after hearing the monster's poignant pleas for sympathy, Frankenstein responds, "There can be no community between you and me" (90), the reader asks "Why?" and fully understands when the monster, finding himself "unsympathised with, wished to tear up the trees, spread havoc and destruction . . . and then to have sat down and enjoyed the ruin" (118).

The reader's "Why?" is answered when Frankenstein, about to destroy the partially assembled female monster, explains that he can never risk setting the monster's progeny loose on the world. In spite of the monster's convincing case for a mate, the reader later accepts Frankenstein's reasoning that, though he has broken the bonds of sympathy with family and friends, his destroying the female monster respects a greater bond, that with civilization itself:

> Even if they were to leave Europe, and inhabit the deserts of the new world, yet one of the first results of those sympathies for which the dæmon thirsted would be children, and a race of devils

would be propagated upon the earth, who might make the very existence of the species of man a condition precarious and full of terror. Had I a right, for my own benefit, to inflict this curse upon everlasting generations? (140)

The repetitions and varieties of sympathetic types in the text had by now taught my students that the concept of sympathy is complex and the need for it universal. Implicit in the sympathies represented by the text is the notion of a hierarchy of sympathetic behavior. In such a hierarchy, one student pointed out, Walton has more right to expect sympathy from his loving sister than from an anonymous reader of his letters, which may explain why the reader is given Margaret's role. Similarly, another student suggested, the blind father of the De Lacey family owes more sympathy to his own children than to the monster, which accounts for his rejecting the monster. Frankenstein's invoking what the reader understands to be the highest order in the hierarchy of sympathies — civilization itself — almost demands the reader's compliance. In fact my students almost unanimously approved Frankenstein's decision to destroy the female monster and most of them unequivocally accepted the reasons he gave for doing so.

Familiarity with film versions of the story, in combination with various textual prompts, makes the events that follow the destruction of the monster's mate predictable, ridiculous, and almost superfluous for the modern reader. When the monster warns, ''I shall be with you on your wedding-night'' (142), the reader never doubts for a moment that it is Elizabeth's and not Frankenstein's life he threatens. In this closing section, the novel becomes the frivolous monster story the reader had expected from the beginning and any real engagement with ethical considerations seems to have ended. My attempts to arouse the students' indignation at Frankenstein's failure to take responsibility for Clerval's death and his reluctance to warn Elizabeth of imminent danger, for example, proved futile. Even Elizabeth's death failed to elicit a serious response from the students. For most of them, the ''apt moral'' Frankenstein had hoped Walton (and through him, presumably, the world) would derive from his story seems to be that in the order of sympathy we owe others, we owe most to the human race. The one event in the closing pages of the novel that held the students' critical attention was Walton's reluctant decision, at the urging of the crew, to turn back and abandon his project. In their view, this decision, paralleling Frankenstein's decision to destroy the monster's prospective companion, respects the appropriate order of sympathy.

Accounting for their final judgment of Victor Frankenstein as an essentially good man, but like the narrator Walton led astray by ambition, most students in the class agreed on several reasons. First, they had been early and repeatedly urged to see him as such a man. Once I had alerted them to the sympathy–education pattern linking Walton, the reader, and Frankenstein, they found it impossible to ignore or be unmoved by it. Furthermore, they reasoned, if the reader is like Walton's sister (as the epistolary format suggests), and Frankenstein is like Walton's brother, then the reader is meant to feel a kinship with Frankenstein.

But the emphatic, almost universal approval the students awarded Frankenstein because he was candid enough to tell his story, including those parts that made him look bad, came from strategies I did not influence and cannot explain. His very willingness to confess made Frankenstein a good person in their eyes. Several pointed out that even the monster's story, engaging as it was, was told to Walton by Frankenstein. Thus, Frankenstein gained credence by portraying the monster sympathetically when it clearly would have been to his advantage (in terms of gaining his listener's sympathy) not to. A few students did notice that Frankenstein's apparently sympathetic rendering of the monster was somewhat undercut by his repeated references to the "dæmon," but those prejudicial epithets did not outweigh Frankenstein's basic "honesty" for them.

Clearly, then, in pointing out the sympathy–education nexus, I had succeeded in alerting the students to rhetorical signposts that in turn provided them an interpretive strategy for arriving at *Frankenstein*'s "apt moral." But just as clearly, the students combined this strategy with a preconceived belief in the inherent value of confession that led them to judge the character Frankenstein differently than I do. Only one student saw Victor Frankenstein as a spoiled young man who brought death and destruction to all who loved him, simply to satisfy an intellectual whim.

The preconceptions students brought to the novel from films may partly account for their willingness to exonerate Frankenstein, for those preconceptions seem to have desensitized them to particulars of his behavior. From the beginning of Chapter I, when the epistolary format of the novel is suppressed, most students disregarded the narrative frames of Frankenstein's and the monster's stories and the complexity those frames suggest to me. That is, they took the stories to be straightforward accounts given directly to the reader by Frankenstein and the monster. Furthermore, although noting the frequent contradictions between what Frankenstein said and what he did, and the similarities between Walton and Frankenstein, they never questioned the reliability of either as a narrator. Nor did they doubt the monster's veracity.

As long as the format, incidents, and characters of the novel seemed radically different from those usually included in Frankenstein films, students seemed to have no trouble distancing themselves from their monster-story expectations. Thus, the Preface and the opening letters were tremendously influential in convincing the students that the story to come would be much more weighty than they had imagined. Mary Shelley's "old-fashioned" writing style and conventionally romantic invocations of nature also contributed to the students' respect for the story's serious theme. They readily sought "levels of meaning" in the opening pages as well as in the various unfamiliar stories embedded within the novel. But as the events in the novel more closely resembled those depicted in films, the students' drive to elicit complex meaning from the text relaxed. For them, Frankenstein's failure to anticipate the monster's murder of Elizabeth, for example, was foolish and predictable, but not particularly significant. As Iser might have predicted, then, *Frankenstein* made the students more aware that texts and cultures impose roles upon individuals that must be challenged. But, as Fish might add, the transformation this interpretive community has undergone is unavoidably constrained by previous interpretive strategies.

WORKS CITED

Fish, Stanley Eugene. *Is There a Text in This Class? The Authority of Interpretive Communities*. Cambridge: Harvard UP, 1980.

Iser, Wolfgang. *The Implied Reader: Patterns of Communication in Prose Fiction from Bunyan to Beckett*. Baltimore: Johns Hopkins UP, 1974.

Richards, I. A. *Practical Criticism*. London: Routledge, 1929.

Psychoanalytic Criticism
and
Frankenstein

WHAT IS PSYCHOANALYTIC CRITICISM?

It seems natural to think about novels in terms of dreams. Like dreams, novels are fictions, inventions of the mind that, although based on reality, are by definition not literally true. Like a novel, a dream may have some truth to tell, but, like a novel, it may need to be interpreted before that truth can be grasped.

There are other reasons why an analogy between dreams and novels seems natural. We can live vicariously through romantic fictions, much as we can through daydreams. Terrifying novels and nightmares affect us in much the same way, plunging us into an atmosphere that continues to cling, even after the last chapter has been read — or the alarm clock has sounded. Thus it is not surprising to hear someone say that Mary Shelley's *Frankenstein* is "like a dream." It describes dreams, it frightens like a nightmare, and it is a structure that allows author and reader to explore wishes, fears, and fantasies.

The notion that dreams allow such psychic explorations, of course, like the analogy between literary works and dreams, owes a great deal to the thinking of Sigmund Freud, the famous Austrian psychoanalyst who in 1900 published a seminal essay, *The Interpretation of Dreams*. But is the reader who calls *Frankenstein* a nightmarish tale a Freudian literary critic? And is it even *valid* to apply concepts advanced in 1900 to a novel written in the first half of the nineteenth century?

To some extent the answer to the first question has to be yes. Freud is one of the reasons it *seems* "natural" to think of literary works in terms of dreams. We are all Freudians, really, whether or not we have read anything by Freud. At one time or another, most of us have referred to ego, libido, complexes, unconscious desires, and sexual repression. The premises of Freud's thought have changed the way the Western world thinks about itself. To a lesser extent, we are all psychoanalytic interpreters as well. Psychoanalytic criticism has influenced the teachers our teachers learned from, the works of scholarship and criticism they read, and the critical and creative writers *we* read as well.

What Freud did was develop a language that described, a model that explained, a theory that encompassed human psychology. Many of the elements of psychology he sought to describe and explain are present in the literary works of various ages and cultures, from Sophocles' *Oedipus Rex* to Shakespeare's *Hamlet* to Mary Shelley's *Frankenstein*. When the great novel of the twenty-first century is written, many of these same elements of psychology will probably inform its discourse as well. If, by understanding human psychology according to Freud, we can appreciate literature on a new level, then we should acquaint ourselves with his insights.

Freud's theories are either directly or indirectly concerned with the nature of the unconscious mind. Freud didn't invent the notion of the unconscious; others before him had suggested that even the supposedly "sane" human mind was conscious and rational only at times, and even then at possibly only one level. But Freud went further, suggesting that the powers motivating men and women are *mainly* and *normally* unconscious.

Freud, then, powerfully developed an old idea: that the human mind is essentially dual in nature. He called the predominantly passional, irrational, unknown, and unconscious part of the psyche the *id*, or "it." The *ego*, or "I," was his term for the predominantly rational, logical, orderly, conscious part. Another aspect of the psyche, which he called the *superego*, is really a projection of the ego. The superego almost seems to be outside of the self, making moral judgments, telling us to make sacrifices for good causes even though self-sacrifice may not be quite logical or rational. And, in a sense, the superego *is* "outside," since much of what it tells us to do or think we have learned from our parents, our schools, or our religious institutions.

What the ego and superego tell us *not* to do or think is repressed, forced into the unconscious mind. One of Freud's most important contributions to the study of the psyche, the theory of repression, goes something like this: much of what lies in the unconscious mind has been put there by consciousness, which acts as a censor, driving underground unconscious or conscious thoughts or instincts that it deems unacceptable. Censored materials often involve infantile sexual desires, Freud postulated. Repressed to an unconscious state, they emerge only in disguised forms: in dreams, in language (so-called Freudian slips), in creative activity that may produce art (including literature), and in neurotic behavior.

According to Freud, all of us have repressed wishes and fears; we all have dreams in which repressed feelings and memories emerge disguised, and thus we are all potential candidates for dream analysis. One of the unconscious desires most commonly repressed is the childhood wish to displace the parent of our own sex and take his or her place in the affections of the parent of the opposite sex. This desire really involves a number of different but related wishes and fears. (A boy — and it should be remarked in passing that Freud here concerns himself mainly with the male — may fear that his father will castrate him, and he may wish that his mother would return to nursing him.) Freud referred to the whole complex of feelings by the word "oedipal," naming the complex after the Greek tragic hero Oedipus, who unwittingly killed his father and married his mother.

Why are oedipal wishes and fears repressed by the conscious side of the mind? And what happens to them after they have been censored? As Roy P. Basler puts it in *Sex, Symbolism, and Psychology in Literature* (1975), "from the beginning of recorded history such wishes have been restrained by the most powerful religious and social taboos, and as a result have come to be regarded as 'unnatural,'" even though "Freud found that such wishes are more or less characteristic of normal human development":

> In dreams, particularly, Freud found ample evidence that such wishes persisted. . . . Hence he conceived that natural urges, when identified as "wrong," may be repressed but not obliterated. . . . In the unconscious, these urges take on symbolic garb, regarded as nonsense by the waking mind that does not recognize their significance. (14)

Freud's belief in the significance of dreams, of course, was no more original than his belief that there is an unconscious side to the psyche. Again, it was the extent to which he developed a theory of how dreams work — and the extent to which that theory helped him, by analogy, to understand far more than just dreams — that made him unusual, important, and influential beyond the perimeters of medical schools and psychiatrists' offices.

The psychoanalytic approach to literature not only rests on the theories of Freud; it may even be said to have *begun* with Freud, who was interested in writers, especially those who relied heavily on symbols. Such writers regularly cloak or mystify ideas in figures that make sense only when interpreted, much as the unconscious mind of a neurotic disguises secret thoughts in dream stories or bizarre actions that need to be interpreted by an analyst. Freud's interest in literary artists led him to make some unfortunate generalizations about creativity; for example, in the twenty-third lecture in *Introductory Lectures on Psycho-Analysis* (1922), he defined the artist as "one urged on by instinctive needs that are too clamorous" (314). But it also led him to write creative literary criticism of his own, including an influential essay on "The Relation of a Poet to Daydreaming" (1908) and "The Uncanny" (1919), a provocative psychoanalytic reading of E. T. A. Hoffmann's supernatural tale "The Sandman."

Freud's application of psychoanalytic theory to literature quickly caught on. In 1909, only a year after Freud had published "The Relation of a Poet to Daydreaming," the psychoanalyst Otto Rank published *The Myth of the Birth of the Hero*. In that work, Rank subscribes to the notion that the artist turns a powerful, secret wish into a literary fantasy, and he uses Freud's notion about the "oedipal" complex to explain why the popular stories of so many heroes in literature are so similar. A year after Rank had published his psychoanalytic account of heroic texts, Ernest Jones, Freud's student and eventual biographer, turned his attention to a tragic text: Shakespeare's *Hamlet*. In an essay first published in the *American Journal of Psychology*, Jones, like Rank, makes use of the oedipal concept: he suggests that Hamlet is a victim of strong feelings toward his mother, the queen.

Between 1909 and 1949 numerous other critics decided that psychological and psychoanalytic theory could assist in the understanding of literature. I. A. Richards, Kenneth Burke, and Edmund Wilson were among the most influential to become interested in the new approach. Not all of the early critics were committed to the approach; neither were all of them Freudians. Some followed Alfred Adler, who believed that writers wrote out of inferiority complexes, and others applied the ideas of Carl Gustav Jung, who had broken with Freud over Freud's emphasis on sex and who had developed a theory of the *collective* unconscious. According to Jungian theory, a great novel like *Frankenstein* is not a disguised expression of Mary Shelley's personal, repressed wishes; rather, it is a manifestation of desires once held by the whole human race but now repressed because of the advent of civilization.

It is important to point out that among those who relied on Freud's models were a number of critics who were poets and novelists as well. Conrad Aiken wrote a Freudian study of American literature, and poets such as Robert Graves and W. H. Auden applied Freudian insights when writing critical prose. William Faulkner, Henry James, James Joyce, D. H. Lawrence, Marcel Proust, and Toni Morrison are only a few of the novelists who have either written criticism influenced by Freud or who have written novels that conceive of character, conflict, and creative writing itself in Freudian terms. The poet H. D. (Hilda Doolittle) was actually a patient of Freud's and provided an account of her analysis in her book *Tribute to Freud*. By giving Freudian theory credibility among students of literature that only they could bestow, such writers helped to endow psychoanalytic criticism with the largely Freudian orientation that, one could argue, it still exhibits today.

The willingness, even eagerness, of writers to use Freudian models in producing literature and criticism of their own consummated a relationship that, to Freud and other pioneering psychoanalytic theorists, had seemed fated from the beginning; after all, therapy involves the close analysis of language. René Wellek and Austin Warren included "psychological" criticism as one of the five "extrinsic" approaches to literature described in their influential book, *Theory of Literature* (1942). Psychological criticism, they suggest, typically attempts to do at least one of the following: provide a psychological study of an individual writer; explore the nature of the creative process; generalize about "types and laws present within works of literature"; or theorize about the psychological "effects of literature upon its readers" (81). Entire books on psychoanalytic criticism even began to appear, such as Frederick J. Hoffman's *Freudianism and the Literary Mind* (1945).

Probably because of Freud's characterization of the creative mind as "clamorous" if not ill, psychoanalytic criticism written before 1950 tended to psychoanalyze the individual author. Poems were read as fantasies that allowed authors to indulge repressed wishes, to protect themselves from deep-seated anxieties, or both. A perfect example of author analysis would be Marie Bonaparte's 1933 study of Edgar Allan Poe. Bonaparte found Poe to be so fixated on his mother that his repressed longing emerges in his stories in images such as the white spot on a black cat's breast, said to represent mother's milk.

A later generation of psychoanalytic critics often paused to analyze the characters in novels and plays before proceeding to their authors. But not for long, since characters, both evil and good, tended to be seen by these critics as the author's potential selves, or projections of various repressed aspects of his or her psyche. For instance, in *A Psychoanalytic Study of the Double in Literature* (1970), Robert Rogers begins with the view that human beings are double or multiple in nature. Using this assumption, along with the psychoanalytic concept of "dissociation" (best known by its result, the dual or multiple personality), Rogers concludes that writers reveal instinctual or repressed selves in their books, often without realizing that they have done so.

In the view of critics attempting to arrive at more psychological insights into an author than biographical materials can provide, a work of literature is a fantasy or a dream — or at least so analogous to daydream or dream that Freudian analysis can help explain the nature of the mind that produced it. The author's purpose in writing is to gratify secretly some forbidden wish, in particular an infantile wish or desire that has been repressed into the unconscious mind. To discover what the wish is, the psychoanalytic critic employs many of the terms and procedures developed by Freud to analyze dreams.

The literal surface of a work is sometimes spoken of as its "manifest content" and treated as a "manifest dream" or "dream story" would be treated by a Freudian analyst. Just as the analyst tries to figure out the "dream thought" behind the dream story — that is, the latent or hidden content of the manifest dream — so the psychoanalytic literary critic tries to expose the latent, underlying content of a work. Freud used the words *condensation* and *displacement* to explain two of the mental processes whereby the mind disguises its wishes and fears in dream stories. In condensation several thoughts or persons may be condensed into a single manifestation or image in a dream story; in displacement, an anxiety, a wish, or a person may be displaced onto the image of another, with which or whom it is loosely connected through a string of associations that only an analyst can untangle. Psychoanalytic critics treat metaphors as if they were dream condensations; they treat metonyms — figures of speech based on extremely loose, arbitrary associations — as if they were dream displacements. Thus figurative literary language in general is treated as something that evolves as the writer's conscious mind resists what the unconscious tells it to picture or describe. A symbol is, in Daniel Weiss's words, "a meaningful concealment of truth as the truth promises to emerge as some frightening or forbidden idea" (20).

In a 1970 article entitled "The 'Unconscious' of Literature," Norman Holland, a literary critic trained in psychoanalysis, succinctly sums up the attitudes held by critics who would psychoanalyze authors, but without quite saying that it is the *author* that is being analyzed by the psychoanalytic critic. "When one looks at a poem psychoanalytically," he writes, "one considers it as though it were a dream or as though some ideal patient [were speaking] from the couch in iambic pentameter." One "looks for the general level or levels of fantasy associated with the language. By level I mean the familiar stages of childhood development — oral [when desires for nourishment and infantile sexual desires overlap], anal [when infants receive their primary pleasure from defecation], urethral [when urinary functions are the locus of sexual pleasure], phallic [when the penis or, in girls, some penis substitute is of primary interest], oedipal." Holland continues by analyzing not Robert Frost but Frost's poem "Mending Wall" as a specifically oral fantasy that is not unique to its author. "Mending Wall" is "about breaking down the wall which marks the separated or individuated self so as to return to a state of closeness to some Other" — including and perhaps essentially the nursing mother ("Unconscious" 136, 139).

While not denying the idea that the unconscious plays a role in creativity, psychoanalytic critics such as Holland began to focus more on the ways in which authors create works that appeal to *our* repressed wishes and fancies. Consequently, they shifted their focus away from the psyche of the author and toward the psychology of the reader and the text. Holland's theories, which have concerned themselves more with the reader than with the text, have helped to establish another school of critical theory: reader-response criticism. Elizabeth Wright explains Holland's brand of modern psychoanalytic criticism in this way: "What draws us as readers to a text is the secret expression of what we desire to hear, much as we protest we do not. The disguise must be good enough to fool the censor into thinking that the text is respectable, but bad enough to allow the unconscious to glimpse the unrespectable" (117).

Whereas Holland came increasingly to focus on the reader rather than on the work being read, others who turned away from character and author diagnosis preferred to concentrate on texts; they remained skeptical that readers regularly fulfill wishes by reading. Following the theories of D. W. Winnicott, a psychoanalytic theorist who has argued that even babies have relationships as well as raw wishes, these textually oriented psychoanalytic critics contend that the relationship between reader and text depends greatly on the text. To be sure, some works fulfill the reader's secret wishes, but others — maybe most — do not. The texts created by some authors effectively resist the reader's involvement.

In determining the nature of the text, such critics may regard the text in terms of a dream. But no longer do they assume that dreams are meaningful in the way that works of literature are. Rather, they assume something more complex. "If we move outward" from one "scene to others in the [same] novel," Meredith Skura writes, "as Freud moves from the dream to its associations, we find that the paths of movement are really quite similar" (181). Dreams are viewed more as a language than as symptoms of repression. In fact, the French structuralist psychoanalyst Jacques Lacan treats the unconscious *as* a language, a form of discourse. Thus we may study dreams psychoanalytically in order to learn about literature, even as we may study literature in order to learn more about the unconscious. In Lacan's seminar on Poe's "The Purloined Letter," a pattern of repetition like that used by psychoanalysts in their analyses is used to arrive at a reading of the story. According to Wright, "the new psychoanalytic structural approach to literature" employs "analogies from psychoanalysis . . . to explain the workings of the text as distinct from the workings of a particular author's, character's, or even reader's mind" (125).

Lacan, however, did far more than extend Freud's theory of dreams, literature, and the interpretation of both. More significantly, he took Freud's whole theory of psyche and gender and added to it a crucial third term — that of language. In the process, he used but adapted Freud's ideas about the oedipal complex and oedipal stage, both of which Freud saw as crucial to the development of the child, and especially of male children.

Lacan points out that the pre-oedipal stage, in which the child at first does not even recognize its independence from its mother, is also a pre*verbal* stage, one in which the child communicates without the medium of language, or — if we insist upon calling the child's communications a language — in a language that can only be called *literal*. ("Coos," certainly, cannot be said to be figurative or symbolic!) Then, while still in the pre-oedipal stage, the child enters the *mirror* stage.

During the mirror period, the child comes to recognize itself and its mother, later other people as well, *as* independent selves. This is the stage in which the child is first able to fear the aggressions of another, desire what is recognizably beyond the self (initially the mother), and, finally, to want to compete with another for the same, desired object. This is also the stage at which the child first becomes able to feel sympathy with another being who is being hurt by a third — to cry, in other words, when another cries. All of these developments, of course, involve projecting beyond the self and, by extension, being able to envision one's own self (or "ego" or "I") as others view one — that is, as *another*. For these reasons, Lacan refers to the mirror stage as the *Imaginary* stage.

The Imaginary stage, however, is usually superseded. It normally ends with the onset of the oedipal stage, which it makes possible. (The Imaginary stage makes possible the oedipal stage insofar as it makes possible not only desire and fear of another but also the sense of another as a rival.)

The oedipal stage, as in Freud, begins when the child, having recognized the self *as* self and the father and mother as *separate* selves, recognizes gender and gender differences between its parents and between itself and one of its parents. For boys, that recognition involves another, more powerful recognition, for the recognition of the father's phallus as the mark of his difference from the mother involves, at the same time, the recognition that his older and more powerful father is also his rival. That, in turn, leads to the understanding that what once seemed wholly his and even undistinguishable from himself is in fact someone else's: something properly to be desired only at a greater distance and in the form of socially acceptable *substitutes*. (The old song "I Want a Girl Just Like the Girl Who Married Dear Old Dad" is a clear and straightforward restatement of the psychoanalytic theory that men's lives are searches for adequate and sufficient substitutes for the lost mother.)

The fact that the oedipal stage roughly coincides with the entry of the child into language is extremely important, even critical, for Lacan. For the linguistic order is essentially a figurative or "Symbolic order"; words are not the things they stand for but are, rather, stand-ins — substitutions — for those things. Hence boys, who in the most critical period of their development have had to submit to what Lacan calls the "Law of the Father" — a law that prohibits direct desire for and communicative intimacy with what has been the boy's whole world — enter more easily into the realm of language and the Symbolic order than do girls, who have never really had to renounce that which once seemed continuous with the self: the mother. The gap that has been opened up for boys, which includes the gap between signs and what they substitute for — the gap marked by the phallus and encoded with the boy's sense of his maleness — has not opened up for girls, or has not opened up in the same way, to the same degree.

Lacan, moreover, takes Freud a step further in the process of making Freud's gender-based psychoanalytic theory a theory of language as well. He suggests that the father does not even have to be present to trigger the oedipal crisis; nor, then, does his phallus have to be seen to catalyze the boy's (easier) transition into the Symbolic order. Rather, he argues, a child's recognition of his or her gender, gender that may be the same as or different from that of the now separate-seeming mother, is intricately tied up with a growing recognition of the system of names and naming. A child has little doubt about who its mother is, but who is its father — and how would one know? The father's claim rests on the mother's *word* that he is in fact the father; the father's relationship to the child is thus established through language and a system of marriage and kinship — names — that in turn is basic to rules of everything from property to law. Thus gender, for Lacan, is intimately connected in the mind of the developing child with names and language. Or, rather, the *male* gender is tied to that world in an association analogously as intimate as is the mother's early, physical (including umbilical) connection with the infant.

Lacan's development of Freud has had several important results. First, his sexist-seeming association of maleness with the Symbolic order, together with his claim that women cannot therefore enter easily into the order, has prompted feminists not to reject his theory out of hand but, rather, to look more closely at the relation between language and gender, language and women's inequality. Some feminists have gone so far as to suggest that the social and political relationships between male and female will not be fundamentally altered until language itself has been radically changed. (That change might begin dialectically, with the development of some kind of "feminine language" grounded in the presymbolic — the literal-to-imaginary — communication between mother and child.)

Second, Lacan's association of the phallus with names, language, and the Symbolic order on which rest all social institutions has led some thinkers — in particular, Marxist critics — to suggest that a revolutionary overthrow of the West's entrenched (patriarchal) ideology would necessarily involve the dismantling of the whole system of marriage, names, and even kinship, on which the present social order rests.

In the essay that follows, David Collings sees *Frankenstein* as a novel consisting of two realms: one proper and public and dominated by language and law (that of Alphonse Frankenstein and the De Lacey family), the other private — even secret — and incommunicable (that of Victor Frankenstein and his monster). These two worlds correspond, in Collings's view, to Lacan's Symbolic and Imaginary orders. In the first world, trials are held and language reigns supreme; the second exists outside society and language, containing only Victor and his double.

Collings, using Lacan's concepts, suggests that Victor's passage from the Imaginary into the Symbolic realms has been incomplete. He points out that we learn near the beginning of the novel that Victor's studies have included "neither the structure of languages, nor the code of governments, nor the politics of various states" (247) — all of which, as Collings points out, are associated with what Lacan calls the Symbolic order.

If Victor had fully and entirely emerged from the Imaginary order and entered the Symbolic, Collings goes on to say, he would have resolved his oedipal conflict by marrying a substitute for his mother. Instead, Victor rejects Elizabeth (whose nature and story nearly double that of his mother) and chooses to look into "the physical secrets of the world" — nature in "her" hiding places (51). Thus, in Collings's words, he continues "spurning the social realm in favor of the Imaginary, bodily mother, whom he attempts to recover by creating the monster" (248). Pointing out that the death of Victor's mother and the later creation of the monster are closely intertwined within the text, Collings goes on to show the numerous ways in which the monster represents not a mother substitute but the body of the mother lost on entrance into the Symbolic order.

Of course, Victor *has* partially emerged from the pre-oedipal mirror stage and entered into some of the terms of the patriarchal or Symbolic order. If he hadn't, he couldn't speak to teachers or function at a university. As a result of the fact that he has partially emerged into the Symbolic order or realm, his attempt to recreate the body of the lost mother is botched — as botched as his passage out of the Imaginary order has been rough and incomplete. His creation ends up resembling his own mirror image more than it does his maternal object, a fact that Collings explains with the help of a Lacanian feminist: "As Luce Irigaray argues, from within the phallocentric regime of the Symbolic order, a genuinely feminine body is inconceivable: woman is either an inferior version of man, or she does not exist." But Victor is incompletely *in* the Symbolic order. "Accordingly, conceiving of woman as both like and unlike 'man,' he produces a monster — a creature who is grotesque precisely because it is, and is not, a 'man'" (249).

Collings goes on to discuss the equally grotesque creation (and destruction) of the "female" monster. He connects Victor's incomplete emergence into the Symbolic order with that of his creator, Mary Shelley. That author, Collings implies without quite stating, was doubly inhibited in her movement from the Imaginary to the Symbolic order, the order governed by patriarchs, their language, and their law. For one thing, her own mother had died in giving birth to her. (It is difficult to begin desiring mother substitutes when the mother herself is, so early, an absence.) For another, Mary Shelley was a woman, and women cannot completely or even genuinely enter the (phallocentric) Symbolic order in the first place, according to Lacanian psychoanalytic theory. (In this sense, they are much like the monster of *Frankenstein*, who is outside the realm of language even though he does learn to use it.)

And it may be, Collings suggests, precisely because Mary Shelley drew upon the Imaginary order that she could create what she created: a novel so strikingly visual, so visually arresting, that — although written in words — it seems almost to belong to the presymbolic order that Lacan calls the Imaginary. Perhaps, Collings even suggests, *Frankenstein* was meant to be a revolt against the Symbolic order — a revolt that, as Victor's activities tell us, is fraught with risks as well as with rewards.

PSYCHOANALYTIC CRITICISM: A SELECTED BIBLIOGRAPHY

Some Short Introductions to Psychological and Psychoanalytic Criticism

Holland, Norman. "The 'Unconscious' of Literature." *Contemporary Criticism*. Ed. Norman Bradbury and David Palmer. Stratford-upon-Avon Series 12. New York: St. Martin's, 1970. 131–54.

Natoli, Joseph, and Frederik L. Rusch, comps. *Psychocriticism: An Annotated Bibliography*. Westport: Greenwood, 1984.

Scott, Wilbur. *Five Approaches to Literary Criticism*. London: Collier-Macmillan, 1962. See the essays by Burke and Gorer as well as Scott's introduction to the section "The Psychological Approach: Literature in the Light of Psychological Theory."

Wellek, René, and Austin Warren. *Theory of Literature*. New York: Harcourt, 1942. See the chapter "Literature and Psychology" in pt. 3, "The Extrinsic Approach to the Study of Literature."

Wright, Elizabeth. "Modern Psychoanalytic Criticism." *Modern Literary Theory: A Comparative Introduction*. Ed. Ann Jefferson and David Robey. Totowa: Barnes, 1982. 113–33.

Freud, Lacan, and Their Influence

Basler, Roy P. *Sex, Symbolism, and Psychology in Literature*. New York: Octagon, 1975. See especially 13–19.

Clément, Catherine. *The Lives and Legends of Jacques Lacan*. Trans. Arthur Goldhammer. New York: Columbia UP, 1983.

Freud, Sigmund. *Introductory Lectures on Psycho-Analysis*. Trans. Joan Riviere. London: Allen, 1922.

Gallop, Jane. *Reading Lacan*. Ithaca: Cornell UP, 1985.

Hoffman, Frederick J. *Freudianism and the Literary Mind*. Baton Rouge: Louisiana State UP, 1945.

Kazin, Alfred. "Freud and His Consequences." *Contemporaries*. Boston: Little, 1962. 351–93.

Lacan, Jacques. *Écrits: A Selection*. Trans. Alan Sheridan. New York: Norton, 1977.

———. *Feminine Sexuality: Lacan and the école freudienne*. Ed. Juliet Mitchell and Jacqueline Rose. Trans. Rose. New York: Norton, 1982.

———. *The Four Fundamental Concepts of Psychoanalysis*. Trans. Alan Sheridan. London: Penguin, 1980.

Meisel, Perry, ed. *Freud: A Collection of Critical Essays*. Englewood Cliffs: Prentice, 1981.

Muller, John P., and William J. Richardson. *Lacan and Language: A Reader's Guide to "Écrits."* New York: International, 1982.

Porter, Laurence M. *The Interpretation of Dreams: Freud's Theories Revisited*. Twayne's Masterwork Studies Series. Boston: G. K. Hall, 1986.

Reppen, Joseph, and Maurice Charney. *The Psychoanalytic Study of Literature*. Hillsdale: Analytic, 1985.

Schneiderman, Stuart. *Jacques Lacan: The Death of an Intellectual Hero*. Cambridge: Harvard UP, 1983.

Selden, Raman. *A Reader's Guide to Contemporary Literary Theory*. Lexington: U of Kentucky P, 1985. See "Jacques Lacan: Language and the Unconscious."

Trilling, Lionel. "Art and Neurosis." *The Liberal Imagination*. New York: Scribner's, 1950. 160–80.

Wilden, Anthony. "Lacan and the Discourse of the Other." In Lacan,

Speech and Language in Psychoanalysis. Trans. Wilden. Baltimore: Johns Hopkins UP, 1981. (Published as *The Language of the Self* in 1968.) 159–311.

Psychoanalysis, Feminism, and Literature

Chodorow, Nancy. *The Reproduction of Mothering: Psychoanalysis and the Sociology of Gender.* Berkeley: U of California P, 1978.

Gallop, Jane. *The Daughter's Seduction: Feminism and Psychoanalysis.* Ithaca: Cornell UP, 1982.

Garner, Shirley Nelson, Claire Kahane, and Madelon Sprengnether. *The (M)other Tongue: Essays in Feminist Psychoanalytic Interpretation.* Ithaca: Cornell UP, 1985.

Irigaray, Luce. *This Sex Which Is Not One.* Trans. Catherine Porter. Ithaca: Cornell UP, 1985.

———. *The Speculum of the Other Woman.* Trans. Gillian C. Gill. Ithaca: Cornell UP, 1985.

Jacobus, Mary. "Is There a Woman in This Text?" *New Literary History* 14 (1982): 117–41.

Kristeva, Julia. *The Kristeva Reader.* Ed. Toril Moi. New York: Columbia UP, 1986. See especially the selection from *Revolution in Poetic Language,* 89–136.

Mitchell, Juliet. *Psychoanalysis and Feminism.* New York: Random House, 1974.

Mitchell, Juliet, and Jacqueline Rose, "Introduction I" and "Introduction II." Lacan, *Feminine Sexuality: Jacques Lacan and the école freudienne.* 1–26, 27–57.

Sprengnether, Madelon. *The Spectral Mother: Freud, Feminism, and Psychoanalysis.* Ithaca: Cornell UP, 1990.

Psychological and Psychoanalytic Studies of Literature

Bettelheim, Bruno. *The Uses of Enchantment: The Meaning and Importance of Fairy Tales.* New York: Knopf, 1976. Although this book is about fairy tales instead of literary works written for publication, it offers model Freudian readings of well-known stories.

Crews, Frederick C. *Out of My System: Psychoanalysis, Ideology, and Critical Method.* New York: Oxford UP, 1975.

———. *Relations of Literary Study.* New York: MLA, 1967. See the chapter "Literature and Psychology."

Hallman, Ralph. *Psychology of Literature: A Study of Alienation and Tragedy.* New York: Philosophical Library, 1961.

Hartman, Geoffrey, ed. *Psychoanalysis and the Question of the Text.* Baltimore: Johns Hopkins UP, 1978. See especially the essays by Hartman, Johnson, Nelson, and Schwartz.

Hertz, Neil. *The End of the Line: Essays on Psychoanalysis and the Sublime.* New York: Columbia UP, 1985.

Holland, Norman N. *Dynamics of Literary Response.* New York: Oxford UP, 1968.

———. *Poems in Persons: An Introduction to the Psychoanalysis of Literature.* New York: Norton, 1973.

Kris, Ernest. *Psychoanalytic Explorations in Art.* New York: International, 1952.

Lucas, F. L. *Literature and Psychology.* London: Cassell, 1951.

Natoli, Joseph, ed. *Psychological Perspectives on Literature: Freudian Dissidents and Non-Freudians: A Casebook.* Hamden: Archon Books–Shoe String, 1984.

Phillips, William, ed. *Art and Psychoanalysis.* New York: Columbia UP, 1977.

Rogers, Robert. *A Psychoanalytic Study of the Double in Literature.* Detroit: Wayne State UP, 1970.

Skura, Meredith. *The Literary Use of the Psychoanalytic Process.* New Haven: Yale UP, 1981.

Strelka, Joseph P. *Literary Criticism and Psychology.* University Park: Pennsylvania State UP, 1976. See especially the essays by Lerner and Peckham.

Weiss, Daniel. *The Critic Agonistes: Psychology, Myth, and the Art of Fiction.* Ed. Eric Solomon and Stephen Arkin. Seattle: U of Washington P, 1985.

Lacanian Psychoanalytic Studies of Literature

Davis, Robert Con, ed. *The Fictional Father: Lacanian Readings of the Text.* Amherst: U of Massachusetts P, 1981.

———, ed. "Lacan and Narration." *Modern Language Notes* 5 (1983): 843–1063.

Felman, Shoshana, ed. *Literature and Psychoanalysis: The Question of Reading: Otherwise.* Baltimore: Johns Hopkins UP, 1982.

Froula, Christine. "When Eve Reads Milton: Undoing the Canonical

Economy." *Canons*. Ed. Robert von Hallberg. Chicago: U of Chicago P, 1984. 149–75.

Homans, Margaret. *Bearing the Word: Language and Female Experience in Nineteenth-Century Women's Writing*. Chicago: U of Chicago P, 1986.

Muller, John P., and William J. Richardson, eds. *The Purloined Poe: Lacan, Derrida, and Psychoanalytic Reading*. Baltimore: Johns Hopkins UP, 1988. Includes Lacan's seminar on Poe's "The Purloined Letter."

Psychoanalytic Readings of *Frankenstein*

Brooks, Peter. "'Godlike Science/Unhallowed Arts': Language and Monstrosity in *Frankenstein*." *New Literary History* 9 (1978): 591–605.

Gilbert, Sandra M., and Susan Gubar. "Horror's Twin: Mary Shelley's Monstrous Eve." Ch. 7 of *The Madwoman in the Attic: The Woman Writer and the Nineteenth-Century Literary Imagination*. New Haven: Yale UP, 1979.

Homans, Margaret. "Bearing Demons: Frankenstein's Circumvention of the Maternal." Homans, ch. 5.

Johnson, Barbara. "My Monster/My Self." *Diacritics* 12 (1982): 2–10.

Knoepflmacher, U. C. "Thoughts on the Aggression of Daughters." In *The Endurance of Frankenstein: Essays on Mary Shelley's Novel*. Ed. George Levine and U. C. Knoepflmacher. Berkeley: U of California P, 1979. 88–119.

Mellor, Anne K. "Possessing Nature: The Female in *Frankenstein*." *Romanticism and Feminism*. Ed. Mellor. Bloomington: Indiana UP, 1988. 220–32.

Moers, Ellen. *Literary Women*. New York: Doubleday, 1977. 90–99.

Rubinstein, Marc. "'My Accursed Origin': The Search for the Mother in *Frankenstein*." *Studies in Romanticism* 15 (1976): 165–94.

A PSYCHOANALYTIC PERSPECTIVE ON *FRANKENSTEIN*

DAVID COLLINGS

The Monster and the Imaginary Mother: A Lacanian Reading of *Frankenstein*

It is all too easy for literary critics to apply their knowledge of psychoanalysis to literary texts by finding in those fictions the complexes that Freud described. Such an approach assumes that psychoanalysis possesses a truth that reveals the meaning of literary texts, a meaning that they themselves did not recognize. But the more closely one examines Freud and psychoanalytic practice, generally, the more one realizes that psychoanalysis itself tells stories, invents scenarios of development, and guesses at meanings and events: it too deals in fictions and cannot entirely rise above the bewildering complexity of the unconscious. Similarly, the more one examines works of literature written before Freud, the more they seem to have been, in some strange way, already aware of psychoanalysis or of the unconscious.

It is best, then, to recognize that literature and psychoanalysis are on a continuum; it is as useful and interesting to interpret psychoanalysis as a form of literature as to interpret literature with the tools of psychoanalysis. Each thus profits from the other without becoming completely subject to the other's authority. Together they demonstrate that there is no discourse against which either must be measured, no final scientific or literary authority that reigns over all. Instead, they show that there is a history of the psyche that takes part in many histories, including those of the family, manners, sexuality, and the body. The works of Freud and Lacan thus arrive late in a long tradition of texts that trace the formation of what we call the unconscious, texts that might well challenge psychoanalysis to alter or expand its theories in many areas.

Psychoanalysis is vulnerable in its treatment of women: both Freud and Lacan are notoriously phallocentric, interpreting the psyche with reference to male development, castration, and the phallus. Thus psychoanalysis and literature can interpret each other fruitfully with a literary text that explores the woman's place in the psyche — a text such as Mary Shelley's *Frankenstein*. Lacan's theory of the Imaginary and Symbolic orders makes apparent a pattern within the novel that pre-Lacanian psychoanalytic readings missed: its persistent contrast between the world of the mirror-image, or double (the Imaginary), and that of kinship, language, and social life (the Symbolic). Yet the novel, in turn, demonstrates that the Symbolic order's insistence on denying the Imaginary comes at the enormous cost of excluding the maternal body. As Mary Shelley's novel suggests that the situation Lacan describes is neither inevitable nor necessary, it opens up new directions for psychoanalytic theory.

Frankenstein, the Monster, and the Imaginary Mother

Within *Frankenstein* the world is divided between the public realm and the private, almost delusional relation between Victor and the monster: in Lacanian terms, between the Symbolic and Imaginary orders. On the one hand, there are Alphonse Frankenstein, dutiful father and judge; the families of the Frankensteins and the De Laceys; the possibility of Victor's marriage with Elizabeth; the responsible science of M. Krempe; and the operation of law in the trial of Justine and the imprisonment of Victor. All these exemplify, in varying degrees, a social order rooted in patriarchal marriage, legality, and genital (phallic) sexuality. On the other hand, there is the curious solitude of Victor and the monster, neither of which can ever belong to a family; their endless fascination with each other; and their utter incapacity to communicate their situation with anyone else, except of course Robert Walton, the novel's narrator. Victor's solitude is so profound that his obsession with the monster and paranoid fear of him would amount to madness were it not that another person, Walton, encounters the monster in the novel's final pages. Victor's obsession with this Imaginary double of the self, outside of society and language, compels him to resist or attack his father, friend, and potential wife whenever they threaten that self.

The Imaginary quality of Victor's solitude is made clear in the early pages of his story. As a young scholar, Victor studies "neither the structure of languages, nor the code of governments, nor the politics of various states," all subjects associated with the Symbolic order, but rather the "physical secrets of the world" (43). Moreover, within the physical sciences, Victor pursues an outmoded, erroneous, semimagical science in defiance of his father's prohibition, as if replaying the oedipus complex in his intellectual pursuits. In an unofficial, magical nature Victor hopes to recover the mother that has been denied or forgotten in much the same way as the alchemy of Agrippa, Paracelsus, and Albertus Magnus has been dismissed by contemporary science. A similar oedipal drama is performed after Victor arrives at the university. The ugly, forbidding M. Krempe scoffs at the alchemists (49), but Waldman indirectly praises them and describes modern chemistry in terms resonant with maternal sexuality: the modern masters "penetrate into the recesses of nature, and show how she works in her hiding places" (51).

Victor's search for a substitute mother does not take the normative oedipal path. Typically, the son relinquishes his mother and desires a person who resembles her. Margaret Homans argues that in effect the son gives up the physical mother and desires a figurative representation of her, a substitute for her in the realm of language or social relations. Homans goes on to propose that Victor's development *is* quite typical, because he attempts to recreate his mother in his scientific, intellectual project and thus in the realm of language (Homans 9–10, 101–2, 107).

But the authorized figure for the mother is Elizabeth, not the monster; her personality and biography almost duplicate Caroline Frankenstein's, as if she is in fact the perfect person to complete the oedipal drama. Victor resists the seemingly inevitable marriage to Elizabeth, leaves home, and chooses another, forbidden erotic object: the mystery of how nature works in "her" hiding places — the mystery of the feminine body. That is, he chooses to take exactly the opposite of the typical path, spurning the social realm in favor of the Imaginary, bodily mother, whom he attempts to recover by creating the monster.

This relation between the mother and monster is made clear in the episodes surrounding Victor's going to the university. The break from the family represents Victor's entrance into the public world and his separation from his mother. Thus her death immediately before his leaving is highly appropriate; it represents Victor's separation from her and the loss consequent on accepting his place in the Symbolic order. Despite himself, Victor must leave her behind, tell himself not to grieve over his loss (47–48), and go on to begin a career. Yet, as we have seen, once he gets to the university he refuses to partake in authorized scientific activities and falls prey to his longing for forbidden knowledge. He identifies with his mother, recovering her body in his own body as he attempts to become pregnant himself, to labor in childbirth, and to watch the child awaken, gesture, and attempt to speak (see 55–59). He also attempts to recreate her by reassembling her dead body, as it were, from "bones from charnel-houses" (56), animating it, and looking up at it (as would a child at its mother) as he lies in bed (58). As Ellen Moers has pointed out, this story of monstrous creation is thus a "birth myth" built around Mary Shelley's own experiences with pregnancy and childbirth (Moers 90–99). It might also describe her attempts to recover a relation to a mother who had always been for her a *dead* mother; perhaps she, like Victor, is compelled to reassemble that impossibly distant body.

In the midst of these depictions of the monster's infantile and maternal attributes comes Victor's dream:

> I thought I saw Elizabeth, in the bloom of health, walking in the streets of Ingolstadt. Delighted and surprised, I embraced her; but as I imprinted the first kiss on her lips, they became livid with the hue of death; her features appeared to change, and I thought that I held the corpse of my dead mother in my arms; a shroud enveloped her form, and I saw the graveworms crawling in the folds of the flannel. (58)

Here the normative shift from mother to lover is reversed: Elizabeth transforms into the dead mother. For Victor, feminine sexuality can never be separated from the Imaginary mother he has lost; as soon as he imagines touching her and taking pleasure in her body, the figurative substitute for her turns back into her physical form. In effect, all women are for him the dead mother, the all-too-physical person he left when he went to the university. It would be impossible for Elizabeth to walk in Ingolstadt without seeming to be a visitor from the dead, a monstrously physical intruder in the world of masculine learning. Nor could the creature whom he created as a result of his rapturous discovery of "the cause of generation and life" (54) awaken without becoming a monster.

Clearly, the turn from erotic ideal to grotesque body horrifies Victor; in this respect he is a responsible citizen of the Symbolic realm, longing for Elizabeth rather than the mother. Yet this horror is so strong, and this dream so necessary, because of his unspeakable desire for the dead mother, for the secret of her body, for that element of her that has no (Symbolic) substitute. Perhaps the real horror is that Victor has learned to dread what he longs for; the only way to articulate his desire for the maternal body is in the very terms that exclude her, much as the only way of recreating her body is with the very tools acquired in the university at the cost of her life. And in these terms, with these tools, Victor cannot even recreate her as a female body: as if in retreat from his mother even on the most primal level, he creates a *male* monster who resembles his own mirror-image more than the mother he desires. As Luce Irigaray argues, from within the phallocentric regime of the Symbolic order, a genuinely feminine body is inconceivable: woman is either an inferior version of man, or she does not exist (Irigaray 11–129). Yet Victor is compelled to imagine this alien, Imaginary mother who no longer quite exists for him. Accordingly, conceiving of woman as both like and unlike "man," he produces a monster — a creature who is grotesque precisely because it is, and is not, a "man."

The Imaginary nature of his relation to the monster is further reinforced in the visual imagery of the passage: when Victor awakens, he sees, "by the dim and yellow light of the moon, as it forced its way through the window shutters," the monster, who fixes on Victor "his eyes, if eyes they may be called. . . ." A peculiar and intense sight dominates in this passage: a haunting light cast on a ghastly figure, framed by the window, who gazes back with inhuman eyes. This seems to be the return of a deeply repressed mirror stage, in which the monster is Victor's own reflection in the window/mirror. As if to emphasize the prelinguistic nature of this moment, Shelley goes on to write: "His jaws

opened, and he muttered some inarticulate sounds, while a grin wrinkled his cheeks'' (58). The truly mirror-like quality of Victor's encounters with the monster is clearer elsewhere in the novel where the nearly
hallucinatory image recurs: at the destruction of the female monster (''I
trembled, and my heart failed within me; when, on looking up, I saw,
by the light of the moon, the dæmon at the casement'' [141]) and,
most clearly, at the death of Elizabeth (164). In all these passages, the
window represents the mirror, a framed surface on which always appears
the nonspeaking face of the other, of the self's dæmonic double. And
each time the monster only grins, even though in the later instances he
is quite capable of speech.

All this is complicated by Mary Shelley's account of the moment
when she conceived the novel:

> When I placed my head on my pillow, I did not sleep, nor could
> I be said to think. My imagination, unbidden, possessed and
> guided me, gifting the successive images that arose in my mind
> with a vividness far beyond the usual bounds of reverie. I saw —
> with shut eyes, but acute mental vision, — I saw the pale student
> of unhallowed arts kneeling beside the thing he had put together.
> . . . I opened [my eyes] in terror. . . . I wished to exchange the
> ghastly image of my fancy for the realities around. I see them
> still; the very room, the dark *parquet,* the closed shutters, with the
> moonlight struggling through, and the sense I had that the glassy
> lake and white high Alps were beyond. (Introduction 22–23)

Shelley's emphasis on the haunting ''vividness'' of this ''acute mental
vision'' locates it outside of ordinary, waking sight in the Imaginary
realm. And even her reference to ''the realities around'' leads her to
further mental images, ''sense[d]'' through the closed shutters, of the
lake and Alps, or perhaps of the Alps reflected in the lake, another kind
of mirror; the intense seeing of the original vision (emphasized through
the repetition of the words ''I saw'') is repeated late in the passage (''I
see them still'').

It is important that this visual imagery is most intense in moments
both of creating (the novel, the monster) and of killing (the female
monster, Elizabeth): by tying together these apparently opposite motifs, this imagery points to the fundamental Imaginary coherence of the
novel. Clearly, for both Shelley and her character Victor Frankenstein,
creation takes place neither in the Symbolic moment of uttering words
(as in *Genesis*) nor even of writing them but in the moment of an astonishing visual literalization when what they ''see'' comes to life. Mellor
has quite justifiably discussed Victor's creation of the monster as a mas-

culine attempt to circumvent the maternal, to usurp and destroy the life-giving power of feminine sexuality (Mellor 220–32). But the strong parallels of the two creation scenes suggest that Victor circumvents Symbolic, married, genital sexuality with an Imaginary sexuality in which the son or daughter can recreate the dead mother in a prelinguistic, visual mode.

Such a reading of the creation scenes would also explain the murder scenes. The female monster and Elizabeth represent not simply feminine sexuality but its function within the Symbolic order: Elizabeth as a married sexual partner blessed by the patriarch Alphonse Frankenstein, and the female monster as someone who will join the monster in creating a new society in South America — a new "chain of existence" (127) which, as Peter Brooks points out, would be a new "systematic network of relation" akin to the Symbolic order (Brooks 593). If we apply this reading to Mary Shelley as author, it suggests that literary creation is for her a form of matricide, of killing the Symbolic mother subordinated to father or husband. Perhaps it is even a way to kill herself as such a mother. Barbara Johnson argues this point, emphasizing the subtle link between the italics in the passages on the creating of the book ("*to think of a story*" [22, 23]) and the killing of Elizabeth ("'*I will be with you on your wedding-night*'" [143, 158]) (Johnson 8–9). One way to understand this point is to say that for Shelley, creating in language threatened her role as a woman expected to create by means of her genital sexuality. To take on the masculine role of author threatened her femininity. But these passages might also suggest that creating in an Imaginary and thus prelinguistic mode threatens the whole language of marriage, filiation, and sexuality defined as the reproduction of the social structure. It threatens not femininity but the patriarchal, Symbolic order that negates and excludes the feminine body.

We do not have to distort the text to arrive at this interpretation. In fact, in both of the passages to which Johnson refers, the italics culminate in a moment of hallucinatory creation or murder, a moment of Imaginary intensity. It is not female authorship as intrusion upon a male domain that kills Elizabeth but Imaginary authorship, a nonlinguistic and nongenital creativity. Victor/Mary murders the woman capable of genital sexuality in order to look up and see the desired mother in the window/mirror. It is almost as if simply by looking in the window/mirror, he/she murders the mother-wife: in this novel, looking in the mirror can kill. The Imaginary pair — Victor Frankenstein and his monster, Mary Shelley and her story — kill all third parties and all systems (like the father's Law) built on the third party. If the Symbolic order excludes and indeed kills the Imaginary mother (Caroline), these children will gain revenge by murdering the Symbolic mother in their turn.

The Monster's Protest

By itself, however, this Imaginary revolt against the Symbolic does not necessarily liberate such children; if anything, it would confine them within the Imaginary order, which could be at least equally oppressive. Shelley makes the horror of this Imaginary entrapment vivid in her account of the monster's experience. By creating an Imaginary figure, Victor gives birth to someone who does not, and cannot, belong in the Symbolic realm. Wherever the monster goes, people reject him immediately because of his monstrous appearance. It seems he will never be anything but this horrible apparition from another psychic space, this embodiment of what everyone represses in order to enter society: the archaic, physical, nameless mother.

That he is this repressed body becomes clear in his version of the mirror stage. Like Milton's Eve, who looks into the pool when she should be gazing at Adam and who is soon taught to set aside her love of her own beauty in favor of the superior, manly strength of her mate (see Gilbert and Gubar 240), the monster looks in the pool and sees there an image that is already monstrous in comparison with "the perfect forms of my cottagers" (101). The monster is an Eve who is never given the chance merely to enjoy his/her own beauty; it is as if s/he has already been taught to love Adam before s/he looks in the pool. As a result, the monster's mirror image is alien to him the first time he sees it: "At first I started back," he says, "unable to believe that it was indeed I who was reflected in the mirror. . ." (101). Even worse, he will soon discover that he is nothing more than what appears in the mirror, as if he is the Eve that God and Adam reject, the image she leaves behind on the water.

Of course, the monster does not accept his exclusively Imaginary status; he longs to enter the social world, to belong to a family, to converse, and to have a sexual partner. He wishes, in short, to enter the Symbolic order. If Victor creates the monster in order to revolt against the Symbolic, the monster protests against being caught in the Imaginary. He understands his condition well: as Peter Brooks points out, early in their conversation high in the Alps when Victor cries out, "'Begone! relieve me from the sight of your detested form,'" the monster replies by placing his hands over Victor's eyes (91), mocking Victor's Imaginary fixation on the *sight* of his form (Brooks 592). In the narrative that follows, the monster attempts to replace his appearance with his words (Brooks 593), just as he attempts to cut across the obsessively dual relation between Victor and himself with his demands for a female partner who could offer him a social and sexual relation. In the end, of course, the monster's appeal fails; although he can speak, he has not truly entered into language, never having received the name of his father Victor, and thus he remains poised on the margins of language.

The story that the monster tells Victor, primarily about his acquisition of language from the De Lacey family, dramatizes this marginal position in language. Crouching there in the lean-to next to the family's cottage, he can listen to everything that people say but cannot participate in their conversations. He can learn the words, but he cannot share in the social exchange of words and must remain a silent, invisible presence unknown to the family. It is no surprise that the monster learns the language along with Safie, as if he, too, is both foreign and a woman. Critics have remarked that he is thus placed in the position of the woman who, like Eve or Mary Shelley, eavesdrops on the conversations of men (see, for example, Gilbert and Gubar 238, Moers 94). As a result, his condition is similar to that of woman in Lacanian theory. As Jacqueline Rose puts it, "woman is excluded *by* the nature of words" but not "*from* the nature of words" (Mitchell and Rose 49), on the one hand being given a sexual and gender identity through the Symbolic processes of language and on the other being excluded from language as it is based in the *father's* name. Oddly enough, he becomes defined by language without receiving the name-of-the-father, in effect dramatizing the condition of women in Western culture, whose names come from men and who thus remain in one sense nameless.

Yet Safie and the monster are not entirely alike. She is accepted into the cottage, after all, while he must remain outside. If Safie represents woman as she is accepted into language and the family, the monster represents what they exclude. He is even more foreign than she, perhaps what will always remain foreign, nameless, and threateningly feminine in her.

Shelley emphasizes the disembodied quality of Symbolic language when she renders the elder De Lacey blind. This father seems to have forgotten about the Imaginary and to live entirely within the world of words. Hardly moving from his place in the cottage, he only speaks, listens to someone read, and teaches people words: like Safie and the monster, he too is a consummate listener, but because he is already the master of the language and need not see the objects to which words refer. In effect, he represents the blindness of language, its apparent indifference to the body and to sight. This old man verges on being the Lacanian father because he has almost ceased to be an actual father and become the name-of-the-father, the father as nothing but names.

Although the father's blindness might indicate that he is so alien-ated from the visual world he need no longer see it, the monster inter-prets that blindness differently. Perhaps the old man, unable to see the monster, will accept him simply because he speaks. Blindness to the Imaginary may allow some tolerance for it. Of course, in the crucial moment of the monster's attempt to be accepted, Felix rushes in and violently ejects the monster from the cottage, and in the following days the entire family, including the father, flees the scene. The monster's failure demonstrates that the father's blindness represents not indiffer-ence but hostility to the body, a determination to render the world blank, as if Victor's cry to the monster (''Begone!'') were the Symbolic father's cry to the entire visible world.

The monster cannot escape this condemnation by turning from the De Laceys to books. Recognizing that he is ''similar, yet at the same time strangely unlike to the beings concerning whom'' he reads in Goethe, Plutarch, or Milton (112), he finds himself once again in an oblique relation to language. If we regard books as language preserved in print, then we can understand why the monster cannot find anyone like himself in them. In these books and this monster we are given two conflicting images of people: one that forgets their bodies and preserves only their words, and the other that despises their words and pieces together only their bodies. The monster embodies precisely what these books have forgotten and buried: everything in human life that cannot be put into words.

The stories that books tell also have a way of replacing the body with words: Milton's *Paradise Lost,* the myth of origins that the monster reads, attributes origins not to physical nature but to the disembodied Word of God at the creation. Milton's God is somewhat like a divine version of the Lacanian father, who lacks any direct physical link with the child and thus establishes his paternal authority through words, claiming that the child belongs to him. But the Miltonic God goes even further, dispensing with nature or any physical force and creating the world out of his own Word, as if no mother of the world were neces-sary. In this text, the Symbolic order substitutes the father's words for the mother's body as origin so radically that the latter almost disappears. The story that the monster finds in Victor's papers is, of course, very different: it tells of a bodily, maternal origin, as if the monster were produced directly out of the mother's body without her even having sex, as if she could create life without the participation of a father. Here we find the opposite of Milton's myth of an exclusively patriarchal origin: a celibate, solitary, exclusively maternal creation. Thus the monster finds his origins in a kind of anti-Symbolic story, indeed an anti-story, which confusedly tells how bodies come from bodies without the need for sex, how no parent claims the child, in effect how the monster has no origin worthy of the name. With such an anti-story in his pocket, the monster must remain nameless, for a name depends upon the myth that one originates in social and sexual relations, in kinship, and thus in language.

It is inevitable, then, that the monster is ejected from the cottage. Safie is welcomed in part because she has a story to tell that establishes her identity. Even though her story depicts the wrongs done to women in a feminist manner reminiscent of the novels written by Mary Shelley's mother, Mary Wollstonecraft, and therefore challenges sexist prejudice outright, it nevertheless remains coherent within broadly social and Symbolic norms. The monster, however, is denied even this form of protest; unaccountable, he has no parents or relations; only an unspeakable secret can explain him. His anti-story would serve to expose him, even to the blind old man, as one who did not belong. Produced in defiance of sexuality and kinship, he was forever cast out of the family at the start. Thus his story, or rather this entire novel, challenges patriarchy on an even more fundamental level than Wollstonecraft does, exposing the prejudice inherent in the Symbolic order itself.

The monster's most obvious difference from Safie, of course, and the one that epitomizes all the rest, is that he is a monster and cannot sustain the invisibility of what the Symbolic order excludes. Simply by showing himself, he loses even his tenuous access to language, because people can see him only as an unspeakably alien figure. Excluded from all families, he begins his journey through the world by exacting revenge against the family. Little William taunts him with the words, "'My papa is a Syndic — he is M. Frankenstein — he will punish you'" (123) and displays his miniature portrait of his mother, in effect bragging about his possession of the father's name, the power of the Law, and the figurative mother. The monster responds as if he is the literal maternal body for which the portrait is the substitute, the prelinguistic mother returned, as it were, from the dead to gain her revenge. He kills William and then places the miniature on Justine, not merely in order to condemn her but unwittingly to demonstrate that she is already condemned by such a picture to silence and death. In this act the monster shows that he need not destroy the family, for it destroys itself; William's mother is already dead, cast out so that her son Victor could become a man. Excluded from the family, the monster condemns it to the condition of excluding him, of missing something he represents. Very well, he seems to say; if you wish to live without me, your Imaginary mother, you will forever lack precisely what you desire, and in place of your women you will have only pictures of the dead.

Henceforth the monster is fated to define himself in relation to Victor, becoming Victor's Imaginary double, the mirror-self that haunts his every step. If, as Lacan suggests, the I is an other, then on some level Victor is the monster, and the monster in turn is Victor. Indeed, in the eyes of the law (which represents the Law of the Symbolic) they are indistinguishable; witnesses in Ireland mistake the dark figure in the boat for Victor (148), and later when Victor tries to gain the law's help in tracking down the monster, the judge assumes he is mad (167). Caught in this relation to the double, each sees the other as his rival self, attacking the other and getting revenge in an endless spiral of violence, each revealing in this way what Lacan identifies as the aggressive, paranoid structure of the ego. Rivalry becomes a directly destructive force, reducing everything to the opposition between the Imaginary pair — an opposition that is never resolved by the intervention of a Symbolic Law but which expires at last only with their deaths.

This Imaginary process of identification and rivalry with the double takes over the novel, as if an anti-Symbolic tale must become an Imaginary one in which one narrator identifies with another, who introduces yet a third, in an endless regress of tale within tale, mirror within mirror. I have no space to repeat here what critics have already discussed: the many resemblances between the narrators Mary Shelley and Margaret Saville (the woman who receives Walton's letters, and whose initials are also M. S.), Mary Shelley and Walton, Walton and Victor, Victor and the monster, the monster and Safie, and Safie and Mary Shelley (see Brooks 603, Rubenstein 168–72). Nor can I review the ways in which characters in the novel are orphaned and motherless (see Gilbert and Gubar 227–28), with the result that they tend to create an identity through finding doubles of themselves in other orphans. I can only point to the psychoanalytic coherence of this duplication of narratives, which, like the monster's tale to Victor in the heart of the novel, follow from and return to Victor's horrified gaze into the monster's face. We read all the stories in the novel as if a hand is over our eyes, too, and at any moment it will be lifted and the novel will transform from something read into someone seen — perhaps someone seen in the mirror.

Frankenstein's Implicit Critique of Lacan

In this essay I have argued that Victor Frankenstein desires the Imaginary mother and that the monster, caught in the Imaginary, wishes to join the Symbolic. Yet ironically, on a more general level, Victor and the monster want the same thing: the recognition by the Symbolic order of the Imaginary mother. The failure of the Symbolic to recognize the mother drives Victor to create a substitute for her and permanently excludes the monster from the society he wishes to join. The novel taken as a whole, then, challenges a very basic but powerful negation of women. It seems that neither the Imaginary, which relies entirely on a physical and/or visual relation to the mother, nor the Symbolic, which subordinates her to the father's Law, recognizes the woman on her own terms. Neither provides a space in which she can speak in her own right. Where might there be such a space? Shelley's novel suggests that it might appear where the Symbolic recognizes and accepts the Imaginary, where it allows the body to speak, the nameless monster to join the family, and the mirror image to be one element of the beloved's face. In such a space the mother would not have to die, even metaphorically, when one enters language, but would remain present in the elements of life that language cannot master and in the physical elements (sounds, disruptions, slippages) within language itself. One would never have to create a monster, a substitute Imaginary mother, because she would always remain accessible within the social realm.

Shelley's novel thus suggests a critique of Lacan's separation of Symbolic and Imaginary. Even though Lacan argues explicitly that the Imaginary remains important after the entrance into the Symbolic, so that they are both present throughout human experience, and that the Mirror stage prepares the subject for Symbolic identifications (see *Écrits* 22–25), his overall separation of the two realms tends to reinforce their differences and blinds him to the ways in which they are everywhere implicated in each other. Shelley exaggerates the way in which the Symbolic excludes the Imaginary in order to point out this problem, as if to suggest, long before Lacan, that the very terms of her novel and of our entire discussion are suspect.

With this critique of such a basic disjunction, the novel challenges many familiar dichotomies explored in this essay. For example, it opens up the possibility of a story that attributes origins neither to the father's word alone nor to the mother's nameless body alone but to the father and the mother together, recognizing thereby the necessarily social *and* physical dimensions of sexuality. Such a tale would have to be written in a language that did not exclude the body but delighted in the body's nonsense: verbal excess, playfulness, even "babytalk." Moreover, this novel also disrupts psychoanalysis itself, the "talking cure," pointing out that in those private sessions the patient finds in the analyst an Imaginary double as well as a version of the Symbolic father. Such a disruption quite naturally extends to the psychoanalytic critic, who may find in this novel not merely another text to be analyzed but a curious rival, perhaps double, of psychoanalytic theory itself.

WORKS CITED

Brooks, Peter. "'Godlike Science / Unhallowed Arts': Language and Monstrosity in *Frankenstein*." *New Literary History* 9 (1978): 591–605.

Gilbert, Sandra M., and Susan Gubar. "Horror's Twin: Mary Shelley's Monstrous Eve." Ch. 7 of *The Madwoman in the Attic: The Woman Writer and the Nineteenth-Century Literary Imagination*. New Haven: Yale UP, 1979.

Homans, Margaret. "Bearing Demons: Frankenstein's Circumvention of the Maternal." *Bearing the Word: Language and Female Experience in Nineteenth-Century Women's Writing*. Ed. Homans. Chicago: U of Chicago P, 1986.

Irigaray, Luce. "The Blind Spot of an Old Dream of Symmetry." In *The Speculum of the Other Woman*. Trans. Gillian C. Gill. Ithaca: Cornell UP, 1985.

Johnson, Barbara. "My Monster / My Self." *Diacritics* 12 (1982): 2–10.

Lacan, Jacques. *Écrits: A Selection*. Trans. Alan Sheridan. New York: Norton, 1977.

Mellor, Anne K. "Possessing Nature: The Female in *Frankenstein*." *Romanticism and Feminism*. Ed. Mellor. Bloomington: Indiana UP, 1988. 220–32.

Mitchell, Juliet, and Jacqueline Rose. "Introduction II." *Feminine Sexuality: Lacan and the école freudienne*. Ed. Mitchell and Rose. New York: Norton, 1982. 27–57.

Moers, Ellen. *Literary Women*. Garden City: Doubleday, 1977.

Rubenstein, Marc. "'My Accursed Origin': The Search for the Mother in *Frankenstein*." *Studies in Romanticism* 15 (1976): 165–94.

Feminist Criticism
and
Frankenstein

WHAT IS FEMINIST CRITICISM?

Feminist criticism comes in many forms, and feminist critics have a variety of goals. Some are interested in rediscovering the works of women writers overlooked by a masculine-dominated culture. Others have revisited books by male authors and reviewed them from a woman's point of view to understand how they both reflect and shape the attitudes that have held women back.

Frankenstein is somewhat anomalous when seen in light of these two, very broadly described areas of feminist critical interest. For one thing, it has hardly been overlooked by the culture: the story of Victor Frankenstein and his "monster" has remained popular for almost two centuries, thanks to numerous hardback and paperback reprintings and a number of film and television adaptations. Less obvious but no less important is the fact that some feminist critics have found in *Franken-stein* a powerful strain of patriarchal ideology and an ambivalent attitude toward women's creativity. The presence of these may be partially attributable to Mary Shelley's position at the edge of a circle of extraordinary poets dominated by Lord Byron and her husband, Percy Bysshe Shelley.

In any case, *Frankenstein* has, in the past twenty years, elicited what might be called hybrid feminist responses. Because of its textual difference, it has interested critics practicing different kinds of feminist criticism. And it has seemed to require of each of them a willingness to adopt the stances and terminologies of feminists doing a different kind of work.

Since the early 1970s three strains of feminist criticism have emerged, strains that can be categorized as French, American, and British. These categories should not be allowed to obscure either the global implications of the women's movement or the fact that interests and ideas have been shared by feminists from France, Great Britain, and the United States. British and American feminists have examined similar problems while writing about many of the same writers and works, and American feminists have recently become more receptive to French theories about femininity and writing. Historically speaking, however, French, American, and British feminists have examined similar problems from somewhat different perspectives.

French feminists have tended to focus their attention on language, analyzing the ways in which meaning is produced. They have concluded that language as we commonly think of it is a decidedly male realm. Drawing on the ideas of the psychoanalytic philosopher Jacques Lacan, French feminists remind us that language is a realm of public discourse. A child enters the linguistic realm just as it comes to grasp its separateness from its mother, just about the time that boys identify with their father, the family representative of culture. The language learned reflects a binary logic that opposes such terms as active/passive, masculine/feminine, sun/moon, father/mother, head/heart, son/daughter, intelligent/sensitive, brother/sister, form/matter, phallus/vagina, reason/emotion. Because this logic tends to group with masculinity such qualities as light, thought, and activity, French feminists have said that the structure of language is phallocentric: it privileges the phallus and, more generally, masculinity by associating them with things and values more appreciated by the (masculine-dominated) culture. Moreover, French feminists believe, "masculine desire dominates speech and posits woman as an idealized fantasy-fulfillment for the incurable emotional lack caused by separation from the mother" (Jones 83).

In the view of French feminists, language is associated with separation from the mother. Its distinctions represent the world from the male point of view, and it systematically forces women to choose: either they can imagine and represent themselves as men imagine and represent them (in which case they may speak, but will speak as men) or they can choose "silence," becoming in the process "the invisible and unheard sex" (Jones 83).

But some influential French feminists have argued that language only *seems* to give women such a narrow range of choices. There is another possibility, namely that women can develop a *feminine* language. In various ways, early French feminists such as Annie Leclerc, Xavière Gauthier, and Marguerite Duras have suggested that there is something that may be called *l'écriture féminine:* women's writing. Recently, Julia Kristeva has said that feminine language is "semiotic," not "symbolic." Rather than rigidly opposing and ranking elements of reality, rather than symbolizing one thing but not another in terms of a third, feminine language is rhythmic and unifying. If from the male perspective it seems fluid to the point of being chaotic, that is a fault of the male perspective.

According to Kristeva, feminine language is derived from the preoedipal period of fusion between mother and child. Associated with the maternal, feminine language is not only threatening to culture, which is patriarchal, but also a medium through which women may be creative in new ways. But Kristeva has paired her central, liberating claim — that truly feminist innovation in all fields requires an understanding of the relation between maternity and feminine creation — with a warning. A feminist language that refuses to participate in "masculine" discourse, that places its future entirely in a feminine, semiotic discourse, risks being politically marginalized by men. That is to say, it risks being relegated to the outskirts (pun intended) of what is considered socially and politically significant.

Kristeva, who associates feminine writing with the female body, is joined in her views by other leading French feminists. Hélène Cixous, for instance, also posits an essential connection between the woman's body, whose sexual pleasure has been repressed and denied expression, and women's writing. "Write your self. Your body must be heard," Cixous urges; once they learn to write their bodies, women will not only realize their sexuality but enter history and move toward a future based on a "feminine" economy of giving rather than the "masculine" economy of hoarding (Cixous 250). For Luce Irigaray, women's sexual pleasure (*jouissance*) cannot be expressed by the dominant, ordered, "logical," masculine language. She explores the connection between women's sexuality and women's language through the following analogy: as women's *jouissance* is more multiple than men's unitary, phallic pleasure ("woman has sex organs just about everywhere"), so "feminine" language is more diffusive than its "masculine" counterpart. ("That is undoubtedly the reason . . . her language . . . goes off in all directions and . . . he is unable to discern the coherence," Irigaray writes [101–03].)

Cixous's and Irigaray's emphasis on feminine writing as an expression of the female body has drawn criticism from other French feminists. Many argue that an emphasis on the body either reduces "the feminine" to a biological essence or elevates it in a way that shifts the valuation of masculine and feminine but retains the binary categories. For Christine Fauré, Irigaray's celebration of women's difference fails to address the issue of masculine dominance, and a Marxist-feminist, Catherine Clément, has warned that "poetic" descriptions of what constitutes the feminine will not challenge that dominance in the realm of production. The boys will still make the toys, and decide who gets to use them. In her effort to redefine women as political rather than as sexual beings, Monique Wittig has called for the abolition of sexual categories that Cixous and Irigaray retain and revalue as they celebrate women's writing.

American feminist critics have shared with French critics both an interest in and a cautious distrust of the concept of feminine writing. Annette Kolodny, for instance, has worried that the "richness and variety of women's writing" will be missed if we see in it only its "feminine mode" or "style" ("Some Notes" 78). And yet Kolodny herself proceeds, in the same essay, to point out that women *have* had their own style, which includes reflexive constructions ("she found herself crying") and particular, recurring themes (clothing and self-fashioning are two that Kolodny mentions; other American feminists have focused on madness, disease, and the demonic).

Interested as they have become in the "French" subject of feminine style, American feminist critics began by analyzing literary texts rather than philosophizing abstractly about language. Many reviewed the great works by male writers, embarking on a revisionist rereading of literary tradition. These critics examined the portrayals of women characters, exposing the patriarchal ideology implicit in such works and showing how clearly this tradition of systematic masculine dominance is inscribed in our literary tradition. Kate Millett, Carolyn Heilbrun, and Judith Fetterley, among many others, created this model for American feminist criticism, a model that Elaine Showalter came to call "the feminist critique" of "male-constructed literary history" ("Poetics" 25).

Meanwhile another group of critics including Sandra Gilbert, Susan Gubar, Patricia Meyer Spacks, and Showalter herself created a somewhat different model. Whereas feminists writing "feminist critique" have analyzed works by men, practitioners of what Showalter used to refer to as "gynocriticism" have studied the writings of those women who, against all odds, produced what she calls "a literature of their own." In *The Female Imagination* (1975), Spacks examines the female literary tradition to find out how great women writers across the ages have felt, perceived themselves, and imagined reality. Gilbert and Gubar, in *The Madwoman in the Attic* (1979), concern themselves with well-known women writers of the nineteenth century, but they too find that general concerns, images, and themes recur, because the authors that they treat wrote "in a culture whose fundamental definitions of literary authority are both overtly and covertly patriarchal" (45).

If one of the purposes of gynocriticism is to (re)study well-known women authors, another is to rediscover women's history and culture, particularly women's communities that have nurtured female creativity. Still another related purpose is to discover neglected or forgotten women writers and thus to forge an alternative literary tradition, a canon that better represents the female perspective by better representing the literary works that have been written by women. Showalter, in *A Literature of Their Own* (1977), admirably began to fulfill this purpose, providing a remarkably comprehensive overview of women's writing through three of its phases. She defines these as the "Feminine, Feminist, and Female" phases, phases during which women first imitated a masculine tradition (1840–80), then protested against its standards and values (1880–1920), and finally advocated their own autonomous, female perspective (1920 to the present).

With the recovery of a body of women's texts, attention has returned to a question raised a decade ago by Lillian Robinson: Doesn't American feminist criticism need to formulate a theory of its own practice? Won't reliance on theoretical assumptions, categories, and strategies developed by men and associated with nonfeminist schools of thought prevent feminism from being accepted as equivalent to these other critical discourses? Not all American feminists believe that a special or unifying theory of feminist practice is urgently needed; Showalter's historical approach to women's culture allows a feminist critic to use theories based on nonfeminist disciplines. Kolodny has advocated a "playful pluralism" that encompasses a variety of critical schools and methods. But Jane Marcus and others have responded that if feminists adopt too wide a range of approaches, they may relax the tensions between feminists and the educational establishment necessary for political activism.

The question of whether feminism weakens or fortifies itself by emphasizing its separateness — and by developing unity through separateness — is one of several areas of debate within American feminism. Another area of disagreement touched on earlier, between feminists who stress universal feminine attributes (the feminine imagination, feminine writing) and those who focus on the political conditions experienced by certain groups of women at certain times in history, parallels a larger distinction between American feminist critics and their British counterparts.

While it has been customary to refer to an Anglo-American tradition of feminist criticism, British feminists tend to distinguish themselves from what they see as an American overemphasis on texts linking women across boundaries and decades and an underemphasis on popular art and culture. They regard their own critical practice as more political than that of American feminists, whom they have often faulted for being uninterested in historical detail. They would join such American critics as Myra Jehlen to suggest that a continuing preoccupation with women writers might create the danger of placing women's texts outside the history that conditions them.

In the view of British feminists, the American opposition to male stereotypes that denigrate women has often led to counterstereotypes of feminine virtue that ignore real differences of race, class, and culture among women. In addition, they argue that American celebrations of individual heroines falsely suggest that powerful individuals may be immune to repressive conditions and may even imply that *any* individual can go through life unconditioned by the culture and ideology in which she or he lives.

Similarly, the American endeavor to recover women's history — for example, by emphasizing that women developed their own strategies to gain power within their sphere — is seen by British feminists like Judith Newton and Deborah Rosenfelt as an endeavor that "mystifies" male oppression, disguising it as something that has created for women a special world of opportunities. More important from the British standpoint, the universalizing and "essentializing" tendencies in both American practice and French theory disguise women's oppression by highlighting sexual difference, suggesting that a dominant system is impervious to political change. By contrast, British feminist theory em-

phasizes an engagement with historical process in order to promote social change.

In *The Proper Lady and the Woman Writer* (1984), Mary Poovey
showed how Mary Shelley's desire to be the latter came constantly into
conflict with the need, conditioned by her masculine-dominated culture, to be the former. In the essay that follows, Johanna M. Smith
builds on Poovey's argument by showing the presence of patriarchal
ideology in the way that *Frankenstein* pictures men and women in "separate spheres" defined not only by the nature of the work done in them
but also by the extent to which language is an available or appropriate
tool.

What Smith goes on to point out, however, is that *Frankenstein* is
deeply conflicted with regard to the patriarchal ideology so deeply inscribed in it. This conflict, evident within the character of Victor Frankenstein, parallels a conflict that can be found in Mary Shelley's private
writings. There, Victor's creator exhibits great uncertainty about her
ability to use language publicly and effectively. There, too, she exhibits
guilt over the degree to which her life as a writer has brought her into
the public sphere and, at the same time, an abiding dissatisfaction with
the traditional domestic roles of daughters and wives.

Mary's ambivalence toward domesticity and public life are thus seen
as being inseparable from the text's ambivalence toward women and
language. *Frankenstein,* Smith points out, is a work made of words by a
woman in which women characters never speak directly; language is
represented as a masculine realm by a woman who, in one sense, lived
by language. The troubled feeling that writing was a masculine activity
may, Smith suggests, have led Mary Shelley, first, to allow her husband
to revise her manuscript version of the novel, bringing it more in line
with his latinate style; later, it may have caused her to allow him to
revise the novel into one that more clearly taught domestic virtues.

Finally, though, Smith sees Mary Shelley effectively resisting patriarchal ideology, rather than merely succumbing to it. For one thing, she
suggests that the author's decision to permit her husband's collaboration may have been less an act of submission than a conscious or subconscious attempt at resistance. By the act, she may have been resisting
not only the convention of seeing creation as the mysterious fulmina-
tion of a single mind but also the conventional notion that language is
tied to gender. Even more provocative is Smith's suggestion that *Frankenstein* counters the notion that women should inhabit a separate
sphere by creating a "feminine patriarch" (in Alphonse, the good fa-

ther) and, later, by connecting the domesticity of Victor's early life with later monstrosities.

In its interest in language, Smith's work bears evidence of the French feminist influence; in its interest in women, creativity, and androgyny, it shows the influence of American gynocriticism. Finally, however, Smith — though an American — writes feminist criticism more nearly on the British model by emphasizing writing and ideology. Ideology not only informs writing but is also resisted and, presumably, changed by the very writing that responds to it.

FEMINIST CRITICISM: A SELECTED BIBLIOGRAPHY

French Feminist Theories

Beauvoir, Simone de. *The Second Sex*. 1953. Trans. and ed. H. M. Parshley. New York: Bantam, 1961.

Cixous, Hélène. "The Laugh of the Medusa." Trans. Keith Cohen and Paula Cohen. *Signs* 1 (1976): 875–94.

Cixous, Hélène, and Catherine Clément. *The Newly Born Woman*. Trans. Betsy Wing. Minneapolis: U of Minnesota P, 1986.

French Feminist Theory. Special issue, *Signs* 7.1 (1981).

Irigaray, Luce. *This Sex Which Is Not One*. Trans. Catherine Porter. Ithaca: Cornell UP, 1985.

Jones, Ann Rosalind. "Writing the Body: Toward an Understanding of *L'Écriture féminine*." Showalter, *New Feminist Criticism* 361–77.

Kristeva, Julia. *Desire in Language: A Semiotic Approach to Literature and Art*. Ed. Leon S. Roudiez. Trans. Thomas Gora, Alice Jardine, and Roudiez. New York: Columbia UP, 1980.

Marks, Elaine, and Isabelle de Courtivron, eds. *New French Feminisms: An Anthology*. Amherst: U of Massachusetts P, 1980.

Moi, Toril, ed. *French Feminist Thought: A Reader*. Oxford: Basil Blackwell, 1987.

British and American Feminist Theories

Belsey, Catherine, and Jane Moore, eds. *The Feminist Reader: Essays in Gender and the Politics of Literary Criticism*. New York: Basil Blackwell, 1989.

Benhabib, Seyla, and Drucilla Cornell, eds. *Feminism as Critique: On the Politics of Gender.* Minneapolis: U of Minnesota P, 1987.

Collins, Patricia Hill. *Black Feminist Thought: Knowledge, Consciousness, and the Politics of Empowerment.* Boston: Unwin Hyman, 1990.

de Lauretis, Teresa, ed. *Feminist Studies/Critical Studies.* Bloomington: Indiana UP, 1986.

Feminist Readings: French Texts/American Contexts. Special issue, *Yale French Studies* 62 (1982). Essays by Jardine and Spivak.

hooks, bell. *Ain't I a Woman?: Black Women and Feminism.* Boston: South End, 1981.

Keohane, Nannerl O., Michelle Z. Rosaldo, and Barbara C. Gelpi, eds. *Feminist Theory: A Critique of Ideology.* Chicago: U of Chicago P, 1982.

Kolodny, Annette. "Dancing Through the Minefield: Some Observations on the Theory, Practice, and Politics of a Feminist Literary Criticism." Showalter, *New Feminist Criticism* 144–67.

The Lesbian Issue. Special issue, *Signs* 9 (Summer 1984).

Malson, Micheline, et al., eds. *Feminist Theory in Practice and Process.* Chicago: U of Chicago P, 1986.

Rich, Adrienne. *On Lies, Secrets, and Silence: Selected Prose, 1966–1979.* New York: Norton, 1979.

Showalter, Elaine. "Toward a Feminist Poetics." Showalter, *New Feminist Criticism* 125–43.

———, ed. *The New Feminist Criticism: Essays on Women, Literature, and Theory.* New York: Pantheon, 1985.

The Feminist Critique

Fetterley, Judith. *The Resisting Reader: A Feminist Approach to American Fiction.* Bloomington: Indiana UP, 1978.

Greer, Germaine. *The Female Eunuch.* New York: McGraw, 1971.

Millett, Kate. *Sexual Politics.* Garden City: Doubleday, 1970.

Robinson, Lillian S. *Sex, Class, and Culture.* 1978. New York: Methuen, 1986.

Wittig, Monique. *Les Guerilléres.* Trans. David Le Vay. 1969. New York: Avon, 1973.

Woolf, Virginia. *A Room of One's Own.* New York: Harcourt, 1929.

Women's Writing and Creativity

Abel, Elizabeth, ed. *Writing and Sexual Difference.* Chicago: U of Chicago P, 1982.

Abel, Elizabeth, Marianne Hirsch, and Elizabeth Langland, eds. *The Voyage In: Fictions of Female Development.* Hanover: UP of New England, 1983.

Auerbach, Nina. *Communities of Women: An Idea in Fiction.* Cambridge: Harvard UP, 1978.

Christian, Barbara. *Black Feminist Criticism: Perspectives on Black Women Writers.* New York: Pergamon, 1985.

Gilbert, Sandra M., and Susan Gubar. *The Madwoman in the Attic: The Woman Writer and the Nineteenth-Century Literary Imagination.* New Haven: Yale UP, 1979.

Jacobus, Mary, ed. *Women Writing and Writing about Women.* New York: Barnes, 1979.

Miller, Nancy K., ed. *The Poetics of Gender.* New York: Columbia UP, 1986.

Newton, Judith Lowder. *Women, Power and Subversion: Social Strategies in British Fiction, 1778–1860.* Athens: U of Georgia P, 1981.

Poovey, Mary. *The Proper Lady and the Woman Writer: Ideology as Style in the Works of Mary Wollstonecraft, Mary Shelley, and Jane Austen.* Chicago: U of Chicago P, 1984.

Showalter, Elaine. *A Literature of Their Own: British Women Novelists from Brontë to Lessing.* Princeton: Princeton UP, 1977.

Marxist and Class Analysis

Barrett, Michèle. *Women's Oppression Today: Problems in Marxist Feminist Analysis.* London: Verso, 1980.

Delphy, Christine. *Close to Home: A Materialist Analysis of Women's Oppression.* Trans. and ed. Diana Leonard. Amherst: U of Massachusetts P, 1984.

Hartsock, Nancy C. M. *Money, Sex, and Power: Toward a Feminist Historical Materialism.* Boston: Northeastern UP, 1985.

Kaplan, Cora. *Sea Changes: Culture and Feminism.* London: Verso, 1986.

Mitchell, Juliet. *Woman's Estate.* New York: Pantheon, 1971.

Newton, Judith, and Deborah Rosenfelt, eds. *Feminist Criticism and Social Change: Sex, Class and Race in Literature and Culture.* New York: Methuen, 1985.

Sargent, Lydia, ed. *Women and Revolution: A Discussion of the Unhappy Marriage of Marxism and Feminism.* Montreal: Black Rose, 1981.

Women's History / Women's Studies

Bridenthal, Renate, and Claudia Koonze, eds. *Becoming Visible: Women in European History.* Boston: Houghton, 1977.

Farnham, Christie, ed. *The Impact of Feminist Research in the Academy.* Bloomington: Indiana UP, 1987.

Kelly, Joan. *Women, History and Theory.* Chicago: U of Chicago P, 1984.

McConnell-Ginet, Sally, et al., eds. *Woman and Language in Literature and Society.* New York: Praeger, 1980.

Mitchell, Juliet, and Ann Oakley, eds. *The Rights and Wrongs of Women.* London: Penguin, 1976.

Newton, Judith L., et al., eds. *Sex and Class in Women's History.* London: Routledge, 1983.

Riley, Denise. *"Am I That Name?": Feminism and the Category of "Women" in History.* Minneapolis: U of Minnesota P, 1988.

Rowbotham, Sheila. *Woman's Consciousness, Man's World.* Harmondsworth: Penguin, 1973.

Schipper, Mineke, ed. *Unheard Words: Women and Literature in Africa, the Arab World, Asia, the Caribbean, and Latin America.* London: Allison, 1985.

Scott, Joan Wallach. *Gender and the Politics of History.* New York: Columbia UP, 1988.

Smith-Rosenberg, Carroll. *Disorderly Conduct: Visions of Gender in Victorian America.* New York: Knopf, 1985.

Feminism and Other Critical Approaches

Armstrong, Nancy, ed. *Literature as Women's History I.* A special issue of *Genre* 19–20 (1986–87).

Diamond, Irene, and Lee Quinby, eds. *Feminism and Foucault: Reflections on Resistance.* Boston: Northeastern UP, 1988.

Feminist Studies 14 (1988). Special issue on feminism and deconstruction.

Gallop, Jane. *The Daughter's Seduction: Feminism and Psychoanalysis.* Ithaca: Cornell UP, 1982.

Keller, Evelyn Fox. *Reflections on Gender and Science.* New Haven: Yale UP, 1985.

Meese, Elizabeth, and Alice Parker, eds. *The Difference Within: Feminism and Critical Theory.* Amsterdam/Philadelphia: John Benjamins, 1989.

Penley, Constance, ed. *Feminism and Film Theory.* New York: Routledge, 1988.

Feminist Criticism of *Frankenstein*

Carson, James B. "Bringing the Author Forward: *Frankenstein* through Mary Shelley's Letters." *Criticism* 30.4 (Fall 1988): 431–53.

Ellis, Kate. "Monsters in the Garden: Mary Shelley and the Bourgeois Family." *The Endurance of Frankenstein*. Ed. George Levine and U. C. Knoepflmacher. Berkeley: U of California P, 1979. 123–42.

Gilbert, Sandra M., and Susan Gubar. *The Madwoman in the Attic: The Woman Writer and the Nineteenth-Century Literary Imagination*. New Haven: Yale UP, 1979. 213–47.

Hatlen, Burton. "Milton, Mary Shelley, and Patriarchy." *Bucknell Review* 28.2 (1983): 19–47.

Hodges, Devon. "*Frankenstein* and the Feminine Subversion of the Novel." *Tulsa Studies in Women's Literature* 2.2 (Fall 1983): 155–64.

Homans, Margaret. *Bearing the Word: Language and Female Experience in Nineteenth-Century Woman's Writing*. Chicago: U of Chicago P, 1986. 110–19.

Mellor, Anne K. *Mary Shelley: Her Life, Her Fiction, Her Monsters*. New York: Methuen, 1988.

A FEMINIST PERSPECTIVE ON *FRANKENSTEIN*

JOHANNA M. SMITH

"Cooped Up": Feminine Domesticity in *Frankenstein*

It is important to note that *Frankenstein* was published anonymously, that its woman author kept her identity hidden. Similarly, no women in the novel speak directly: everything we hear from and about them is filtered through the three masculine narrators. In addition, these women seldom venture far from home, while the narrators and most of the other men engage in quests and various public occupations. These facts exemplify the nineteenth century's emerging doctrine of "separate spheres," the ideology that split off the (woman's) domestic sphere from the (man's) public world and strictly defined the "feminine" and "masculine" traits appropriate to each sphere. My essay will analyze the operations of this ideology in the writing of *Frankenstein* and in the novel itself.

From the novel's women we may infer that Mary Shelley approved the separate-spheres doctrine; Elizabeth, for example, fully embodies the ideologically correct feminine qualities Victor — and the author — attribute to her. Yet it is equally clear that Elizabeth and the domestic sphere she represents fail signally in their raison d'être, which is to prepare young men like Victor to resist the temptations of the public sphere. *Frankenstein* shows that the private virtues inculcated through domestic affection cannot arm men against the public world unless men emulate these feminine and domestic qualities. Although Victor waxes eloquent on the domestic "lesson of patience, of charity, and of self-control" taught him as a child (40), his quest for scientific glory shows that none of this lesson took; and while he often reiterates his "warmest admiration" (129) for Elizabeth's qualities, he perceives them not as a model but as a "reward" and "consolation" for his trials (131). Through these contradictions the novel may be suggesting that domestic affection can achieve its educational aim only if it is "hardy enough to survive in the world outside the home" (Ellis, "Monsters" 140); but *Frankenstein* also dramatizes how all but impossible is that aim.

The problem is that the domestic ideology is bifurcated: the home is to provide not only a moral education for involvement in the public world but also a shelter against this world. Instead of a nursery of virtue, then, the home could become, as one of domesticity's stoutest ideologues put it, a "relief from the severer duties of life" (Ellis, *Women* 12); a man could thus "pursue the necessary avocation of the day" but also "keep as it were a separate soul for his family, his social duty, and his God" (Ellis, *Women* 20). Although written some twenty years after *Frankenstein,* this picture of a man with two separate souls perfectly represents a contradictory domestic ideology and its product, a Victor divided between his masculine "necessary avocation" of scientific glory and his admiration of Elizabeth's feminine domesticity.

Feminist criticism of *Frankenstein* has addressed the similar conflict between public and private that troubled Victor's creator. Mary Shelley's 1831 introduction states her desire for the public fame both her parents had achieved by writing, but she adds that her private, domestic role — "the cares of a family" — kept her from pursuing this goal (20). Even when she went public with *Frankenstein* in 1818, she remained to some extent private by publishing it anonymously. Several possible explanations of this desire for privacy suggest themselves. While Mary claimed that she withheld her name out of respect for those "from whom I bear it" (*Letters* 1.71), she may also have feared a repetition of the public contumely directed at both of her parents as well as their writings. The experience of her husband Percy and their friend Byron, two published poets whose work and unconventional lives had been vilified by critics, must have intensified these fears. And, although by 1818 she was legally married, her experience of publicity after eloping — she knew the rumors that her father had sold her to Percy (*Letters* 1.4) — may have made her especially wary of inviting public attention. Finally, Mary's caution could well have been gender-specific: she may have wanted to prevent critics from dismissing her as a woman writer.

Several elements of this last possibility — the terms of such a critical judgment, Mary Shelley's own view of women's writing, the difficulty of writing her way out of the woman's private into the man's public sphere — are well illustrated by the peregrinations of a letter she wrote to Percy. On September 30, 1817, the letter's date, *Frankenstein* was at the publisher, halfway between a private and a public state; Percy Shelley, not Mary, was in London editing the proofs. In her letter Mary animadverted at some length on the politics of a pamphlet by the radical William Cobbett. Percy apparently showed these private comments on public affairs to their mutual friend Leigh Hunt, editor of the *Examiner*. Without informing Mary, Hunt published her comments in the October 15 *Examiner;* he did not name her but did note her gender, describing her as "a lady of what is called a masculine understanding, that is to say, of great natural abilities not obstructed by a *bad* education" (*Letters* 1.54, fn. 2). Mary's letter reads somewhat breathlessly — like much of the manuscript *Frankenstein,* for instance, it is punctuated only by dashes — and she felt it "cut a very foolish figure" in print (*Letters* 1.53). Had she known Hunt planned to make her comments public, she told Percy, she would have written with "more print-worthy dignity"; instead, the letter was "so femeninely [sic] expressed that all men of letters will on reading it acquit me of having a *masculine* understanding."

The incident of the letter and its author's response illuminate several of her difficulties as a woman writer. To begin with, she would come up against one element of the separation of spheres, namely a strict ideological distinction of "masculine" from "feminine" qualities. In Hunt's editorial note, for instance, "great natural abilities" are gendered; that is, they are equated with "a masculine understanding." If "obstructed" by the "bad" education most women could expect to receive, these abilities would be feminized — that is, obscured and weakened. For Mary Shelley to name herself as *Frankenstein's* author, then, would be to endanger her status as honorary man, to risk having her "masculine understanding" impugned as "femininely expressed."

Writing a novel of "print-worthy dignity" had already presented its author with similar problems. As I have noted (see p. 11), her domestic duties interfered with the time available for writing, and as editor her husband may have been a further impediment. Mary Poovey has cogently argued that Mary Shelley's own editing of the 1831 *Frankenstein* was meant to bring her younger, unorthodox self into line with the conventional image of a proper lady, and it seems to me that a similar image-making motivated Percy's revisions of his wife's manuscript. In some ways, of course, his idea of a proper lady diverged wildly from contemporary ideology; after he and Mary eloped, for instance, he suggested to his wife Harriet that she join them. Nonetheless, Percy Shelley shared his culture's desire to mold women according to a masculine idea of femininity, a narcissistic complement to masculine traits. Such narcissism colored his view of his relationship with Mary: they were so "united," he wrote, that in describing her "excellencies" he seemed to himself "an egoist expatiating upon his own perfections" (qtd. in Spark 21). His editing displays the same self-satisfied desire to "unite" Mary's work to his, to see his perfections mirrored in her manuscript.

While some of Percy Shelley's changes are clarifications and others are grammatical, even these minimal alterations show his desire to control the text and shape it in his own image. As he consistently changes Mary's dashes to colons and semicolons, for instance, or her coordinating "that" to the subordinating "which," he is imposing his order on her ideas. More striking are his revisions of her language. Anne K. Mellor has exhaustively documented the extent to which Percy altered Mary's straightforward and colloquial diction into a more ponderous and latinate prose,[1] and my own examination of the rough-draft and fair-copy manuscripts confirms that he is largely responsible for what George Levine calls the novel's "inflexibly public and oratorical" style (3). This "public" style is masculine — the product of a public-school and university education, available only to men, which taught writing by using Latin prose as a model — and so it confers "print-worthy dignity" on what might otherwise seem "femininely expressed."

Where Percy Shelley's changes extended beyond clarification, grammar, and diction, Mellor charges that they "actually distorted the meaning of the text" (62). I will return to this questionable notion that any text has a single meaning, but certainly Percy's heavy editorial hand marks the novel throughout. He rewrote some sections extensively; his fair copy of the conclusion (from Victor's death on) significantly revises

[1]See Mellor 58–69 and Appendix. Murray 62–68 prints a useful side-by-side listing of the rough draft, fair copy, and 1831 revisions.

the rough draft; and his wife gave him "carte blanche to make what alterations you please" while he was editing certain sections of the proofs (*Letters* 1.42).

Accustomed as we are to regarding authorship as independent creation we may wonder why Mary Shelley allowed her husband to rewrite her novel in these fairly substantial ways. Every writer knows how dispiriting it is to have one's deathless prose altered, no matter how kindly — especially when, as in Mary's case, the alterations come from a more experienced and thus (presumably) authoritative writer. Yet most writers have also felt the benefits of what might be called a collaborative editing, one that does not "distort" a text's single meaning but rather teases out its several inchoate or chaotic possibilities. It is at least arguable, then, that Mary acceded to her husband's changes not simply out of "deference to his superior mind" (Mellor 69) but also because she viewed him as a collaborator. Moreover, if Percy's revisions were in some ways protective coloration, they were also empowering: his attentions must have encouraged her to believe that she "possessed the promise of better things hereafter" (Introduction 20) and to produce a substantial body of "better things" after his death.

But the issue of a man's influence on a woman writer remains complicated. Mary Shelley felt unable "to put [her]self forward unless led, cherished & supported," and she perceived this need for support as feminine, "the woman's love of looking up and being guided" (*Journal* 555). It might be, then, that this ideology of dependent femininity rendered her unable to write her own text without her husband's help. Moreover, collaboration forced by a more dominant writer on a less powerful and perhaps unwilling "partner" is a kind of rape; if *Frankenstein* is the product of such a union, then it evinces a debilitating femininity. But to perceive writing as noncollaborative, as a necessarily independent act, betokens a concept of masculinity that raises another set of problems. One has only to think of Victor as self-sufficient "author"[2] — of the monster (91), "unalterable evils" (84), and "[his] own speedy ruin" (92) — to see such authorship as a monstrous, masculine version of creativity. If Mary Shelley rejected this view of creation as autochthonous, of a work as wholly self-engendered, *Frankenstein* becomes "an incipient critique of the individualistic notion of

---

[2]Mellor 65 argues that Percy Shelley introduced all uses of the word "author." Granted I am not a handwriting expert, the manuscript evidence for this assertion does not seem to me conclusive; moreover, even if it were he who introduced the word, surely Mary Shelley would have had her own ideas of what it connoted.

originary creativity" (Carson 436). By welcoming help, then, she challenged a destructive version of "masculine understanding." But even if her collaboration was willing, it could be seen as self-suppression, an acceptance of "feminine" weakness: as the journal entry cited above shows, a woman of her time was *conditioned* to think she needed a man's help. From this perspective, her willingness to accept her husband's revisions is analogous to the novel's oppressively feminine women: all are efforts to straddle the line between public and private, to ensure that a masculine understanding is expressed without feminine obstructions but with feminine propriety.

This "but"-laden formulation leaves the question of Percy Shelley's influence open, and I have done so deliberately — partly because editing this book showed me the difficulty of distinguishing between encouragement and coercion, partly because we cannot ascertain Mary Shelley's motives with any certainty, but mainly because the problem of influence shows that the relations between prescribed femininity and women's actual experience are so convoluted as to resist single-answer formulations.

If we now turn from the author to her novel, we can see how domestic relationships in *Frankenstein* embody this complex and uneasy negotiation between ideology and experience.

The Frankenstein home seems a model of ideologically correct relationships. Not only are Alphonse and Caroline happily married, as parents they are "possessed by the very spirit of kindness and indulgence" (43). Together, we are told, they guide Victor with "a silken cord" (40); they are joint "agents and creators" of his childhood joys (43); and he derives as much pleasure from his father's "smile of benevolent pleasure" (40) as from his mother's "tender caresses." This shared parenting shows that men as well as women have an important domestic role; indeed, insofar as Alphonse is a Good Father, he is feminine. His nurturant qualities were commonly associated with femininity, and it is significant that he has "relinquished all his public functions," withdrawn from the man's sphere of government into the woman's domestic sphere. Yet he also fulfills the traditional masculine role of protector toward his wife, by rescuing her from want and "shelter[ing] her, as a fair exotic is sheltered by the gardener, from every rougher wind." In these ways Alphonse becomes a sort of feminine patriarch, and his gentle rule by "silken cord" is the reverse of paternal tyranny.

Also ideologically sound is the harmony produced among the household's children by their opposite yet complementary traits.

Where the original manuscript focused on diversity, the final version was revised to focus on harmony. In the rough draft, for instance, an electrical storm produced "a very different effect" on each child: Victor wanted "to analyze its causes," Henry "said that the fairies and giants were at war," and Elizabeth "attempted a picture of it" (Abinger Dep.c.477/1, p. 45). Although the 1831 *Frankenstein* retains such differences between Elizabeth and Victor, the focus shifts to how "diversity and contrast . . . drew us nearer together" (42). Elizabeth accepts "with a serious and satisfied spirit the appearance of things" while Victor "delight[s] in investigating their causes," but no "disunion or dispute" mars this gender difference between feminine passivity and masculine activity. Here as throughout the novel, gender opposites are represented as complements. The young Victor Frankenstein and his friend Henry Clerval actively prepare for public futures while Elizabeth simply exists as a domestic icon, but what might seem an *opposition* between separate spheres is rewritten as complementary *difference*. In other words, while Elizabeth is little more than "the living spirit of love" (43), as such she has feminine functions. Her "sympathy," smile, etc. are "ever there to bless and animate" Henry and Victor; she teaches Henry "the real loveliness of beneficence" (43), and she keeps Victor from becoming "sullen" and "rough" by "subdu[ing him] to a semblance of her own gentleness"(43).

In Henry, moreover, Victor has a paradigm for the successful complementarity of masculine and feminine traits within himself. While Henry wants to be one of "the gallant and adventurous benefactors of our species" (43), he is also a domestic benefactor: as Victor's "kind and attentive nurse" (61) at Ingolstadt, he fulfills the role Elizabeth wished for herself (63). In addition, he tempers his masculine "passion for adventurous exploit" (43) with Elizabeth's feminine desire that he make "doing good the end and aim of his soaring ambition." Unlike Victor's "mad enthusiasm" (154), Henry's "wild and enthusiastic imagination was chastened by the sensibility of his heart" (133). Clearly, Victor's "eager desire" to learn "the *physical* secrets of the world" should have been balanced by Henry's preoccupation with "the *moral* relations of things" (43; emphasis added).

Why, then, does this domestic enclave of virtue not protect Victor? Why does he not remain within the boundaries marked off by the "silken cord" of domestic affection? Why does he not profit from the "lesson of patience, of charity, of self-control" taught by his parents and embodied in his friends, Elizabeth and Henry? The answers lie in

Victor's complicated relations to nature, feminized domesticity, and masculine science.

For Victor, nature is "maternal" (87), and its life-giving and "kindly influence" has a domestic equivalent in Elizabeth's feminine fosterage. Just as Elizabeth "subdued Victor to a semblance of her own gentleness," so a "cloudless blue sky" can bestow "a tranquillity to which [he] had long been a stranger" (132); just as Elizabeth can "inspire [him] with human feelings" (159), so a "divine spring" can "revive" in him "sentiments of joy and affection" (62). In these moods of openness to nature, Victor is feminized into passive tranquillity and domestic affection. In other moods, however, he thrills to a more masculine nature; when he experiences a storm in the Alps, for instance, "This noble war in the sky elevated my spirits" (72). It is this idea of war, of attempted conquest or dominion, that most frequently informs Victor's masculine attitude toward nature. It is no accident, then, that he chooses the masculine realm of science as a means of discovering and thereby mastering the secrets of feminine nature. From childhood Victor had regarded the world as "a secret which I desired to divine"; repeatedly he tells us of his obsessive curiosity about "the hidden laws of nature" (42), his "eager desire" to learn "the secrets of heaven and earth" (43), his "fervent longing to penetrate the secrets of nature" (44). Because "her immortal lineaments were still a wonder and a mystery" to him (45), this unknown nature offers a field for the masculine mastery promised by scientific knowledge.[3] At Ingolstadt M. Waldman assures him that modern scientists can "penetrate into the recesses of nature and show how she works in her hiding-places" (51), and so Victor determines to "pursue nature to her hiding-places"(56).

Now, this language describing masculine penetration of feminine nature may be scientific, but it also sounds insistently sexual; to post-Freudian ears, it may suggest a woman writer's uneasiness with masculine sexuality.[4] But another explanation may lie in Mary Shelley's conflicted desire both to achieve public fame by writing and to escape the consequent publicity by remaining in the private sphere. If Percy Shel-

[3]Mellor's Chapter 5 fully documents the masculinist language of domination used by the scientists Mary consulted while writing *Frankenstein;* on more recent uses of such language, see Kranzler.

[4]There is some biographical evidence for this view. In 1815 Percy was apparently urging Mary toward an affair with his friend T. J. Hogg, who was nothing loath; this combined sexual pressure may have been at least unsettling for Mary, at worst the same kind of masculine domination that Victor wants to impose on nature. See *Letters* 1.6–14; the most even-handed treatment of this episode is Spark 40–46.

ley's "incitement" (23) reinforced her "persistent association of writing with an aggressive quest for public notice" (Poovey 121), then writing *Frankenstein* must have seemed to *invite* the consequent invasions by publicity. The novel's language of penetration, that is, may have less to do with sexuality per se than with a woman writer's fear that walled-off domesticity cannot guarantee the privacy it promises. More troubling would be the possibility that, if writing masculinizes, then it might make a woman Victor-like, aggressive, a scientific violator of domesticity's secrets.

But if domesticity can be penetrated, especially from within, does this not suggest that it was never inviolable, that its apparent strengths were in fact its weaknesses or even its immanent destruction? This question moves back toward the problem of feminized domesticity, and here we need to look again at Alphonse's role as feminine patriarch. While Victor says that Waldman's promises of scientific prowess were "enounced to destroy me" (51), he blames not Waldman but his father. Instead of offhandedly dismissing Cornelius Agrippa as "sad trash" (44), Victor complains, Alphonse should have explained that modern science "possessed much greater powers" than Agrippa's outmoded alchemical methods; Victor would then have bowed to the authority of paternal knowledge and "possibl[y]" escaped "the fatal impulse that led to my ruin" (44). Well, maybe. But if the revelation of modern science's "new and almost unlimited powers" (51) is an "evil influence" when it comes from M. Waldman (49), it would be no less evil coming from the elder Frankenstein. Significant here are the author's revisions rendering Alphonse "not scientific" (45). She omitted from the rough draft both his scientific experiments and his wish that Victor attend lectures in natural philosophy, and she altered the decision to send Victor to university, originally made by "my father," to the wish of "my parents" (Abinger Dep.c.477/1, pp. 6, 47). All these changes suggest that the author intended to reduce Alphonse's culpability for Victor's skewed science.

Yet Alphonse *does* contribute to Victor's ruin, not because he is a bad scientist but because he is a good father. What I am suggesting is a destructive domesticity enforced by the feminized patriarch. Despite Victor's insistence on his perfect childhood, his relation to his "remarkably secluded and domestic" upbringing (48) is in fact conflicted. On the one hand, he is "reluctant" to leave home for Ingolstadt, where he must become "[his] own protector"; on the other, he has "longed to enter the world," to no longer be "cooped up" by domesticity and its protections. In a novel ostensibly written to exhibit "the amiableness of domestic affection" (Preface 25),[5] Victor's admission jars: can it be that his home is too domestic, his feminized father too protective?

Although Victor insists on his "gratitude" for his parents' care (43), we may speculate that this very gratitude has made him feel "cooped up." Gratitude, no matter how heartfelt, implies obligation, which in turn implies the power of the person to whom one is grateful or obligated. The insistence on gratitude and obligation induces a bookkeeping mentality that permeates all the relations in this novel. Victor acknowledges Henry Clerval's nursing by asking "How shall I ever repay you?" (62); Felix De Lacey views Safie as "a treasure which would fully reward his toil and hazard" in rescuing her father (108); when shot by the peasant, the monster fumes that "the reward of [his] benevolence" is "ingratitude" (122). This emotional quid pro quo is most evident, however, in the novel's domestic relations. In these terms the Frankenstein family is "a paradigm of the social contract based on economic terms" (Dussinger 52), for kinship and domestic affection are "secondary to the indebtedness incurred by promises exchanged for gifts." That is, in this family what seems freely given in fact requires something in exchange, so that the relation between parents and children is one of "unpayable debt."

Rather than Victor's picture of a gentle patriarch guiding by "silken cord," what then emerges is a cord or bond of constricting domestic relations. Among the Frankensteins, a gift requires gratitude and so produces a sense of obligation that can be discharged only by endless repetition of this pattern. Victor's parents had "a deep consciousness of what they *owed* towards the being to which they had *given* life" (40). To them the child was

> the innocent and helpless creature *bestowed* on them by Heaven,
> . . . whose future lot it was in their hands to direct to happiness
> or misery, according as they fulfilled their duties towards me. (40;
> emphases added)

Caroline and Alphonse pay off their debt of gratitude to "heaven" by fulfilling the duties they owe their child. Victor in turn owes gratitude for the life "given" him and for his parents' care, but their power and

---

[5]In her 1831 introduction Mary Shelley claims that Percy Shelley wrote this Preface, but an 1817 journal entry suggests otherwise. On May 14 she writes "S. [i.e., Percy] reads History of Fr[ench] Rev[olution] and corrects F[rankenstein]. write Preface. — Finis" (*Journal* 169). The verb "write" indicates that the omitted subject of this sentence is not Percy but "I"; this may be a slip of the pen, but if not it is interesting to speculate why Mary remembered Percy and not herself as the author of the Preface.

his consequent obligations form the cord that, no matter how silken, confines and encloses him within the family. Hence he repeats this domestic pattern when he contemplates creating a new species, and his view of the parent–child relation revealingly focuses on himself as patriarch. The members of his new species "would *owe* their being to me," he gloats, and so "[n]o father could *claim* the *gratitude* of his child so completely as I should deserve theirs" (55; emphases added). Alphonse may have seemed a gentle patriarch, but Victor's words suggest there was an iron hand in this velvet glove: a father can *claim* gratitude from the child who owes existence to him.

Judged simply from this paternal point of view, there is a certain logic in Victor's abandonment of the "child" he created: if the sheer bestowal of existence is a sufficient claim to gratitude, why be an Alphonse-like Good Father? Of course, in abandoning the monster Victor forgets the distinction he had earlier made between merely claiming gratitude and really deserving it. To deserve gratitude, parents must "fulfill their duties" toward their child; because Victor does not do so, he is a Bad Father and his child is not embodied filial gratitude but "my own vampire, my own spirit . . . forced to destroy all that was dear to me" (73). But if a bad father produces a bad child, and Victor like the monster is a bad child, does this not suggest that Alphonse too was a bad father, that he somehow failed to fulfill his duties toward his child? Or was it *fulfilling* those duties that made him a bad father? In other words, can the ideologically correct Good Father be so nurturant that he becomes a Bad Father? If so, then Alphonse's paternal protection is as damaging to his child as Victor's paternal indifference is to his. In other words, while the monster becomes monstrous in part because he has been denied parental care, Victor becomes monstrous in part because he has been *given* this care and made subject to the attendant obligations. In this reading, the "spirit" that Victor releases through the monster is the masculinity so "cooped up" by Alphonse's feminized domesticity that it breaks out as "the male principle in its extreme, monstrous form" (Veeder 190). Hence Victor can enter the masculine sphere of science only by destroying the feminine sphere, and that includes his feminized father. Victor's kinship to the monster reveals the dark side of the Frankenstein family's oppressive domesticity and too-nurturant patriarch.

But Victor is not the only victim of this pattern of domestic indebtedness: it is the novel's women who are literally destroyed by it. In the relations of Caroline, Elizabeth, and Justine to the Frankenstein family, we can again see something excessive, something too enveloping in Frankensteinian domesticity. Certainly the image of Caroline as Alphonse's "fair exotic" (39) suggests a hot-house atmosphere, and when she transplants the "garden rose" Elizabeth (41) to the Frankenstein home as Victor's "more than sister" (42), "the amiableness of domestic affection" comes precariously close to incest. Of course Elizabeth is not literally Victor's sister, and he later assures his father that he loves her not as a brother but as a husband (129). But pursuing the hint of incest will clarify how blood kinship among the Frankensteins is secondary to familial indebtedness; we can then see how the resulting insistent domesticity kills off the novel's women.

Class selection determines which women are worthy to enter the upper class Frankenstein family; as Anca Vlasopolos suggests, this criterion is "a form of aristocratic protectionism that encourages, in fact engineers, incest" (126) by closing the family off from otherness or difference. Although plunged into straw-plaiting poverty by her father's business failure, Caroline's lineage and beauty mark her as still deserving the "rank and magnificence" he once enjoyed (38); by marrying her, then, Alphonse is restoring the status quo, rescuing Caroline from the otherness of a working-class milieu and returning her to her proper place. This pattern is even more overt in the adoption of Elizabeth. Because Elizabeth is "of a different stock" from her rude guardians (40), Caroline rescues this nobleman's daughter from the lower orders and then uses the "powerful protection" (41) of the Frankenstein family to restore Elizabeth to her proper status. Difference is further excluded as Elizabeth takes on all the family's feminine roles; Victor's "more than sister" and destined to be his wife, she also becomes Caroline by "supply[ing her] place" as mother after her death (47). Although Justine is brought less fully into the family, she is perhaps the most Frankensteinized: when Caroline rescues her from a Bad Mother, Justine so "imitate[s] her phraseology and manners" (64) as to become her clone. The Frankenstein family's incestuous pattern of reproducing itself by excluding difference could hardly be clearer. And although none of these women is a born Frankenstein, they all — unlike Victor — fully internalize the family pattern of gratitude that enforces obligation.

This insistent replication of the grateful icon of domesticity shows how completely the pattern of indebtedness permeates the Frankenstein definition of femininity. Caroline is an especially rich example of this definition. We first see her as a daughter; even though her father's culpably "proud and unbending disposition" (38) forces her into his (masculine) role of breadwinner, the daughterly "tenderness" that discharges obligations to even a bad father (39) ensures her elevation to Frankenstein status. After Alphonse becomes her "protecting spirit," Caroline almost literally owes all she has to this marriage, and his oppressive benevolence constitutes another silken cord of enjoined gratitude. When she tries to discharge her obligations by "act[ing] in her turn the guardian angel to the afflicted" (40) — that is, by becoming a Frankenstein — her benevolence takes the usual form of enforced gratitude and obligation. When she gives Justine an education, for instance, "this benefit was fully repaid" (64) when Justine becomes "the most grateful little creature in the world." And when Caroline tries to discharge her debt to Alphonse by rescuing Elizabeth as she herself was rescued, she eventually pays with her life when she catches scarlet fever while nursing her protegée; unlike Victor, she has learned her own lesson "of patience, of charity" only too well.

A similar sacrifice is Elizabeth. Indebted to Caroline for rescue from peasant life, she must discharge this debt by taking Caroline's place as the Frankenstein ideal of femininity. As "a shrine-dedicated lamp in our peaceful home" (43) and "the tie of our domestic comfort and the stay of [Alphonse's] declining years," she is embodied domesticity. She is also Victor's "possession" (41), as he puts it: "my pride and my delight," "mine to protect, love, and cherish." But just as Alphonse's "protecting spirit" is ultimately responsible for Caroline's death, so Victor fails signally to "protect and cherish" his wife. His dream, that his kiss kills Elizabeth and turns her into his dead mother, is proleptic of the price she must pay for being Caroline's "pretty present" to him (41): in the form of the monster, Victor's aggressive masculinity murders the domestic femininity that had tried to "subdue [him] to a semblance of her own gentleness."

Justine is perhaps the most pathetic victim of this pattern of replicated femininity. Exhausted by her Caroline-like maternal care in searching for William, she falls asleep and so becomes the monster's prey. Her likeness to Caroline reminds him that he is "forever robbed" of any woman's "joy-imparting smiles" (123), so he determines that "she shall atone" for all women's indifference. While Justine suffers here from being Caroline's stand-in, more generally her crime is being seductive; according to this masculine logic, women are "to blame for having been desired" (Jacobus 133). To the townspeople, however, the crime for which Justine must "atone" is "blackest ingratitude" toward her benefactors (79). Once again the portrait of Caroline seals Justine's fate: planted on her by the monster, it becomes circumstantial evidence of this ingratitude. Elizabeth's statement of her own and Caroline's kindness to their servant backfires; Justine, like Caroline and Elizabeth, must pay her obligations to the Frankensteins with her life, and furthermore dies all but convinced "that I was the monster" of ingratitude she is accused of being (80). These dramatic ironies, one victimized woman convicting another and that second victim convicting herself, in fact convict the Frankenstein family of omnivorous benevolence. Victor is right to call himself Justine's murderer (149), for it is the masculinity he represents that destroys its own creation of perfect femininity.

Victor's creation and destruction of the female monster is a kind of parody of these three women's fates. From watching the De Laceys and Safie, the monster learns to value the delights of domesticity they represent but also learns that he is "shut out" from such intercourse (106); hence he asks Victor for a mate with whom to "interchange [the] sympathies necessary for my being" (124). Given the failure of his exchange of sympathies with the De Laceys, it is more than a little ironic that the monster should make this request. And his desire for a female complement, a woman "as hideous as myself" (125), parodies not only Victor's insistence on Elizabeth's complementary relationship to himself, but also Victor's bride-to-be as both the creation and the gift of his parents. This traffic in women via Frankensteinian quid pro quo is at its most overt in the murders of the monsterette and Elizabeth: deprived of a bride by Victor, the monster retaliates by killing Victor's bride. Victor, of course, assumes that he and not Elizabeth will be the monster's target, and in one sense he is correct: like the monsterette's, Elizabeth's creation and murder show that women function not in their own right but rather as signals of and conduits for men's relations with other men.

Against this dreary record of dead women we may place Safie. Her mother was rescued from slavery just as Caroline was rescued from poverty (Ellis, "Monsters" 141), but there the resemblance ends. From her mother Safie learns "to aspire to higher powers of intellect and an independence of spirit" (108); hence she flouts her father's "tyrannical mandate" (110) against marrying Felix and travels across Europe to rejoin him. Both her maternal inspiration and her active adventurousness contrast with Caroline's influence on her passive "daughters" Elizabeth and Justine. Unlike their iconic femininity, Safie is "subtly androgynous" (Rubinstein 189); we might see her as a female Henry, combining the standard feminine "angelic beauty" (103) with a masculine energy and enterprise lacking in the novel's other women. But the challenge she might represent to conventional ideas of femininity is in effect "absorbed" by various cultural norms (Vlasopolos 132). In the first place, her desire to marry Felix has a class bias, for she is "en-chant[ed]" (109) by the prospect of "tak[ing] a place in society." In addition, unlike Henry or Walton she seeks adventure not for its own sake or to benefit humankind but to get a man. This is not to say that Walton's quest is unambiguously benevolent: like Victor's desire to "pioneer a new way" (51) and thus achieve "more, far more" than his predecessors, Walton's urge to "confer on all mankind" (26) an "inestimable benefit" is motivated at least as much by a self-absorbed itch for glory as by humanitarianism. It is nonetheless true that Safie, albeit much less drastically than the Frankenstein women, represents the view that women are "relative creatures" whose value derives from "promoting the happiness of others" (Ellis, *Women* 48, 16). It is thus apt that she joins the De Lacey family, for while their interactive domes-tic style stands in stark contrast to the rigid gift/debt structure of the Frankensteins, still it is a conventionally separate-spheres arrangement: Felix is "constantly employed out of doors" (98), for instance, while his sister Agatha's work consists of "arranging the cottage" (97). More-over, just as Victor's family attempts to make a select few women into Frankensteins, so the De Lacey family circle opens only to admit the beautiful Safie. That Felix, like Victor, excludes the ugly monster indi-cates again how strictly men control where "the amiableness of domes-tic affection" is allowed to operate.

By using several feminist methodologies — studying one woman writer's experience of domestic and public roles, analyzing the cultural formation and literary representation of these gender roles — I have been reading *Frankenstein* as a woman's text concerned with women's issues. While Victor's story shows that the constraints of domesticity bear down hard on men, it is clear that the novel's women — who must not only create the familial sanctuary and sacrifice themselves to main-tain it but also be punished for its failures — take the heavier share of the burden. If *Frankenstein* is about Victor, it is also about what his monstrous masculinity does to women, and even though none of these women speaks directly, Mary Shelley's novel speaks to us for them.

WORKS CITED

Carson, James B. "Bringing the Author Forward: *Frankenstein* through Mary Shelley's Letters." *Criticism* 30.4 (Fall 1988): 431–53.

Dussinger, John A. "Kinship and Guilt in Mary Shelley's *Franken-stein.*" *Studies in the Novel* 8 (1976): 38–55.

Ellis, Kate. "Monsters in the Garden: Mary Shelley and the Bourgeois Family." Levine and Knoepflmacher 123–42.

Ellis, Sarah Stickney. *The Women of England: Their Social Duties and Domestic Habits.* 1838. In *The Select Works of Mrs. Ellis.* New York: Langley, 1854.

Jacobus, Mary. "Is There a Woman in This Text?" *New Literary History* 14.1 (Autumn 1982): 117–41.

Kranzler, Laura. "Frankenstein and the Technological Future." *Foundation* 44 (Winter 1988–89): 42–49.

Levine, George. "The Ambiguous Heritage of *Frankenstein.*" Levine and Knoepflmacher 3–30.

Levine, George, and U. C. Knoepflmacher, eds. *The Endurance of Frankenstein: Essays on Mary Shelley's Novel.* Berkeley: U of California P, 1979.

Mellor, Anne K. *Mary Shelley: Her Life, Her Fiction, Her Monsters.* New York: Routledge, 1988.

Murray, E. B. "Shelley's Contribution to Mary's *Frankenstein.*" *Keats–Shelley Memorial Bulletin* 29 (1978): 50–68.

Poovey, Mary. *The Proper Lady and the Woman Writer: Ideology as Style in the Works of Mary Wollstonecraft, Mary Shelley, and Jane Austen.* Women in Culture and Society series. Chicago: U of Chicago P, 1984. 114–42.

Rubinstein, Marc A. "'My Accursed Origin': The Search for the Mother in *Frankenstein.*" *Studies in Romanticism* 15 (Spring 1976): 165–94.

Shelley, Mary. *The Journals of Mary Wollstonecraft Shelley.* Ed. Paula R. Feldman and Diana Kilvert-Scott. Oxford: Clarendon, 1987.

———. *The Letters of Mary Wollstonecraft Shelley.* Ed. Betty T. Bennett. 3 vols. Baltimore: Johns Hopkins UP, 1980–1988.

Spark, Muriel. *Mary Shelley.* Rev. ed. London: Sphere–Penguin, 1987.

Veeder, William. *Mary Shelley and "Frankenstein": The Fate of Androgyny.* Chicago: U of Chicago P, 1986.

Vlasopolos, Anca. "*Frankenstein's* Hidden Skeleton: The Psycho-Politics of Oppression." *Science-Fiction Studies* 10.2 (July 1983): 125–36.

Marxist Criticism
and
Frankenstein

WHAT IS MARXIST CRITICISM?

To be a modern Marxist literary critic, it is not necessary to be a political revolutionary. Nor is it necessary to like only those literary works with a radical social vision or to dislike books that represent or even reinforce a middle-class, capitalist world-view. It is necessary, however, to adopt what most students of literature would consider a radical definition of the purpose and function of literary criticism.

More traditional forms of criticism, according to the Marxist critic Pierre Macherey, "set . . . out to deliver the text from its own silences by coaxing it into giving up its true, latent, or hidden meaning." Inevitably, however, non-Marxist criticism "intrude[es] its own discourse between the reader and the text" (qtd. in Bennett 107). Marxist critics, by contrast, do not attempt to discover hidden meanings in texts. Or, if they do, they do so only after seeing the text, first and foremost, as a material product to be understood in broadly historical terms. That is to say, a literary work is first viewed as a product *of* work (and hence of the realm of production and consumption we call economics). Second, it may be looked upon as a work that *does* identifiable work of its own. At one level, that work is usually to enforce and reinforce the prevailing ideology, that is, the network of conventions, values, and opinions to which the majority of people uncritically subscribe.

This does not mean that Marxist critics merely describe the obvious. Quite the contrary: the relationship that the Marxist critic Terry Eagleton outlines in *Criticism and Ideology* (1978) between the soaring cost of books in the nineteenth century, the growth of lending libraries, the practice of publishing "three-decker" novels (so that three borrowers could be reading the same book at the same time), and the changing *content* of those novels is highly complex in its own way. But the complexity Eagleton finds is not that of the deeply buried meaning of the text. Rather, it is that of the complex web of social and economic relationships that were prerequisite to the work's production. Marxist criticism does not seek to be, in Eagleton's words, "a passage from text to reader." Instead, "its task is to show the text as it cannot know itself, to manifest those conditions of its making (inscribed in its very letter) about which it is necessarily silent" (43).

As everyone knows, the original Marxist was none other than Karl Marx, the nineteenth-century German philosopher best known for writing *Das Kapital*, the seminal work of the communist movement. What everyone doesn't know is that Marx was also the first Marxist literary critic (much as Sigmund Freud, who psychoanalyzed E. T. A. Hoffmann's supernatural tale "The Sandman," was the first Freudian literary critic). During the 1830s Marx wrote critical essays on writers such as Goethe and Shakespeare (whose tragic vision of Elizabethan disintegration he praised).

The fact that Marxist literary criticism began with Marx himself is hardly surprising, given Marx's education and early interests. Trained in the classics at the University of Bonn, Marx wrote literary imitations, his own poetry, a failed novel, and a fragment of a tragic drama (*Oulanem*) before turning to contemplative and political philosophy. Even after he met Friedrich Engels in 1843 and began collaborating on works such as *The German Ideology* and *The Communist Manifesto*, Marx maintained a keen interest in literary writers and their works. He and Engels argued about the poetry of Heinrich Heine, admired Hermann Freiligrath (a poet critical of the German aristocracy), and faulted the playwright Ferdinand Lassalle for writing about a reactionary knight in the Peasants' War rather than about more progressive aspects of German history.

As these examples suggest, Marx and Engels would not — indeed, could not — think of aesthetic matters as being distinct and independent from such things as politics, economics, and history. Not surprisingly, they viewed the alienation of the worker in industrialized, capitalist societies as having grave consequences for the arts. How can people mechanically stamping out things that bear no mark of their producer's individuality (people thereby "reified," turned into things themselves) be expected to recognize, produce, or even consume things of beauty? And if there is no one to consume something, there will soon be no one to produce it, especially in an age in which production (even of something like literature) has come to mean *mass* (and therefore profitable) production.

In *The German Ideology* (1846), Marx and Engels expressed their sense of the relationship between the arts, politics, and basic economic reality in terms of a general social theory. Economics, they argued, provides the "base" or "infrastructure" of society, but from that base emerges a "superstructure" consisting of law, politics, philosophy, religion, and art.

Marx later admitted that the relationship between base and superstructure may be indirect and fluid: every change in economics may not be reflected by an immediate change in ethics or literature. In *The Eighteenth Brumaire of Louis Bonaparte* (1852), he came up with the word *homology* to describe the sometimes unbalanced, often delayed, and almost always loose correspondence between base and superstructure. And later in that same decade, while working on an introduction to his *Political Economy,* Marx further relaxed the base–superstructure relationship. Writing on the excellence of ancient Greek art (versus the primitive nature of ancient Greek economics), he conceded that a gap sometimes opens up between base and superstructure — between economic forms and those produced by the creative mind.

Nonetheless, *at* base the old formula was maintained. Economics remained basic and the connection between economics and superstructural elements of society was reaffirmed. Central to Marxism and Marxist literary criticism was and is the following "materialist" insight: consciousness, without which such things as art cannot be produced, is not the source of social forms and economic conditions. It is, rather, their most important product.

Marx and Engels, drawing upon the philosopher Friedrich Hegel's theories about the dialectical synthesis of ideas out of theses and antitheses, believed that a revolutionary class war (pitting middle-class capitalists against a proletarian, antithetical class) would lead eventually to the synthesis of a new social and economic order. Placing their faith not in the idealist Hegelian dialectic but, rather, in what they called "dialectical materialism," they looked for a secular and material salvation of humanity — one in, not beyond, history — via revolution and not via divine intervention. And they believed that the communist society eventually established would be one capable of producing new forms of consciousness and belief and therefore, ultimately, great art.

The revolution anticipated by Marx and Engels did not occur in their century, let alone lifetime. When it finally did take place, it didn't happen in places where Marx and Engels had thought it might be successful: the United States, Great Britain, and Germany. It happened, rather, in 1917 Russia, a country long ruled by despotic czars, but also enlightened by the works of powerful novelists and playwrights, including Chekhov, Pushkin, Tolstoy, and Dostoyevsky.

Perhaps because of its significant literary tradition, Russia produced revolutionaries like Nikolai Lenin, who shared not only Marx's interest in literature but also his belief in literature's ultimate importance. But it was not without some hesitation that Lenin endorsed the significance of texts written during the reign of the czars. Well before 1917 he had questioned what the relationship should be between a society undergoing a revolution and the great old literature of its bourgeois past.

Lenin attempted to answer that question in a series of essays on Tolstoy that he wrote between 1908 and 1911. Tolstoy — the author of *War and Peace* and *Anna Karenina* — was an important nineteenth-century Russian writer whose views hardly accorded with those of young Marxist revolutionaries. Continuing interest in a writer like Tolstoy may be justified, Lenin reasoned, given the primitive and unenlightened economic order of the society that produced him. Since superstructure usually lags behind base (and is therefore usually *more* primitive), the attitudes of a Tolstoy look relatively progressive when viewed in light of the unenlightened, capitalist society out of which they arose.

Moreover, Lenin also reasoned, the writings of the great Russian realists would *have* to suffice, at least in the short run. Lenin looked forward, in essays like "Party Organization and Party Literature," to the day in which new artistic forms would be produced by progressive writers with revolutionary political views and agendas. But he also knew that a great proletarian literature was unlikely to evolve until a thoroughly literate proletariat had been produced by the educational system.

Lenin was hardly the only revolutionary leader involved in setting up the new Soviet state who took a strong interest in literary matters.

In 1924 Leon Trotsky published a book called *Literature and Revolution,* which is still acknowledged as a classic of Marxist literary criticism.

Trotsky worried about the direction in which Marxist aesthetic theory seemed to be going. He responded skeptically to groups like Proletkult, which opposed tolerance toward pre- and nonrevolutionary writers, and which called for the establishment of a new, proletarian culture. Trotsky warned of the danger of cultural sterility and risked unpopularity by pointing out that there is no necessary connection between the quality of a literary work and the quality of its author's politics.

In 1927 Trotsky lost a power struggle with Josef Stalin, a man who believed, among other things, that writers should be "engineers" of "human souls." After Trotsky's expulsion from the Soviet Union, views held by groups like Proletkult and the Left Front of Art (LEF), and by theorists such as Nikolai Bukharin and A. A. Zhdanov, became more prevalent. Speaking at the First Congress of the Union of Soviet Writers in 1934, the Soviet author Maxim Gorky called for writing that would "make labor the principal hero of our books." It was at the same writer's congress that "socialist realism," an art form glorifying workers and the revolutionary State, was made Communist party policy and the official literary form of the USSR.

Of those critics active in the USSR after the expulsion of Trotsky and the unfortunate triumph of Stalin, two critics stand out. One, Mikhail Bakhtin, has had his greatest impact on non-Marxist criticism; his influence is discussed in "What Is Cultural Criticism?" in this volume (p. 312). The other sane and subtle critic who managed to survive Stalin's dictatorship and his repressive policies was Georg Lukács. A Hungarian who had begun his career as an "idealist" critic, Lukács had converted to Marxism in 1919; renounced his earlier, Hegelian work shortly thereafter; visited Moscow in 1930–1931; and finally emigrated to the USSR in 1933, just one year before the First Congress of the Union of Soviet Writers met.

Lukács was far less narrow in his views than the most strident Stalinist Soviet critics of the 1930s and 1940s. He disliked much socialist realism and appreciated prerevolutionary, realistic novels that broadly reflected cultural "totalities" — and were populated with characters representing human "types" of the author's place and time. (Lukács was particularly fond of the historical canvasses painted by the early-nineteenth-century novelist Sir Walter Scott.) But like his more rigid and censorious contemporaries, he drew the line at accepting nonrevolutionary, modernist works like James Joyce's *Ulysses.* He condemned movements like Expressionism and Symbolism, preferring works with "content" over more decadent, experimental works characterized mainly by "form."

With Lukács its most liberal and tolerant critic from the early 1930s until well into the 1960s, the Soviet literary scene degenerated to the point that the works of great writers like Franz Kafka were no longer read, either because they were viewed as decadent, formal experiments or because they "engineered souls" in "nonprogressive" directions. Officially sanctioned works were generally ones in which artistry lagged far behind the politics (no matter how bad the politics were).

Fortunately for the Marxist critical movement, politically radical critics *outside* the Soviet Union were free of its narrow, constricting policies and, consequently, able fruitfully to develop the thinking of Marx, Engels, and Trotsky. It was these non-Soviet Marxists who kept Marxist critical theory alive and useful in discussing all *kinds* of literature, written across the entire historical spectrum.

Perhaps because Lukács was the best of the Soviet communists writing Marxist criticism in the 1930s and 1940s, non-Soviet Marxists tended to develop their ideas by publicly opposing those of Lukács. German dramatist and critic Bertolt Brecht countered Lukács by arguing that art ought to be viewed as a field of production, not as a container of "content." Brecht also criticized Lukács for his attempt to enshrine realism at the expense not only of other "isms" but also of poetry and drama, both of which had been largely ignored by Lukács.

Even more outspoken was Brecht's critical champion Walter Benjamin, a German Marxist who, in the 1930s, attacked those conventional and traditional literary forms conveying a stultifying "aura" of culture. Benjamin praised Dadaism and, more important, new forms of art ushered in by the age of mechanical reproduction. Those forms — including radio and film — offered hope, he felt, for liberation from capitalist culture, for they were too new to be part of its stultifyingly ritualistic traditions.

But of all the anti-Lukácsians outside the USSR who made a contribution to the development of Marxist literary criticism, the most important was probably Théodor Adorno. Leader since the early 1950s of the Frankfurt school of Marxist criticism, Adorno attacked Lukács for his dogmatic rejection of nonrealist modern literature and for his belief in the primacy of content over form. Art does not equal science, Adorno insisted. He went on to argue for art's autonomy from empirical forms of knowledge, and to suggest that the interior monologues of modernist works (by Beckett and Proust) reflect the fact of modern alienation in a way that Marxist criticism ought to find compelling.

In addition to turning against Lukács and his overly constrictive canon, Marxists outside the Soviet Union were able to take advantage of insights generated by non-Marxist critical theories being developed in post–World War II Europe. One of the movements that came to be of interest to non-Soviet Marxists was structuralism, a scientific approach to the study of humankind whose proponents believed that all elements of culture, including literature, could be understood as parts of a system of signs. Using modern linguistics as a model, structuralists like Claude Lévi-Strauss broke the myths of various cultures down into "mythemes" in an attempt to show that there are structural correspondences or homologies between the mythical elements produced by various human communities across time.

Of the European structuralist Marxists, one of the most influential was Lucien Goldmann, a Rumanian critic living in Paris. Goldmann combined structuralist principles with Marx's base–superstructure model in order to show how economics determines the mental structures of social groups, which are reflected in literary texts. Goldmann rejected the idea of individual human genius, choosing to see works, instead, as the "collective" products of "trans-individual" mental structures. In early studies, such as *The Hidden God* (1955), he related seventeenth-century French texts (such as Racine's *Phèdre*) to the ideology of Jansenism. In later works, he applied Marx's base–superstructure model even more strictly, describing a relationship between economic conditions and texts unmediated by an intervening, collective consciousness.

In spite of his rigidity and perhaps because of his affinities with structuralism, Goldmann came to be seen in the 1960s as the proponent of a kind of watered-down, "humanist" Marxism. He was certainly viewed that way by the French Marxist Louis Althusser, a disciple not of Lévi-Strauss and structuralism but rather of the psychoanalytic theorist Jacques Lacan and of the Italian communist Antonio Gramsci, famous for his writings about ideology and "hegemony." (Gramsci used the latter word to refer to the pervasive, weblike system of assumptions and values that shapes the way things look, what they mean, and therefore what reality *is* for the majority of people within a culture.)

Like Gramsci, Althusser viewed literary works primarily in terms of their relationship to ideology, the function of which, he argued, is to (re)produce the existing relations of production in a given society. Dave Laing, in his book on *The Marxist Theory of Art* (1978), has attempted to explain this particular insight of Althusser's by saying that ideologies, through the "ensemble of habits, moralities, and opinions" that can be found in any literary text, "ensure that the work-force (and those responsible for re-producing them in the family, school, etc.) are maintained in their position of subordination to the dominant class" (91). This is not to say that Althusser thought of the masses as a brainless multitude following only the dictates of the prevailing ideology: Althusser followed Gramsci in suggesting that even working-class people have some freedom to struggle against ideology and change history. Nor is it to say that Althusser saw ideology as being a coherent, consistent force. In fact, he saw it as being riven with contradictions that works of literature sometimes expose and even widen. Thus Althusser followed Marx and Gramsci in believing that although literature must be seen in *relation* to ideology, it — like all social forms — has some degree of autonomy.

Althusser's followers included Pierre Macherey, who in *A Theory of Literary Production* (1966) developed Althusser's concept of the relationship between literature and ideology. A realistic novelist, he argued, attempts to produce a unified, coherent text, but instead ends up producing a work containing lapses, omissions, gaps. This happens because within ideology there are subjects that cannot be covered, things that cannot be said, contradictory views that aren't recognized as contradictory. (The critic's challenge, in this case, is to supply what the text cannot say, thereby making sense of gaps and contradictions.)

But there is another reason why gaps open up and contradictions become evident in texts. Works don't just reflect ideology (which Goldmann had referred to as "myth" and which Macherey refers to as a system of "illusory social beliefs"); they are also "fictions," works of art, *products* of ideology that have what Goldmann would call a "worldview" to offer. What kind of product, Macherey implicitly asks, is identical to the thing that produced it? It is hardly surprising, then, that Balzac's fiction shows French peasants in two different lights, only one of which is critical and judgmental, only one of which is baldly ideological. Writing approvingly on Macherey and Macherey's mentor Althusser in *Marxism and Literary Criticism* (1976), Terry Eagleton says: "It is by giving ideology a determinate form, fixing it within certain fictional limits, that art is able to distance itself from [ideology], thus revealing . . . [its] limits" (19).

A follower of Althusser, Macherey is sometimes referred to as a "post-Althusserian Marxist." Eagleton, too, is often described that way, as is his American contemporary, Fredric Jameson. Jameson and

Eagleton, as well as being post–Althusserians, are also among the few Anglo-American critics who have closely followed and significantly developed Marxist thought.

Before them, Marxist interpretation in English was limited to the work of a handful of critics: Christopher Caudwell, Christopher Hill, Arnold Kettle, E. P. Thompson, and Raymond Williams. Of these, Williams was perhaps least Marxist in orientation: he felt that Marxist critics, ironically, tended too much to isolate economics from culture; that they overlooked the individualism of people, opting instead to see them as "masses"; and that even more ironically, they had become an elitist group. But if the least Marxist of the British Marxists, Williams was also by far the most influential. Preferring to talk about "culture" instead of ideology, Williams argued in works such as *Culture and Society 1780–1950* (1958) that culture is "lived experience" and, as such, an interconnected set of social properties, each and all grounded in and influencing history.

Terry Eagleton's *Criticism and Ideology* (1978) is in many ways a response to the work of Williams. Responding to Williams's statement, in *Culture and Society,* that "there are in fact no masses; there are only ways of seeing people as masses" (289), Eagleton writes: "That men and women really are now unique individuals was Williams's (unexceptionable) insistence; but it was a proposition bought at the expense of perceiving the fact that they must mass and fight to achieve their full individual humanity. One has only to adapt Williams's statement to 'There are in fact no classes; there are only ways of seeing people as classes' to expose its theoretical paucity" (*Criticism* 29).

Eagleton goes on, in *Criticism and Ideology,* to propose an elaborate theory about how history — in the form of "general," "authorial," and "aesthetic" ideology — enters texts, which in turn may revivify, open up, or critique those same ideologies, thereby setting in motion a process that may alter history. He shows how texts by Jane Austen, Matthew Arnold, Charles Dickens, George Eliot, Joseph Conrad, and T. S. Eliot deal with and transmute conflicts at the heart of the general and authorial ideologies behind them: conflicts between morality and individualism, individualism and social organicism and utilitarianism.

As all this emphasis on ideology and conflict suggests, a modern British Marxist like Eagleton, even while acknowledging the work of a British Marxist predecessor like Williams, is more nearly developing the ideas of continental Marxists like Althusser and Macherey. That holds, as well, for modern American Marxists like Fredric Jameson. For although he makes occasional, sympathetic references to the works of

Williams, Thompson, and Hill, Jameson makes far more *use* of Lukács, Adorno, and Althusser as well as non-Marxist structuralist, psychoanalytic, and poststructuralist critics.

In the first of several influential works, *Marxism and Form* (1971), Jameson takes up the question of form and content, arguing that the former is "but the working out" of the latter "in the realm of superstructure" (329). (In making such a statement Jameson opposes not only the tenets of Russian Formalists, for whom content had merely been the fleshing out of form, but also those of so-called vulgar Marxists, who tended to define form as mere ornamentation or windowdressing.) In his later work *The Political Unconscious* (1981), Jameson uses what in *Marxism and Form* he had called "dialectical criticism" to synthesize out of structuralism and poststructuralism, Freud and Lacan, Althusser and Adorno, a set of complex arguments that can only be summarized reductively.

The fractured state of societies and the isolated condition of individuals, he argued, may be seen as indications that there originally existed an unfallen state of something that may be called "primitive communism." History — which records the subsequent divisions and alienations — limits awareness of its own contradictions and of that lost, Better State, via ideologies and their manifestation in texts, whose strategies essentially contain and repress desire, especially revolutionary desire, into the collective unconscious. (In Conrad's *Lord Jim,* Jameson shows, the knowledge that governing classes don't *deserve* their power is contained and repressed by an ending that metaphysically blames Nature for the tragedy and that melodramatically blames wicked Gentleman Brown.)

As demonstrated by Jameson in analyses like the one mentioned above, textual strategies of containment and concealment may be discovered by the critic, but only by the critic practicing dialectical criticism, that is to say, a criticism aware, among other things, of its *own* status as ideology. All thought, Jameson concludes, is ideological; only through ideological thought that knows itself as such can ideologies be seen through and eventually transcended.

In the Marxist interpretation of *Frankenstein* that follows, Warren Montag begins his interpretive encounter with Mary Shelley's novel by arguing that a literary work creates the illusion of autonomy while depending, in fact, on history for meaning. (He thus steers a course between Althusser, for whom literary works are at least semiautonomous, and critics like Eagleton, for whom they are not.) Montag proceeds, then, by attempting to "ascertain . . . the character of the second decade of the nineteenth century and more generally the period of English (and to a certain extent European) history between the French Revolution of 1789 and the period of relative social stability that set in with the passage of the Reform Bill in 1832 in England" (300).

Using the text to establish that the novel is set in the 1790s, the period of the French Revolution, Montag shows how the novel at once reveals and masks that fact, telling us that Victor Frankenstein is planning to create his monster one hundred and fifty years *after* the *English* Revolution (of 1642). The passage referring to that earlier revolt against monarchy turns out to be surprisingly conservative in its implications — *oddly* conservative, in fact, given Mary Shelley's supposed radicalism. Montag explains that conservatism by remounting E. P. Thompson's argument that the French Revolution had produced a kind of monster in Europe, a mood of amorality and anarchy that had infected England and come to raise fears, even among some radicals, that England itself was on the brink of chaos.

After all, the formation of the working class *as* a class had led to revolutionary working-class political movements such as the Luddite movement, which in turn had led to violent mass demonstrations and machine-smashing incidents. These movements and incidents had shown English working people to be militant and combative toward the middle class as well as toward the aristocracy. Mary Shelley had seen this as well as anyone, and the sight could only have made her fearful, if also excited. "Shelley's work," according to Montag, "is incontestably interwoven in this history: it bears witness to the birth of that monster, simultaneously the object of pity and fear, the industrial working class" (303).

We come to realize as we follow Montag's argument further, however, that to read *Frankenstein* as a work in which monster equals proletariat is to read as a somewhat simplistic Marxist critic. So Montag proceeds to another level of the text, as well as to other levels of Marxist critical discourse that we may associate with Macherey, Eagleton, and Jameson. To find the history in the text — rather than seeing the text as a simpleminded allegory of history — Montag goes back to it in search of "the contradictions, discrepancies, and inconsistencies that the work displays but does not attempt to address or resolve" (306). In doing so, he begins practicing a form of Marxism that combines Macherey's conviction that the profoundest historical meaning of a work lies in what the work *cannot* say, what ideology of the day will not *let* it say, with a neo-Hegelian interest in form. For the telling contradictions Montag finds in *Frankenstein,* the discrepancies that hide what it cannot say as often involve disruptions of aesthetic unity as they do contradictory ideas or "contents."

What *Frankenstein* leaves out — what is conspicuously and significantly absent — is not that in creating a working class, England has created a monster. That, rather, is what the work virtually says outright. It is, rather, that science, or more precisely the technology that the Age of Reason has made possible (and that the Enlightenment would tell us will assure human progress), can in fact be alienating and dehumanizing, could in fact cause society to grow, if anything, weaker and turn human beings into a lower form of life. In making that absence in the text present, Marxist criticism surely makes *Frankenstein* present in the temporal as well as in the spatial sense — that is, as a work able to speak provocatively of and to the historical epoch in which it is now being read.

MARXIST CRITICISM: A SELECTED BIBLIOGRAPHY

Marx, Engels, Lenin, and Trotsky

Engels, Friedrich. *The Condition of the Working Class in England.* Ed. and trans. W. O. Henderson and W. H. Chaloner. Stanford: Stanford UP, 1968.

Lenin, V. I. *On Literature and Art.* Moscow: Progress, 1967.

Marx, Karl. *Selected Writings.* Ed. David McLellan. Oxford: Oxford UP, 1977.

Trotsky, Leon. *Literature and Revolution.* New York: Russell, 1967.

General Introductions to and Reflections on Marxist Criticism

Bennett, Tony. *Formalism and Marxism.* London: Methuen, 1979.

Demetz, Peter. *Marx, Engels and the Poets.* Chicago: U of Chicago P, 1967.

Eagleton, Terry. *Marxism and Literary Criticism.* Berkeley: U of California P, 1976.

Fokkema, D. W., and Elrud Kunne-Ibsch. *Theories of Literature in the Twentieth Century: Structuralism, Marxism, Aesthetics of Reception, Semiotics.* New York: St. Martin's, 1977. See ch. 4, "Marxist Theories of Literature."

Frow, John. *Marxism and Literary History*. Cambridge: Harvard UP, 1986.

Jefferson, Ann, and David Robey. *Modern Literary Theory: A Critical Introduction*. Totowa: Barnes, 1982. See the essay "Marxist Literary Theories" by David Forgacs.

Laing, Dave. *The Marxist Theory of Art*. Brighton, Eng.: Harvester, 1978.

Selden, Raman. *A Reader's Guide to Contemporary Literary Theory*. Lexington: U of Kentucky P, 1985. See ch. 2, "Marxist Theories."

Slaughter, Cliff. *Marxism, Ideology and Literature*. Atlantic Highlands: Humanities, 1980.

Some Classic Marxist Studies and Statements

Adorno, Théodor. *Prisms*. Trans. Samuel and Shierry Weber. Cambridge: MIT P, 1982.

Althusser, Louis. *For Marx*. Trans. Ben Brewster. New York: Pantheon, 1969.

Althusser, Louis, and Etienne Balibar. *Reading Capital*. Trans. Ben Brewster. New York: Pantheon, 1971.

Auerbach, Erich. *Mimesis: The Representation of Reality in Western Literature*. Trans. Willard R. Trask. Princeton: Princeton UP, 1953.

Bakhtin, Mikhail. *Rabelais and His World*. Cambridge: MIT P, 1968.

Benjamin, Walter. *Illuminations*. Ed. with intro. by Hannah Arendt. Trans. H. Zohn. New York: Harcourt, 1968.

Caudwell, Christopher. *Illusion and Reality*. New York: Russell, 1955.

———. *Studies in a Dying Culture*. London: Lawrence, 1938.

Goldmann, Lucien. *The Hidden God*. New York: Humanities, 1964.

———. *Towards a Sociology of the Novel*. London: Tavistock, 1975.

Gramsci, Antonio. *Selections from the Prison Notebooks*. Ed. Quintin Hoare and Geoffrey Nowell Smith. New York: International, 1971.

Kettle, Arnold. *An Introduction to the English Novel*. New York: Harper, 1960.

Lukács, Georg. *The Historical Novel*. Trans. H. and S. Mitchell. Boston: Beacon, 1963.

———. *Studies in European Realism*. New York: Grosset, 1964.

———. *The Theory of the Novel*. Cambridge: MIT, 1971.

Marcuse, Herbert. *One-Dimensional Man*. Boston: Beacon, 1964.

Thompson, E. P. *The Making of the English Working Class*. New York: Pantheon, 1964.

———. *William Morris: Romantic to Revolutionary*. New York: Pantheon, 1977.

Williams, Raymond. *Culture and Society 1780–1950*. New York: Harper, 1958.

———. *The Long Revolution*. New York: Columbia UP, 1961.

———. *Marxism and Literature*. Oxford: Oxford UP, 1977.

Wilson, Edmund. *To the Finland Station*. Garden City: Doubleday, 1953.

Studies by and of Post-Althusserian Marxists

Dowling, William C. *Jameson, Althusser, Marx: An Introduction to "The Political Unconscious."* Ithaca: Cornell UP, 1984.

Eagleton, Terry. *Criticism and Ideology: A Study in Marxist Literary Theory*. London: Verso, 1978.

———. *Exiles and Émigrés*. New York: Schocken, 1970.

Jameson, Fredric. *Marxism and Form: Twentieth-Century Dialectical Theories of Literature*. Princeton: Princeton UP, 1971.

———. *The Political Unconscious: Narrative as a Socially Symbolic Act*. Ithaca: Cornell UP, 1981.

Macherey, Pierre. *A Theory of Literary Production*. Trans. G. Wall. London: Routledge, 1978.

Marxist Readings of *Frankenstein*

Hatlen, Burton, "Milton, Mary Shelley, and Patriarchy." *Bucknell Review* 28.2 (1983): 19–47.

Michie, Elsie B. "Production Replaces Creation: Market Forces and *Frankenstein* as Critique of Romanticism." *Nineteenth-Century Contexts* 12.1 (1988): 27–33.

Moretti, Franco. *Signs Taken for Wonders: Essays in the Sociology of Literary Forms*. Trans. Susan Fischer, David Forgacs, and David Miller. London: Verso, 1983. See especially 83–90.

O'Flinn, Paul. "Production and Reproduction: The Case of *Frankenstein*." *Literature and History* 9.2 (1983): 194–213.

Vlasopolos, Anca. "*Frankenstein*'s Hidden Skeleton: The Psycho-Politics of Oppression." *Science-Fiction Studies* 10.2 (1983): 125–36.

A MARXIST PERSPECTIVE
ON *FRANKENSTEIN*

WARREN MONTAG

"The Workshop of Filthy Creation":
A Marxist Reading of *Frankenstein*

The literary work, perhaps because of its physical appearance, presents itself as an autonomous artifact bearing within it all that is necessary to decipher the secrets that it seems to contain. A Marxist reading of a literary work begins with a refusal of this illusion of autonomy and seeks instead to restore to the work that peculiar form of dependence that its very structure is designed to mask or deny. For the literary text is in no way independent of the historical moment in which it emerged. It is not a closed, self-contained whole whose meaning would derive from itself alone. On the contrary, it is no more than a "node within a network" (Foucault 19). The work is bound both to the literary and nonliterary discourses with which it coexists (and in relation to which alone it possesses a meaning), and to the "non-discursive" social, economic, and political practices that make discourse possible.

We are thus obliged to begin our investigation of Mary Shelley's *Frankenstein* by ascertaining the character of the second decade of the nineteenth century, and more generally the period of English (and to a certain extent European) history between the French Revolution of 1789 and the period of relative social stability that set in with the passage of the Reform Bill in 1832 in England. Even the most cursory examination of this singular period reveals that its key themes are precisely those of *Frankenstein:* there is everywhere a sense of monstrous forces unwittingly conjured up in order to serve the project of progress and the Enlightenment but which have ultimately served to call that very project into question.

The French Revolution, unquestionably the major event of the period, had apparently come to a close just prior to the publication of *Frankenstein,* with the final defeat of Napoleon in 1815. Jean-Jacques Lecercle has demonstrated that although not once mentioned in *Frankenstein,* the French Revolution is nevertheless alluded to (Lecercle 1988). Walton's letters to his sister are dated but with the decade and year omitted (for example, 28 March 17—). A passage that occurs rather late in the text, however, allows us to determine the years during which the action of the novel takes place. Victor Frankenstein, accompanied by his friend Henry Clerval, journeys to Scotland seeking a remote spot in which he can work to fulfill his promise to create a mate to relieve the monster's terrible solitude. When they stop briefly in Oxford, Frankenstein records the following sentiments:

> As we entered this city, our minds were filled with the remembrance of the events that had been transacted there more than a century and a half before. It was here that Charles I. had collected his forces. This city had remained faithful to him, after the whole nation had forsaken his cause to join the standard of parliament and liberty. (136)

Frankenstein's meditation on the Revolution of 1642 in England locates the narrative in the 1790s, placing it in the midst of the French Revolution. It is indeed remarkable that the work refers to a revolution that occurred "more than a century and a half before" rather than to the most important event of contemporary history. But the absence of the French Revolution from the text is not the only surprising fact in this passage. Its tone is unexpectedly sympathetic to Charles I, a monarch typically regarded by Whigs (the moderates of the day), let alone the Radicals of Shelley's circle, as the very figure of a tyrant. His absolutist policies, his refusal to base his rule on the consent of Parliament, his abolition of religious freedom were all held to be the causes of the English civil war that began in 1642 and ended in 1649 when Charles was executed by order of Parliament.

Two discrepancies have thus appeared: (1) the substitution of English revolution of a hundred and fifty years earlier for the French; (2) a brief commentary on the English civil war that is at odds with everything we know of Mary Shelley's political sympathies. But these discrepancies are precisely what will allow us to proceed from the work to the history on which it depends and which made it possible. For the English and the French revolutions together were the most developed and elaborate social and political "experiments" in modern history and both had "failed," both were attempts to create social orders based on justice or (especially in the case of the French Revolution) reason that had collapsed into tyranny or chaos. The movements that destroyed (or attempted to destroy) absolutist monarchies were usually led by new elites (the rural or urban bourgeoisie: landowners, merchants, and financiers) whose access to political power was blocked by the old regime. In order to overthrow the old state and to create a system that more adequately represented their interests, the new elites were forced to mobilize the plebeian masses (peasants, workers, and the urban poor). But in doing so they found that they had conjured up a monster that, once unleashed, could not be controlled. It was widely felt, even by those sympathetic to such experiments, that the mass mobilizations necessary to destroy the old order effectively blocked the creation of the new. Unleashing the power of the multitude had led to anarchy, and to the proliferation of innumerable demands that went far beyond what was rational or even "just" (according to the norms of middle-class revolutionaries). The dreams of progress toward a rational state faded in the face of what appeared to be the unpredictable, seemingly "irrational" character of the activity of the masses. The Enlightenment, far from having led to the reign of reason, had unloosed elemental forces deaf to the appeals of the morality that had liberated them in the first place. Accordingly, a general demoralization followed the close of the French Revolution, creating an atmosphere in which the Enlightenment was called radically into question and with it the notion of history conceived as progress toward a world organized on the basis of reason.

And the close of the French Revolution did little to resolve this dilemma. Instead, it was displaced to England which, following the Napoleonic wars, itself entered a period of social crisis the character of which only further underscored these questions. According to historian E. P. Thompson, "it is as if the English nation entered a crucible in the 1790s and emerged after the wars in a different form" (191). This crucible, often referred to as the industrial revolution, was anything but a period of smooth evolution. First, the era was marked by the sudden emergence of new technologies whose origins seemed inexplicable to contemporaries, appearing to herald a world utterly unlike what had gone before. As a contemporary commentator, Cooke Taylor, noted in 1843: "the steam engine had no precedent and the spinning-jenny is without ancestry . . . they sprang into sudden existence like Minerva from the brain of Jupiter" (qtd. in Thompson 190). Before the paradox of technologies created by human beings but whose nature seemed to defy human understanding, the mind sought refuge in the familiar language of mystery and miracle.

But these new technologies and the industrial systems they made possible were perhaps less disturbing than their effects on the lives of the laboring population. Increased unemployment, falling wages, rising prices for food and other necessities: these were the conditions that grew alongside the prosperity of the employing class. This contradictory development of capitalism meant that the peace and social harmony associated with a rural economy had been replaced by the apparently insurmountable conflict of the industrial order: "the cotton-mill is seen as the agent not only of industrial but also social revolution, producing not only more goods but also the labor movement itself" (192). For Thompson, "the outstanding fact of the period between 1790 and 1830 is the formation of 'the working class'" (194), a social force conscious of its own interests as opposed to the interests of the dominant classes and which further began to act on the basis of these interests.

The English working class had entered the political stage, but in forms that could only appear monstrous to contemporary observers. The first wave of this movement, from 1811 to 1813, consisted of the mass action of workers bent on resisting the introduction of new technologies, particularly into the textile industry. By reducing the numbers of workers necessary to the production process, new industrial developments added to what was already a crisis of unemployment. This movement amounted to a clandestine army under the command of the mythical General Ludd (in fact no such leader existed). The "Luddites" sacked factories, and smashed the new "labor saving machines." As their movement receded in the face of violent repression on the part of the British state, it was quickly succeeded by a wave of popular agitation against high prices and rents. Mass demonstrations were common, violent confrontations with the state only slightly less so. It was a time when talk of the threat or hope of revolution (according to one's perspective) was common. At the very moment that *Frankenstein* was published, the British state suspended various civil rights (including that of habeas corpus) in order more effectively to counter the growing combativity of the unemployed and the working poor.

Mary Shelley's work is incontestably interwoven in this history: it bears witness to the birth of that monster, simultaneously the object of pity and fear, the industrial working class (Moretti). A dense network of resemblances appears to allow us to identify Frankenstein's monster with the emergent proletariat. The monster is monstrous by virtue of its being artificial rather than natural; lacking the unity of a natural organism, the monster is a factitious totality assembled from (the parts of) a multitude of different individuals, in particular, the "poor," the urban mass that, because it is a multitude rather than an individual, is itself as nameless as Frankenstein's "creation." It is also significant that the term "creation" is used at all to describe the origins of the monster. For the monster is a product rather than a creation, assembled and joined together not so much by a man (if such were the case the monster might be allotted a place in the order of things) as by science, technology, and industry, whose overarching logic subsumes and subjects even the greatest geniuses. In fact, Frankenstein the man struggles

against Frankenstein the practitioner of science and servant of technological progress only finally to prove no more than an unwitting instrument of this progress. In this way the very notion of progress, a central
ideological representation of the perpetual revolutionizing of the means
by which goods are produced necessary to the development of capitalism, becomes problematic. Technological and industrial progress has
produced a monster, an artificial being as destructive as it is powerful.
The very logic of capitalism has produced the means of its own destruction: the industrial working class, that fabricated collectivity whose interests are irreconcilable with those of capital and which is thus rendered
monstrous in the eyes of its creators. The development of capitalism,
then, does not correspond to a logic at all, except perhaps a dialectical
logic capable of grasping the manner in which the production of wealth
engenders terrible poverty, and in which the greater the intelligence of
the machine the more stunted the mind of the worker.

But of course, Mary Shelley is not content to denounce "the hideous progeny" of the first phase of industrial capitalism. For the monster is no less contradictory than the process that created it. Far from
being simply the object of horror, the monster, so eloquent in describing his suffering and solitude, also elicits pity, if not exactly sympathy.
Shelley thus lends her voice to the voiceless, those who, bowed and
numbed by oppression and poverty, cannot speak for themselves.

The same ambivalence, the same combination of pity and fear is to
be found in "The Mask of Anarchy," a poem by Percy Bysshe Shelley
for which Mary Shelley wrote an explanatory note. The poem was written in response to the Peterloo massacre of 1819 and describes the
"slavery" of the "men of England." Starvation, poverty, injustice, and
the violence of the ruling class and its state will cause the masses to
"Feel revenge/Fiercely thirsting to exchange/Blood for blood — and
wrong for wrong." Shelley concludes the stanza with the admonition,
"Do not thus when ye are strong." Sympathy circumscribed by fear,
finally conditional, an appeal to reason and law that is unconvincing
even in the poem's own terms, "The Mask of Anarchy" with its refrain, "ye are many — they are few," fears nothing so much as the ever
present possibility of the irrational (although objectively determined)
violence of the "sleeping giant," the British working class and a repetition of the Terror of the French Revolution. Is not *Frankenstein* this
very dilemma presented as a fable?

Considered in this way, the work assumes a kind of coherence that
in turn derives from the "class location" of the author. *Frankenstein*
seems to center on the emergence of the industrial working class as a

political and social force, seen in the light of the French and perhaps even British revolutions by the "progressive" artist: unable finally to identify with the proletariat and to adopt its point of view, even the radicals of Mary Shelley's milieu are constrained to regard it as a monster. If Marxist criticism worked this way it would resemble a kind of decoding. The critic replaces the apparent with the real and the mythological with the historical: the monster *is* the proletariat. History disguised as the novel remains only to be unmasked by the reader.

But such a reading is too simple; to stop here would be to reduce the literary work to a mere allegory structured by a set of symbolic equivalences: the monster equals the proletariat. Conceived in this way the work remains outside history, which is alluded to even as it is concealed. But a Marxist reading demands a more complex conception of the work. For Marxism is above all a materialism. All that exists, including art and culture, necessarily possesses a material existence. From a materialist point of view, the literary work cannot somehow exist outside of history and even less outside of reality. It cannot be collapsed into or reduced to something "more real" than itself, that is, history. When we say that literary works are historical by their very nature we mean that history is as present in them as outside of them, that we do not leave the work in search of its historical meaning but seek the meaning of its historical existence within it.

For Marxism, history is a struggle between antagonistic social forces. Further, this struggle is inescapable: it is present in every cultural artifact, every intellectual enterprise. But the struggle is not the same throughout history, it takes many forms and involves many actors. It follows no rules and obeys no logic. Literary works are not simply expressions of some invariable, essential contradiction, they are singular, specific realizations of a struggle whose character is perpetually transformed by its own activity.

Thus, if we are to seek the signs of the historicity of the work within it, this historicity will inescapably be present in the form of a conflict. This conflict, however, is not merely or even primarily present in the content of the work, but rather in the very letter of the text. While literary works have, since Aristotle, been defined by their coherence, by their formal resolution of internal contradictions and antagonisms, Marxism asks us to understand them on the basis of the specific conflicts that have generated them and that every work, no matter how apparently coherent, embodies and perhaps transforms but cannot resolve. Most often these contradictions are not what the work is about at all; instead they constitute symptomatic antagonisms that disrupt the unity that the text appears to display. From a Marxist point of view, an adequate reading of *Frankenstein* will therefore refrain from the enterprise of establishing correspondences between the apparently parallel worlds of literature and history and will instead seek to grasp the way in which history is present in the text as a force or motor ("class struggle is the motor of history," as Marx and Engels wrote in *The Communist Manifesto)*. History sets the work against itself and splits it open, forcing it to reveal all that it sought to deny but cannot help revealing by the very fact of this denial. We will begin by posing the question the answer to which we have already begun to formulate: What are the contradictions, discrepancies, and inconsistencies that the work displays but does not address or attempt to resolve?

This question brings us immediately into conflict with the form of the work. For Frankenstein's life, at least as he narrates it from his deathbed, possesses an absolute coherence. His every thought, word, and deed are revealed to have been steps toward a destiny that awaited him from the very beginning. He is able to see that he has always lived according to laws of whose existence he had been unaware, seeking without knowing it an end that would mean his destruction: "Destiny was too potent, and her immutable laws had decreed my utter and terrible destruction" (46).

But his destiny is neither personal nor individual: Frankenstein has been the instrument of science. A seemingly chance encounter with the works of Cornelius Agrippa, his father's too casual dismissal of Agrippa, the reduction of a tree to splinters by lightning, the decision to attend the University of Ingolstadt: each of these moments was a ruse of scientific and technological progress, realizing itself through him but without his knowing it. His life as it is narrated assumes a nightmarish coherence; every experience, sensation, and feeling was a step on the road to his damnation. Although he once dreamed of creating a race that would worship him as master, he realizes as he lies dying that his relation to science ought rather to be described as a state of servitude. The ironic reversal of Frankenstein's position is perhaps clearest when his creation, far more powerful than he, calls him "slave."

Irony is natural to this dialectic of science, the essence of which is as manifest in violence as in peace, in destruction as in creation. Indifferent to human law and morality, science finally counterposes its own order to that of humankind. *Frankenstein* thus rejects the most fundamental myths of the Enlightenment, the notion that scientific and economic progress will continually improve the condition of humankind, the idea that once the barriers to knowledge are pushed aside, the conditions for perpetual peace and a universal harmony will have been established. Once we have stepped away from the false supports, the dogmas and formulas that prevented us from thinking on our own, once we have taken as our creed the Kantian motto *sapere aude,* "dare to know" (Kant 1970), we will not have achieved the freedom we dreamed of but merely a new kind of servitude. For knowledge has a logic of its own, within which humankind may play only an instrumental role. There is no longer any such thing as progress in the singular; there is a plurality of progresses, some antithetical to others. No longer does the progress of science and, by extension, reason necessarily entail an improvement of the human conditions. Scientific and technological progress does not strengthen human institutions by reaffirming the community of free and rational individuals but instead introduces separateness, division, and antagonism into the social world. From the moment Frankenstein surrenders to the "enticements of science" he is irrevocably divided from his family and friends. Even the University of Ingolstadt fails to provide anything like an academic community. It is a world of separate, solitary scientists. Krempe and Waldman seem scarcely to know each other. Upon entering the portals of science, Frankenstein experiences a solitude matched only by that of his creation.

The monster in its turn is not so much the creation that Frankenstein constantly calls it, as a product, the product of reason. In fact, the frequent recourse to theological terminology (which places Frankenstein in the position of a tragic god who is the prisoner of providence) may once again be regarded as a symptom: it masks the extent to which Frankenstein has himself been created, hailed into existence in order to hasten the realization of a reason whose ends are unknowable to him. Reason is always in the process of becoming real and its realization may well involve the production of monsters or a displacing of the human by the inhuman. For in the process, which in its largest sense is nothing other than history itself, humankind is in no way central. Humanity's greatest achievement may have been to hasten its own destruction.

Frankenstein has thus been led inescapably to the threshold represented by "the workshop of filthy creation":

> In a solitary chamber, or rather cell, at the top of the house, and separated from all the other apartments by a gallery and staircase, I kept my workshop of filthy creation: my eye-balls were starting in their sockets in attending to the details of my employment. The dissecting room and the slaughter-house furnished many of my materials; and often did my human nature turn with loathing from my occupation, whilst, still urged on by an eagerness which

perpetually increased, I brought my work near to a conclusion.
(56)

The narrative pauses at this threshold; the reader is not conducted into
the "workshop." At this point the narrative digresses into moral commentary until Frankenstein uncharacteristically refers to the presence of
Walton, his listener: "Your looks remind me to proceed." But his narrative does not begin again from where it left off. Instead it begins with
his work completed: "It was on a dreary night of November, that I
beheld the accomplishment of all my toils" (57). Utterly absent from
the narrative is any description or explanation of the process by which
the monster was created. The sequences so central to the film versions
of Shelley's tale, in which the mystery of technology is reaffirmed
through iconic figures of electric arcs and bubbling chemicals, have no
place at this point or any other of Mary Shelley's narrative. The process
of production is evoked but never described, effectively presenting us a
world of effects without causes. In this sense, Victor's capacity for denial, his ability to forget after the initial shock that his creation runs
amok, resembles the movement of the text itself, which "turns away"
at certain key points, omitting every description of the technology so
central to the tragedy of Victor Frankenstein and his creation.

In no sense can this omission be regarded as mistake or failure on
Mary Shelley's part. On the contrary, the omission recurs throughout
the work with a regularity that renders it integral to the work as a whole.
At the same time it should not be dismissed as an authorial choice,
an intentional abbreviation of the narrative for the sake of brevity or
coherence. For as was evident in the sequence described above, this
omission appears as a gap in the narrative that is filled in or covered
over by a digression that is marked as a deviation by the narrative itself.
Technology and science, so central to the novel, are present only in
their effects; their truth becomes visible only in the face of their hideous
progeny and is written in the tragic lives of those who serve them.

If we now return to the passage above, we may see the way in which
the systematic suppression of the scientific and the technological functions at an even more primary level. The passage begins by evoking the
solitary separateness of Frankenstein's labor. He works in a "solitary
chamber," a term of description that is replaced by the apparently more
accurate "cell." The textual movement from chamber to cell is important. For if "cell" is a synonym for "solitary chamber," it adds certain
associations that link Frankenstein's solitude to that of a monk in a
monastery or a prisoner in prison. We understand the metaphor of the

prison cell: Frankenstein has always been a prisoner, and perhaps most when he believed himself to be free (of familial and social obligations), forced to labor on a project of whose ultimate meaning he remained ignorant. Thus, shortly after this passage, he compares himself to "one doomed by slavery to toil in the mines" (57).

But the idea of a monk's cell presents more difficulty insofar as it is incompatible with Frankenstein's scientific activity. The kind of discoveries made by monks in the closed world of their cells were precisely those of Cornelius Agrippa, the fantastic, exploded systems that were the empty creations of deluded minds. But this coupling of the religious and the scientific is far from unusual in the text as a whole. For just as the narrative cannot describe any scientific activity, so it cannot speak of the scientific without first clothing it in theological terms. The narrative thereby protects itself from the reality that it describes by casting a veil over that reality: it must continue to cover that which it reveals.

In this way, the stark heterogeneity of the phrase "workshop of filthy creation" is placed clearly in relief. Here, the incompatible worlds of industry (workshop) and theology (creation) collide. The material activity associated with the workshop, the work of manufacture, is immediately supplanted by the immateriality of creation as the text itself turns with loathing from the images that it produces. Like the dissecting room and the slaughterhouse, the "details of his employment" are too frightening to reproduce. As Victor speaks, his "eyes swim with the remembrance" and he frequently turns away from the reality of his own activity. Thus the technology so central to the Promethean drama is in one sense utterly absent from the work.

If we have argued that this absence is neither a fault for which the author might be reproached (for example, Mary Shelley was ignorant of scientific procedure and the technologies of her time) nor simply a stylistic choice (for example, the descriptions are in no way "essential" to the narrative and would at best be superfluous) but highly symptomatic, it is not simply because the narrative "stumbles" and digresses at the threshold of the "workshop of filthy creation." For this absence is doubled by another: the world that this "modern Prometheus" inhabits is not modern at all. Frankenstein's world is a world without industry, a rural world dominated by scenes of a sublime natural beauty in which not a single trace of Blake's "dark satanic mills" is to be found. Although Frankenstein is reared in Geneva and educated at Ingolstadt, although he and Clerval visit London, Oxford, and Edinburgh, there are no significant descriptions of the urban world, none certainly to match the frequent portraits of natural vistas and rural scenes. London,

at a time of explosive growth and development (cf. Wordsworth's treatment of London in the *Prelude*), is not described at all although he
and Clerval passed "some months" there (135). Further, there are no
workers or work. The peasants who appear intermittently throughout
the novel are either engaged in various forms of recreation or, as turns
out to be the case with the De Lacey family, they are not peasants at
all.

The effect of this suppression of the urban and the industrial is to
render Frankenstein's labor as well as the product of that labor, the
monster, all the more incongruous. He is the sole embodiment of the
industrial in an otherwise rural world, and this is the source of his monstrousness. At one point, the monster makes explicit his identification
with the working class:

> I learned that the possessions most esteemed by your fellow-crea-
> tures were high and unsullied descent united with riches. A man
> might be respected with only one of these advantages; but, with-
> out either, he was considered, except in very rare instances, as a
> vagabond and a slave, doomed to waste his powers for the profits
> of the chosen few! And what was I? Of my creation and my crea-
> tor I was absolutely ignorant; but I knew that I possessed no
> money, no friends, no kind of property. . . . When I looked
> around, I saw and heard of none like me. Was I then a monster,
> a blot upon the earth, from which all men fled, and whom all
> men disowned? (106)

It is at this point that we see most clearly the associations that link
the image of the monster to the industrial proletariat: an unnatural being, singular even in its collective identity, without a genealogy and belonging to no species. Its tragic fate is all the more pitiable in that it is
necessary, and in the grand scheme of things, just and proper. If the
proletariat speaks (like the monster always through an intermediary),
the reader, like Frankenstein and Walton, must resist its eloquence:
"hear him not" (174). At the same time, however, Frankenstein's
monster is finally not identified with the working class of Mary Shelley's
time but with its absence. For the narrative precisely suppresses all that
is modern in order to render this being inexplicable and unprecedented,
a being for whom there is no place in the ordered world of nature. If
the modern (the urban, the industrial, the proletarian) were allowed to
appear, the monster would no longer be a monster; no longer alone
but part of a "race of devils," his disappearance would change nothing.
Instead, the mass is reduced to the absolute singularity of Franken-

stein's creation, which is therefore not so much the sign of the proletariat as of its unrepresentability. Written before the notion of a postcapitalist order (a society ruled by the workers themselves) could be articulated but at a time when the oppressive and dehumanizing effects of capitalism were all too obvious, the work can do no better than to turn backward toward a time of mutual (if unequal) obligation, to a time before the creation of monsters by the industrial order, a time when the human was regulated by the natural. But if a certain historical reality is inscribed within the work as a monster to be expelled into "darkness and distance" (just as Frankenstein himself "forgets" his "hideous progeny" immediately after bringing it into this world), the act of repression can only postpone its inevitable return.

WORKS CITED

Foucault, Michel. *The Archaeology of Knowledge.* Trans. A. M. Sheridan Smith. New York: Pantheon, 1972.

Kant, Immanuel. "What Is Enlightenment?" *Political Writings.* Cambridge: Cambridge UP, 1970.

Lecercle, Jean-Jacques. *Frankenstein.* Paris: Presses Universitaires de France, 1988.

Moretti, Franco. *Signs Taken for Wonders.* London: New Left, 1983.

Thompson, E. P. *The Making of the English Working Class.* New York: Vintage, 1963.

Cultural Criticism
and
Frankenstein

WHAT IS CULTURAL CRITICISM?

What do you think of when you think of culture? The opera or ballet? A performance of a Mozart symphony at Lincoln Center, or a Rembrandt show at the Metropolitan Museum of Art? Does the phrase "cultural event" conjure up images of young people in jeans and T-shirts or of people in their sixties dressed formally? Most people hear "culture" and think "High Culture." Consequently, most people, when they first hear of cultural criticism, assume it would be more formal than, well, say, formalism. They suspect it would be "highbrow," in both subject and style.

Nothing could be further from the truth. In fact, one of the goals of cultural criticism is to oppose Culture with a capital C, in other words, that *view* of culture which always and only equates it with what we sometimes call "high culture." Cultural critics want to make the term *culture* refer to *popular* culture as well as to that culture we associate with the so-called classics. Cultural critics are as likely to write about "Star Trek" as they are to analyze James Joyce's *Ulysses*. They want to break down the boundary between high and low, and to dismantle the hierarchy that the distinction implies. They also want to discover the (often political) reasons *why* a certain kind of aesthetic product is more valued than others.

A cultural critic writing on a revered classic might concentrate on a movie or even comic strip version. Or she might see it in light of some more common form of reading material (a novel by Jane Austen might be viewed in light of Gothic romances or ladies' conduct manuals), as the reflection of some common cultural myths or concerns (*Huckleberry Finn* might be shown to reflect and shape American myths about race, concerns about juvenile delinquency), or as an example of how texts move back and forth across the alleged boundary between "low" and "high" culture. A history play by Shakespeare, as one group of cultural critics has pointed out, may have started off as a popular work enjoyed by working people, later become a "highbrow" play enjoyed only by the privileged and educated, and, still later, due to a film version produced during World War II, become popular again — this time because it has been produced and viewed as a patriotic statement about England's greatness during wartime (Humm 6–7). Even as this introduction was being written, cultural critics were analyzing the "cultural work" being done cooperatively by Mel Gibson and Shakespeare in Franco Zeffirelli's recent movie, *Hamlet.*

In combating old definitions of what constitutes culture, of course, cultural critics sometimes end up combating old definitions of what constitutes the literary canon, that is, the once-agreed-upon honor roll of Great Books. They tend to do so, however, neither by adding books (and movies and television sitcoms) *to* the old list of texts that every "culturally literate" person should supposedly know, nor by substituting for it some kind of Counterculture Canon. Rather, they tend to combat the canon by critiquing the very *idea* of canon. Cultural critics want to get us away from thinking about certain works as the "best" ones produced by a given culture (and therefore as the novels that best represent American culture). They seek to be more descriptive and less evaluative, more interested in relating than rating cultural products and events.

It is not surprising, then, that in an article on "The Need for Cultural Studies," four groundbreaking cultural critics have written that "Cultural Studies should . . . abandon the goal of giving students access to that which represents a culture." Instead, these critics go on to argue, it should show works in reference to other works, economic contexts, or broad social discourses (about childbirth, women's education, rural decay, etc.) within whose contexts the work makes sense. Perhaps most important, critics doing cultural studies should counter the prevalent notion that culture is some wholeness that has already been formed. Culture, rather, is really a set of interactive *cultures,* alive and growing and changing, and cultural critics should be present- and even future-oriented. Cultural critics should be "resisting intellectuals," and cultural studies should be "an emancipatory project" (Giroux 478–80).

The paragraphs above are peppered with words like *oppose, counter, deny, resist, combat, abandon,* and *emancipatory.* What such words suggest — and quite accurately — is that a number of cultural critics view themselves in political, even oppositional, terms. Not only are cultural critics likely to take on the literary canon while offering political readings of popular films, but they are also likely to take on the institution of the university, for that is where the old definitions of culture as High Culture (and as something formed and finished and canonized) have been most vigorously preserved, defended, and reinforced.

Cultural critics have been especially critical of the departmental structure of universities, for that structure, perhaps more than anything else, has kept the study of the "arts" more or less distinct from the study of history, not to mention from the study of such things as television, film, advertising, journalism, popular photography, folklore, current affairs, shoptalk, and gossip. By doing so, the departmental structure of universities has reasserted the high/low culture distinction, implying that all the latter subjects are best left to historians, sociologists, anthropologists, linguists, and communication theorists. But such a suggestion, cultural critics would argue, keeps us from seeing the aesthetics of an advertisement as well as the propagandistic elements of a work of literature. For these reasons, cultural critics have mixed and matched the most revealing analytical procedures developed in a variety of disciplines, unabashedly jettisoning the rest. For these reasons, too, they have formed — and encouraged other scholars to form — networks other than and outside of those enforced departmentally.

Some initially loose interdisciplinary networks have, over time, solidified to become Cultural Studies programs and majors, complete with courses on comics and surveys of soaps. As this has happened, a significant if subtle danger has arisen. Cultural critics, Richard Johnson has warned, must strive diligently to keep cultural studies from becoming a discipline unto itself — one in which students encounter cartoons as a canon and belief in the importance of such popular forms as an "orthodoxy" (39). The only principles that critics doing cultural studies can doctrinally espouse, Johnson suggests, are the two that have thus far been introduced: namely, the principle that "culture" has been an "inegalitarian" concept, a "tool" of "condescension," and the belief that a new, "interdisciplinary (and sometimes antidisciplinary)" approach to *true* culture (that is, to the forms in which culture actually lives now) is required now that history and art and media are so complex and inter-related (42).

Johnson, ironically, played a major part in the institutionalization of cultural studies. Together with Stuart Hall and Richard Hoggart, he developed the Centre for Contemporary Cultural Studies, founded by Hoggart and Hall at Birmingham University, in England, in 1964. The fact that the Centre was founded in the mid-1960s is hardly surprising; cultural criticism, based as it is on a critique of elitist definitions of culture, spoke powerfully to and gained great energy and support from a decade of student unrest and revolt. The fact that the first center for cultural studies was founded in England, in Europe, is equally unsurprising. Although the United States has probably contributed more than any other nation to the *media* through which culture currently lives, critics in Europe, drawing upon the ideas of both Marxist and non-Marxist theorists, first articulated the need for something like what we now call cultural criticism or cultural studies. Indeed, to this day, European critics are more involved than Americans, not only in the analysis of popular cultural forms and products but also in the analysis of human subjectivity or consciousness *as* a form or product of culture. ("Subjectivities," Johnson argues, are "produced, not given, and are . . . objects of inquiry" inevitably related to "social practices," whether those involve factory rules, supermarket behavior patterns, reading habits, advertisements watched, myths perpetrated, or languages and other signs to which people are exposed [44–45].)

Among the early continental critics now seen as forerunners of present-day cultural critics were those belonging to the *Annales* school, so-called because of the name of the journal that Marc Bloch and Lucien Febvre launched, in France, in 1929: *Annales: Economies, Sociétés, Civilisations*. The *Annales* school critics greatly influenced later thinkers like Michel Foucault, who, in turn, influenced other *Annales* thinkers such as Roger Chartier, Jacques Ravel, François Furet, and Robert Darnton. Both first- and second-generation *Annales* school critics warn against the development of "topics" of study by cultural critics — unless those same critics are bent on "developing . . . [a] sense of cohesion or inter-action between topics" (Hunt 9). At the same time, interested as they are in cohesion, *Annales* school critics have warned against seeing the "rituals and other forms of symbolic action" as "express[ing] a central, coherent, communal meaning." They have reminded us that texts affect different readers "in varying and individual ways" (Hunt 13–14).

Michel Foucault is another strong, continental influence on present-day cultural criticism — and perhaps *the* strongest influence on American cultural criticism and the so-called new historicism, an interdisciplinary form of historical criticism whose evolution has often paralleled that of cultural criticism. Influenced by early *Annales* critics and contemporary Marxists (but neither an *Annales* critic nor a Marxist himself), Foucault sought to study cultures in terms of power relationships. Unlike Marxists and some *Annales* school critics, he refused to see power as something exercised by a dominant over a subservient class. Indeed, he emphasized that power is not just *repressive* power: a tool of conspiracy by one individual or institution against another. Power, rather, is a whole complex of forces; it is that which produces what happens.

Thus even a tyrannical aristocrat does not simply wield power, for he is empowered by "discourses" — accepted ways of thinking, writing, and speaking — and practices that amount to power. Foucault tried to view all things, from punishment to sexuality, in terms of the widest possible variety of discourses. As a result, he traced the "genealogy" of topics he studied through texts that more traditional historians and literary critics would have overlooked, looking at (in Lynn Hunt's words) "memoirs of deviants, diaries, political treatises, architectural blueprints, court records, doctors' reports — appl[ying] consistent principles of analysis in search of moments of reversal in discourse, in search of events as loci of the conflict where social practices were transformed" (Hunt 39). Foucault tended not only to build interdisciplinary bridges but also, in the process, to bring into the study of culture the "histories of women, homosexuals, and minorities" — groups seldom studied by those interested in culture with a capital C (Hunt 45).

Of the British influences on cultural studies and criticism as it is today, several have already been mentioned. Of those who have not, two early forerunners stand out. One of these, the Marxist critic E. P. Thompson, revolutionized study of the industrial revolution by writing about its impact on human attitudes, even consciousness. He showed how a shared cultural view, specifically that of what constitutes a fair or just price, influenced crowd behavior and caused such things as the food riots and rick burnings of the nineteenth century. The other, even greater, early British influence on contemporary cultural criticism and cultural studies was the late Raymond Williams. In works like *The Long Revolution* and *Culture and Society: 1780–1950,* Williams demonstrated that culture is not a fixed and finished but, rather, a living and changing thing. One of the changes he called for was the development of a common socialist culture.

Like Marxists, with whom he often both argued and sympathized, Williams viewed culture in relation to ideologies, what he termed the "residual," "dominant," or "emerging" ways of viewing the world held by classes or individuals holding power in a given social group. But unlike Thompson and Richard Hoggart, he avoided emphasizing *social* classes and class *conflict* in discussing those forces most powerfully shaping and changing culture. And, unlike certain continental Marxists, he could never see the cultural "superstructure" as being a more or less simple "reflection" of the economic "base." Williams's tendency was to focus on people as people, on how they experience conditions they find themselves in and creatively respond to those conditions in their social practices. A believer in the resiliency of the individual, he produced a body of criticism notable for what Hall has called its "humanism" (63).

As is clear from the paragraphs above, the emergence and evolution of cultural studies or criticism are difficult to separate entirely from the development of Marxist thought. Marxism is, in a sense, the background to the background of most cultural criticism, and some contemporary cultural critics consider themselves Marxist critics as well. Thus, although Marxist criticism and its most significant practitioners are introduced elsewhere in this volume, some mention of Marxist ideas — and of the critics who developed them — is also necessary here. Of particular importance to the evolution of cultural criticism are the works of Walter Benjamin, Antonio Gramsci, Louis Althusser, and Mikhail Bakhtin.

Bakhtin was a Russian, later a Soviet, critic so original in his thinking and wide-ranging in his influence that some would say he was never a Marxist at all. He viewed language — especially literary texts — in terms of discourses and dialogues *between* discourses. Within a novel written in a society in flux, for instance, the narrative may include an official, legitimate discourse, plus another infiltrated by challenging comments and even retorts. In a 1929 book on Dostoyevsky and a 1940 study *Rabelais and His World*, Bakhtin examined what he calls "polyphonic" novels, each characterized by a multiplicity of voices or discourses. In Dostoyevsky the independent status of a given character is marked by the difference of his or her language from that of the narrator. (The narrator's voice, too, can in fact be a dialogue.) In works by Rabelais, Bakhtin finds that the (profane) language of the carnival and of other popular festivities play against and parody the more official discourses, that is, of the magistrates or the Church. Bakhtin influenced modern cultural criticism by showing, in a sense, that the conflict between "high" and "low" culture takes place not only between classic and popular texts but also between the "dialogic" voices that exist within all great books.

Walter Benjamin was a German Marxist who, during roughly the same period, attacked certain conventional and traditional literary forms that he felt conveyed a stultifying "aura" of culture. He took this position in part because so many previous Marxist critics and, in his own day, Georg Lukács, had seemed to be stuck on appreciating nineteenth-century realistic novels — and opposed to the modernist works of their own time. Benjamin not only praised modernist movements, such as Dadaism, but also saw as hopeful the development of new art forms utilizing mechanical production and reproduction. These forms, including radio and films, offered the promise of a new definition of culture via a broader, less exclusive domain of the arts.

Antonio Gramsci, an Italian Marxist best known for his *Prison Notebooks* (first published as *Lettere dal caracere* in 1947), critiqued the very concept of literature and, beyond that, of culture in the old sense, stressing not only the importance of culture more broadly defined but the need for nurturing and developing proletarian, or working-class, culture. He suggested the need to view intellectuals politically — and the need for what he called "radical organic" intellectuals. Today's cultural critics calling for colleagues to "legitimate the notion of writing reviews and books for the general public," to "become involved in the political reading of popular culture," and, in general, to "repoliticize . . . scholarship" have often cited Gramsci as an early advocate of their views (Giroux 482).

Finally, and most important, Gramsci related literature to the ideologies of the culture that produced it and developed the concept of "hegemony," a term he used to describe the pervasive, weblike system of meanings and values — ideologies — that shapes the way things look, what they mean and, therefore, what reality *is* for the majority of people within a culture. Gramsci did not see people, even poor people, as the helpless victims of hegemony, as ideology's idiotic robots. Rather, he believed that people have the freedom and power to struggle against ideology, to alter hegemony. As Patrick Brantlinger has suggested in *Crusoe's Footprints: Cultural Studies in Britain and America* (1990), Gramsci's thought is unspoiled by the "intellectual arrogance that views the vast majority of people as deluded zombies, the victims or creatures of ideology" (100).

Of those Marxists who, after Gramsci, explored the complex relationship between literature and ideology, the French Marxist Louis Althusser also had a significant impact on cultural criticism. Unlike Gramsci, Althusser tended to see ideology in control of people, and not vice versa. He argued that the main function of ideology is to reproduce the society's existing relations of production, and that that function is even carried out in most literary texts, although literature is relatively autonomous from other "social formations." Dave Laing has explained Althusser's position by saying that the "ensemble of habits, moralities, and opinions" that can be found in any work of literature tend to "ensure that the work-force (and those responsible for re-producing them in the family, school, etc.) are maintained in their position of subordination to the dominant class" (91).

In many ways, though, Althusser is as good an example of where Marxism and cultural criticism part ways as he is of where cultural criticism is indebted to Marxists and their ideas. For although Althusser did argue that literature is relatively autonomous — more independent of ideology than, say, Church, press, or State — he meant by literature not just literature in the narrow sense but something even narrower. He meant Good Literature, certainly not the popular forms that present-day cultural critics would want to set beside Tolstoy and Joyce, Eliot and Brecht. Those popular fictions, Althusser assumed, were mere packhorses designed (however unconsciously) to carry the baggage of a culture's ideology, mere brood mares destined to reproduce it.

Thus, while cultural critics have embraced *both* Althusser's notion that works of literature reflect certain ideological formations *and* his notion that, at the same time, literary works may be relatively distant from or even resistant to ideology, they have rejected the narrow limits within which Althusser and other Marxists have defined literature. In "Marxism and Popular Fiction" (1986), Tony Bennett uses "Monty Python's Flying Circus" and another British television show, "Not the 9 o'clock News," to argue that the Althusserian notion that all forms of popular culture are to be included "among [all those] many material forms which ideology takes . . . under capitalism" is "simply not true." The "entire field" of "popular fiction" — which Bennett takes to include films and television shows as well as books — is said to be "replete with instances" of works that do what Bennett calls the "work" of "distancing." That is, they have the effect of separating the audience from, not rebinding the audience to, prevailing ideologies (249).

Although there are Marxist cultural critics (Bennett himself is one, carrying on through his writings what may be described as a lover's quarrel with Marxism), most cultural critics are not Marxists in any strict sense. Anne Beezer, in writing about such things as advertisements and women's magazines, contests the "Althusserian view of ideology as the construction of the subject" (qtd. in Punter 103). That is to say, she gives both the media she is concerned with and their audiences more credit than Althusserian Marxists presumably would. Whereas they might argue that such media make people what they are, she points out that the same magazines that may, admittedly, tell women how to please their men may, at the same time, offer liberating advice to women about how to preserve their independence by not getting too serious romantically. And, she suggests, many advertisements advertise their status as ads, just as many people who view or read them see advertising as advertising and interpret it accordingly.

The complex and subtle sort of analysis that Beezer has brought to bear on women's magazines and advertisements has been focused on paperback romance novels by Tania Modleski and Janice Radway, in *Loving with a Vengeance* (1982) and *Reading the Romance* (1984), respectively. Radway, a feminist cultural critic who uses but finally exceeds Marxist critical discourse, points out that many women who read romances do so in order to carve out a time and space that is wholly their own, not to be intruded upon by their husband or children. Also, Radway argues, such novels may end in marriage, but the marriage is usually between a feisty and independent heroine and a powerful man she has "tamed," that is, made sensitive and caring. And why do so many such stories involve such heroines and end as they do? Because, Radway demonstrates through painstaking research into publishing houses, bookstores, and reading communities, their consumers *want* them to be that way. They don't buy — or, if they buy they don't recommend — romances in which, for example, a heroine is raped: thus, in time, fewer and fewer such plots find their way onto the racks by the supermarket checkout.

Radway's reading is typical of feminist cultural criticism in that it is *political* — but not exclusively about oppression. The subjectivities of women may be "produced" by romances — that is, their thinking is governed by what they read — but the same women also govern, to some extent, what gets written or produced, thus doing "cultural work" of their own. Rather than seeing all forms of popular culture as manifestations of ideology, soon to be remanifested in the minds of victimized audiences, non-Marxist cultural critics tend to see a sometimes disheartening but always dynamic synergy between cultural forms and the culture's consumers.

Mary Poovey does this in *The Proper Lady and the Woman Writer* (1984), a book in which she traces the evolution of female "propriety." Poovey closely connects the proprieties taught by eighteenth-century women who wrote conduct manuals, ladies' magazines, and even novels with patriarchal notions of women and men's *property*. (Since property was inherited, an unfaithful woman could threaten the disposition of a man's inheritance by giving birth to children who were not his. Therefore, writings by women that reinforced proprieties also shored up the proprietary status quo.) Finally, though, Poovey also shows that some of the women writers who reinforced proprieties and were seen as "textbook Proper Ladies" in fact "crossed the borders of that limited domain" (40). They may have written stories showing the audacity, for women, of trying to lead an imaginative, let alone audacious, life beyond the bounds of domestic propriety. But they did so imaginatively and audaciously.

Whereas Mary Poovey, in *The Proper Lady and the Woman Writer,* viewed *Frankenstein* in terms of its relation to conduct manuals and novels by Jane Austen, most cultural critics who have written about Mary Shelley's best-known novel have instead read it in the context of a very different popular form: the Gothic tale. Paul O'Flinn, for instance, begins his essay on "Production and Reproduction: The Case of *Frankenstein*" by pointing out that the novel was published in the same year as a famous attack on the fifty-year-old tradition of Gothic fiction.

In the essay that follows, Lee E. Heller begins by treating *Frankenstein* as Gothic fiction and by suggesting that the interesting thing about Gothic is its "existence in both 'highbrow' and popular forms." What is true of Gothic in general, Heller goes on to argue, is especially true of *Frankenstein,* which in its book and movie versions has cut a wide swath of audience appeal through boundaries that usually prove impenetrable. Although it remains a classic, *Frankenstein* is also, quite clearly, a fit subject for the new cultural criticism.

Heller next places the *Frankenstein* "original" in the cultural contexts of a late-eighteenth-century debate about education and literacy. This was a period during which the "reading class" had grown to include most of the middle class, a fact that at once had allowed the novel to emerge (as a form, it is more dedicated to representing ordinary life than is poetry) and which, at the same time, had set off a somewhat moralistic debate about what constitutes proper entertainment for readers in need of instruction. That debate had been intensified by the advent of Gothic fiction, the audience for which tended to be more female than male and less prosperous than the audiences of, say, Fielding and Smollett. Should such an audience be reading a kind of writing that seemed only to excite the emotions needlessly and not to instruct? Perhaps because many people were answering that question in the negative, the Gothic evolved to combine the moral elements of the "serious" eighteenth-century novel with the entertaining, escapist excitement that it had come to be known for.

Heller's interest in audience — and in the novel as a consumer product — is as typical for a critic practicing cultural criticism as is her interest in a text that defies the boundaries between "Literature" and popular fiction. So, of course, is her concern with the "cultural work" (Jane Tompkins's phrase) done by a given form in a given historical moment. What makes Heller's version of the new cultural criticism particularly complex and exciting is that she identifies *within* a given literary form (here Gothic) three distinguishable *forms* of that form (horror Gothic, sentimental-educational Gothic, and "high" philosophical Gothic), each of which is then shown to have been doing a different kind of cultural work for a different class or kind of audience — but all within the same text.

Thus, she explains *Frankenstein*'s ability to persist in popularity over the centuries, among a range of socioeconomic classes and via a variety of forms, by showing it to be a hybrid form, a variegated thread twisted together of sensational, middle-class sentimental, and philosophical strands. In the process, she provides a strikingly original reading, one that shows not only how a cultural debate lies behind a text but also how it is foregrounded within the text. For she shows that *Frankenstein* is as much about good and bad education, salutary books, and (Cornelius Agrippa's) corrupting, "sad trash," as it is about ghouls and their horrifying acts.

Finally, though, Heller's work represents cultural criticism at its best by virtue of the fact that it sets the text in its later historical periods, including our own. Through her essay, we can see the radical metamorphosis of its meaning and function in subsequent film versions (from the 1931 classic through the crop of "Freddie" and "Jason" movies); the changing ways in which we have used the word *Frankenstein* to speak of historical figures and atrocities (from Adolf Hitler to the atom bomb to the monstrous "wildings" that have been committed in Central Park). Thus, Heller makes *Frankenstein* speak in a way that critics taking other approaches to the novel can only hope to make it speak, for she shows *all* Frankensteins to be *versions* of *Frankenstein* and shows how the current version speaks now.

CULTURAL CRITICISM:
A SELECTED BIBLIOGRAPHY

General Introductions to
Cultural Criticism, Cultural Studies

Brantlinger, Patrick. *Crusoe's Footprints: Cultural Studies in Britain and America*. New York: Routledge, 1990.

Desan, Philippe, Priscilla Parkhurst Ferguson, and Wendy Griswold. "Editors' Introduction: Mirrors, Frames, and Demons: Reflections on the Sociology of Literature." *Literature and Social Practice*. Ed. Desan, Ferguson, and Griswold. Chicago: U of Chicago P, 1989. 1–10.

Eagleton, Terry. "Two Approaches in the Sociology of Literature." *Critical Inquiry* 14 (1988): 469–76.

Giroux, Henry, David Shumway, Paul Smith, and James Sosnoski. "The Need for Cultural Studies: Resisting Intellectuals and Oppositional Public Spheres." *Dalhousie Review* 64.2 (1984): 472–86.

Gunn, Giles. *The Culture of Criticism and the Criticism of Culture*. New York: Oxford, 1987.

Hall, Stuart. "Cultural Studies: Two Paradigms." *Media, Culture and Society* 2 (1980): 57–72.

Humm, Peter, Paul Stigant, and Peter Widdowson, eds. *Popular Fictions: Essays in Literature and History*. New York: Methuen, 1986. See especially the intro. by Humm, Stigant, and Widdowson, and Tony Bennett's essay "Marxism and Popular Fiction." 237–65.

Hunt, Lynn, ed. *The New Cultural History: Essays*. Berkeley: U of California P, 1989.

Johnson, Richard. "What Is Cultural Studies Anyway?" *Social Text: Theory/Culture/Ideology* 16 (1986–87): 38–80.

Pfister, Joel. "The Americanization of Cultural Studies." *Yale Journal of Criticism* 4 (1991): 199–229.

Punter, David, ed. *Introduction to Contemporary Critical Studies*. New York: Longman, 1986. See especially Punter's "Introduction: Culture and Change" 1–18, Tony Dunn's "The Evolution of Cultural Studies" 71–91, and the essay "Methods for Cultural Studies Students" by Anne Beezer, Jean Grimshaw, and Martin Barker 95–118.

Cultural Studies:
Some Early British Examples

Hoggart, Richard. *Speaking to Each Other*. 2 vols. London: Chatto, 1970.
———. *The Uses of Literacy: Changing Patterns in English Mass Culture*. Boston: Beacon, 1961.

Thompson, E. P. *The Making of the English Working Class*. New York: Pantheon, 1977.

——. *William Morris: Romantic to Revolutionary*. New York: Pantheon, 1977.

Williams, Raymond. *Culture and Society, 1780–1950*. New York: Harper, 1958.

——. *The Long Revolution*. New York: Columbia UP, 1961.

Cultural Studies:
Continental and Marxist Influences

Althusser, Louis. *For Marx*. Trans. Ben Brewster. New York: Pantheon, 1969.

Althusser, Louis, and Etienne Balibar. *Reading Capital*. Trans. Ben Brewster. New York: Pantheon, 1971.

Bakhtin, Mikhail. *The Dialogic Imagination: Four Essays*. Ed. Michael Holquist. Trans. Caryl Emerson. Austin: U of Texas P, 1981.

——. *Rabelais and His World*. Cambridge: MIT, 1968.

Benjamin, Walter. *Illuminations*. Ed. with intro. by Hannah Arendt. Trans. H. Zohn. New York: Harcourt, 1968.

Bennett, Tony. ''Marxism and Popular Fiction.'' Humm, Stigant, and Widdowson.

Foucault, Michel. *Discipline and Punish: The Birth of the Prison*. Trans. Alan Sheridan. New York: Pantheon, 1978.

——. *The History of Sexuality*, Vol. 1. Trans. Robert Hurley. New York: Pantheon, 1978.

Gramsci, Antonio. *Selections from the Prison Notebooks*. Ed. Quintin Hoare and Geoffrey Nowell Smith. New York: International, 1971.

Modern Cultural Studies:
Selected British and American Examples

Colls, Robert, and Philip Dodd, eds. *Englishness: Politics and Culture, 1880–1920*. London: Croom Helm, 1986.

Modleski, Tania. *Loving with a Vengeance: Mass-Produced Fantasies for Women*. Hamden: Archon, 1982.

Poovey, Mary. *Uneven Developments: The Ideological Work of Gender in Mid-Victorian England*. Chicago: U of Chicago P, 1988.

Radway, Janice. *Reading the Romance: Women, Patriarchy, and Popular Literature*. Chapel Hill: U of North Carolina P, 1984.

Cultural Studies of *Frankenstein*

Baldick, Chris. *In Frankenstein's Shadow: Myth, Monstrosity, and Nineteenth-Century Writing*. Oxford: Clarendon, 1987.

Bewell, Alan. "An Issue of Monstrous Desire: Frankenstein and Obstetrics." *Yale Journal of Criticism* 2.1 (1988): 105–28.

LaValley, Albert J. "The Stage and Film Children of *Frankenstein:* A Survey." *The Endurance of Frankenstein*. Ed. George Levine and U. C. Knoepflmacher. Berkeley: U of California P, 1979. 243–89.

O'Flinn, Paul. "Production and Reproduction: The Case of *Frankenstein.*" *Literature and History* 9.2 (1983): 194–213.

Poovey, Mary. *The Proper Lady and the Woman Writer: Ideology as Style in the Works of Mary Wollstonecraft, Mary Shelley, and Jane Austen*. Chicago: U of Chicago P, 1984. See especially ch. 4: "'My Hideous Progeny': The Lady and the Monster."

Rieder, John. "Embracing the Alien: Science Fiction in Mass Culture." *Science-Fiction Studies* 9.1 (March 1982): 26–37.

Spivak, Gayatri Chakravorty. "Three Women's Texts and a Critique of Imperialism." *Critical Inquiry* 12.1 (1985): 243–61.

Vlasopolos, Anca. "*Frankenstein*'s Hidden Skeleton: The Psycho-Politics of Oppression." *Science-Fiction Studies* 10.2 (1983): 125–36.

A CULTURAL PERSPECTIVE ON *FRANKENSTEIN*

LEE E. HELLER

Frankenstein and the Cultural Uses of Gothic

Mary Shelley's tale of creation and destruction has claimed a central place in Anglo-American culture since its first publication in 1818. Along the way, *Frankenstein* has come to stand for the genre we call Gothic. Yet it is hard to define Gothic in any single way, for its conventions and their meanings depend upon the historical, ideological context in which they were created and construed. Cultural criticism endeavors to reconstruct Gothic, as far as it can, by exploring the ways in which its writers and readers understood its intention and its impact.

Gothic fiction as it emerged from 1760 to 1820 was associated with the development of new forms of popular literature. The emergence of accessible reading matter intended to entertain was linked with the extension of literacy to new classes of readers; in turn, concerns about reading and its uses were part of larger debates over education, the location of power in society, and the nature and control of individual behavior. The development of Gothic fiction, and of Mary Shelley's novel, takes its meaning from the tensions informing these cultural concerns about human nature, its potentials and limits, and the forces that go into its making.

The redefinition of human nature and its possible shaping through education was a crucial concern for eighteenth-century British culture. John Locke's *Essay Concerning Human Understanding* (1689) popularized the notion that character is acquired rather than innate. Personality and conduct could be created, or at least controlled, by controlling experience: "of all the Men we meet with," Locke wrote elsewhere, "Nine Parts of Ten are what they are, Good or Evil, useful or not, by their Education. . ." (qtd. in Axtell 114). Rousseau's *Emile,* published seventy years later, offered "a textbook of how to educate for the development of natural virtue" (Silver 18): it emphasized the importance of childhood experience in determining adult behavior, and identified education as the essential tool for forming—and reforming—cultural values. Mary Shelley's parents, Mary Wollstonecraft and William Godwin, and the circle of Jacobin radical writers sympathetic to the egalitarian ideas of the French Revolution, reinforced Rousseau's view of the perfectibility of human character while resisting his elitism and gender biases; they argued for the use of education to reform the economic and social status of women and workers.

Education came increasingly to bear the weight of anxieties about control of those who had no tradition of formal education, and who therefore seemed most vulnerable to social instability and most dangerous if formed for ill: middle-class children, women, and the working class. And the area in which they were least protected and most open to influence was the newly acquired literacy that was growing rapidly amid precisely these three groups. Even conservative opponents of radical reform, like Hannah More, acknowledged the formative power of education, and more specifically reading, as a powerful tool for social control. More's works attempted to determine the values and conduct of these new readers by determining what they read: she wrote *Strictures on the Modern System of Female Education, with a View of the Principles and Conduct Prevalent among Women of Rank and Fortune* (1799) as a reply to and attack on Wollstonecraft's egalitarianism and feminism, while her Cheap Repository Tracts, aimed at preventing the spread of reformist ideology in juvenile and working-class readers, borrowed form and style from popular street literature in order to work against the very reforms that popular literacy implied.

Books, it seemed, could shape people's lives. That this was perceived to be the case was evident in the boom in conduct manuals — self-help books giving instruction in everything from childrearing to family religion — for newly literate, rising middle-class readers lacking institutions to educate them in their new social roles. But if books could provide guidance, they could also lead readers astray. The capacity to read could be acquired without institutional guidance (radical or conservative), through a growing array of material cheaply available, highly appealing, and of uncertain moral influence. For publisher William Dicey this was a point in favor of his street literature, with its stories of crimes and fantastic romance; he advertised his broadsides by claiming:

> the use of these Old Songs is very great, in respect that many Children never would have learn'd to Read, had they not took a delight in poring over Jane Shore, or Robin Hood &c. which has insensibly stole into them a Curiosity and Desire of Reading other the like Stories. . . . (qtd. in Vincent 226)

Conduct manuals, with their interest in the impact of reading on the formation of character, reflected the conservative effort to control the spread of literacy via the very literature that Dicey praised. They defined the proper use of literacy by excluding such street literature as inappropriate to the upwardly mobile values of their aspiring readers, advising what should and shouldn't be read, and by whom.

The different kinds of Gothic fiction that emerged in the late eighteenth century reflected the perceived vulnerabilities of their intended readers. Gothic achieved a measure of respectability only in the "sentimental Gothic" form popularized by Ann Radcliffe, whose plots were little more than scary versions of the didactic novel's lessons about women's proper marital choices. In general, however, Gothic fiction was considered proof of the dangerous influence of the wrong kind of books on susceptible readers. Even the radical Jacobins objected to its misuse of literacy's power. Mary Wollstonecraft attacked Charlotte Smith's Gothic stories for their tendency "to debauch the mind" so that "duties are neglected, and content despised" (qtd. in Roper 126), while Thomas Holcroft objected to Gothic precisely in terms of the power of reading to shape character: "It contributes to keep alive that superstition which debilitates the mind. . . . The good writer teaches the child to become a man; the bad and indifferent best understand the reverse art of making a man a child" (qtd. in Roper 125). Reviewers worried in particular about the malleability of unsophisticated readers seduced by material like William Dicey's broadsides and the popular "blue books" or "shilling shockers" (cheap redactions of Gothic tales of the supernatural or of violent crime). Such trash, even when a stern moral was tacked on, was clearly sensational in purpose and effect; and thus it was a threat to the innocent, unguided minds of middle-class schoolboys, fragile young women, and the newly literate laborer.

James Lackington, the London bookseller, observed in his 1791 autobiography that "[t]he poorer sorts of farmers, and even the poor country people in general, who before that period spent their winter evenings in relating stories of witches, ghosts, hobgoblins, &c. now shorten the winter nights by hearing their sons and daughters read tales, romances, &c." (qtd. in Leavis 132). Thus oral stories of the supernatural and the sensational, transferred to print in the form of chapbooks and shilling shockers, made the transition to literate culture via a new generation of rising and increasingly urban readers, and connected elite literate with subordinate illiterate classes. This "horror Gothic"[1] — popularized by Matthew "Monk" Lewis and German supernatural fiction — borrowed from oral storytelling and the street literature of the poor: broadsides of criminal confessions, Newgate biographies (histories of the lives of criminals), and newspaper accounts of supernatural events and horrendous violence. To hostile reviewers, horror Gothic was obscene and immoral, emphasizing sexual misconduct, criminality, and antiaristocratic sentiment. It seemed to prove that expanding literacy meant that new classes of readers were bringing their vulgar, indecent, even anarchic tastes with them.

Despite, or perhaps because of, its controversial cultural status, it was horror Gothic that provided the conventions for the form of Gothicism developed by novelists interested in politics and human psychology. In "philosophical Gothic," as we might call it, "the laws of nature are represented as altered, not for the purpose of pampering the imagination with wonders, but in order to shew the probable effect which

---

[1] I am relying here on the very helpful distinctions among Gothic types described by Hume (2).

the supposed miracles would produce on those who witnessed them" ("Remarks on *Frankenstein*" 613). Philosophical Gothic made explicit the concerns about character, conduct, and education that underlay the emergence of popular Gothic fiction; in place of the machinery of sentimental and horror Gothic, it explored the horrific elements of human personality, and the forces — including education and reading — that go into their creation. Philosophic Gothic did not simply provide education, like its sentimental counterpart, or seem, like horror Gothic, to subvert it; it offered a kind of scientific study of the making of human beings. Its principal representatives were William Godwin, author of the influential novel *Caleb Williams, or Things as They Are* (1794); the American Charles Brockden Brown, Godwin's disciple and author of *Wieland*, a study of the forces involved in the making of a mass murderer; and Mary Shelley.

Early reviews of *Frankenstein* indicate that its first readers assessed it in terms of cultural concerns about the formation of character and the role of reading. The *Quarterly Review* announced that "it inculcates no lesson of conduct, manners, or morality; it cannot mend, and will not even amuse its readers, unless their taste have been deplorably vitiated" (385).[2] A more open-minded reader recognized its philosophical thrust — "All these monstrous concepts are the consequences of the wild and irregular theories of the age" (*Edinburgh Magazine* 253) — but went on to characterize those theories, and the novel, as misguided. It was only fellow novelist Sir Walter Scott, in an unsigned review in *Blackwood's Magazine,* who recognized the intellectual function of this "more philosophical and refined use of the supernatural," in which "the pleasure ordinarily derived from the marvellous incidents is secondary to that which we extract from observing how mortals like ourselves would be affected . . ." ("Remarks on *Frankenstein*" 613).[3]

Frankenstein's focus is on human nature and on the possibility of controlling experience in order to shape character and cultural values. More specifically, it focuses on the problematic influence of experience — both social and literary — on those vulnerable, unstable groups

[2]Percy Shelley's preface to the 1818 edition of *Frankenstein*, written as if by Mary Shelley, anticipates such reactions, and asserts the text's conformity to cultural expectations about fiction and moral instruction: its "moral tendencies," he wrote, are directed "to the exhibition of the amiableness of domestic affection, and the excellence of universal virtue" (7).

[3]Robert Spector, in his bibliography of criticism of English Gothic fiction, attributes this review to Scott.

around whom cluster cultural concerns about education and reading. Although Mary Shelley does not seem explicitly to raise issues of class and gender, her novel is very much about controlling the formation of character among potentially dangerous and endangered social groups.

The text describes again and again the process by which individual characters are formed, via types who represent the vulnerable groups described above — sentimental young women (representing concerns about class and gender), bourgeois boy children, and self-taught nameless, classless men. Mary Shelley spends the least time describing the education of women, but as with the male characters whose stories we will hear in more detail, she repeats one version of female upbringing. Caroline Beaufort is the model of virtuous femininity rescued from class degradation; in Mary Shelley's 1831 revision, Caroline seeks out other girls similarly situated, rescuing them from lower class influences and educating them in the virtues of a specifically bourgeois domesticity. Thus she finds Elizabeth, whose seemingly innate, upper-class feminine virtue makes her shine amid a family of "dark-eyed, hardy little vagrants" (40). Once under proper middle-class guidance — neither with peasants nor with Italian aristocrats (as in the original 1818 text)[4] — she is the perfect domestic woman: daughter, sister, friend, and wife-to-be.

Justine Moritz is also saved and educated by Victor's mother, whose very "phraseology and manners" she imitates (64). Justine's social status as servant and member of the lower class reflects cultural anxieties about women's vulnerability and the stabilizing role of a bourgeois domestic education. Like Caroline and Elizabeth before her, Justine represents female upward mobility, as becomes apparent when Elizabeth explains Caroline's adoption of Justine by praising Geneva's flexible class boundaries: "there is less distinction between the several classes of its inhabitants; and the lower orders being neither so poor nor so despised, their manners are more refined and moral" (64). (The anxieties surrounding such flexibility are revealed by the fact that it is Justine — painted as a lower-class woman whose education fails to take — who is accused of, and dies for, William's murder.) Elizabeth's observation about class flexibility seems to apply only to women in the novel, and reflects the text's definition of ideal female experience as bourgeois: where women are concerned, class and gender roles depend on a foun-

[4]Several subsequent references are to the edition of the 1818 text edited by James Rieger (see Works Cited). I rely primarily on the 1831 edition of the novel, but with reference to the first edition of 1818, in order to assess how differences in the two versions of the novel help to elicit its essential interest in cultural concerns about education, literacy, and conduct.

dation in a good education consisting of models of bourgeois domestic virtue. Thus educated, women fulfill and are fulfilled by their social roles, and so pose little danger of disrupting the culture and its values.

Women, once guided into good conduct, are less actors in the drama of education than they are objects acted upon by men, whose deeds then reveal *their* character. Symbols of the ideal merger of gender and class identity, women's vulnerabilities to men's misconduct reflect cultural anxieties about social order and the education of bourgeois and working-class boys. Though virtuous, Justine is wrongly executed for murdering little William, while the perfect Elizabeth is the final and most intimate victim of the monster's revenge: both women, representing social ideals, suffer the consequences of the combined miseducations of the middle-class boy (Victor) and the nameless upstart (the monster). It seems ironic, given that Mary Shelley was the daughter of a feminist educator and novelist and that she kept such careful records of her own reading in her journals, but the novel is less engaged by the education and reading of its women than by the education of the central male figures whose stories supply the main structure of the text.[5]

The novel's structural unity is supplied by the autobiographical narratives of the parallel figures of Walton, Victor, and the monster, and in particular by their educations. The first two offer varieties (Henry Clerval would be a third) of the ambitious, talented individual whose energy is dedicated to serving humanity.[6] Walton is our introduction to the type: he is engaged in a daring endeavor—"I preferred glory to every enticement that wealth placed in my path" (27)—and expects to achieve extraordinary things, to confer "inestimable benefit . . . on all mankind to the last generation, by discovering a passage near the pole . . . or by ascertaining the secret of the magnet. . ." (26). Victor, too, is nobly ambitious: "wealth was an inferior object; but what glory would attend the discovery, if I could banish disease from the human frame, and render man invulnerable to any but a violent death!" (45).

[5]There is biographical support for Mary Shelley's characterization of the subordination of female to male educational experience: her journal kept as careful track of her husband's reading as of her own and noted her dependency on his guidance of and involvement in her reading.

[6]Judith Wilt refers to these three figures as types of the "Shelleyan doomed seeker" (69–70), and I think she is right to see them as representatives of an abstract notion of human potential in search of fulfillment. Certainly Walton, Victor, and the monster are variants on the romantic theme — embodied also by Goethe's Faust and the Werther about whom the Monster reads — of uncontainable human desire. But the cultural-critical reading I offer here places the novel in the context of more historically local concerns about how specifically identified social groups — women and the rising working class — might use, or abuse, their power.

Although they seem to abjure the pursuit of wealth, they are all three quintessentially bourgeois in status, as is clear from the example of Clerval, the merchant's son. In the 1818 version Victor describes him as "the image of my former self" (Rieger 155), while the 1831 text conflates material success with humanitarian ambition, describing Clerval's desire to "visit India, in the belief that he had . . . the means of materially assisting the progress of European colonisation and trade" (135). The sons of successful but not aristocratic fathers, these figures direct their self-creating energies toward enterprises that unite personal gain to cultural progress, expanding humanity's power over the material world.

Each narrator explains himself in terms of his childhood education — and in particular, his reading. Walton describes how books, the primary tools of his self-education, have shaped him and his choices. He characterizes himself as "passionately fond of reading" (27) but adds that as a boy he was "self-educated: for the first fourteen years of my life I ran wild on a common, and read nothing but our uncle Thomas's books of voyages" (29). He bemoans this neglect: "Now I am twenty-eight, and am in reality more illiterate than many schoolboys of fifteen" (29). His goals, both noble and dangerous, are the product of the unguided childhood reading that has been almost the sole influence over him.

By contrast, the world in which Victor grows up seems at first an educator's paradise, with all the elements necessary to turn happy children into virtuous adults. Everyone and everything is in perfect concord: "Such was our domestic circle, from which care and pain seemed for ever banished. My father directed our studies, and my mother partook of our enjoyments" (Rieger 37). The 1831 edition heightens the ideal nature of that parental authority: "We felt that they were not the tyrants to rule our lot according to their caprice, but the agents and creators of the many delights which we enjoyed" (43). The Frankenstein children are products of an educational system based on an ideal, partly Rousseauian pedagogy: "Our studies were never forced; and by some means we always had an end placed in view, which excited us to ardour in the prosecution of them" (Rieger 31). This happy family lives in Geneva (Rousseau's ideal middle-class polity), a republic composed of virtuous burghers like Alphonse Frankenstein, with "simpler and happier manners than those which prevail in the great monarchies that surround it" (64).

Victor, the promising eldest son of a virtuous public servant, credits his parents with close guidance of his education. But the event that shapes his future actions is a chance encounter with a book — the work of Cornelius Agrippa, the medieval natural philosopher. He calls it, and the other books he is led to read, "wild fancies" (44); like Walton's sea stories, and like Gothic fiction itself, they are unsanctioned, dangerously exciting explorations of the mysterious. And they have obvious power: although Alphonse Frankenstein and M. Krempe dismiss them as worthless, they start Victor down the path that results in his awful discovery.

Victor's reaction to Agrippa is partly determined by his father's careless dismissal of the book as "sad trash" (44). He intimates that his father is one of many instructors who "utterly neglect" their responsibility to direct "the attention of their pupils to useful knowledge" (Rieger 32):

> If, instead of this remark, my father had taken the pains to explain to me, that the principles of Agrippa had been entirely exploded, and that a modern system of science had been introduced . . . I should certainly have thrown Agrippa aside. . . . It is even possible, that the train of my ideas would never have received the fatal impulse that led to my ruin. (44)

As Walton disobeys his father's injunction against seafaring, so Victor disobeys his father's will in pursuing his interest; further, he seems to imply that his father is responsible for that act, and for its consequences. The novel thus raises explicitly the central issue of dangerous conduct and its causes. Who is responsible for the train of events beginning with Victor's reading of Agrippa, and ending with the annihilation of the entire Frankenstein family?

Critics have tried to find someone to blame for the horrific events of the novel — bad parents (Walton's neglectful uncle, Alphonse for failing to monitor Victor, even Clerval's insensitive father), or rebellious sons (Walton for acting against his father's dying "injunction," Victor for disbelieving and in effect disobeying his father). Such critics have then read these as variants on the neglectful Victor-as-father and his rebellious monster-son. Certainly the novel is critical of irresponsible instruction. In addition to emphasizing the consequences of Alphonse's carelessness, Mary Shelley offers us models of bad and good pedagogy. At Ingolstadt M. Krempe ridicules Victor's reading as "nonsense," with the consequence that, like Alphonse, he turns Victor back to those "exploded systems" (49). M. Waldman on the other hand is an inspiring instructor, who succeeds not by mocking Victor's favorite philosophers but by seeing the same potential in the new chemistry. In fact, Waldman says that chemistry offers a *better* field for such ambitions:

"[T]hese philosophers . . . have indeed performed miracles. They penetrate into the recesses of nature, and show how she works in her hiding places. . . . They have acquired new and almost unlimited powers . . ." (50–51).

If Waldman's good pedagogy guides Victor in the direction of great achievements in the field of chemistry, it is this new expertise, combined with his earlier ambition to conquer death, that leads to Victor's discovery and the train of consequences which follow. Given Waldman's contributory role, then, we must reject the simplistic notion that bad teaching or the wrong kind of reading is to blame. We need to consider instead the difficulty of controlling the experiences, including reading, that affect the shaping of character, and the extent to which individuals are themselves responsible for their actions.

What we realize first is that "education" is partly accidental; as Victor discovers Cornelius Agrippa by chance, so the accident by which he learns about electricity in the 1818 version of the novel "explodes" his faith in alchemical texts and temporarily turns him away from his fatal path. Then Alphonse's plans to send Victor to more modern science courses — which, presumably, would have made Victor's change permanent — are frustrated by "[s]ome accident, which prevented my attending these lectures until the course was nearly finished" (Rieger 36). The 1831 version of the novel emphasizes the image of the vulnerable unguided child: "I was left to struggle with a child's blindness, added to a student's thirst for knowledge" (45). But it also complicates the issue of character's origins by adding Victor's apparently innate longing to penetrate the secrets of nature, and by making Alphonse scientifically uninformed rather than careless. The revised text seems to emphasize fate; Victor mentions a "guardian angel of my life" trying to "avert the storm that was even then hanging in the stars," and claims that "[d]estiny was too potent . . ." (46). What I would argue is not that Mary Shelley literally means to abandon materialist concepts of character in favor of a fatalistic mysticism, but that her increasing emphasis on destiny, as well as on inherent tendencies of character, is metaphoric for the inaccessibility of character — as the product of complex forces that include predispositions and accidents — to human control. No one person is to blame for flawed character and bad actions, the novel then seems to say, but a combination of social, familial, and literary experiences, some within our control, some not: "Thus strangely are our souls constructed, and by such slight ligaments are we bound to prosperity or ruin" (46).

As Victor's education parallels Walton's, so the monster's echoes that of his maker — and in his we see explicit cultural anxieties about social disorder, criminal potential, and the relation between reading and experience. Victor's (mis)education reflects specific anxieties about bourgeois childrearing; the monster represents both the abstract concept of natural "man" and his social equivalent in late eighteenth-century England — the culturally displaced, newly literate rising worker lacking class traditions to guide or guard him. The monster calls his story "an account of the progress of my intellect" (111); it is exemplary simultaneously of eighteenth-century psychological theories of the mind as *tabula rasa*, political theories of the development of class identity and social hierarchy, and historically specific cultural concerns about the violent potential of the rising lower class.

The creature's sensory development, described from the moment of "birth" as it were, echoes Locke's notion of sensory experience as the source of thought: "A strange multiplicity of sensations seized me, and I saw, felt, heard, and smelt, at the same time; and it was, indeed, a long time before I learned to distinguish between the operations of my various senses" (92). As presocial man, he is a model for Rousseau's noble savage, creating social ties out of initial equality and finding in society only injustice.[7] But the monster is also the type of the classless, placeless, self-taught upstart. Lacking parentage or identity, he is on the move in search of means to survive (like the displaced rural peasants migrating to cities and industrial towns). Poor and untaught, he educates himself in a rural hovel, with the De Lacey family as examples of appropriate lower-class virtue — because they are not really lower class, but good bourgeoisie who preserve the domestic virtues despite their reduced circumstances. (One is reminded here of Caroline Beaufort, that model of good character and embodiment of ideal middle-class conduct.) Ugly yet hardy, he is like the little vagrants from whose home Elizabeth Lavenza is removed or like the "horrid and slimy" peasants whom Mary Shelley described, in language prophetic of her novel, in her journal for 1814: "our only wish was to absolutely annihilate such uncleanly animals, to which we might have addressed the Boatman's speech to Pope — 'Twere easier for God to make entirely new men than attempt to purify such monsters as these'" (Jones 12).

As with Walton and Victor, we see in the story of the monster the complex question of reading, experience, and character. Books literally shape his initial conception of reality, giving him the ideological con-

---

[7]For more on Mary Shelley's reading in these areas and its impact on *Frankenstein*, see Pollin.

cepts by which to explain the social behavior he witnesses. He learns language by watching Felix read Volney's *Ruins of Empires,* and understands Safie's story alongside that book. As one critic notes, the monster's first education, via Safie and her assigned reading, is in class identity — and in his own apparent lack thereof (O'Flinn 28): he learns from Felix's teaching of Safie that "the possessions most esteemed by your fellow-creatures were high and unsullied descent united with riches" (106), and he defines himself by contrast: "And what was I? . . . I knew that I possessed no money, no friends, no kind of property" (106).

Against the reality of social injustice is set the ideality of the three books that so profoundly influence the monster's desires and his consequent actions: Goethe's *Sorrows of Werther,* Plutarch's *Lives,* and Milton's *Paradise Lost* (also the source of the novel's controversial epigraph). *The Sorrows of Werther* offers the monster models for ideal feeling: "The gentle and domestic manners it described, combined with lofty sentiments and feelings, which had for their object something out of self, accorded well with my experience among my protectors, and with the wants which were for ever alive in my own bosom" (112). He learns republican values from Plutarch: "I was of course led to admire peaceable law-givers, Numa, Solon, and Lycurgus, in preference to Romulus and Theseus . . ." (112). And he learns good and evil from Milton, identifying with both Adam and Satan: he too came forth potentially perfect, acquiring knowledge "of a superior nature" (113), but like Milton's Satan he is embittered by experience of his inequality; and like Adam, knowledge (in the form of experience) contradicts and debases his initial virtues (which his books have taught him). It is the gap between the ideal offered by this reading, and the reality that he confronts, that precipitates the monster's crisis of identity and values: "As I read, however, I applied much personally to my own feelings and condition. I found myself similar, yet at the same time strangely unlike to the beings concerning whom I read. . . . Who was I? What was I? Whence did I come? What was my destination?" (112). It is the gap between what he has been taught to value, and what experience teaches him he can have, that will propel him into assaults on the social order via its ideal representation — the Frankenstein family.

As with Victor and Walton, it is possible to blame the irresponsibility of the parent-creator for the actions of his creature. Victor clearly was derelict in abandoning what was in effect a helpless outcast infant. Again, however, the issue is more complicated than this. We learn from the monster that a variety of factors have produced him. His tendency toward goodness is reinforced by good romantic books, but they are contradicted by experiences of injustice — by the De Laceys' rejection, by the violence of the peasant who shoots him, by the revulsion of William, all of whom repay his good deeds with hostility. What makes the monster's case hopeless is that there is no way to reconcile what he learns from books with what he experiences in his social relations; as long as he appears horrid and slimy, people (meaning the exemplary bourgeois families he wants to join) will fear and reject him, and the rules of conduct about which he reads will not apply to him. Even the promise of new social relations, via the wife he demands from his creator, is uncertain; Victor's fears that she will reject him, or that both will be unsatisfied, echo cultural anxieties about the rising lower classes' ability to assimilate to middle-class society. In this the monster is a symbol of the violent potential of social instability, and of the danger posed by the discontinuity between the ideals that books imagine and the reality that such readers must confront.

Frankenstein is Gothic because its stories of education become stories of crime — committed not just by the monster, but by Victor, who calls himself the murderer of both William and Justine and feels "as if I had committed some great crime . . ." (138). The monster represents the criminal potential of the uncontrolled, perhaps uncontrollable lower classes, formed by the contradictory lessons of social and literary experience; Victor's transgression represents the potential of even bourgeois men of talent, as products of the complex forces that make up early experience, to become a danger to the very social order they desire to serve. In the novel's analysis of the role of reading in the formation of character and conduct, we see the working out of cultural concerns in which it is itself — as that controversial thing, a Gothic novel — implicated, looking for ways to explain how education in general, and books in particular, contribute to individual behavior and the construction of identity.

Mary's father, William Godwin, in *The Enquirer: Reflections on Education, Manners, and Literature,* wrote that "[w]hen a child is born, one of the earliest purposes of his instructor ought to be, to awaken his mind, to breathe a soul into the, as yet, unformed mass" (2); however, he added:

> [w]e are too confident in our own skill, and imagine our science to be greater than it is. . . . The world, instead of being, as the vanity of some men has taught them to assert, a labyrinth of which they hold the clue, is in reality full of enigmas which no penetration of man has hitherto been able to solve. (16–17)

If his daughter's novel, which she dedicated to her father, has affinities with crime literature and today's horror films, in which violence is committed upon the undeserving by the unmotivated, it is in this sense that character is finally enigmatic, and our control over its formation tenuous at best.

The most widely known version of *Frankenstein* is not Mary Shelley's novel but the 1931 Universal Studios film, directed by James Whale, whose revisions of the story reflect both departures from and the persistence of concerns about the nature and origins of character and the limits on our control over it. The most important revisions were made in the two central characters: the monster "was simplified to a creature of brute primitive force and emotions" while "Victor Frankenstein was assimilated to the myth of the godless and 'presumptive' scientist, tampering with nature's secrets" (LaValley 249). These changes reflect significant differences in the way that early nineteenth- and early twentieth-century Anglo-American culture understood human personality and the power to shape it.

Instead of autobiographical education narratives, criminality frames the story from the opening scene, replacing those narratives as the central structure of the text. Frankenstein, renamed Henry, is now explicitly criminal; the movie opens with him and Fritz (the proverbial hunchbacked assistant) hiding at the fringes of a funeral, waiting to steal a corpse. They then cut down a hanged man to see if they can use his brain. And brains themselves are classified into normal and abnormal, socially upright and criminal, inherently virtuous and innately evil. It is a significant accident (like yet unlike the accidents that determine character in the novel) that Fritz drops the "good" brain, and so must steal the "bad" one for implantation.

Although Henry dismisses the brain's criminality by claiming that it is just tissue, the brain functions as the equivalent to Mary Shelley's long story of social experience in conflict with reading. If, as the film's Waldman claims in his medical lecture, personality and action are inscribed in the very physical folds of the brain, then we can explain behavior by the very factors that limit our control over it. The monstrousness of Frankenstein's monster emphasizes this aspect of the story. Although he initially seems submissive and obedient, even childlike in his delight with flowers, he nonetheless drowns little Maria, probably without intending violence but effecting it nevertheless. Nor can he claim to have been neglected by his creator: the film's Frankenstein is weak, but he does not reject his creation until after it has murdered

Fritz and menaced himself; and even then, he leaves it in the hands of his own teacher. The monster's criminal brain is the only possible cause of his unmotivated, uncontrollable, and deeply threatening violence. Heredity and physiology are destiny.

As with the monster, changes in the characterization of Franken-stein reflect crucial shifts in cultural concepts of personality. His educa-tion too is omitted; we get no sense of what led him to the "mad dream" that drives him. But where Victor was nobly ambitious in his goals, discussions of Henry's character focus on his sanity. Elizabeth reports his erratic behavior: "He said he was on the verge of a discovery so terrific that he doubted his own sanity. There was a strange look in his eyes." When "Victor Moritz" (Henry Clerval rebaptized) accuses Frankenstein of madness, the latter decides to prove that he is sane: "A moment ago you said I was crazy. Tomorrow we'll see about that." The message conveyed by this talk of madness, and by subsequent events, is that Frankenstein is not in control of his own diseased psyche or the thing that he has made. We see this most clearly in his empty boast that "I made [the creature] with these hands, and with these hands I'll de-stroy him"; he threatens, but he is physically helpless in the creature's hands. The illusion of human power over oneself and over life, an illu-sion conveyed by the spectacle of technology and ambition apparently gratified, is destroyed by the reality of a monstrosity outside our power to change or control.

These changes in the representation of human personality and po-tential make sense given the context in which the film was made. The cultural understanding of what makes people who they are, and the extremes of which they are capable, had been reshaped in the century since the publication of Mary Shelley's novel by new theories of the origin of the species, the elements of human psychology, and the nature of identity as determined by gender, class, and race. Early twentieth-century American culture experienced the culmination of those changes in the context of World War I and the social and economic disruptions of the Depression, both of which offered simultaneous examples of hu-man powerlessness and unprecedented human brutality. Ideologies of racism promoted the idea that character is genetically determined, and that social order depends on controlling those whom race-heritage makes dangerous. The Scopes Monkey Trial of 1925 raised related cul-tural anxieties about the Darwinian view that the human species origi-nated not in a first, perfect man, but in lower (monstrous) animal forms; and it represented the battle over what version of human nature would be taught to, and used to teach, America's children. Such concerns resulted in the eugenics movements of the 1920s and 1930s, which advocated selective human breeding in order to weed out the bad and improve the species as a whole; in Europe, these movements culminated in the racial typing, sterilizations, and genocide practiced in Hitler's Germany. What comes through in the 1931 version of *Franken-stein* is a sense of profound cultural anxiety about the inability to do more than watch as human beings enact a physiologically determined criminal potential.

The persistence of *Frankenstein* is not a result of some eternal truth that the text achieves, but of its representation of concerns at the center of Anglo-American culture. Differences within that culture, the conse-quence of changing historical circumstances, are evident in turn in changes in the uses and versions of the story. Gothic itself, in all its types, reflects different cultural anxieties, focused around the kinds of disorder to which the community felt vulnerable — disorder based on new classes of readers empowered by their literacy and endangered by what it might teach them; on fears of what these new readers, especially from the lower classes, might bring with them in the way of criminality threatening to run amok; and, for twentieth-century ideologies of hu-man personality, on fears of the uncontrollable insanity and criminality imprinted in our animal being. In our postatomic culture genetic engi-neering suggests both a new way to control human destiny and an even greater sense of the physical determinism behind the illusion of choice.

WORKS CITED

Axtell, James L., ed. *The Educational Writings of John Locke*. Cam-bridge: Cambridge UP, 1968.

Edinburgh Magazine and Literary Miscellany 2 (March 1818): 249–53. Review of *Frankenstein*.

Godwin, William. *The Enquirer. Reflections on Education, Manners, and Literature. In a Series of Essays*. Philadelphia: For Robert Campbell by John Bioren, 1797.

Jones, Frederick L., ed. *Mary Shelley's Journal*. Norman: U of Oklahoma P, 1957.

Hume, Robert D. "Gothic versus Romantic: A Reevaluation of the Gothic Novel." *PMLA* 84 (1969): 282–90.

LaValley, Albert J. "The Stage and Film Children of *Frankenstein:* A Survey." *The Endurance of Frankenstein: Essays on Mary Shelley's Novel.* Ed. George Levine and U. C. Knoepflmacher. Berkeley: U of California P, 1979. 243–89.

Leavis, Q. D. *Fiction and the Reading Public.* London: Chatto, 1939.

O'Flinn, Paul. "Production and Reproduction: The Case of *Frankenstein.*" *The Study of Popular Fiction: A Source Book.* Ed. Bob Ashley. Philadelphia: U of Pennsylvania P, 1989. 23–39.

Pollin, Burton. "Philosophical and Literary Sources for *Frankenstein.*" *Comparative Literature* 17 (1965): 97–108.

Quarterly Review 18 (January 1818): 379–85. Review of *Frankenstein, or the Modern Prometheus.*

"Remarks on *Frankenstein, or the Modern Prometheus;* a Novel." *Blackwood's Magazine* 2 (March 1818): 613–20.

Roper, Derek. *Reviewing before the Edinburgh, 1788–1802.* Newark: U of Delaware P, 1978.

Shelley, Mary. *Frankenstein; or, the Modern Prometheus* (The 1818 Text). Ed. James Rieger. 1974; Chicago: U of Chicago P, 1982.

Silver, Harold. *English Education and the Radicals, 1780–1850.* London: Routledge, 1975.

Spector, Robert Donald. *The English Gothic: A Bibliographic Guide to Writers from Horace Walpole to Mary Shelley.* Westport: Greenwood, 1984.

Vincent, David. *Literacy and Popular Culture: England, 1750–1914.* Cambridge: Cambridge UP, 1989.

Whale, James, dir. *Frankenstein.* Universal Studios, 1931.

Wilt, Judith. *Ghosts of the Gothic: Austen, Eliot, and Lawrence.* Princeton: Princeton UP, 1980.

Glossary of Critical
and Theoretical Terms

Most terms have been glossed parenthetically where they first appear in the text. Mainly, the glossary lists terms that are too complex to define in a phrase or a sentence or two. A few of the terms listed are discussed at greater length elsewhere (feminist criticism, for instance); these terms are defined succinctly and a page reference to the longer discussion is provided.

AFFECTIVE FALLACY   First used by William K. Wimsatt and Monroe C. Beardsley to refer to what they regarded as the erroneous practice of interpreting texts according to the psychological responses of readers. "The Affective Fallacy," they wrote in a 1946 essay later republished in the *Verbal Icon* (1954), "is a confusion between the poem and its *results* (what it *is* and what it *does*). . . . It begins by trying to derive the standards of criticism from the psychological effects of a poem and ends in impressionism and relativism." The affective fallacy, like the intentional fallacy (confusing the meaning of a work with the author's expressly intended meaning), was one of the main tenets of the New Criticism, or formalism. The affective fallacy has recently been contested by reader-response critics, who have deliberately dedicated their efforts to describing the way individual readers and "interpretive communities" go about "making sense" of texts.

See also: Authorial Intention, Formalism, Reader-Response Criticism.

AUTHORIAL INTENTION   Defined narrowly, an author's intention in writing a work, as expressed in letters, diaries, interviews, and conversations. Defined more broadly, "intentionality" involves unexpressed motivations, designs, and purposes, some of which may have remained unconscious.

The debate over whether critics should try to discern an author's intentions (conscious or otherwise) is an old one. William K. Wimsatt and Monroe C. Beardsley, in an essay first published in the 1940s, coined the term "intentional fallacy" to refer to the practice of basing interpretations on the expressed or implied intentions of authors, a practice they judged to be erroneous. As proponents of the New Criticism, or formalism, they argued that a work of literature is an object in itself and should be studied as such. They believed that it is sometimes helpful to learn what an author intended, but the critic's real purpose is to show what is actually in the text, not what an author intended to put there.

See also: Affective Fallacy, Formalism.

BASE *See* Marxist Criticism.

BINARY OPPOSITIONS *See* Oppositions.

BLANKS *See* Gaps.

CANON Since the fourth century, used to refer to those books of the Bible that the Christian church accepts as being Holy Scripture. The term has come to be applied more generally to those literary works given special status, or "privileged," by a culture. Works we tend to think of as "classics" or the "Great Books" produced by Western culture — texts that are found in every anthology of American, British, and world literature — would be among those that constitute the canon.

Recently, Marxist, feminist, minority, and Third World critics have argued that, for political reasons, many excellent works never enter the canon. Canonized works, they claim, are those that reflect — and respect — the culture's dominant ideology and/or perform some socially acceptable or even necessary form of "cultural work." Attempts have been made to broaden or redefine the canon by discovering valuable texts, or versions of texts, that were repressed or ignored for political reasons. These have been published both in traditional and in nontraditional anthologies. The more outspoken critics of the canon, especially radical critics practicing cultural criticism, have called into question the whole concept of canon or "canonicity." Privileging no form of artistic expression that reflects and revises the culture, these critics treat cartoons, comics, and soap operas with the same cogency and respect they accord novels, poems, and plays.

See also: Cultural Criticism, Feminist Criticism, Ideology, Marxist Criticism.

CONFLICTS, CONTRADICTIONS *See* Gaps.

CULTURAL CRITICISM A critical approach that is sometimes referred to as "cultural studies" or "cultural critique." Practitioners of cultural criticism oppose "high" definitions of culture and take seriously popular cultural forms. Grounded in a variety of continental European influences, cultural criticism nonetheless gained institutional force in England, in 1964, with the founding of the Centre for Contemporary Cultural Studies at Birmingham University. Broadly interdisciplinary in its scope and approach, cultural criticism views the text as the locus and catalyst of a complex network of political and economic discourses. Cultural critics share with Marxist critics an interest in the ideological contexts of cultural forms. See "What Is Cultural Criticism?" page 312.

DECONSTRUCTION A poststructuralist approach to literature that is strongly influenced by the writings of the French philosopher Jacques Derrida. Derrida, who coined the term "deconstruction," suggested that the Western mind tends to think in terms of binary oppositions (light/dark, masculine/feminine, cause/effect, presence/absence). When we read, consequently, we look for ways in which a text means one thing and not another.

Derrida attempts to show, in readings of Rousseau's *Confessions* and Plato's *Phaedrus,* that texts can defy logic's "law" of noncontradiction. They can mean both "A" and "not-A"; they can mean opposite things at the same time. "What Derrida does in his reading of Plato," Barbara Johnson explains, "is to unfold dimensions of Plato's *text* that work against the grain of (Plato's own) Platonism." J. Hillis Miller, the leading American practitioner of deconstruction, points out that "deconstruction is not a dismantling of the structure of a text but a demonstration that it has already dismantled itself."

Deconstruction is, in part, a response to structuralism and to formalism. Formalists relied on close readings of individual works to determine meaning-giving patterns of imagery, sound, rhythm, allusion, and other rhetorical devices. Although they were interested in ambiguities, they tended to resolve ambiguity in interpretation. Structuralists relied on the linguistic theory of Ferdinand de Saussure and also on semiotics or semiology (the study of signs) in their attempt to identify the organizing principles, not only of individual works but also of whole classes of stories or myths.

Deconstructors, like structuralists, are highly interested in linguistic theory and its implications for literary criticism. Like formalists they practice close reading, often devoting several intricate paragraphs to a single, ambiguous passage. But there most of the similarities end. Deconstructors tend to leave a work ambiguous or "undecidable"; indeed, they would subvert the search for *the* structure of a passage, or work, or set of works. They would suspend the quest for *the* form or pattern of artistic effects that makes a text mean black and not white, life and not death, one thing and not another. They would have us see that, as Jonathan Culler puts it, when "one speaks of the structure of a literary work, one does so from a certain vantage point: one starts with notions of the meaning or effects of a poem and tries to identify the structures responsible for those effects. Possible configurations or patterns that make no contributions are rejected as irrelevant."

Deconstruction has fostered a body of highly imaginative, even playful, works of criticism: essays and books that some (including some deconstructors) would call metafictions, that is, fictions about fictions. Deconstruction has also proved useful to critics who are interested in political problems and relationships — both within literary works and in the world they represent. To feminist critics, for example, the same "logic" that Derrida would call into question can cause us to see women as women and men as men, and not to see instructive connections, say, between white women and minority men. To a new historicist critic, the same deconstructive moves that can reveal the "other side" of a text may also help reveal what *else* the past may have to tell us.

See also: Feminist Criticism, Formalism, New Historicism, Oppositions, Semiotics, Structuralism.

DIALECTIC Originally developed by Greek philosophers, mainly Socrates and Plato, as a form and method of logical argumentation; the term later came to denote a philosophical notion of evolution. The German philosopher G. W. F. Hegel described dialectic as a process whereby a thesis, when countered by an antithesis, leads to the synthesis of a new idea. Karl Marx and Friedrich Engels, adapting Hegel's idealist theory, used the phrase "dialectical materialism" to discuss the way in which a revolutionary class war might lead to the synthesis of a new social economic order. The American Marxist critic Fredric Jameson has coined the phrase "dialectical criticism" to refer to a Marxist critical approach that synthesizes structuralist and poststructuralist methodologies.

See also: Marxist Criticism, Structuralism, Poststructuralism.

DIALOGIC *See* Discourse.

DISCOURSE Used specifically, can refer to (1) spoken or written discussion of a subject or area of knowledge; (2) the words in, or text of, a narrative as opposed to its story line; or (3) a "strand" within a given narrative that argues a certain point or defends a given value system.

More generally, "discourse" refers to the language in which a subject or area of knowledge is discussed or a certain kind of business is transacted. Human knowledge is collected and structured in discourses. Theology and medicine are defined by their discourses, as are politics, sexuality, and literary criticism.

A society is generally made up of a number of different discourses or "discourse communities," one or more of which may be dominant or serve the dominant ideology. Each discourse has its own vocabulary, concepts, and rules, knowledge of which constitutes power. The psychoanalyst and psychoanalytic critic Jacques Lacan has treated the unconscious as a form of discourse, the patterns of which are repeated in literature. Cultural critics, following Mikhail Bakhtin, use the word "dialogic" to discuss the dialogue *between* discourses that takes place within language or, more specifically, a literary text.

See also: Cultural Criticism, Ideology, Narrative, Psychoanalytic Criticism.

FEMINIST CRITICISM An aspect of the feminist movement whose primary goals include critiquing masculine-dominated language and literature by showing how they reflect a masculine ideology; writing the history of unknown or undervalued women writers, thereby earning them their rightful place in the literary canon; and helping create a climate in which women's creativity may be fully realized and appreciated. See "What Is Feminist Criticism?" page 259.

FIGURE *See* Metaphor, Metonymy, Symbol.

FORMALISM Also referred to as the New Criticism, formalism reached its height during the 1940s and 1950s but it is still practiced today. Formalists treat a work of literary art as if it were a self-contained, self-referential object. Rather than basing their interpretations of a text on the reader's response, the author's stated intentions, or parallels between the text and historical contexts (such as the author's life), formalists concentrate on the relationships *within* the text that give it its own distinctive character or form. Special attention is paid to repetition, particularly of images or symbols, but also of sound effects and rhythms in poetry.

Because of the importance placed on close analysis and the stress on the text as a carefully crafted, orderly object containing observable formal patterns, formalism has often been seen as an attack on Romanticism and impressionism, particularly impressionistic criticism. It has sometimes even been called an "objective" approach to literature. Formalists are more likely than certain other critics to believe and say that the meaning of a text can be known objectively. For instance, reader-response critics see meaning as a function either of each reader's experience or of the norms that govern a particular "interpretive community," and deconstructors argue that texts mean opposite things at the same time.

Formalism was originally based on essays written during the 1920s and 1930s by T. S. Eliot, I. A. Richards, and William Empson. It was significantly developed later by a group of American poets and critics, including R. P. Blackmur, Cleanth Brooks, John Crowe Ransom, Allen Tate, Robert Penn Warren, and William K. Wimsatt. Although we associate formalism with certain principles and terms (such as the "Affective Fallacy" and the "Intentional Fallacy" as defined by Wimsatt and Monroe C. Beardsley), formalists were trying to make a cultural statement rather than establish a critical dogma. Generally Southern, religious, and culturally conservative, they advocated the inherent value of literary works (particularly of literary works regarded as beautiful art objects) because they were sick of the growing ugliness of modern life and contemporary events. Some recent theorists even suggest that the rising popularity of formalism after World War II was a feature of American isolationism, the formalist tendency to isolate literature from biography and history being a manifestation of the American fatigue with wider involvements.

See also: Affective Fallacy, Authorial Intention, Deconstruction, Reader-Response Criticism, Symbol.

GAPS When used by reader-response critics familiar with the theories of Wolfgang Iser, refers to "blanks" in texts that must be filled in by readers. A gap may be said to exist whenever and wherever a reader perceives something to be missing between words, sentences, paragraphs, stanzas, or chapters. Readers respond to gaps actively and creatively, explaining apparent inconsistencies in point of view, accounting for jumps in chronology, speculatively supplying information missing from plots, and resolving problems or issues left ambiguous or "indeterminate" in the text.

Reader-response critics sometimes speak as if a gap actually exists in a text; a gap is, of course, to some extent a product of readers' perceptions. Different readers may find gaps in different texts, and different gaps in the same text. Furthermore, they may fill these gaps in in different ways, which is why, a reader-response critic might argue, works are interpreted in different ways.

Although the concept of the gap has been used mainly by reader-response critics, it has also been used by critics taking other theoretical approaches. Practitioners of deconstruction might use "gap" when speaking of the radical contradictoriness of a text. Marxists have used the term to speak of everything from the gap that opens up between economic base and cultural superstructure to the two kinds of conflicts or contradictions to be found in literary texts. The first of these, they would argue, results from the fact that texts reflect ideology, within which certain subjects cannot be covered, things that cannot be said, contradictory views that cannot be recognized as contradictory. The second kind of conflict, contradiction, or gap within a text results from the fact that works don't just reflect ideology: they are also fictions that, consciously or unconsciously, distance themselves from the same ideology.

See also: Deconstruction, Ideology, Marxist Criticism, Reader-Response Criticism.

GENRE A French word referring to a kind or type of literature. Individual works within a genre may exhibit a distinctive form, be governed by certain conventions, and/or represent characteristic subjects. Tragedy, epic, and romance are all genres.

Perhaps inevitably, the term "genre" is used loosely. Lyric poetry is a genre, but so are characteristic *types* of the lyric, such as the sonnet, the ode, and the elegy. Fiction is a genre, as are detective fiction and science fiction. The list of genres grows constantly as critics establish new lines of connection between individual works and discern new categories of works with common characteristics. Moreover, some writers form hybrid genres by combining the characteristics of several in a single work.

Knowledge of genres helps critics to understand and explain what is conventional and unconventional, borrowed and original, in a work.

HEGEMONY Given intellectual currency by the Italian communist Antonio Gramsci, the word (a translation of *egemonia*) refers to the pervasive system of assumptions, meanings, and values — the web of ideologies, in other words — that shapes the way things look, what they mean, and therefore what reality *is* for the majority of people within a given culture.

See also: Ideology, Marxist Criticism.

IDEOLOGY A set of beliefs underlying the customs, habits, and/or practices common to a given social group. To members of that group, the beliefs seem obviously true, natural, and even universally applicable. They may seem just as obviously arbitrary, idiosyncratic, and even false to outsiders or members of another group who adhere to another ideology. Within a society, several ideologies may coexist, or one or more may be dominant.

Ideologies may be forcefully imposed or willingly subscribed to. Their component beliefs may be held consciously or unconsciously. In either case, they come to form what Johanna M. Smith has called "the unexamined ground of our experience." Ideology governs our perceptions, judgments, and prejudices — our sense of what is acceptable, normal, and deviant. Ideology may cause a revolution; it may also allow discrimination and even exploitation.

Ideologies are of special interest to sociologically oriented critics of literature because of the way in which authors reflect or resist prevailing views in their texts. Some Marxist critics have argued that literary texts reflect and reproduce the ideologies that produced them; most, however, have shown how ideologies are riven with contradictions that works of literature manage to expose and widen. Still other Marxists have focused on the way in which texts themselves are characterized by gaps, conflicts, and contradictions between their ideological and anti-ideological functions.

Feminist critics have addressed the question of ideology by seeking to expose (and thereby call into question) the patriarchal ideology mirrored or inscribed in works written by men — even men who have sought to counter sexism and break down sexual stereotypes. New historicists have been interested in demonstrating the ideological underpinnings not only of literary representations but also of our interpretations of them. Fredric Jameson, an American Marxist critic, argues that all thought is ideological, but that ideological thought that knows itself as such stands the chance of seeing through and transcending ideology.

See also: Cultural Criticism, Feminist Criticism, Marxist Criticism, New Historicism.

IMAGINARY STAGE According to Lacanian psychoanalytic theory, the pre-oedipal, prelinguistic stage of child development that precedes the Symbolic stage. During the Imaginary stage, also called the mirror stage, the child conceives of the mother and indeed of the entire world as being indistinguishable from the self.

See also: Psychoanalytic Criticism, Symbolic Stage.

IMPLIED READER A phrase used by some reader-response critics in place of the phrase "the reader." Whereas "the reader" could refer to any idiosyncratic individual who happens to have read or to be reading the text, "the implied reader" is *the* reader intended, even created, by the text. Other reader-response critics seeking to describe this more generally conceived reader have spoken of the "informed reader" or the "narratee," who is "the necessary counterpart of a given narrator."

See Reader-Response Criticism.

INTENTIONAL FALLACY *See* Authorial Intention.

INTENTIONALITY *See* Authorial Intention.

INTERTEXTUALITY The condition of interconnectedness among texts. Every author has been influenced by others, and every work contains explicit and implicit references to other works. Writers may consciously or unconsciously echo a predecessor or precursor; they may also consciously or unconsciously disguise their indebtedness, making intertextual relationships difficult for the critic to trace.

Reacting against the formalist tendency to view each work as a free-standing object, some poststructuralist critics suggested that the meaning of a work only emerges intertextually, that is, within the context provided by other works. But there has been a reaction, too, against this type of intertextual criticism. Some new historicist critics suggest that literary history is itself too narrow a context and that works should be interpreted in light of a larger set of cultural contexts.

There is, however, a broader definition of intertextuality, one that refers to the relationship between works of literature and a wide range of narratives and discourses that we don't usually consider literary. Thus defined, intertextuality could be used by a new historicist to refer to the significant interconnectedness between a literary text and nonliterary discussions of or discourses about contemporary culture. Or it could be used by a poststructuralist to suggest that a work can only be recognized and read within a vast field of signs and tropes that is *like* a text and that makes any single text self-contradictory and "undecidable."

See also: Discourse, Formalism, Narrative, New Historicism, Poststructuralism, Trope.

MARXIST CRITICISM An approach that treats literary texts as material products, describing them in broadly historical terms. In Marxist criticism, the text is viewed in terms of its production and consumption, as a product *of* work that does identifiable cultural work of its own. Following Karl Marx, the founder of communism, Marxist critics have used the terms "base" to refer to economic reality and "superstructure" to refer to the corresponding or "homologous" infrastructure consisting of politics, law, philosophy, religion, and the arts. Also following Marx, they have used the word "ideology" to refer to that set of cultural beliefs that literary works at once reproduce, resist, and revise. See "What Is Marxist Criticism?" page 286.

METAPHOR The representation of one thing by another related or similar thing. The image (or activity or concept) used to represent or "figure" something else is known as the "vehicle" of the metaphor; the thing represented is called the "tenor." In other words, the vehicle is what we substitute for the tenor. The relationship between vehicle and tenor can provide much additional meaning. Thus, instead of saying, "Last night I read a book," we might say, "Last night I plowed through a book." "Plowed through" (or the activity of plowing) is the vehicle of our metaphor; "read" (or the act of reading) is the tenor, the thing being figured. The increment in meaning through metaphor is fairly obvious. Our audience knows not only *that* we read but also *how* we read, because to read a book in the way that a plow rips through earth is surely to read in a relentless, unreflective way. Note that in the sentence above, a new metaphor — "rips through" — has been used to explain an old one. This serves (which is a metaphor) as an example of just how thick (another metaphor) language is with metaphors!

Metaphor is a kind of "trope" (literally, a "turning," i.e., a figure that alters or "turns" the meaning of a word or phrase). Other tropes include allegory, conceit, metonymy, personification, simile, symbol, and synecdoche. Traditionally, metaphor and symbol have been viewed as the principal tropes; minor tropes have been categorized as *types* of these two major ones. Similes, for instance, are usually defined as simple metaphors that usually employ "like" or "as" and state the tenor outright, as in "My love is like a red, red rose." Synecdoche involves a vehicle that is a *part* of the tenor, as in "I see a sail" meaning "I see a boat." Metonymy is viewed as a metaphor involving two terms commonly if arbitrarily associated with (but not fundamentally or intrinsically related to) each other. Recently, however, deconstructors such as Paul de Man and J. Hillis Miller have questioned the "privilege" granted to metaphor and the metaphor/metonymy distinction or "opposition." They have suggested that all metaphors are really metonyms and that all figuration is arbitrary.

See also: Deconstruction, Metonymy, Oppositions, Symbol.

METONYMY The representation of one thing by another that is commonly and often physically associated with it. To refer to a writer's handwriting as his or her "hand" is to use a metonymic "figure" or "trope." The image or thing used to represent something else is known as the "vehicle" of the metonym; the thing represented is called the "tenor."

Like other tropes (such as metaphor), metonymy involves the replacement of one word or phrase by another. Liquor may be referred to as "the bottle," a monarch as "the crown." Narrowly defined, the vehicle of a metonym is arbitrarily, not intrinsically, associated with the tenor. In other words, the bottle just happens to be what liquor is stored in and poured from in our culture. The hand may be involved in the production of handwriting, but so are the brain and the pen. There is no special, intrinsic likeness between a crown and a monarch; it's just that crowns traditionally sit on monarchs' heads and not on the heads of university professors. More broadly, "metonym" and "metonymy" have been used by recent critics to refer to a wide range of figures and tropes. Deconstructors have questioned the distinction between metaphor and metonymy.

See also: Deconstruction, Metaphor, Trope.

NARRATIVE   A story or a telling of a story, or an account of a situation or of events. A novel and a biography of a novelist are both narratives, as are Freud's case histories.

Some critics use the word "narrative" even more generally; Brook Thomas, a new historicist, has critiqued "narratives of human history that neglect the role human labor has played."

NEW CRITICISM   *See* Formalism.

NEW HISTORICISM   One of the most recent developments in contemporary critical theory, it is still evolving and thus somewhat difficult to define precisely. But all practitioners of new historicism share certain convictions, one of which is that literary critics need to develop a high degree of historical consciousness. Another belief shared by new historicists is that literature should not be viewed apart from other human creations, artistic or otherwise. Rather, it and they should be viewed as artifacts mirroring and influencing the ideology of their place and time. Jerome McGann, following Mikhail Bakhtin, has recently suggested that historically conscious critics come to know both the "point of origin" and "point of reception" of a work. To know both fully, a critic would need to be familiar not only with biography, bibliography, and expressions of authorial intention but also with the interpretive history of the work, the ideology of the place and period in which it was written, and the historical (and ideological) conditions governing his or her *own* era, society, and interpretive strategies.

The notion that literary criticism should be conscious of history is, of course, not a new one. Until the advent of formalism — with its conception of the text as a freestanding, self-referential object — critics had commonly related literary works to their authors' lives and times. But the criticism being written now is different in kind from the old historical criticism. It may presuppose familiarity with Marx, or with psychoanalytic or poststructuralist theory. It is often achronological and sometimes less oriented toward establishing "facts" and chronicling "events" than was the old historical criticism, perhaps because of its authors' acute awareness of the extent to which all views of the past are historically determined. Finally, the new historicism differs from the old in its reliance on sociological and anthropological theory. Due in large part to Clifford Geertz's influence, new historicists such as Stephen Greenblatt have produced a body of "anthropological criticism" in which old distinctions between art and politics, history and theater, the literary and the nonliterary, have all but been erased. Literary devices are viewed as being continuous with other representational practices within a culture. The production of a play by Shakespeare has been shown to be as much a political act as a queen's coronation was an intricate and lavish piece of symbolic theater.

The writings of French thinker Michel Foucault have also influenced the development of the new historicism. As much an archaeologist as a historian and as much a philosopher as either, Foucault sees history in terms of power relationships. He doesn't see it as a development toward the present; neither does he view it as a string of causes and effects. Rather, he connects a given historical development, such as the disappearance of public torture, with a web of other economic, political, and social factors, each of which is bound up with the others and as much a response as a catalyst.

The tendency to blur edges or erase boundaries — whether between causes and effects, history and the other social sciences, artistic and political representation, or the study of literature and the study of culture — is at the heart of the new historicism. This tendency to search for what new historicists would call a "decentered" perspective is also reflected in (and a reflection of) the view that our own place and time do not afford us a privileged vantage point from which to view other periods or cultures.

See also: Authorial Intention, Deconstruction, Formalism, Ideology, Poststructuralism, Psychoanalytic Criticism.

OPPOSITIONS A concept highly relevant to linguistics, since linguists maintain that words (such as "black" and "death") have meaning not in themselves, but in relation to other words ("white" and "life"). Jacques Derrida, a poststructuralist philosopher of language, has suggested that in the West we think in terms of these "binary oppositions" or dichotomies, which on examination turn out to be evaluative hierarchies. In other words, each opposition — beginning/end, presence/absence, or consciousness/unconsciousness — contains one term that our culture views as superior and one term that we view as negative or inferior.

Derrida has "deconstructed" a number of these binary oppositions, including two — speech/writing and signifier/signified — that he believes to be central to linguistics in particular and Western culture in general. He has concurrently critiqued the "law" of noncontradiction, which is fundamental to Western logic. He and other deconstructors have argued that a text can contain opposed strands of discourse and, therefore, mean opposite things: reason *and* passion, life *and* death, hope *and* despair, black *and* white. Traditionally, criticism has involved choosing between opposed or contradictory meanings and arguing that one is present in the text and the other absent.

French feminists have adopted the ideas of Derrida and other deconstructors, showing not only that we think in terms of such binary oppositions as male/female, reason/emotion, and active/passive, but that we also associate reason and activity with masculinity and emotion and passivity with femininity. Because of this, they have concluded that language is "phallocentric," or masculine-dominated.

See also: Deconstruction, Discourse, Feminist Criticism, Poststructuralism.

POSTSTRUCTURALISM The general attempt to contest and subvert structuralism initiated by deconstructors and certain other critics associated with psychoanalytic, Marxist, and feminist theory. Structuralists, using linguistics as a model and employing semiotic (sign) theory, posit the possibility of knowing a text systematically and revealing the "grammar" behind its form and meaning. Poststructuralists argue against the possibility of such knowledge and description. They counter that texts can be shown to contradict not only structuralist accounts of them but also themselves. In making their adversarial claims, they rely on close readings of texts and on the work of theorists such as Jacques Derrida and Jacques Lacan.

Poststructuralists have suggested that structuralism rests on distinctions between "signifier" and "signified" (signs and the things they point toward), "self" and "language" (or "text"), texts and other texts, and text and world that are overly simplistic, if not patently inaccurate. Poststructuralists have shown how all signifieds are also signifiers, and they have treated texts as "intertexts." They have viewed the world as if it *were* a text (we desire a certain car because it *symbolizes* achievement) and the self as the subject, as well as the user, of language; for example, we may shape and speak through language, but it also shapes and speaks through us.

See also: Deconstruction, Feminist Criticism, Intertextuality, Psychoanalytic Criticism, Semiotics, Structuralism.

PSYCHOANALYTIC CRITICISM Grounded in the psychoanalytic theories of Sigmund Freud, it is one of the oldest critical methodologies still in use. Freud's view that works of literature, like dreams, express secret, unconscious desires led to criticism that interpreted literary works as manifestations of the authors' neuroses. More recently, psychoanalytic critics have come to see literary works as skillfully crafted artifacts that may appeal to *our* neuroses by tapping into our repressed wishes and fantasies. Other forms of psychological criticism that diverge from Freud, although they ultimately derive from his insights, include those based on the theories of Carl Jung and Jacques Lacan. See "What Is Psychoanalytic Criticism?" page 230.

READER-RESPONSE CRITICISM An approach to literature that, as its name implies, considers the way readers respond to texts, as they read. Stanley Fish describes the method by saying that it substitutes for one question, "What does this sentence mean?" a more operational question, "What does this sentence do?" Reader-response criticism shares with deconstruction a strong textual orientation and a reluctance to define a single meaning for a work. Along with psychoanalytic criticism, it shares an interest in the dynamics of mental response to textual cues. See "What Is Reader-Response Criticism?" page 205.

SEMIOLOGY, SEMIOTIC *See* Semiotics.

SEMIOTICS The study of signs and sign systems and the way meaning is derived from them. Structuralist anthropologists, psychoanalysts, and literary critics developed semiotics during the decades following 1950, but much of the pioneering work had been done at the turn of the century by the founder of modern linguistics, Ferdinand de Saussure, and the American philosopher Charles Sanders Peirce.

Semiotics is based on several important distinctions, including the distinction between "signifier" and "signified" (the sign and what it points toward) and the distinction between "langue" and "parole." *Langue* (French for "tongue," as in "native tongue," meaning language) refers to the entire system within which individual utterances or usages of language have meaning; *parole* (French for "word") refers to the particular utterances or usages. A principal tenet of semiotics is that signs, like words, are not significant in themselves, but instead have meaning only in relation to other signs and the entire system of signs, or langue.

The affinity between semiotics and structuralist literary criticism derives from this emphasis placed on langue, or system. Structuralist critics, after all, were reacting against formalists and their procedure of focusing on individual words as if meanings didn't depend on anything external to the text.

Poststructuralists have used semiotics but questioned some of its underlying assumptions, including the opposition between signifier and signified. The feminist poststructuralist Julia Kristeva, for instance, has used the word "semiotic" to describe feminine language, a highly figurative, fluid form of discourse that she sets in opposition to rigid, symbolic masculine language.

See also: Deconstruction, Feminist Criticism, Formalism, Poststructuralism, Oppositions, Structuralism, Symbol.

SIMILE   *See* Metaphor.

SOCIOHISTORICAL CRITICISM   *See* New Historicism.

STRUCTURALISM   A science of humankind whose proponents attempted to show that all elements of human culture, including literature, may be understood as parts of a system of signs. Structuralism, according to Robert Scholes, was a reaction to "'modernist' alienation and despair."

Using Ferdinand de Saussure's linguistic theory, European structuralists such as Roman Jakobson, Claude Lévi-Strauss, and Roland Barthes (before his shift toward poststructuralism) attempted to develop a "semiology" or "semiotics" (science of signs). Barthes, among others, sought to recover literature and even language from the isolation in which they had been studied and to show that the laws that govern them govern all signs, from road signs to articles of clothing.

Particularly useful to structuralists were two of Saussure's concepts: the idea of "phoneme" in language and the idea that phonemes exist in two kinds of relationships: "synchronic" and "diachronic." A phoneme is the smallest consistently significant unit in language; thus, both "a" and "an" are phonemes, but "n" is not. A diachronic relationship is that which a phoneme has with those that have preceded it in time and those that will follow it. These "horizontal" relationships produce what we might call discourse or narrative and what Saussure called "parole." The synchronic relationship is the "vertical" one that a word has in a given instant with the entire system of language ("langue") in which it may generate meaning. "An" means what it means in English because those of us who speak the language are using it in the same way at a given time.

Following Saussure, Lévi-Strauss studied hundreds of myths, breaking them into their smallest meaningful units, which he called "mythemes." Removing each from its diachronic relations with other mythemes in a single myth (such as the myth of Oedipus and his mother), he vertically aligned those mythemes that he found to be homologous (structurally correspondent). He then studied the relationships within as well as between vertically aligned columns, in an attempt to understand scientifically, through ratios and proportions, those thoughts and processes that humankind has shared, both at one particular time and across time. One could say, then, that structuralists followed Saussure in preferring to think about the overriding langue or language of myth, in which each mytheme and mytheme-constituted myth fits meaningfully, rather than about isolated individual paroles or narratives. Structuralists followed Saussure's lead in believing what the poststructuralist Jacques Derrida later decided he could not subscribe to — that sign systems must be understood in terms of binary oppositions. In analyzing myths and texts to find basic structures, structuralists tended to find that opposite terms modulate until they are finally resolved or reconciled by some intermediary third term. Thus, a structuralist reading of *Paradise Lost* would show that the war between God and the bad angels becomes a rift between God and sinful, fallen man, the rift then being healed by the Son of God, the mediating third term.

See also: Deconstruction, Discourse, Narrative, Poststructuralism, Semiotics.

SUPERSTRUCTURE *See* Marxist Criticism.

SYMBOL A thing, image, or action that, although it is of interest in its own right, stands for or suggests something larger and more complex — often an idea or a range of interrelated ideas, attitudes, and practices.

Within a given culture, some things are understood to be symbols: the flag of the United States is an obvious example. More subtle cultural symbols might be the river as a symbol of time and the journey as a symbol of life and its manifold experiences.

Instead of appropriating symbols generally used and understood within their culture, writers often create symbols by setting up, in their works, a complex but identifiable web of associations. As a result, one object, image, or action suggests others, and often, ultimately, a range of ideas.

A symbol may thus be defined as a metaphor in which the "vehicle," the thing, image, or action used to represent something else, represents many related things (or "tenors") or is broadly suggestive. The urn in Keats's "Ode on a Grecian Urn" suggests many interrelated concepts, including art, truth, beauty, and timelessness.

Symbols have been of particular interest to formalists, who study how meanings emerge from the complex, patterned relationships between images in a work, and psychoanalytic critics, who are interested in how individual authors and the larger culture both disguise and reveal unconscious fears and desires through symbols. Recently, French feminists have also focused on the symbolic. They have suggested that, as wide-ranging as it seems, symbolic language is ultimately rigid and restrictive. They favor semiotic language and writing, which, they contend, is at once more rhythmic, unifying, and feminine.

See also: Feminist Criticism, Metaphor, Psychoanalytic Criticism, Trope.

SYMBOLIC STAGE According to Lacanian psychoanalytic theory, the stage in which the child (especially the male child) learns that what had seemed wholly his and even undistinguishable from himself (i.e., the mother) is in fact someone else's: something to be desired only in the form of socially acceptable substitutes. That recognition, according to Jacques Lacan, facilitates the child's entrance into language, for words themselves are not the things they stand for but, rather, are substitutes for those things. The Symbolic stage, which corresponds with what Freud called the oedipal stage, follows a pre-oedipal stage that Lacan termed the "Imaginary stage."

See also: Psychoanalytic Criticism.

SYNECDOCHE *See* Metaphor, Metonymy.

TENOR *See* Metaphor, Metonymy, Symbol.

TROPE A figure, as in "figure of speech." Literally a "turning," i.e., a turning or twisting of a word or phrase to make it mean something else. Principal tropes include metaphor, metonymy, simile, personification, and synecdoche.

See also: Metaphor, Metonymy.

VEHICLE *See* Metaphor, Metonymy, Symbol.

About the Contributors

THE VOLUME EDITOR

Johanna M. Smith is an assistant professor of English at the University of Texas at Arlington, where she teaches eighteenth- and nineteenth-century literature. She has written on novels by Jane Austen, Harriet Beecher Stowe, Joseph Conrad, and Raymond Chandler and has completed a book on sister-brother incest in nineteenth-century texts. She is currently working on a study of representations of nineteenth-century working-class politics.

THE CRITICS

David Collings is an assistant professor of English at Bowdoin College, where he teaches gender theory and romanticism. He has published on Samuel Taylor Coleridge and is completing a book on William Wordsworth.

Lee E. Heller is an assistant professor in the School of Humanities and Arts at Hampshire College, where she teaches courses in American literature. She has published studies on the novels of Henry James and Herman Melville and is preparing a book on the novel as popular literature.

Mary Lowe-Evans is an associate professor of English at the University of West Florida, where she teaches poetry, Irish studies, and nineteenth-century literature. She has published several studies on James Joyce, including her book, *Crimes Against Fecundity: Joyce and Population Control* (1989). Currently she is researching the influence of *Frankenstein* on Conrad's *Heart of Darkness*.

Warren Montag is an assistant professor of English at Occidental College, where he teaches Restoration and eighteenth-century literature. His articles on Marxism, psychoanalysis, and postmodernism have appeared in *Rethinking Marxism, Minnesota Review,* and *Quarterly Review of Film Studies*. He is at work on a book about Jonathan Swift.

THE SERIES EDITOR

Ross C Murfin, general editor of *Case Studies in Contemporary Criticism,* is dean of the College of Arts and Sciences at the University of Miami and professor of English. He has taught at Yale University and the University of Virginia and published scholarly studies on Joseph Conrad, Thomas Hardy, and D. H. Lawrence.